YOU HAVE TO FIGHT BETTER.

We'll teach you where to hit them to do the most damage, and how to tell when they're getting ready to breathe or spin around, when to get in close, and when to get away. You'll slow the dragons down, and spill more of their blood than you would otherwise. That's all we can promise.

You have to give them the walls and courtyards, and fight on inside your great keep and the vaults beneath. Make the dragons fight us on foot, at close range, on ground we know better than they do. Set traps and ambuscades. That way, we can hold them back for a long time.

Keep fighting outdoors, and we won't last another tenday.

THE YEAR OF ROGUE DRAGONS

Richard Lee Byers

Book 1
The Rage

Book 11
The Rite
January 2005

Book 111
The Ruin
May 2006

Realms of the Dragons
Edited by Philip Athans

Realms of the Dragons 11
Edited by Philip Athans
May 2005

Other FORGOTTEN REALMS Titles by Richard Lee Byers

R.A. Salvatore's War of the Spider Queen, Book I
Dissolution

The Rogues
The Black Bouquet

Sembia
The Shattered Mask

FORGOTTEN REALMS®

THE RITE

THE YEAR OF ROGUE DRAGONS

book 11

Richard Lee Byers

Wizards
OF THE COAST™

THE RITE
The Year of Rogue Dragons, Book II
©2005 Wizards of the Coast, Inc.

Distributed in the United States by Holtzbrinck Publishing. Distributed in Canada by Fenn Ltd.

Distributed to the hobby, toy, and comic trade in the United States and Canada by regional distributors.

Distributed worldwide by Wizards of the Coast, Inc. and regional distributors.

Printed in the U.S.A.

Cover art by Matt Stawicki
Map by Dennis Kauth
First Printing: January 2005
Library of Congress Catalog Card Number: 2004113602

9 8 7 6 5 4 3 2 1

ISBN-10: 0-7869-3581-2
ISBN-13: 978-0-7869-3581-9
620-17641-001-EN

U.S., CANADA,
ASIA, PACIFIC, & LATIN AMERICA
Wizards of the Coast, Inc.
P.O. Box 707
Renton, WA 98057-0707
+1-800-324-6496

EUROPEAN HEADQUARTERS
Wizards of the Coast, Belgium
T Hofveld 6d
1702 Groot-Bijgaarden
Belgium
+322 467 3360

Visit our web site at **www.wizards.com**

For Bruce, Liz, and Heather

Acknowledgments
Thanks to Phil Athans, my editor,
and to Ed Greenwood, for his help and inspiration.

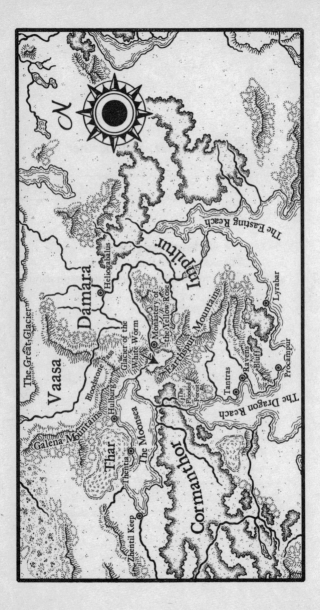

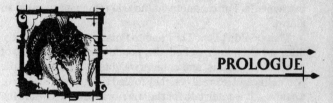

2 & 3 Mirtul, the Year of Rogue Dragons (1373 DR)

To Fodel's chagrin, Natali saw them first. He was the one who knew they were coming, but still, it was his fellow sentry with her keen eyes who spotted an outstretched wing momentarily blocking the light of a star, or perhaps the leading edge of the dark mass creeping over the ground—Fodel could tell by the way she gasped and snatched for the bugle hanging at her hip.

Fodel whipped out his dagger and thrust at the slender redhead's sunburned neck, at the bare flesh between mail and helmet. Thanks be to the Sacred Ones, the point drove home before she could blow a note. Warm blood sprayed out and spattered his hand. The brass horn fell clanking onto the wall-walk.

Fodel winced at the clatter, but maybe no one had heard. He grabbed the corpse before it could collapse and make even more racket, wrestled it to the edge of the battlement, and shoved it over the merlons. It landed with a thud on the ground outside the castle.

He scurried for the stairs leading down into the bailey. Avarin met him in the courtyard and with a nod, conveyed the message that he, too, had killed his companion up on the battlements. For the moment, no one remained to raise an alarm.

That couldn't last. They had to finish their work quickly. Still, as they approached the ponderous mechanisms of windlasses, chains, and counterweights that controlled the portcullis and iron valves, they forced themselves to slow to a saunter. It wouldn't do for the warriors stationed inside the gate to discern their urgency.

The North had reached that time of year when spring ruled the day but winter had yet to relinquish its grip on the night. Accordingly, the two common soldiers and the officer of the watch, a Paladin of the Golden Cup clad in gilt-trimmed knightly trappings, stood huddled around a crackling fire. At first they oriented on Fodel and Avarin, but in a casual sort of way. When the duo stepped into the circle of wavering firelight, though, the paladin peered at them intently.

"Is that blood?" he asked.

Fodel glanced down at himself and saw that it was. He had splotches of Natali's gore all over his chest, where his war cloak didn't cover. Somehow, in his excitement, he hadn't realized.

"Yes," he said, "you see . . ."

He couldn't think of a plausible explanation, but hoped it didn't matter. Maybe he just needed to keep babbling until he and Avarin closed to striking distance.

The knight's eyes narrowed, and Fodel knew the game was up. Ilmater's holy warriors could look into a man's soul when they deemed it necessary, and the officer was surely gazing into his. Fodel flailed his knife arm out from under his mantle and rushed in stabbing.

The paladin caught the first thrusts on his small round

wood-and-leather shield. At the same time, he called, "Treachery! Treachery at the gate!"

Magically amplified, the words boomed loud as thunder. Fodel had no doubt they'd rouse the entire garrison. That meant he and Avarin had, at most, a minute or so left to accomplish their purpose. Fodel feinted with the knife, then kicked the paladin's knee. The knight reeled off balance with his broadsword still halfway in its scabbard. Fodel kicked again, dropped his foe onto his back, flung himself on top of him, and stabbed until the paladin stopped moving.

Hands gripped Fodel's forearm. He jerked around and nearly slashed with the knife before realizing that it was Avarin who'd taken hold of him. His comrade had killed the two men-at-arms and was attempting to haul him to his feet.

"Come on!" Avarin said.

They scrambled on to the windlass that would lift the portcullis. Thanks to the cunning of the dwarves who'd built the contraption, two men could operate it without strain. Still, such was Fodel's desperation that it seemed to take forever to hoist the massive steel grille.

Next, they shifted the bar sealing the gates, which squealed in its brackets despite the grease. That alone didn't make the thick iron leaves movable. Their sheer weight and the enchantments the king's wizards had cast on them could hold them shut. Accordingly, Fodel and Avarin rushed to another windlass, grasped the handles, and heaved.

"Stop!" a soprano voice shouted.

The gate was in effect a sort of tunnel passing through the thick granite wall. Fodel looked around and saw the archers, crossbowmen, and spellcasters assembled in the courtyard just outside, each ready to shoot the traitors down with shaft or spell.

"Come away from the mechanism," the magician, a thin, aging woman with braided hair, continued. She was still in her nightgown, with only a knit shawl wrapped around her shoulders to ward off the chill.

Come away? Fodel thought. Why? They'd only kill him anyway. Better, then, to go down fighting, striving to do what he'd come so close to accomplishing. He threw his weight against the windlass, and Avarin did the same. A first crossbow bolt, precursor to the volley to follow, streaked past Fodel's head.

Fire, dazzling bright, roared down from the sky to engulf men-at-arms and paladins, wizards and clerics, who screamed, floundered, burned, and died. Those defenders who happened to be standing outside the perimeter of the blast, and who thus survived it, goggled upward to see what had so unexpectedly attacked them. What they saw there drove some mad with fear and made them bolt. The rest, the bravest, prepared to strike back.

With a jolt that shook the earth and knocked men staggering, a gigantic dragon slammed down amid the litter of burning corpses. Its scales were a dull, deep red, and its blank eyes glowed like orbs of molten lava. With a claw it pulled a knight's guts out of his belly. Its serpentine tail lashed, shattering an archer's legs. Biting, its fangs sheared off the top half of a wizard's torso.

The defenders managed to do the wyrm some little harm in return. An arrow pierced one of its scalloped neck frills. Bellowing the name of his god, a Paladin of the Golden Cup swung his greatsword and cut a gash in the dragon's flank. The wizard in the shawl thrust out her hands and encrusted the monster's neck and one wing in frost, which seemed to sting it. The dragon hissed in fury. Blood oozed from its scales, not as a result of any injury but as a manifestation of some magic of its own, and slathered it in a dark, shiny wetness. It lunged, snapped, and raked at its adversaries even more savagely than before.

At which point Fodel abruptly realized that the surviving defenders were so busy fighting the wyrm that they'd forgotten all about him and Avarin.

"Let's get it open," he said, and he and his comrade hauled on the windlass anew. One of the iron leaves swung inward, and cheering and howling, stunted goblins, pig-faced orcs, and a miscellany of bigger, more fearsome creatures surged through. A towering hill giant with thick, long arms, a low forehead, and lumpish features spotted Fodel and Avarin and rushed them. It swung its crude warhammer over its head.

"We're friends!" Fodel cried. "We opened the gate for you!"

The giant only sneered.

But then, in the blink of an eye, Sammaster appeared between the huge marauder and its intended victims. Many an observer might have regarded him as an even more alarming apparition than the giant, for his spiked gold crown and the rest of his jeweled regalia did nothing to blunt the horror of his withered skull-face and skeletal limbs. But Fodel had never been so glad to see anyone in his life.

"They are friends," the undead wizard said. "Go make yourself useful. Pulp some paladins or something."

The giant inclined its head in a servile fashion and shambled away to do its master's bidding.

"Thank you!" Fodel said. "I thought—"

Sammaster silenced him by raising a bony finger. "Be careful what you say," the enchanter whispered. "Remember that to you, I'm the First-Speaker of our fellowship, but to our allies here, I'm Zhengyi, their fallen Witch-King risen from the Abyss to lead them to victory. Convenient, isn't it, that to most eyes, one lich looks like another."

"Thank you for sending the dragon to help us." Fodel wondered how Sammaster had known they needed succor, but probably that was no great trick for a master wizard. "I'm sorry we couldn't open the gate secretly, the way we were supposed to."

"No matter. I thought to take the fortress with more finesse and less brute force, but the important thing is that we've taken it. Look for yourself."

Fodel gazed out into the courtyard and saw that Sammaster was correct. The king's men had no hope of contending with the dragon and the invading horde of goblin kin simultaneously. Most of the men-at-arms were dead, the rest, routing. Perhaps a handful would escape the citadel and lose themselves in the night, but that didn't matter.

Earlier, the castle called the Vaasan Gate, where the Cult of the Dragon had likewise insinuated its agents, had fallen, enabling Sammaster to lead the orcs and giants of the desolate territory to the northwest into Bloodstone Pass. Marching at maximum speed under cover of darkness, the invaders had ignored the various setlements in the valley to reach the Damaran Gate in advance of any warning that aught was amiss, and they'd taken possession of that fortification as well.

Well, actually, only the eastern tip of it. The Damaran Gate was a mammoth construction of wall and watchtowers three miles long, with castles anchoring the ends, and it was the lesser of these that Sammaster had overthrown. But that was enough to open Damara to the hosts of savage creatures who'd lusted to take their vengeance on it ever since the king slew their overlord and drove them out of his dominions fourteen years before.

Fodel was a Damaran himself, and for a moment, felt a vague pang of regret over the slaughter and ruin to come. Then he reminded himself of the glorious future that awaited him and all who believed in Sammaster's teachings, and the emotion faded.

—————ecoe—————

The company had ridden hard for two days, but, Igan reflected, no one would know it from the way Gareth Dragonsbane sat tall and easy in the saddle. Trying to copy the brawny, handsome, blond-bearded warrior as a squire was supposed to emulate the knight he served—especially if said knight also happened to be a Paladin of the Golden Cup, a celebrated hero, and the King of Damara—the gangly youth with the pox-scarred face sat up straighter, too.

"They're coming," said Mor Kulenov, one of the senior wizards, a pudgy little man with a billy-goat beard. Presumably some spell alerted him to the enemy's approach.

"It's a bad idea," grumbled Drigor Bersk, "fighting dragons in the dark." Scar-faced and hulking, stronger than most men-at-arms, the priest of Ilmater was a dauntless terror in battle, but had a habit of predicting doom before the hostilities commenced.

"It's either stop them here and now," Dragonsbane said, "or let them rampage through Ostrav. The village is just beyond those hills. Besides, dragons are big, Drigor. You won't have any trouble picking them out, even at night." He raised his voice and called, "All right, gentlemen, this is where we make our stand. You know what to do, so take your positions, and may the Crying God bless us all."

Maneuvering with practiced efficiency, the company of six hundred riders dispersed itself into a number of smaller units arrayed across the heath. It was a looser formation than the king might have chosen to meet another foe, but it was bad tactics to bunch up when fighting dragons.

Though he'd skirmished with orcs and bandits, Igan had never even seen a drake. He looked forward to it with a mix of eagerness and dry-mouthed trepidation, despite the fact that he still might not behold a living wyrm up close. His master had assigned him to help guard four of the magicians, a contingent positioned to the rear of most of the men-at-arms, and it was entirely possible no dragon would attack so far behind the front line.

Like the majority of mounts, even war-horses, Rain, Igan's dappled destrier, quite possibly lacked the courage to stand before a dragon. Accordingly, Igan tied him up, then, carrying his lance to use as a spear, took up his position in front of the warlocks. After that, he had little to do but wait and imagine his comrades making their preparations for combat out there in the dark. Archers were surely stringing their bows, warriors tightening the pommels of their swords, clerics praying for the blessing of Ilmater and the other gods of light, and mages conjuring wards of their own. Indeed, flickers of silver, blue, and greenish light across the moor gave evidence of spellcasting.

One of the magicians stalked up to Igan and the other men who were his protectors. His squint, the tight set of his jaw, and the tension in his shoulders gave him a clenched, dyspeptic look that was habitual. Igan knew the wizard's name was Sergor Marsk, but little else about him.

"Stand a few yards farther forward," Sergor said.

The sergeant, a short, wiry man with a bushy white mustache, a gimpy leg, and a missing pinkie likely severed on some forgotten battlefield, said, "We're better able to guard you if we stay close."

"Do as I say!" Sergor snapped, and perhaps realizing how sharp he'd sounded, continued in a more moderate tone. "We'll be conjuring forces that could hurt you if you stand too near, and the dragons won't molest us anyway. They won't even see us."

"Have it your way," the sergeant said. "You heard him, boys. Move thataway." The line shifted forward.

Sergor returned to his colleagues, murmured words of power, and brandished a scrap of fleece. The air rippled and turned colder for a second, and the four warlocks twisted into the form of a cart heaped high with baggage. Igan assumed that in actuality, the mages were still there, hidden behind an illusion.

"That's odd," he said, frowning.

"What is?" the sergeant replied.

"If Goodman Marsk wanted to conjure a veil, why not hide all of us behind it, wizards and guards alike?"

The old soldier snorted. "It probably never occurred to him. High-and-mighty magicians don't give a rat's whisker about folk who can't cast spells. The sooner you learn that, the better off—Oh, Tempus, here they come!"

Igan jerked around. At first glance, he spotted half a dozen dragons, a couple soaring, one, cloaked in shimmering light, proceeding over the ground in a series of prodigious bounds aided by snaps of its wings, and the others striding as fast as a horse could run. One of the striders glowed like a hot coal. All had presumably fallen prey to the Rage, the madness that made wyrms rampage across country killing everything in their path.

The king's men were elite warriors all. Even so, a few threw down their weapons and shields and ran, overwhelmed by fear. Others lost control of the panicked steeds whose mettle they'd trusted too well, and the destriers bore them helplessly away. But most of the company stood its ground.

Volleys of arrows thrummed and whistled through the air, and flares of fiery breath leaped and hissed in answer. The first dying men and horses screamed. The air above the heath sparkled and rippled, and Igan felt a momentary surge of vertigo, as a number of spellcasters conjured attacks all at once. One of the flying dragons fell and hit the earth with a crash. Warriors cheered, but the celebration was premature. The wyrm heaved itself to its feet, shook itself like a wet hound, and charged the nearest group of humans.

Igan realized something else that struck him as peculiar. "The mages we're guarding haven't attacked yet."

"They're working on it, I expect," the sergeant said. "I guess some spells take longer than others."

"How can they even see past the illusion Goodman Marsk conjured to pick a target?"

"I reckon they can do it because they're wizards. Now stop worrying about their job and do yours. Which is to shut up and stand ready."

Embarrassed, Igan resolved to do just that, for after all, he didn't know himself why he was so concerned with what the warlocks were or weren't doing. It was just a manifestation of his jitters, he supposed.

A sinuous shadow at the heart of a bulb of glowing light, the leaping dragon—a fang dragon, if Igan wasn't mistaken—rushed at the archers who were harrying it. Swirling tendrils of black mist appeared in its path, and five radiant spheres, each a different color, hurtled at it. Unfortunately, the spell effects failed to hinder it in the slightest. To Igan, it looked as if the curls of mist and brilliant orbs withered out of existence on contact with the reptile's shimmering aura, before they could touch its body.

The archers scattered, but they weren't all quick enough. The fang dragon pounced in among them and started killing. It struck so fast its motions were a blur, and every snatch of its talons, snap of its jaws, flick of a wing, or lash of its tail left at least one man mangled on the ground.

A party of lancers charged it. Their course carried them in front of the drake that was blazing hot, casting them briefly into vivid silhouette, enabling Igan to pick out Dragonsbane galloping a pace or two in advance of the others. The youth smiled, anticipating the deadly blow his master was about to strike, for how could it be otherwise? The king's very name bespoke his skill at slaying wyrms.

Then the greatest champion in Damara swayed like a cripple in his saddle. The point of his lance flopped down to catch in the ground, and the pressure tumbled him backward over his horse's rump. The knights riding closest to him hauled on their reins to keep from trampling him, and veered into the comrades on their other flanks. Other lancers, focused on the fang dragon, raced on without realizing anything was wrong.

"Ilmater's tears!" Igan cried. "What happened?"

"A dragon struck him down with a spell," the sergeant answered. "They're sorcerers, you know."

Igan did know, but he still wasn't sure the older warrior was correct. It was his impression that all the drakes had been busy with other targets at that particular moment.

Something implored him to act. It might have been the whisper of a god or merely the urging of his own folly, but either way, he meant to heed it. He dropped the long, heavy lance—a good weapon for fending off a dragon but otherwise awkward for a combatant afoot—drew his broadsword, wheeled, and strode toward the illusory cart. The sergeant called after him, but Igan ignored him.

The interior of the phantasm resembled an artist's palette, but with all the dabs of luminous, multicolored paint twisting and crawling around one another. Fortunately, the space was only a few feet across. Two more strides carried Igan out the other side before he could lose either his bearings or the contents of his stomach.

When he emerged, a single glance confirmed the worst of his suspicions. One of the mages lay dead or at least insensible on the ground. After striking him down, his companions had proceeded to the real point of their treachery.

Pulling as if it were a garrote, Sergor held the end of a thin black cord in either fist. In the middle, the tight coils cutting into it, hung an entangled rag doll. Though the figure was crudely fashioned, its tinsel crown, fringe of yellow beard, and the golden chalice emblem stitched to its torso made it plain it represented the king. The other two traitorous warlocks stood facing it, crooning to it in some sibilant, esoteric language, weaving their hands in cabalistic passes. Their fingers left fleeting smears of deeper blackness on the night.

Igan rushed in. He wanted to kill Sergor first, but the wizard saw him coming, squawked a warning to his fellows, and scrambled backward out of range. Igan had to content himself with a thrust at a different target. The traitor was still turning when the point drove into his side. He crumpled.

As Igan yanked his blade free, Sergor's other comrade jabbered a rhyme. Something flickered at the edge of the squire's vision. He pivoted in time to see the jagged length of conjured ice fly at him, but not in time to dodge. The missile exploded against his chest. Though the shards failed to pierce his breastplate, a pang of ghastly cold stabbed through his torso and doubled him over.

As he struggled against shock, he heard both magicians chanting, and realized with a surge of dread that he couldn't reach either one in time to stop his conjuring. He would have to endure two more magical attacks.

Then, however, the sergeant strode out of the illusory cart. Judging by the way he goggled, he hadn't realized anything was amiss. He'd simply come to drag an errant squire back to his assigned duty. But he only needed an instant to recover from his surprise. Then he lowered his spear, ran forward, and rammed it into the belly of the mage who'd produced the dart of ice.

That disrupted the one casting, but Sergor finished a split second later. He thrust out his hand and a bolt of yellow flame leaped from his fingertips. Igan tried to jump aside, but the fire brushed him anyway, searing him.

Refusing to let the pain balk him, Igan charged. Sergor scrambled backward and commenced a rhyme. His hands swirled in a complex figure. Power howled through the air. But the whine died abruptly when Igan's sword smashed through the warlock's ribs.

As soon as Sergor collapsed, Igan felt the fierce heat gnawing at the left side of his body. He dropped and rolled until the fire went out. By that time the sergeant was standing beside him.

"What is all this?" the old warrior asked.

"A rag doll . . . we have to find it . . . Sergor must have dropped it so he could throw other—"

Igan saw the doll and snatched it up.

The black cord still cut into the cloth figure even though no one was pulling on the ends. Igan hauled off his steel gauntlet so he could use his fingertips more deftly, and with considerable difficulty, stripped the binding coils away. Then he ran back through the illusory cart to survey the battlefield.

He cursed when it appeared that the king was as crippled as before. Some of his retainers were trying to hoist the big man in his heavy plate over the back of his horse so they could take him to safety. Others had positioned themselves between the fang dragon and the stricken monarch. The gigantic reptile, still cloaked in its shimmering aura of protection, lunged, raked, and bit amid a shambles of shredded human and equine corpses.

A rider on the wyrm's flank chopped at its foreleg with an axe. In response, the drake simply shifted the limb and brushed the axeman and his mount. An armored knight and charger might have been able to withstand such a comparatively light bump, except that the edges of a fang dragon's scales were as sharp as blades. They stripped away the steel and leather layers of protection to flay the flesh beneath.

The dragon snatched up another warrior in its jaws, chewed, swallowed, then pounced at the knot of men surrounding the king. Its bulk smashed through the final rank of defenders, reducing the scene to chaos. Men dropped, pulped and shattered. Horses bolted. The wyrm was within easy reach of Dragonsbane, and those who'd hoped to remove the king from harm's way had no choice but to turn and fight.

Igan looked around, hoping to see other men-at-arms rushing to the king's aid. Nobody was. They were busy fighting the other wyrms.

Igan snatched up the lance he'd dropped and ran for Rain, still tethered among a dozen other horses to the twisted steel stake his rider had screwed into the ground. The sergeant scrambled after him. They untied their mounts and swung themselves into their sadles, but the older warrior's steed balked at going any closer to the dragons. Igan was on his own.

As he galloped onto the field, the fang dragon steadily obliterated the king's defenders, one every heartbeat or so.

"Steady, Rain," Igan crooned. "Steady, good boy, don't be scared, just do it the way we practiced. . . ."

The closer he rode to the dragon, the better he could see it, and the more hideous it became. Its hide was dark and mottled, and bony spurs projected from its joints. The tail forked into two long, bladelike projections, and the orange eyes smoldered. Resisting his swelling dread as best he could, Igan galloped to within several yards of it, and it turned its glittering gaze on him.

Rain whinnied in terror as some magical force the wyrm had invoked heaved him and his rider twenty feet into the air. It slammed them down again a second later.

Igan lay on his side. For a moment, he couldn't remember

why, where he was, or what was happening. Then he realized that when the dragon had dashed him and Rain to the ground, it must have knocked him unconscious for a time. He was lucky it hadn't done worse than that, almost certainly luckier than poor Rain, who sprawled motionless, his weight pressing down on his rider's leg.

Igan kicked his feet out of the stirrups, then awkwardly squirmed and dragged himself out from under the destrier. By the time he stood up, the dragon, intent on other foes, had pivoted away from him. Still, he had to take a steadying breath, gathering his courage, before he could bring himself to poise the lance and run at the creature.

It sensed him coming, swung back toward him, but not quite quickly enough. By more good fortune, the lance punched through what must have been a thin spot in its scales and jabbed deep into the base of its neck. The drake let out a weak hiss, stamped, reached in a shuddering, faltering way to seize Igan in its jaws, then flopped over onto its flank.

It occurred to Igan then that he likely had won his spurs today, but he didn't even care. Only Dragonsbane mattered. He scurried to his master, helped to carry him from the field, and stayed with him for the remainder of the battle, watching as various learned folk attended him. At first the clerics worked alone. Then, when their efforts proved unavailing, they sent for wizards to help them.

That was no use, either.

Out on the heath, the company slew the last surviving dragon, and Drigor turned to the onlookers and announced what everyone already realized: "I don't understand. His Majesty isn't dead. He isn't even wounded. But neither Master Kulenov nor I can rouse him."

—————✦—————

Cloaked in the diminutive form of an aged gnome with nut-brown, wrinkled skin, Lareth, King of Justice, sovereign of the gold dragons of Faerûn—indeed, of all metallic wyrms, until the present crisis passed—sat on an outcropping, watched the morning sun creep higher into a clear blue sky, and wondered about the taste of human flesh.

He'd never sampled it, of course, or the meat of any sentient creature, even a slinking goblin or brutish orc. No metal dragon had. It was against their laws, to the extent that such proud and independent beings could be said to have any.

He'd never questioned the wisdom of such a prohibition, but now he didn't see the point of it. Naturally no dragon of goodly character would eat a human of similar inclinations, but if you had to kill a wicked man to stop him from doing evil, wherein lay the harm of devouring the body afterward?

Was the meat so succulent that the wyrm might develop a compulsion to eat it on a regular basis? Lareth tried to imagine a feast as delicious as that, the sweet, warm, bloody flesh melting on his tongue, the dainty bones cracking between his fangs and giving up their marrow—

And avidity gave way to a surge of nausea. Lords of light, what was the matter with him?

Of course, he knew the answer. It was the Rage, madness and bloodlust nibbling at his mind. He needed to rest, but first he'd have to wake another sentinel to take his place.

Knowing he'd sleep better in his natural form, he swelled into a gleaming, sinuous creature with a gold's characteristic "catfish whiskers," twin horns sweeping back from the skull, and wings that sprouted at the shoulders to extend almost all the way down to the tip of the tail. He turned, spread his pinions, and leaped upward. Below him, in a valley nestled among the frigid peaks called the Galenas, dozens of his kin lay slumbering, their scales—gold, brass, silver, bronze, or copper—glittering in the sun.

Furling his wings, Lareth landed beside a fellow gold nearly as huge as himself. It was Tamarand, first among the lords. Tamarand was snoring, an odd little puff and whistle that made Lareth smile for a moment. Then he recited the incantation Nexus, greatest of all draconic wizards, had taught him. Power groaned through the air, and tufts of coarse mountain grass caught fire.

Tamarand's blank, luminous amber eyes fluttered open. He heaved himself to his feet, then inclined his head in a show of respect.

"Your Resplendence . . ."

"I need you to take over for a while," Lareth said. "I . . . the frenzy was . . ." He realized he didn't need or want to explain the shameful impulse that had crept unbidden into his mind. "Just take over."

Tamarand eyed him. "Are you all right?"

Under the circumstances, the question shouldn't have annoyed Lareth, but it did anyway. It even made fire warm his throat and brought smoke fuming out of his maw and nostrils before he stifled the emotion.

"I'm fine. It's just . . . you know what it is. This is why we take turns standing watch. Because it's dangerous for any of us to remain awake for too long at a stretch."

"Of course."

"Lay the enchantment on me, and—"

Lareth heard wings lashing overhead, and peered up at the sky to see Azhaq swooping lower. A member of the martial fellowship of silvers called the Talons of Justice, Azhaq was one of the few metallic drakes who enjoyed Lareth's permission to stay awake and wander abroad.

Lareth should have greeted Azhaq with the decorum befitting their respective stations, but he was too eager to hear what the shield dragon, as silvers were often called, had to say. Before Azhaq's talons even touched the earth, the King cried, "Give me your news. Did you find Karasendrieth, or any of the other rogues?"

Smelling like rain as his species often did, the broad argent plates on his head reflecting the sun, Azhaq folded his wings and inclined his head. "No, Your Resplendence. The Rage has plunged the North into madness. Flights of our evil kindred lay waste to the land. The Zhentarim and other cabals of wicked men strive to turn the chaos to their own advantage.

Suffice it to say, amid all the terror and confusion, it's difficult to pick up a trail."

Lareth bared his fangs in a show of frustration. "Then why have you returned," he asked, "if not to report success?"

Azhaq lowered his wedge-shaped head with its high dorsal frill in a rueful gesture. "I had to come. The frenzy has its claws in me. I need to sleep, and perhaps it's just as well. On my flight north, I saw something you ought to know about. The creatures of Vaasa have breached the fortifications in Bloodstone Pass. They're pouring into Damara."

"Impossible," Lareth said. "They could never take the Gates, certainly not without the Witch-King to lead them, and Zhengyi is gone."

"I don't know how they managed it," Azhaq said, "but they did, and Damara was already in desperate straits, fighting off dragon flights. I don't know how the humans can deal with hordes of orcs as well."

"It's a pity," Lareth said, "but there's nothing we can do about it at the moment."

"With respect, Your Resplendence," Azhaq said, "I think there might be. Surely the dragons sleeping here can withstand the Rage for just another day or two of wakefulness. That could be all the time we need to turn the goblins back."

"No," Lareth snapped. "Too risky. We stick to our plan."

"Plans must sometimes change to fit changing circumstances," Azhaq said.

Lareth's fire rose in his throat and warmed his mouth. "Wings of our ancestors," he snarled, "why didn't I see it before? You and Karasendrieth were comrades in your time."

His eyes like pools of quicksilver, Azhaq blinked in what was surely feigned confusion. "What? No . . . never."

"Since the day I sent you to deal with her, you've caught up with her *twice*—"

"No, only once!"

"—and she 'escaped' both times. It can only be because

you permitted it! You're her accomplice, working to undermine me from within my own court."

Lareth reared to blast forth his flame. Realizing he was in actual danger, Azhaq crouched, his wings unfurling with a snap, as he prepared to spring.

Tamarand lunged between the two combatants. Lareth scrambled, trying to reach a position from which he could expel his fiery breath without hitting his meddling fool of a lieutenant, while Azhaq attempted a corresponding maneuver.

Wings spread to their fullest to make his body a more effective screen, scuttling to keep the king and the Talon separated, Tamarand bellowed, "Llimark! Llimark! Llimark!"

Angry though he was, the shouted name finally registered with Lareth, and he understood he'd been confused. It was Llimark, one of his own golds, who'd been Karasendrieth's friend, and Llimark who, at his monarch's behest, had attempted to bring her to heel the first time. Just as he'd maintained, Azhaq had only caught up with the dragon bard on a single occasion, later on.

The Talon was no liar, and likely wasn't a traitor, either. Lareth abandoned his combative posture and stood still. When Azhaq discerned as much, he too dropped his guard. Tamarand warily edged out from between the other two wyrms.

"My friend," Lareth said, "I'm truly sorry."

"You have nothing to apologize for," Azhaq replied, albeit somewhat stiffly. "It was the frenzy prompting you."

"Yes," said Lareth, "and it shows just how close to the edge all of us truly are. This is why we don't dare fly to the aid of Damara."

Azhaq grimaced. "I suppose."

"Gareth Dragonsbane is a great leader. He saved his people once, and he'll do it again, even without our help. Now lie down and sleep until someone wakes you to take a turn at watch."

Once the silver was asleep, Lareth turned to Tamarand.

"Thank you," said the king. "You saved me from a terrible mistake."

"It's always my honor to serve you," Tamarand said. "I'm just glad I was able to react quickly enough, because I certainly didn't foresee the need."

Lareth felt a pang of annoyance. "What are you getting at?"

"You know Llimark quite well, and you've invested countless hours reflecting on Karasendrieth and all reports concerning her. For you to become muddled in that particular way . . ."

"Must mean the Rage has crippled my mind? That it's time for the first of my Lords to take my place? Is that what you're implying?"

"No, Your Resplendence. By no means."

"Our folk elected me King of Justice because I'm the oldest and thus, the strongest, not only in body but in mind and spirit. I can withstand frenzy better than anyone else."

"I *know* that. It's just that you've stood almost as many watches as the rest of us put together. Perhaps the strain is telling on even you. Perhaps you should rest for a good long while."

Lareth did his best not to feel doubted, mistrusted, and betrayed. He struggled to believe Tamarand meant well.

"Lie down," Lareth said.

Tamarand peered at him and asked, "What?"

"You heard me. I'm going to put you back to sleep. You think I'm displaying signs of instability, but in fact, you are. You don't recognize it because that's the insidious nature of the affliction."

"Was I irrational when I stopped you from attacking Azhaq without cause?"

"No, but you are now."

"When you roused me, you said it was because you yourself needed rest."

"I was suffering dark fancies, the same kind that plague us all. It's nothing I can't endure for a while longer."

"But you don't have to! If you don't trust me, wake Nexus, or one of the others."

Lareth hesitated. "Well, I admit, that makes sense. As soon as you're asleep, I will."

Then Tamarand hesitated. "Your Resplendence . . ."

"Lie down, old friend. I know your mind is in turmoil, but trust me, as we have always trusted one another down the centuries. Or are you turning rogue on me as well?"

Tamarand stood silent for a moment or two, then said, "Of course, I trust and obey you, my liege, as I have always done."

Lareth cast the enchantment of slumber on Tamarand then returned to the outcropping where he liked to perch. He experienced a twinge of guilt at lying to his lieutenant, but realized he simply didn't feel inclined to sleep quite yet. Besides, it truly did make sense for the strongest to stand guard as much as possible and so shield lesser drakes from the ravages of frenzy.

It occurred to Lareth that he ought to resume his gnome disguise. Wearing the shape of one of the small folk enhanced a dragon's ability to resist the Rage. But he didn't feel like doing that, either. He was too tense, too frustrated by Karasendrieth's continued defiance, and vexed by Tamarand's questioning of his competence. At the moment, forsaking his draconic body would make him feel weak and vulnerable, and he very much wanted to feel strong.

❧

Sammaster stood on a ledge in the morning light and watched the orcs stream like ants through Bloodstone Pass. With their access to the lands beyond secured, some of the goblin kin were attacking the various settlements inside the valley. From on high, the battles looked like black twitching knots on the ground. Pillars of gray smoke from burning villages and isolated crofts billowed up to foul the sky.

At first, Sammaster felt satisfied. He didn't know if the brutish inhabitants of Vaasa would actually succeed in conquering Damara, but he didn't care. His only purpose had been to plunge the region into a bloody chaos that would inhibit any effort to find the source of the secret power he'd mastered and halt the process he'd set in motion. Until such time as it didn't matter anymore. Until he and the Cult of the Dragon had created enough dracoliches to subjugate the world and grind humans, dwarves, orcs, giants, and all other races into subservience.

Gradually, though, as was often the case when, to all appearances, everything was going well, the dead man felt contentment eroding into doubt. So many times before, he'd imagined himself on the brink of triumph, only to have one or another of his countless enemies, all the folk who feared and envied his incomparable intellect and magical prowess, thwart and humiliate him, sundering him from the mortal plane for decades, or plunging him into self-loathing and despair.

This time, he reassured himself, he'd planned so well and acquired a tool so powerful that he couldn't possibly fail, yet even so, he wondered. He knew that somewhere there existed an unknown adversary who'd stolen the notes he'd cached in Lyrabar. For a variety of reasons, no one could decipher those pages, and even if somebody managed, it was inconceivable that he could put the information to use in the relatively brief time remaining. But still, if anyone did. . . . !

Sammaster had already decided he couldn't spare the time to hunt down the thief. Though his cultists were useful in their fashion, there were too many tasks across the length and breadth of Faerûn that only the lich himself could perform if his schemes were to come to fruition. As he brooded, it occurred to him that he could take one additional measure to guarantee no one else would discover his secret, if only to buttress his peace of mind.

He swept his skeletal hands through an intricate pass and said, "Come to me, Malazan."

The red dragon would heed the call wherever she was, and sense in which direction she ought to travel. Since no compulsion was involved, Sammaster could only hope she would choose to heed him. Under normal circumstances, the reptile probably would, but if she happened to be berserk in the midst of combat, her scales sweating blood and her already awesome strength and ferocity amplified to preternatural levels, that would be a different matter.

Soon a crimson dot rose up from one of the watchtowers along the Damaran Gate, circled, and soared in Sammaster's direction. The lich's eyes were shriveled, decaying things, but their vision was keener than in life, and he soon discerned a superficial cut on Malazan's shoulder, and a trivial tear in one membranous wing. As he'd expected, she had done more fighting since he'd seen her last, but if she'd chosen to invoke the demonic fury that was her particular gift, the fit had already passed.

Wings snapping and pounding, disturbing the air and making Sammaster's regal purple cloak billow and flap, Malazan settled on the ledge, which was only just broad enough to contain her immensity. As had become his habit, Sammaster scrutinized her features and posture, looking for warning signs that she was about to go mad.

He'd armored her mind, and the minds of all the Sacred Ones with whom he'd come in recent contact, against the Rage, but the protection wouldn't hold forever. The curse cast by the ancient elves, the mythal he'd adapted to his own purposes, was too strong, and growing stronger by the hour. His wizardry notwithstanding, he would prefer not to be caught off guard if a dragon should lapse into frenzy.

Malazan looked all right, though.

"Good morning, Milady," the lich said.

"Your orcs now control almost the entire length of the Damaran Gate," she said. "Only the larger castle remains in human hands, and I trust we can take it within a few days."

"You needn't concern yourself with that. Even if the occupants manage to hold out indefinitely, it will do nothing to hinder our plans."

" 'Our plans,' " Malazan echoed. "*Your* plans, you mean. I still don't understand why you want goblins scurrying all over Damara."

"As I explained, war serves our purposes. It will distract the likes of the Chosen and the Paladins of the Golden Cup from seeking out and destroying our hidden sanctuaries, thus denying you and your kin the opportunity to become undead and so escape eternal madness."

"I suppose," Malazan said. "In any case, now that I've accomplished the task you set me, it's time for me to repair to one of the havens myself."

It gratified Sammaster to glimpse how eager the red was to commence the process of transformation, how profoundly she feared the Rage. That was the point of all his work, to make her and the other chromatics feel that way.

They couldn't all become dracoliches right away, however. The process was too lengthy, difficult, and expensive, and the cult's resources, too limited. Sammaster reckoned that while wyrms like Malazan waited their turns, he might as well make use of them.

"I have one more task for you first," he said.

Malazan's lambent eyes glared. A drop of blood oozed from her scaly brow.

"Something else needs destroying," the lich went on. "It shouldn't take long. I'm not sending you alone."

"I'm tired of you presuming to *send* me at all. You're the servant of dragonkind, not our master."

"I acknowledge it proudly. It is, however, equally true that I'm your friend and savior, and as such, have earned your respect. Now, you have three choices: You can simply renounce me and my followers, and in time succumb to the Rage. Or, if you want to punish me for what you see as my impertinence, we can fight. I warn you, though, that I've slain many wyrms before you—bronzes, silvers, and even golds—and that even if you manage to destroy me, once again, the end result will be that you fall into frenzy. Or, you can cooperate, perform one more piddling chore to our mutual benefit, and claim your immortality."

Malazan spat a tongue of yellow flame, but not at Sammaster.

"What do you want me to do?" the dragon growled.

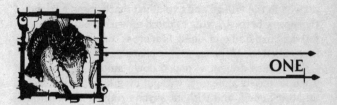

ONE

19 Mirtul, the Year of Rogue Dragons

The sailors cried out at the sight of the dot sweeping through the blue sky above the northern shore. Taegan Nightwind, whose avariel eyes were sharper than a human's, made haste to reassure his companions: "It's a metallic dragon. Brass, I think."

"What's the difference?" said Phylas, he of the shaggy hair and surly disposition, and Taegan had to admit he had a point. In such a grim time as the Rage, any wyrm, even a member of a species generally considered benign, could pose a danger.

The weather-beaten, almost toothless captain of the fishing vessel, however, chose to take the crewman to task.

"Swallow your tongue," he said, which was evidently a Moonsea way of rebuking someone for speaking out of turn. "Not all dragons have turned wicked. Think of Kara."

Despite his general distemper, Phylas had the grace to look abashed.

From what Taegan had gathered, Kara, Dorn Graybrook, Will Turnstone, Pavel Shemov, and Raryn Snowstealer had done Elmwood a considerable service by ridding it of a force of occupying Zhents. Accordingly, when the winged elf arrived in the village and explained that he was a friend of those very heroes, trying to catch up with them, the townsfolk had insisted on helping him cross the great freshwater lake called the Moonsea free of charge.

The brass dragon swooped down among the towers of Thentia and disappeared, without breathing fire or casting an attack spell, and without anyone ringing an alarm bell or shooting arrows at it. Presumably it was one of Kara's rogues, carrying some new bit of information to the town's community of wizards, those eccentric, fiercely independent arcanists who, by Pavel's reckoning, constituted the best hope of unraveling the mysteries of the Rage before it was too late. The locals had likely grown accustomed to the wyrms coming and going.

His iridescent scales rippling with rainbows, silvery butterfly wings beating, Jivex flew across the deck. He too was a drake, a faerie dragon, though the members of his particular forest-dwelling species were tiny compared to their colossal kindred. From the tip of his snout to the end of his constantly flicking tail, Jivex was only as long as Taegan's arm.

"You see," Jivex said, jerking his head in the direction of the since-vanished brass dragon, "that's how creatures with wings are supposed to get around. We ought to try it sometime."

The reptile had suffered a bout of seasickness during the first few hours of the voyage, and in consequence had evidently resolved to despise all boats forever after.

"I humbly beg your problem," Taegan replied, "for selecting this mode of transport. Silly me, I thought it might be imprudent to fly out over a large body of open water with no clear idea how far it was to the other shore, and nowhere to set down if our strength flagged."

Jivex snorted. "Well, can we get off the boat now?"

Taegan realized that was a good idea. Why creep slowly on into port when their wings could carry them there in a fraction of the time?

He turned to the captain and said, "With your kind permission, I believe we will take our leave now."

"It's all right with us," the sailor said. "The sooner we get back to netting fish, the better off we'll be."

"Well, then, Sune bless you all."

Taegan leaped up from the deck, pounded his black-feathered wings to gain altitude, caught an updraft, and flew on over the purple-blue water. The sun warmed his outstretched pinions. Maybe spring truly had arrived, even in the chilly northern lands.

His wings a platinum blur, Jivex took up a position beside Taegan, close enough for the two to converse.

"What will Thentia be like?" asked the drake.

"I've never been there. All I know about the place is that it's famous for its wizards." Taegan's fancy warmed to the idea. "So probably, the dogs and cats can talk, every woman saunters about cloaked in glamours to make her look as delectable as Lady Firehair herself, and the alchemists amuse themselves by turning all base metals into gold. Naturally, no one has to do any work. The mages have conjured demon slaves to perform every task, from chopping wood to swamping out the privies."

"Do you really think the wizards can stop the Rage?"

Taegan realized from the unaccustomed plaintive note in his companion's voice that Jivex was looking for reassurance. He must have suffered nightmares again the past night.

"I'm sure they can," the avariel lied. "What one wizard can do, even if the mage in question is Sammaster, a whole coven of them can surely undo."

They soared on over the docks and on into the center of Thentia. Peering down at the narrow, muddy streets and steeply pitched shingled rooftops, Taegan saw no wonders to betray the fact that the place was home to a plenitude of powerful mages. Thentia seemed a typical Moonsea town, a raw, rugged place that, for the most part, looked as if it had been knocked down and rebuilt so many times that the inhabitants had learned not to invest any time in creating ornate architecture or other civic amenities.

It did have a couple notable structures, though. One was a white marble temple whose stained glass windows bore the eyes-and-stars symbol of Selûne, goddess of the moon. Another was a tower painted in the most garish manner imaginable, with vertical streaks of red, yellow, and orange. The brass dragon had landed in the spire's courtyard and crouched with its head and neck stuck through the principal entry. As Taegan and Jivex swooped lower, the wyrm flattened its wings against its back and crawled completely inside, passing through the high, wide double doors with scarcely an inch to spare.

Taegan landed and started to follow, with Jivex flitting along beside him. A burly doorman with battered ears and a broken nose, clad in livery of the same bright hues disfiguring the tower, started to block the way, then goggled as he took a better look at the newcomers.

"The avariel," he said.

Taegan didn't actually like being called an avariel. Years before, he'd thrown in his lot with the human race, which, in his view, had built a splendid civilization while his own timid, primitive folk hid from the rest of the world. But he supposed that in this situation, the important thing was that the servant had heard about the winged elf who'd acquired Sammaster's folio.

"That's correct," he said, "I'm Maestro Taegan Nightwind." Maestro of nothing, some might say, since the Cult of the Dragon burned his fencing academy to the ground, but entitled to the honorific of a master-of-arms nonetheless.

"And I'm Jivex," the faerie dragon declared, "Lord of the Gray Forest. Well, part of it. Sort of."

"Kara said you might come," the doorman said, "when you finished your work in Impiltur."

"When we parted, I had no idea I'd do any such thing, so I can only marvel at her perspicacity," Taegan said with a grin. "Is she here? Or Dorn, or Pavel?"

The big man shook his head. "No, none of them. They've all traveled to one godsforsaken place or another, looking for the information the wizards need."

"Well, I suppose it doesn't really matter. I actually came to join the search for knowledge. I simply need the wizards to assign me a task."

"I'm sure Firefingers—Flammuldinath Thuldoum, my master—will be glad to oblige."

Dorn had mentioned "Firefingers," and Taegan suddenly understood the colors of the tower, and of the doorman's livery. "Your employer painted his home to resemble a flame," he said.

"Well, obviously," said Jivex in a superior tone. "*I* saw that right away."

The doorman tried to smother a smile. "I'll show you in."

At its base, the tower swelled into a ground floor the size of a villa. Once he entered, Taegan observed that much of the space constituted a single room, one Firefingers had evidently dedicated to the effort to end the Rage. The leaves from Sammaster's folio lay scattered across several long tabletops, mingled with books, scrolls, scribbled notes, quills, and inkwells. Charcoal rubbings of inscriptions from ruins and tombs hung along the high plaster walls, among jottings and diagrams scrawled in multicolored chalk. The mages had likewise drawn intricate pentacles and conjuror's circles in the open space in the middle of the floor.

Taegan was reasonably certain he could spend tendays poring over the scholars' work and emerge little wiser than before. He actually enjoyed considerable mastery of the specialized swordsman's magic called bladesong, but that scarcely provided the breadth or depth of esoteric knowledge that a genuine wizard possessed. He could only hope that Dorn's "partners," who had for some years created the enchanted weapons the half-golem and his comrades used as beast hunters for hire, knew what they were doing.

What they were doing at the moment, of course, was conferring with the brass dragon. Hunkered in the center of the room, its smooth, massive head plates nearly bumping the ceiling even so, the wyrm gleamed yellow in the white light of the floating orbs that provided illumination. Sharp blades grew from the underside of its lower jaw like extra fangs.

A dozen mages clustered around the brass, too many for Taegan to take in all at once, but a few stood out from the crowd. Robed in scarlet, gold, and orange, the stooped, wrinkled codger with the white beard must be Firefingers. He looked like some fortunate child's doting grandfather. In contrast, the colleague at his side, a beefy, middle-aged man with a square, florid face, slicked-back raven hair, and a patch covering his left eye, carried himself with an air of prickly self-importance. An elf with an alabaster complexion, a slender frame, and pointed ears like Taegan's own listened to the conversation with his head cocked and a frown of concentration. A small, impish-looking lass in the silvery robes of a priestess of the Moonmaiden—she must be clever, if, young as she was, she'd mastered arcane and divine magic both—took notes on a slate, the chalk scritch-scritching away. While in a corner, apart from the rest, head bowed, stood a figure so thoroughly shrouded in a cloak and cowl that Taegan couldn't tell if it was male or female, human, elf, or orc.

"Wait here," said the doorman, "and I'll announce you." He strode away.

"This is stupid," Jivex said. "We could announce ourselves."

"It's a custom," Taegan said. "People of a certain stature have servants to—"

The brass roared, the bellow deafening in the enclosed space, and cocked its head back. Fighting the Cult of the Dragon in the Gray Forest, Taegan had faced enough hostile wyrms to understand what was happening. The brass was about to discharge its breath weapon.

The air was warm, and even in the foothills of the harsh Galenas, patches of new green softened the stark contours of the slopes, while a first sprinkling of tiny white and purple wildflowers adorned the winding, ascending trail. Kara's throbbing soprano voice made the landscape even more beguiling. Wearing her willowy human form, partly to shield herself from the Rage, mounted on a white mare, her flowing silver-blond hair shining in the sun, the dragon bard sang a poignant song of love lost and ultimately regained.

As was often the case, to Dorn, the pleasures inherent in the moment felt like mockery, and why not? The simple truth was that things had turned to dung as usual. He, Kara, Raryn, and Chatulio wanted to reach their destination quickly, yet the need to avoid a flight of frenzied dragons had forced them north, off their chosen route and away from their goal. Moreover, he suspected that they were lost, despite Raryn's uncanny sense of direction and Kara's assurances that she knew the Galenas well.

So glum was his humor that he almost told Kara to hold her tongue. Not long ago, he would have, particularly since she was really a dragon. He had, after all, spent decades hating wyrms, and indeed, despised them still. But since meeting Kara there were times when the loathing softened, moments when it even felt mean and wrong. It disturbed him to imagine that he might one day lose it entirely. It was who he was.

Then Chatulio hissed, "Enough!"

Though no shapeshifter like Kara, the copper dragon was a master of illusion, and he wore the semblance of Dorn's huge—and comically ugly—swaybacked, cross-eyed, scrofulous piebald stallion. No actual horse, even the strongest, could have carried the weight of the half-golem's massive frame and enchanted iron arm and leg up and down the steep trails for very long.

Everyone else regarded the copper in surprise. Dorn belatedly realized that, wallowing in his own foul mood, he hadn't noticed that Chatulio hadn't cracked a joke or played a prank in several hours. That, coupled with the display of ill temper, was cause for concern.

"Rage eating at you?" asked Raryn, seated on his shaggy brown pony. As always, it was difficult to tell where the squat arctic dwarf's long white hair and goatee left off and his polar bear fur tunic began. His exposed skin was a flaking, sunburned red that would have been excruciating for a human, but caused his folk no distress whatsoever.

"What do you think?" Chatulio snarled. "Of course it is, and that constant shrillness scraping at my brain . . ." He drew in a long breath and let it out slowly. "I'm sorry, bluebird. I didn't mean it. You know I love your singing."

"It's all right," Kara said. "Too much of anything, even music, can wear on the nerves. I just went on and on because it helps me quell the frenzy in myself. Why don't we play the riddle game instead?"

Chatulio snorted. "We'd better play teams, and each partner up with one of the small folk. Otherwise, they won't stand a—"

"Hush!" said Raryn, holding up one broad, stubby-fingered hand. The dragons possessed inhumanly acute senses, but the dwarf ranger, relaxed as he often looked, was ever vigilant, and evidently he'd detected some sign of possible danger even before his reptilian comrades.

After another moment, Dorn heard the same thing: clopping hooves, the creak of leather, and the clink of metal—riders coming down the trail.

He cast about for a place to hide, but didn't see one.

Discerning the tenor of his thoughts, Kara said, "Chatulio or I can cast a magical concealment."

"And what then?" asked Dorn. "They'll just bump into us, unless we turn and flee before them, back the way we came—or unless you sprout your wings and we all fly away, leaving the mounts behind. I say, let's not bother. It's people approaching, not crazed wyrms. We have no reason to think they mean us ill, and if they do, I reckon we can handle it."

"Sounds all right to me," said Raryn.

They headed cautiously on up the trail, rounded a bend, and came face to face with eight mounted warriors.

By the look of their mismatched weapons and armor, kits plainly assembled from whatever gear they could get, the men-at-arms likely constituted the retinue of the petty lord of some tiny fiefdom thereabouts. The rider in the lead, a stout, graying man with a hawk-and-lily device painted on his kite shield, was evidently the nobleman himself, considering that a youth who strongly resembled him was carrying a banner embroidered with the same arms.

Their spears and swords ready to hand, the men-at-arms eyed Dorn and his companions askance. The half-golem was used to it. His grotesque appearance, the talons and knuckle-spikes on his oversized iron fist and the gray metal half-mask encasing his left profile, often made strangers shy away from him. But even after all those years, it still brought a twinge of resentment jabbing through his guts.

"It's all right," said Kara, holding up her empty hands to convey peaceful intentions. "We're simply travelers, the same as you." Maybe she was using magic to allay the warriors' misgivings, but if so, the charm was subtle enough that Dorn couldn't tell.

The nobleman studied her face for another moment, then waved his hand. His entourage relaxed.

"Well met," he said. "My name is Josef Darag, master of Springhill. The lad is my son, Avel."

Kara made the introductions on her side.

"What can you tell us," Josef asked, "of the road that lies ahead?"

"There was a dragon flight to the south," Raryn said, "but as long as you stay on this trail, you may be all right."

Josef smiled a mirthless smile and said, "I suppose that in these times, that's as much reassurance as anyone can expect."

"What waits ahead of us?" asked Dorn.

"Trouble," Josef said. "The Bandit Army has overrun a village."

Dorn frowned. "The which?"

"Just brigands, basically," Josef said, "for all their pretensions, who operate out of a hidden stronghold to the north. The king's men have wiped out scores of them, but never seem to catch them all. By now, the ones up ahead are taking their pleasure with the captive women, and torturing folk to find out the location of any hidden wealth.

"We almost rode right into the middle of the trouble," the noble continued, "but at the last second, Avel made out what was going on, and we turned around before the raiders saw us. Luckily, we knew of another path that let us swing wide of the village. You can use it, too. When you come to the fork, go left."

"Thank you for the advice," Kara said, then hesitated. "But I don't understand. Surely you and your followers are some of 'the king's men,' too. How can you turn your backs and leave the villagers to their fate?"

Josef glared. "Are you presuming to instruct me on my duty?"

"You have the air of a valiant knight," Kara replied. "I'm sure you require no such instruction from me or anyone."

"Well, you're right!" Josef took a breath, then continued in a softer tone, one that perhaps betrayed a hint of shame. "When we left Springhill, we were riding out to help our neighbors, to help all Damara, despite the risk involved in leaving our own home all but unguarded. We meant to join one of the companies the king was assembling to fight the dragons."

"What changed?" Raryn asked.

"We heard that the Witch-King has risen, taken the Gates, and led his orcs into Damara once more. And Dragonsbane is dead. His officers deny it, but the word's gotten out."

Raryn scratched the chin concealed within his short ivory beard and said, "Seems to me that gave you even more reason to go ahead and enlist in your band of warriors."

"You're an outlander," Josef said, "so you don't understand. The king was the only champion who could defeat Zhengyi, just as he was the only leader who could make the dukes forget their squabbles and stand together to serve the common weal. Without him, Damara will fall apart. By all accounts, it's happening already. That means every lord must concentrate on protecting his own vassals, and I'm working on getting home to look after mine. So perhaps you could let us by."

"As you wish," Kara said. She guided her mare to the edge of the trail, and Raryn followed suit with his pony. Chatulio naturally needed no prompting, though it must have taken some effort for him to make sure none of Josef's company brushed against an unseen folded wing, scaly flank, or serpentine tail.

Once the warriors disappeared around the bend, Dorn growled, "Wonderful. It sounds like nobody can travel anywhere in Damara without wading through goblins, bandits, necromancers, and the Beastlord only knows what else. And according to Pavel, we seekers have plenty of sites to visit hereabouts."

"It can't be much worse than contending with dragon cultists and Zhents," Raryn said. "We'll solve the problems as they come, the way we always do. The one we're facing now is that village."

"If a Damaran knight thinks it's none of his business," Dorn said, "then it's certainly not ours, either. Our job is stopping the Rage, and if we let every farmer's hard luck distract us . . ." He spat. "Ah, to the Abyss with it. It's just a few bandits. It'll probably take less time to smash through them than it would to go the long way around."

Kara gave him a smile of approval and amusement, too, as if his initial display of reluctance had been a kind of private joke between the two of them. It made him uncomfortable, and his impulse was to turn away, but he surprised himself by responding with a fleeting twitch of a grin instead.

Pavel paced back and forth and turned in circles, his gold-plated, garnet-studded sun amulet, symbol of Lathander, god of the dawn, clasped in one leather-gloved hand. Using the sensitivities his prayers had given him, the priest probed at the eroded stubs of what had once been standing stones, the patch of barren ground supporting them, and even the scummy, malodorous green surface of the lake that bordered it. By rights, his magically enhanced perceptions should reveal any hidden opening or lingering aura of enchantment in the area.

"Well?" Will demanded. Clad in his brigandine, warsling dangling from his belt and his seemingly oversized curved, broad-bladed hunting sword hanging at his hip, the halfling with his black lovelocks stood holding his dappled pony and Pavel's roan gelding while keeping an eye out for trouble. The two hunters had already discovered that in the so-called "Great Gray Land" of Thar, a hilly, windswept desolation inhabited primarily by orcs and ogres, danger was always close at hand.

"Nothing," Pavel admitted.

"Charlatan," Will sneered, but without the usual gusto. He was evidently discouraged, too, so much so that even their perpetual mock feud was losing its power to amuse.

"We can keep trying tomorrow," Pavel said. "After I pray for more divinatory spells at dawn."

"We've already been around the whole lake," said Will.

"I know."

Pavel walked to his horse, lifted a canteen from the saddle, and took a drink. The water, which he'd conjured into existence after they'd failed to find a wholesome-looking natural source, had grown lukewarm, but eased his dusty throat nonetheless.

"Maybe we should give up on this site," the halfling said. "You said yourself, Sammaster probably explored some places where there was nothing to find, or where the information was the same as what he'd already picked up elsewhere."

"True," Pavel said, "but he wrote fifteen pages about this site, wherever it is. We can't afford to ignore it."

"We can't afford to spend years looking, either. So for once in your worthless life, you'd better come up with an idea."

Pavel only prayed he could, for his present failure had cured him of the cockiness from which he'd suffered ever since figuring out how to use Sammaster's indecipherable notes. That success had made the priest of the Morninglord feel very clever indeed, until he and Will had come to Thar only to find nothing at all where, Pavel had been certain, an important site supposedly awaited them.

His horse abruptly raised its head high. Its nostrils flared, and trying to back up, the animal pulled on its reins, dragging Will off balance. Pavel grabbed hold of the horse's halter.

"Something's coming," he said, keeping his voice low.

"It's nice you can figure *something* out," Will said. "If it's obvious enough." He pointed. "See that hump of ground with the thorn bushes on top? We can hide behind it."

They urged their mounts to the cover. Pavel, who didn't trust the skittish animals to keep quiet, murmured a prayer and swept his pendant through a mystic pass, scribing a symbol on the air. Points of light burned inside the garnets, and the moan of the wind and every other noise abruptly fell silent. While the spell lasted, no sound could exist in the space where the hunters crouched, which meant none could exit it to betray their presence, either.

Pavel peered out at the ground along the shore, just in time to see a troupe of ogres tramp into view. Half again as tall as a tall man, long-armed, short-legged, covered in moles and warts, ogres were marauding, barbaric worshipers of the powers of darkness and a perennial scourge to humanity.

But the band didn't look as if it would bother anybody anytime soon. Apparently survivors of an encounter with one or more Rage-maddened wyrms, many limped, or bore ghastly wounds, huge, suppurating burns or long, bloody gashes. Perhaps the ogres had forsaken their usual territory to march to what they hoped would be a place of greater safety.

In any event, only one of the brutes still carried itself with the air of belligerent arrogance Pavel would have expected. The largest, a male, swaggered at the head of the procession, its oversized head with its bristling mane thrust forward, the fangs of its protruding lower jaw jutting over its upper lip. Like many of its fellows, it too bore a fearsome wound, but not a recent one. At some point, something had torn the right side of the ogre's face open. As a result, too much of the eyeball showed, especially at the bottom, and the entire orb was a bloody red. The giant-kin wore only a bearskin wrapped around its waist, the better, Pavel assumed, to display the sigils of Vaprak and other malevolent spirits branded into its flesh—it must be the clan shaman.

Pavel waited for the ogres to trudge out of sight, then gestured to convey the idea that he and Will needed to shadow them. Unable to ask verbal questions or argue inside the pocket of silence, the halfling settled for giving his human partner a dubious look, then shrugged and patted the pouch on his belt, reflexively making sure he still had a good supply of skiprocks for his sling.

━━━━━ ∞∞∞ ━━━━━

The mages of Thentia might be powerful, but they could be surprised like anyone else. Startled by the brass dragon's sudden aggressive display, they froze.

Taegan drew his cut-and-thrust sword and leaped. Wings pounding, he hurtled forward over the worktables and chalked pentacles on the floor. Jivex streaked along beside him. They reached the brass an instant before it would otherwise have spewed its fire. The avariel drove his point into its haunch, and Jivex bathed a patch of its scales in his own sparkling—and if they were very lucky, euphoria-inducing—breath.

Its sweeping tail smashing furniture and knocking mages off their feet, the brass rounded on its attackers without bothering to spit flame at its original targets. As Taegan had feared, the immense yellow wyrm looked anything but giddy. Jivex's breath was potent against hobgoblins and such, but less efficacious against drakes a hundred times larger than himself.

"Watch out!" Taegan shouted, springing to one side.

The plume of flame erupted from the brass an instant later, and missed him by inches. Squinting against the brilliance of the flare, he couldn't see Jivex, and didn't know whether the faerie dragon had successfully dodged.

Taegan kept on scrambling, trying to stay ahead of the wheeling brass's jaws and foreclaws, and jabbered an incantation. He didn't have any enchantments in place to enhance his prowess—he hadn't expected to require them—but he needed to conjure some quickly, before his adversary overwhelmed him.

Power whined through the air, and the brass struck at him like an adder. He saw that it was going to miss, though, no doubt because of his first trick. At the moment, it was seeing him slightly offset from his actual location. Its prodigious fangs clashed shut on empty air, and before it could whip its head away, he cut at its throat. Unfortunately, the sword glanced off its scales.

At the same instant, Jivex, seemingly unharmed, soared up behind the brass and hovered, staring at it intently. Probably he was trying to use one of his magical abilities against the larger wyrm, but to no apparent effect. The brass flicked a wing, and Jivex had to break off the effort to dodge the huge vaned membrane with the tarnished-looking green edge that would otherwise have swatted him like a fly.

Taegan spread his pinions and flew. He had to keep moving, too, didn't dare let the brass maneuver into a position where it could use its fangs, claws, flame, and other attacks to best effect. His subtle defensive illusion wouldn't save him from that. As he climbed almost to the ceiling, then dived nearly to the floor, trying to confuse his adversary, he recited another incantation, and caught a glimpse of some of the mages.

It didn't look as if any of them were dead, or even maimed. He and Jivex had succeeded in keeping the brass's attention locked on them. But he almost regretted that because, instead of attacking the crazed wyrm, a number of the wizards were fleeing. A couple blinked out of sight, translating themselves to some safe location. Others scurried along the wall, making for the door.

Though not everyone was running. The man with the eye patch and the lass dressed in a moon priestess's silvery vestments were throwing spells at the brass. Unfortunately, they didn't seem to be hurting or hindering it any more than Jivex had.

Meanwhile, Firefingers battled a different foe. The brass's blast of fiery breath had set books and documents alight. Indeed, if unchecked, the blaze might well spread to devour Sammaster's notes themselves and all the scholarly resources the mages were using to try to make sense of them. Weaving his arms in cabalistic passes, the old man in the garish robes crooned to the flames, coaxing and cajoling them. A bit at a time, the blue and yellow tongues floated up away from the paper and drifted to envelop his hands, which burned like torches.

The brass spun and whipped its tail at Taegan. Caught by surprise, he only just dodged, and in so doing, lost track of the wizards.

On the final word of his own conjuration, he swiped powdered lime and carbon down his blade, and the steel glittered and burned cold beneath his touch. While the spell lasted, his sword would be sharper than any ordinary blade.

The room, spacious as it was, was only barely large enough to accommodate a flyer his size. With difficulty, he zigzagged through the air to befuddle his foe, and spotted Jivex clinging to the larger drake's spine. Tearing with his talons, he swooped to the brass's flank, and thrust his sword between its ribs.

The brass jerked and roared. Taegan yanked his weapon free, mindful not to stop moving, and flew on toward its tail.

He began another spell, one intended to make him preternaturally fast.

Wind howled through the room. A brutal downdraft smashed Taegan to the floor and slammed the breath out of him. Heedless of the darts of ice and scarlet light battering it, the brass, which had no doubt conjured the artificial gale, glowered at him. Its long throat swelled.

It was about to breathe out another cone of flame, and with the screaming wind still pressing down on him, he couldn't dodge fast or far enough to evade it. He rolled, fetched up under a table, and hacked at the legs on one end. Though his sword was scarcely intended for such a task, its magically honed edge served to chop through the wood. That side of the table crashed down, cutting off his view of the brass.

The wyrm's breath engulfed the floor in a mass of flame that blistered him and filled his lungs with excruciating heat. Still, his makeshift shield blocked out the worst of it, and a moment later, the fierce winds halted as suddenly as they'd begun. Evidently one of the mages had countered the dragon's power with his own.

Maybe the sudden cessation of the winds had caught the wyrm by surprise. If so, it was possible that Taegan could rush in close and strike a telling blow while it was distracted. He scuttled out from under the table, leaped up, and flew at the reptile through the countless papers, embers, and scraps of ash adrift in the air.

He'd guessed correctly. The brass had turned away from him to lunge at Firefingers. Taegan's blade punched deep into its breast. It jerked back around, reaching for him with its claws, and Jivex balked it by whizzing into position to scrabble at its eye. Jaws gaping, it whipped its head around to snap at the faerie dragon, at which point sheets of liquid hammered from the empty air like rain from a tiny, invisible cloud. Where the torrent washed over the brass, its flesh smoked, sizzled, and charred.

The yellow drake collapsed, rolled, and convulsed, nearly crushing Taegan beneath its bulk before he flew clear. The reptile kept thrashing for half a minute, then finally slumped inert. The stink of its acid-seared flesh combined with the smoke in the air to sting the fencing teacher's eyes and put a vile taste in his mouth.

At least the room wasn't on fire anymore. Firefingers had collected all the leaping, rustling flames. Still murmuring words of power, he rubbed his hands together as if he was washing them, and the blaze went out. His skin wasn't even pink from the heat.

The elf wizard hurried over to Taegan. Seen up close, his fair complexion had a slight bluish tinge, as did his shoulder-length dark hair. Something about his pleasant, forthright face reminded the avariel of Amra, the kindly elf ghost, if that was the right word, he'd encountered in the Gray Forest.

"How badly are you hurt?" the magician asked.

Taegan tried to respond, but a fit of coughing overwhelmed him.

"It's all right," said the elf. "One of us is a healer, and happily"—he pulled a wry face—"she's one of the ones who didn't run. Sinylla, come here, please!"

The moon priestess hurried in their direction.

"The body!" Firefingers panted. "Don't let the leakage dirty any papers!"

"I'll get rid of it," said the one-eyed man. He started the process by murmuring a rhyme and lashing his hand through a complex pattern, whereupon the brass shrank to a fraction of its former size.

The elf wizard looked sadly at the ravaged, diminished remains. "Poor Samdralyrion," he sighed. "To all appearances, he was one of the most stable of all Kara's allies. I didn't notice any warning signs at all. The Rage took him all at once, in a heartbeat."

Taegan frowned at the suspicion that popped into his head.

Dorn stood in his customary fighting stance, iron half forward, vulnerable human parts behind, long, heavy hand-and-a-half sword cocked back in his fist of flesh and bone. The two bandits edged apart, trying to flank him, and he lunged and snapped his massive metal arm in a backhand blow. His target likely didn't expect anyone who looked so ponderous to pounce that quickly, and the attack caught him by surprise. The knuckle-spikes smashed his skull, and he dropped.

The other raider turned tail. Dorn started to pursue, but then Kara stopped singing her battle anthem to snarl instead. Alarmed, the half-golem pivoted in her direction.

Lithe and lightning-quick, a sparkling crystal-blue in her dragon form, Kara was fighting in front of one of the sod huts that comprised the village. As far as Dorn could tell, nothing had hurt her, nor had any worthy foe appeared to challenge her. Rather, all the surviving brigands in her vicinity were routing. Yet she'd abandoned her music to growl like an angry beast.

As Dorn had predicted, two dragons and a pair of warriors as able as Raryn and himself had experienced no real difficulty defeating a motley band of marauders. Yet the situation had presented a genuine peril nonetheless, the risk that the excitement of combat would cause one or both of the drakes to succumb to the Rage.

Dorn had to stop Kara before the fury deepened, before she gobbled down one of the bandits, lashed out at her own allies, or attacked the villagers.

"Kara!" he called. "Kara!"

She whipped around to face him, amethyst eyes glaring.

He set his bloody sword down on the ground. Fresh gore stimulated the Rage, and he wished he could thoroughly clean his iron hand as well, but knew there wasn't time.

He eased toward Kara, murmuring to her in as soothing a manner as he could manage: "It's all right, the fight's over, you can stop now. Just breathe slowly, and calm down. You can shake the anger off, I've seen you do it before."

She shuddered and bared her fangs. The air smelled like an approaching storm. He was only a few paces in front of her, and drawing nearer with every step. If she chose to attack him with her breath weapon, a plume of vapor charged with the essence of lightning, it would be all but impossible to dodge.

He kept on closing the distance anyway, though he wasn't sure why. It didn't seem as if his prattle was having any effect. In another moment or so, she was going to snap.

Dorn wracked his brain for a way to reach her, and after what felt like a long time, an idea came to him. He sucked in a breath and started singing one of the first songs he'd ever heard her perform, the one about flying high on the wind and beholding all Faerûn spread out below.

As he could have predicted, it sounded awful, harsh and off key, the rhythm stumbling. He hadn't tried to sing since the day the red slaughtered his parents. The impulse was something the wyrm had ripped away along with his arm and leg.

But bad as it sounded, it gradually stopped Kara's shaking. When, still singing, he drew near enough, he gingerly stroked the song dragon's mask.

Kara sighed, closed her eyes, and shrank, melting into her human guise. When the transformation was complete, she put her arms around him and clasped him tight.

"Thank you," she said.

As always, her touch made him feel soft and strange inside, and that was disturbing. Still, he suffered the embrace for a moment or two before breaking it off.

"You would have mastered the frenzy anyway," he said.

"Perhaps not. It's growing worse."

"I know, which means I was wrong to let you fight an unnecessary battle."

Kara smiled and said, "As if you could have stopped me."

Dorn felt his lips stretch into an answering grin. "Well, there is that." Then he was uncomfortable once more, and needed the moment to end. "We should find out what's happening."

She lowered her head as if to conceal a change of expression. "Yes, of course."

It only took a few moments to determine that Raryn and Chatulio were unharmed, and that the copper had resisted the frenzy. After that, the seekers turned their attention to the villagers.

The simple folk cringed from them, despite their efforts on their behalf. It put a bitter taste in Dorn's mouth, but he figured they were right to fear any wyrm in a time of Rage, and knew only too well that he himself resembled some sort of troll or demon. Even an arctic dwarf like Raryn was an oddity in the hinterlands of Damara, hence an object of mistrust.

Kara sang a rhyming couplet under her breath, and she grew even fairer than before. Dorn had to struggle not to stare at her. Yet the transformation did more than enhance her beauty. She seemed manifestly virtuous, a saintly creature whose every word carried the weight of wisdom and truth.

Cloaked in the enchantment, she was able to allay the villagers' fears and begin the work of setting the hamlet to rights, assigning tasks as necessary. Soon, folk who were still well tended those who were injured. Women cooked, and herders set forth to round up scattered sheep and goats. Employing his illusions, Chatulio created the equivalent of a comical puppet show to help the younger children forget the horrors they'd witnessed. When her other self-assumed responsibilities allowed, Kara devoted herself to those hardest hit by the cruelty and bereavement they'd suffered. She listened to their anguish, held their hands, and murmured words of solace.

Dorn watched it all at a distance, feeling that he had no aid to give. He had no knack for speaking gently. All he knew was how to kill.

In time, Raryn strolled up to loiter beside him. The dwarf still had spatters of bandit blood on his cheeks and in his white goatee. The gleaming head of his bone-handled ice-axe, however, was clean. The ranger was scrupulous about caring for his gear. He'd once explained that on the Great Glacier, where he'd spent his youth, weapons and tools were too hard to come by to treat carelessly.

The two hunters watched Kara discover a maimed dog in the shadow of a hunt, soothe it with her voice and caress, then kill it suddenly and cleanly with a thrust of her knife.

"She's a good woman," Raryn said.

"She's not a woman at all," Dorn replied

"Near enough." The dwarf grinned. "By my standards, anyway. Of course, tribal legend has it that some of my forefathers married bears."

Dorn grunted.

"Starting off," Raryn said, "you hated her just for being a dragon, but I don't think that's true anymore."

"Maybe not."

"So I ask, what are you waiting on? This is risky business, chasing all over the North with mad wyrms and other dangers lurking at every turn, sticking our noses into accursed crypts and haunted tombs. I like to think we're tough enough to win through, but I wouldn't bet my mother's teeth on it."

"You're imagining something that isn't there. I may not hate Kara, but I don't desire a creature like her, either."

Raryn shrugged his massive shoulders. "Fair enough, if you truly feel she isn't right for you. I'm just worried the real problem is that, deep down, you think you aren't good enough for her. If so, you're mistaken."

An hour later, they were traveling again, on a trace the villagers claimed was a shortcut to their destination. Apparently they were nearly there. Raryn and Kara had known where they were headed after all.

Accordingly, Dorn was eager to reach the place, but his enthusiasm curdled when they crested a hill and he caught his first glimpse of the gray crags, the imposing walls and spires hewn from the same rock, and the white expanse of ice. Specks of color glittered on the landscape far ahead, and if he could even see them at such a distance, Dorn knew they must be huge.

With his keen eyes, Raryn could make them out more clearly.

"Bugger," said the dwarf.

TWO

20 Mirtul, the Year of Rogue Dragons

Though the upper levels of Firefingers's tower weren't as large as the ground floor, they were so spacious Taegan suspected the wizard had cast an enchantment to make them larger inside than out-. The dining hall had room for all of Thentia's two dozen mages, and the old man had invited each and every one of them to breakfast with him before undertaking the chore of setting their dragon-damaged workroom to rights.

Taegan and Jivex sat as honored guests at their host's right hand. The elf mage Rilitar Shadowwater, was on the other side of them, probably because Firefingers assumed Taegan would enjoy the company of a member of his own race, albeit a different branch of it.

Rilitar seemed to believe the same thing, though in fact, his familiarity made Taegan feel somewhat edgy. Or maybe it was the tense atmosphere afflicting the gathering as a whole. Some of the mages who'd stood their ground to fight the brass dragon plainly disdained the colleagues who'd fled, while the latter resented any implication of cowardice, however justified it seemed.

Indeed, Phourkyn One-eye was engaged in a particularly vitriolic exchange with Scattercloak, the warlock who went about ever muffled in a gray mantle and hood. Scattercloack sat with his meal untouched lest, in the act of eating, he give someone a glimpse of his face.

"I did not flee," insisted Scattercloak in an androgynous, uninflected tenor voice. "I simply veiled myself in invisibility. That's why you didn't notice me afterward."

"Liar," Phourkyn sneered, a streak of light glinting on his oily black hair.

"Retract that."

"No."

Taegan's professional experience enabled him to recognize the preliminaries to a violent altercation when he saw them. But before the situation could deteriorate any further, Baelric, Firefingers's brawny doorman, strode into the hall in a manner that commanded attention.

Facing his master, he announced, "The Watchlord is here."

Firefingers blinked. "Really? Well, show him in."

Baelric ushered a middle-aged, solidly built, dour-looking man into the room. The newcomer was fancily dressed by Moonsea standards, though no rake in fashionable Lyrabar would have been impressed. He wore a chain of office dangling on the breast of his black velvet doublet, and at his side he carried a gold-hilted sword in a golden scabbard—likely another symbol of authority. A clerk and a pair of halberdiers trailed along behind him. All the mages rose to greet him, though some performed the courtesy in a perfunctory manner.

"My dear Gelduth," Firefingers said, beaming, "this is an unexpected honor. We'll set a place."

"I didn't come to eat," the Watchlord said. "I came—" His head snapped around to stare at Jivex, who sat on his haunches on the linen tablecloth behind the plate he'd just finished licking clean.

Prompted by Sune-only-knew what witless impulse, Jivex spread his silvery wings. Taegan grabbed him by the neck an instant before he could take flight. Jivex glared at him indignantly.

"The man's afraid of you," Taegan whispered. "Approach him, and he's liable to take a swipe at you with his sword." He gave Gelduth a smile. "This is Jivex, Lord. He's a friend to humans and other civilized folk."

The small dragon twisted, brought a hind foot into proximity with Taegan's hand, and gave him a stinging scratch across the wrist.

"Indeed." Gelduth pivoted back toward Firefingers and said, "I came to talk to you—all of you, even though by rights I should be able to summon you to attend me in the Watchlord's tower, at my convenience. But we all know how that generally works out, don't we?"

"Gelduth Blackturret's pretty much a figurehead," Rilitar whispered to Taegan, "and some wizards don't show him much respect. A mistake, in my view, precisely because he is the spokesman for the old families, and they really do run Thentia. Besides, he does a good job of protecting the outlying farms when the orcs come sniffing around."

"Well, at least let me get you a chair," said Firefingers to the Watchlord, and Baelric hurried away to fetch one.

"We have to talk," Gelduth persisted, "about all these dragons coming and going. I've told you before, it worries me. The noble Houses don't like it, either. Not when wyrms are running amok and laying waste to all Faerûn. But everyone accepted the situation because you assured us your dragons were safe. Now I understand that the one who arrived yesterday went berserk."

"Regrettably," said Firefingers, "that's true."

"Then I'm going to have to bar all drakes from Thentia."

Some of the mages scowled and exclaimed at that, though the show of dismay was less than unanimous. Affronted, Jivex hissed.

"My dear friend," Firefingers said, "I've told you, we're seeking a cure for the Rage. That's important work, and it absolutely requires that we consult with dragons. We'll lose precious time if you force us to relocate our operation."

"I don't see," Phourkyn said, "that this posturing oaf can 'force' us to do anything. We mages are the real power in Thentia. Apparently, because we don't abuse our strength, some folk underestimate it, but I can remedy that."

He gestured, and a pair of glass vials appeared in his hand. Blue smoke curled around his fingers.

Sinylla Zoranyian, the lass who'd healed Taegan's blisters, and who sat across the room from Phourkyn with two other petite priestesses to whom she bore a familial resemblance, sprang to her feet.

"No!" she cried.

Rilitar leaped up, too, and snatched out the topaz-tipped oak wand he wore sheathed like a dagger on his belt.

Phourkyn gave them both a sneer. "I would have changed him back," he said, "but have it your way."

The vials vanished from his grasp.

"If you'd actually cursed me," grated Gelduth to Phourkyn, "I guarantee you, the entire city would have taken it as an act of treason, and none of you, even the most powerful, could survive for long with every hand against you."

"Phourkyn's ill-considered jest has angered you," Firefingers said, "and I don't blame you. But surely we've no need to bandy threats about."

"I'm speaking bluntly," the Watchlord said, "because apparently it's the only way to stab through your conceit and make you hear. The rest of Thentia puts up with a good deal from you lot and your lunatic experiments. We tolerate foul stenches, flying rats, milk that spurts from the udder already sour, and shoes that clomp around all night by themselves. But we won't suffer slaughter and destruction that a bit of simple prudence might have prevented."

"Lord Blackturret," said Taegan, "I realize you don't know me, but I implore you to reconsider. I was present when the brass dragon lapsed into frenzy. Firefingers and his circle killed it easily, before it could harm anyone or escape the building. Surely that demonstrates their ability to manage any potential hazard."

"What if the wyrm had gone mad before it reached the tower," Gelduth said, "or immediately after it departed?"

Taegan smiled. "Well, having observed a fair number of dragons lost to frenzy, I can assure you, the creature wouldn't have been subtle about it. The whole town would have heard it roaring and smashing about. Whereupon the wizards, many of whom can transport themselves instantly from one location to another, would have rushed to the scene to eliminate the threat."

"Maybe it is certain they could overcome a drake," Gelduth said, "but you can't tell me it might not kill some people first."

"True," the avariel said, "but I ask you to balance the danger against the potential benefit. This Rage is more terrible than any in memory, and your part of the North is crawling with wyrms. Surely you've heard about the devastating attacks on Teshwave and Melvaunt. It's only a matter of time before an entire flight of dragons hurls itself at Thentia. Unless, that is, your mages can quell the frenzy first."

"Maestro Nightwind's right," Rilitar said. "We enchanters are your best hope, as we've always been Thentia's bulwark against the Zhents and all the other folk who wish it ill. By Corellon's silver sword, we understand that our fellow citizens are frightened. Rest assured, we are, too. But we beg you to trust us. We haven't let you down yet, have we?"

The Watchlord glowered for a time. Finally he said, "I'll think more on this, and let you know my decision."

He stalked out of the chamber, followed once again by his attendants.

"That," said Sinylla, a hint of laughter in her voice, "is how a dignitary lets you know he's changed his mind. It would wound his pride to admit it outright."

"He's changed it for now," Phourkyn said. "If another of our wyrms goes mad, he'll change it back again, and pleading won't sway him. You should have let me teach him some respect."

"I'm sorry," Firefingers said, "that's not how things are done in my home."

"Has it occurred to anyone," asked Scattercloak, "that Gelduth Blackturret may have a point?"

Firefingers's faded blue eyes narrowed beneath their scraggly white brows. "How do you mean?"

"To dissuade the Watchlord," Scattercloak said, "Maestro Nightwind made us out to be invincible dragon slayers. But the truth is, the brass might have killed us all if he and his companion hadn't intervened."

Jivex preened at this acknowledgment of his valor.

"I was right," Phourkyn said, "you are a coward."

"Only idiots," the shrouded wizard said, "have no fear of dragons."

Some of his fellows muttered in agreement.

"It was a fluke," said Rilitar, "that Samdralyrion snapped precisely when he did."

"Perhaps we can look forward to more such flukes," said a small, plump wizard clad all in white with azure trim, "considering that the Rage keeps waxing stronger. What if we do welcome a dragon into town, it goes mad and kills an innocent, and everyone holds us responsible? I fled here after deserting the Cloaks, with half of Mulmaster on my tail. Thentia is my sanctuary. I don't want the nobles to cast me out."

From the murmur of sympathy, Taegan gathered that a good many of the wizards were, for all their arcane might, fugitives and refugees of one sort or another.

"You presumably don't want scores of dragons to destroy Thentia, either," Rilitar said.

"That might never happen," said one of the silver-robed priestesses.

"Or it may," Taegan said, "unless you prevent it."

"But can we?" Scattercloak replied. "So far, we've made little progress."

"As Kara and the other seekers recover more information," the bladesinger said, "that will change."

"We don't know that," said the magician in white. "All we do know is that one of us has already died investigating this matter, and that many more could have perished yesterday."

Phourkyn made a spitting sound. "True wizards are willing to risk their lives to discover new lore."

Taegan turned to Rilitar and whispered, "Who died, and how?"

"Her name was Lissa Uvarrk," Rilitar said, "a gnome, quite adept at transmutation. She was working alone at home when, as best we can judge, she called up a spirit that slipped the leash. It ripped her apart and burned her, too." Then one of Scattercloak's remarks snagged his attention, and he leaned forward, eager to refute it.

The argument rambled on for a couple more minutes, growing steadily more contentious, until the warlocks were shouting all at once. Finally Firefingers rose from his ornately carved high-backed chair and snapped the fingers of both hands. A spherical blast of flame exploded above his head. The flash was blinding, the boom, deafening. Startled, everyone else fell silent.

"We made a promise," the old man said, "to aid Karasendrieth, and I intend to honor it. A great deal—perhaps even the fate of the world—depends on it. If you're the wizards I think you are, you'll do the same. If not, then all you need do to keep yourselves safe—until a dragon flight targets Thentia, anyway—is refuse to help any further. No one can force you. But if anyone does intend to turn his back on this enterprise, do it now. Leave my house, and don't come back. You won't be welcome in the future."

Taegan could see that Firefingers had timed his ultimatum well. Despite all the complaints and misgivings, nobody had yet mustered the resolve to walk out, and so everyone stayed put. For the moment. Firefingers gave them all a grandfatherly smile.

"Splendid. I knew I could count on you. Hurry and eat, your meal is getting cold." The wrinkled, white-bearded mage turned to Taegan and Jivex and said, "When we finish here, we can go to my study and decide on an errand for you. Since you can fl—"

Taegan interrupted the old man by lurching forward and coughing into his napkin, and kept on hacking until Firefingers and Rilitar were peering at him with concern.

"Are you all right?" Firefingers asked.

"Yes," Taegan wheezed, dabbing at his eyes. "Well, no, not entirely. When Jivex and I fought green dragons in Impiltur, I inhaled a bit of their poison. My lungs haven't been the same since, and I fear the smoke and cinders I breathed in yesterday damaged them still further. In all candor, I doubt I'm fit enough to continue my travels at present. May I please avail myself of your hospitality for a few more days?"

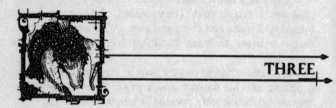

THREE

25 Mirtul, the Year of Rogue Dragons

Lying on his belly, Will peered down at the ogres shambling along the bottom of the ravine. Some of them glanced up from time to time, but didn't see him. The gorge was too deep, and he was too adept at hiding.

Still, shadowing giant-kin through unfamiliar territory was demanding, nerve-wracking work, and particularly unpleasant when one couldn't see a point to it. As Will mounted his pony and rode back to the spot where Pavel waited, he could feel his patience fraying thin.

"Did you get lost?" Pavel asked in a nasty tone. The lanky cleric stood holding his roan horse in a stand of gnarled, stunted trees. His days in Thar had given a haggard edge to his keen, handsome features. The hem of his cloak and stray strands of his hair stirred in the chilly, fitful breeze.

"Nice," said Will. "You loaf up here while I do the work, but naturally, it doesn't stop you griping."

"I wasn't complaining that you took your time," said the priest. "I was honestly worried about you. The feebleminded can come to grief when they go off by themselves."

"You'd know, I suppose," Will replied. "Your ogres are headed down a gully. We can parallel their track by keeping to the high ground. If you, in your idiocy, still think it's worth doing."

"That rat pellet you call a brain hasn't squeezed out any better ideas." As if he'd suddenly glimpsed something from the corner of his eye, Pavel pivoted and peered upward. "Get under cover!"

Will leaped off the pony, and he and the priest dragged their mounts into the center of the twisted trees. It was difficult. The low-hanging branches swiped and jabbed at the animals, who tried to balk.

It was only when he'd concealed himself and the pony as well as possible that Will took the time to look for whatever Pavel had spotted. After a second, he saw it too, a serpentine, bat-winged shape wheeling against the leaden, overcast sky.

The wyrm was azure. Blues were desert-dwellers, and Will had never encountered one before. He wondered if, maddened by the Rage, the reptile had wandered all the way from far Anauroch in search of prey.

Wherever it had come from, he wished it hadn't.

"These trees are miserable cover," he whispered. The branches above them had begun to put forth new leaves, but not in any great profusion. "Can you do something?"

"I could try," Pavel said, "but a patch of fog suddenly billowing into existence might catch the creature's attention all by itself. We're better off just crouching low and keeping still. I will wrap us in silence, to keep the animals quiet."

He gripped his sun amulet, murmured a prayer, and the world hushed, though Will could still feel his heart pounding in his chest.

Finally, inevitably, the moment he dreaded arrived. The blue swooped lower . . . but not at them. It had spotted the ogres instead, and was making a pass over the ravine. Will heaved a sigh of relief.

Somewhat to the halfling's surprise, the blue didn't attack at once. Rather, it climbed high into the sky again, then circled. The gray clouds started changing, massing into looming shapes like anvils. Light flickered in their bellies. The wind blew harder, flinging grit into the air.

Pavel tied his horse to a branch, then beckoned for Will to follow him. Keeping low, the halfling obeyed, but only until they'd skulked to the edge of the trees, where he heard the wind howling, and the ogres clamoring down in their gorge. The blue hadn't yet attacked them with fang, talon, or breath weapon, but it had done something on its initial pass. Will just hadn't been able to tell. In any case, the important thing was that he and Pavel could talk.

"Hold it!" he said. "What do you think you're doing, breaking cover?"

"If we're lucky," said Pavel, "the blue won't notice us. It's busy changing the weather."

"But why risk it?"

"To help the ogres," Pavel replied as he crept forward.

"I've never hated you," observed Will, following, "as much as I do right now."

As they stalked toward the ravine, Will felt as exposed and vulnerable as ever in his life. Even an expert housebreaker generally required cover to go undetected, and the barren moor had little to offer. He silently prayed to Brandobaris, Master of Stealth, to hide him and his demented friend, too.

And perhaps the god heard, for the blue didn't dive at them. Not yet.

As they reached the ravine, thunder boomed. Will peered cautiously over the edge, then narrowed his eyes in surprise. Because to all appearances, the terrain at the bottom had changed, from hard, pebbly ground to muck, patches of which steamed, bubbled, and looked as if they'd burn the foot of anyone who trod in them. Stranger still, the lower portions of the gully walls had disappeared to reveal further expanses of the same hellish mud flats. Most of the ogres regarded the altered landscape with alarm and confusion. The shaman with the blood-red eye chanted and lashed his flint-tipped spear through a mystic pass, but whatever magic he was attempting, it didn't seem to be working.

"The blue cast an illusion." said Pavel.

"Obviously," said Will, "but why?"

Raindrops started falling.

"For that," said the priest.

He brandished his pendant, recited a prayer, and grew taller, more impressive, the very definition of strength and wisdom. It was a glamour he used to make it easier to influence others. He stood up straight, revealing himself to the ogres. From the way the long-armed brutes with their warty hides gawked, it was obvious they could see him, though Will suspected that from their vantage point, Pavel appeared to be floating in midair.

"What you're seeing isn't real," Pavel called. Lightning flared, thunder roared, and the rain started hammering down in earnest. "You're still in the ravine. Grope around, find the walls, and climb out, or at least, partway up."

His magically augmented force of personality wasn't enough to deflect the ogres' reflexive hatred of humans. Several heaved their long, heavy spears. He had to leap backward to avoid being spitted.

Will was still hunkered down behind a bump in the ground. He popped up just long enough to spin his warsling and let fly. The skiprock cracked into one ogre's skull, then rebounded to strike another in the ear. The brutes lurched off balance, their heads bloodied.

"I'll kill the next fool who raises a weapon," he shouted.

Pavel stepped back to the brink of the gully. "You're caught in an illusion."

The ogre with the crimson eye snarled like a beast. "I know that, sun priest, but I can break us free. My god is stronger than yours." He gripped his spear in both oversized knotted fists and raised it over his head in what was plainly the start of an invocation.

"I didn't cause this," Pavel said, "a dragon did." That made the shaman hesitate, and his followers babble. "The point was to disorient you and stop you from moving, and to hold you in place for the next attack. It's coming now. Listen, and you'll hear it."

Will strained, and after a moment caught the sound despite the intermittent bang of thunder and the constant drumming of the rain. It was a steady roaring, hurtling down the channel below him.

The shaman heard it, too. "Feel around!" he shouted. "Grab on to something and climb, if you can!"

The ogres had perhaps three seconds to obey his commands. Then the wall of water raced into view.

Will knew that even the torrential rain couldn't have produced a flash flood so quickly. The blue must have employed still more magic to amplify the force and volume of the surging water. It slammed into the ogres like a battering ram and swept over them like an avalanche, so that all but the few who'd managed to clamber highest on the invisible walls were lost from sight. The halfling was certain the rest were as good as dead.

But when the water level dropped, he saw he was mistaken. Some ogres lay broken or had simply disappeared, but the majority, reeling, coughing, and sputtering, remained. They wouldn't for long, though, unless they pulled themselves together.

"Get ready to fight!" he shouted. "The dragon's coming right behind the flood. It's almost on top of you!"

He couldn't see the blue yet. The sheets of rain hid it. But it would follow up fast.

Still knee-deep in streaming water, the ogres lifted their spears, stone axes, and war clubs.

"Spread out!" Pavel shouted, and some of them waded apart.

A moment later, a vertical thunderbolt blazed down the gully and through the midst of them. Those whom it struck were charred black and killed. The ogres on the periphery of the dazzling, sizzling flare, or who received some of its force through the water on the ground, jerked in agony.

The blue lunged into view. Perhaps because the ravine was too narrow for it to comfortably spread its wings, it had opted to fight on the ground. It raked, and tore one still-paralyzed ogre apart; struck, and bit another in two.

The giant-kin plainly needed someone to buy them time to rally. Will had no idea it was going to be him until he leaped over the edge of the ravine.

Will was an accomplished climber and acrobat. Still, as he half rolled, half scrambled down the nearly vertical slope, he was pushing his skills to the limit. The rocky outcroppings were slick with rain, and once he dropped low enough to enter the heart of the illusion, he couldn't even see them anymore. He had to rely on pure instinct to snatch for handholds in what appeared to be empty air.

Somehow he found the first of them, then realized he couldn't just tumble on down to the gully floor and attack the dragon's belly as he'd initially intended. The water was deep enough to submerge him completely, and would likely sweep him away. He certainly wouldn't be able to fight.

In desperation, he kicked off from the slope, trying to turn his barely controlled fall into a leap that would carry him where he needed to land. He slammed down atop the blue's heaving back at the juncture of the wings. He grabbed hold of a scale to anchor himself, drew his hornblade, an enchanted, exquisitely balanced halfling sword, and plunged it into the dragon's flesh.

The blue jerked, nearly breaking his grip on it. The enormous, wedge-shaped head with its ragged ears and the long horn jutting up from the tip of the snout swiveled around. It jaws gaped, and it struck.

Will flipped backward to avoid the attack, and would scarcely have been surprised if he'd kept on helplessly rolling right off the dragon's bucking, rain-slick back. But he grabbed, managed to grip another scale, and stabbed with the hunting sword. Striking a shower of popping sparks, a tiny fraction of the lightning that was a part of the blue's essence, the point glanced off the creature's natural armor.

The dragon stretched its neck back, reaching with its jaws. The angle was awkward for it, but it was renewing the attack so quickly that Will scarcely had time to find his balance, while the shuddering, inclined surface beneath him was treacherous in the extreme. Dodging would be even harder. Maybe too hard.

But before the blue could strike, a glowing mace, red like the sun at dawn, appeared above its head. The hovering weapon swung despite the lack of a corporeal hand to wield it and bashed the wyrm's mask. At the same time, a ball of flame splashed against the blue's sinuous neck. Will knew Pavel had conjured the former attack, and assumed the ogre with the red eye was responsible for the latter.

The assaults must have hurt. The blue snapped its head forward and charged, rushing the shaman, whose hand burned like a torch. The sudden jerk nearly broke Will's grip on the wyrm's hide, but not quite, and he stabbed once more, driving the point several inches into into flesh. For a moment, the sword seemed to vibrate in his grip, and the muscles in his arm jumped and clenched.

A rank of ogres with leveled spears stood between the blue and their leader. It smashed through, trampling one defender to pulp, but at least they'd slowed it momentarily, and driven a couple lances into its chest. The shaman retreated and lobbed more fire. Other giant-kin splashed through the stream to engage their colossal foe. Pavel's mace of light streaked through the air and bashed the reptile in one slit-pupiled eye. At the same time, the human discharged a bright ray of light from his out-thrust hand. The beam burned a hole in the dragon's wing.

Will kept on cutting and stabbing. He rather hoped the blue had forgotten him, but no. The end of its sinuous tail suddenly whipped up and around to flick him away like a troublesome fly. He wrenched himself aside to avoid the first swat and leaped over the second one. He knew he couldn't keep dodging for long.

Then, however, raising a prodigious splash, the blue fell on its belly. Apparently the ogres had wounded at least two of its legs to such a degree that they couldn't support it anymore. The wyrm's wings pounded as it tried to take flight, but it couldn't quite manage without a running or jumping start.

The blue laid about furiously. More ogres perished, seared and withered by a fresh blast of lightning from its maw, torn to pieces between its fangs, or shattered by hammering blows of its tail. It just wouldn't stop, wouldn't even falter.

The shaman ran at it, rammed his spear into the base of its neck, and scrambled on to fling himself at its chest. The giant-kin's body sported countless stiff spikes like a porcupine's quills. No doubt he'd sprouted them via enchantment, and as he slammed himself repeatedly against the dragon, the spines stabbed it again and again.

The blue lurched partway onto its side and lifted its fore-leg to claw at the shaman. But before it could, Pavel's flying mace smashed it in the center of its brow. Bone crunched. The creature convulsed, nearly flinging the halfling from his perch.

The blue spat another thunderbolt, but into the air, not at any foe. Then the head at the end of the long neck toppled into the coursing stream like a collapsing tower. Rustling, an enormous wing flopped down, too, after which the drake lay motionless.

The shaman clambered up over the blue's carcass toward Will. The halfling had no choice but to fight. With the water still high, and giant-kin gathered all around, he had nowhere to run.

"Stop!" Pavel shouted. The command carried a palpable charge of magic, and the shaman froze in place.

Will considered cutting him down before mobility returned, but instinct stayed his hand.

"If you have any sense," Pavel called, "you can see that we want to be your friends. We've been trailing you for days, waiting for an opportunity to make contact."

"Without you dumping our arses in the stewpot," muttered Will.

The shaman glowered up at Pavel, then finally growled, "Climb down, little sun priest, and we'll talk."

———— ✑✑ ————

Wearing her dragon form, perched on a mountainside with her companions, Kara took a final look at the scene across the valley. She didn't look hopeful. The situation hadn't changed for the better since she'd first observed it.

Sure enough, her keen sight confirmed the discouraging truth. The Monastery of the Yellow Rose, a huge fortress perched atop a different peak overlooking the shining white expanse of the Glacier of the White Worm, was still besieged. A score of dragons, a motley collection of reds, fangs, and other species, crawled or lay motionless about the landscape, while several others glided in circles overhead, watching the stronghold from on high. The only time the vista had materially changed had been when the wyrms mounted an assault, an attack so furious it was a miracle of valor that the monks had managed to repel it, their massive fortifications notwithstanding.

"Are we sure we all want to do this?" Kara asked. "It will be dangerous, and if we do get in, it may well be impossible to get out again."

Dorn shrugged. "Pavel's convinced Sammaster spent a long time in the monastery—in disguise, I guess—learning something important, and I think this proves it. Those wyrms don't look like they're in frenzy. They're too patient. I think they're still sane, and the lich sent them here to make sure nobody else gets a chance to read whatever he discovered."

"He likely found out somebody stole his folio," said Raryn, leaning on his harpoon. "We expected it to happen eventually.

Now he's trying to cover his trail."

"Anyway," said Dorn, "if this is a site that he particularly wants to keep people out of, then plainly, we need to find out what's inside."

"But you and Raryn aren't scholars," Kara said. "You likely won't be able to contribute much to the research."

"We can stand with you against whatever trouble rears its head," Dorn replied. "It's what we came to do."

Raryn nodded and said, "We'll stick."

Kara sighed. "I just think—"

"Enough!" Chatulio snapped. Having abandoned the appearance of a horse, he too stood revealed as the dragon he was. His bright blue eyes, shining orange scales, and the gap in his upper front teeth usually made him look merry—to other wyrms, anyway—but at the moment, they didn't mask his irritability. "The small folk are set on coming, so let's get on with it."

Plainly, the Rage was eating at him. At least Kara had her human guise to armor her much of the time, but Chatulio could only resist the madness by simple force of will. She was worried about him, but knew it would be useless to speak of it

"All right," she said, crouching low. "We'll get ready."

Dorn swung himself onto her back, and Raryn clambered onto Chatulio. The copper chanted an incantation. Rainbows rippled through the air, a tingling danced across Kara's scales, and at the end, Chatulio and Raryn faded away.

They weren't really gone. The master illusionist had simply veiled himself and the dwarf in invisibility. In fact, he'd done the same for Kara and Dorn, though the effect didn't keep the song dragon and half-golem from seeing themselves.

"I'm going," Chatulio said.

A snap of wings revealed he'd taken flight. Kara flexed her legs, leaped, and followed him.

Dorn sat on her back more easily than the first time she'd carried him. She wondered wistfully if he could ever come to love flying the way she did.

She found an updraft and rode it high above the mountains, so high the air must have been brutally cold for a human, though Dorn didn't complain. As per the plan, Chatulio rose with her. If she listened intently, she could hear the occasional rustle of his pinions.

Once they'd ascended high enough, they winged their way toward the monastery, making their approach far above the gliding, wheeling chromatic wyrms. If they descended in a tight spiral, it might be possible to slip past them undetected—or so they hoped. A huge red peered upward. Plainly, the drake had sensed the presence of the newcomers even from far below.

Kara was bitterly disappointed, but also recognized that in a sense, she and her comrades were lucky the chromatic wyrms had detected them before they even started their descent. The fact that they were still hundreds of yards above the foe might allow them to escape unharmed.

Kara lifted one wing and dipped the other, turning, preparing to withdraw. Meanwhile, the red snarled words of power. At the spell's conclusion, magic throbbed through the cold, thin mountain air, and Chatulio and Raryn popped into view.

Kara gasped, and Dorn cursed, but not because they could see their friends. Visible or not, Chatulio and Raryn might still have been able to get away safely. Rather, it was because, talons poised for combat, the copper was diving to engage the chromatics, carrying the dwarf helplessly along.

Malazan beat her wings, climbing, searching for an updraft. She coveted the satisfaction of killing the copper all by herself, before any of her comrades could fly high and close enough to get in on the sport.

The red needed some diversion to make her forget her frustrations. She'd initially assumed that she and the other chromatics could take the monastery in a day or two. She'd likewise expected that, since she was the oldest dragon present and manifestly the greatest in might and cunning, all the others would grovel to her and give her their unquestioning obedience. Sadly, she'd known disappointment on all counts.

Of course, time would change everything for the better. The stronghold must fall eventually, Sammaster's human lackeys would transform her, and possessed of a dracolich's power, she'd slaughter any wyrm who'd shown her less than absolute subservience. After that, her reputation secure, she could go home to her lair and the treasure horde she loved above all things.

Soon, she promised herself. But in the meantime, killing one of her metallic cousins might brighten her mood.

The enchantment she'd cast in the air around the monastery to keep anyone from escaping via spells of flight and concealment, didn't allow her to see the copper's companion, but it gave her a general sense of the creature's location. Thus, she knew it when that wyrm dived, plummeting even faster than its comrade, and she laughed with delight. It wouldn't matter even if the second wyrm was an ancient gold. Two metal drakes still wouldn't be able to defeat the half dozen chromatics Malazan had in the air. Apparently the Rage had both newcomers too addled to care how gravely they were outnumbered, and so they were both going to die.

She felt less pleased, though, when the wyrm who was still invisible started to chant in a high, sweet, vibrant voice that suggested she was probably a song dragon. Malazan recognized a spell of coercion when she heard it, and realized the reptile had dived not to hurl herself into a suicidal battle but to get close enough to constrain the copper's will.

The copper jerked as the charm sunk its claws into his mind. "Flee!" the song dragon cried. "Escape!"

He obediently pounded his wings to arrest his plunging descent.

Too late, Malazan thought. He'd already swooped too low, and so, for that matter, had the song drake. If they exerted themselves, the chromatics could catch both of them. The red roared to her subordinates, urging them to fly faster and climb higher. Then she snarled a spell to wipe away the song dragon's concealment, bringing her slim blue-diamond body shimmering into view. The singer had a rider, too, a grotesque hulk who appeared to be half human meat and half iron.

One of Malazan's minions sent a mote of yellow light streaking upward at the copper. He veered, dodging, and when the spark exploded into a mass of flame, he was at the periphery of the blast. It still must have seared him, but even the odd-looking white-haired, ruddy-faced dwarf on his back survived.

The crystal-blue dragon sang, holding a single throbbing note that became a prodigious thunderclap. The deafening peal drove a lance of pain through Malazan's ears and made her flounder in the air. Some of her worthless minions swerved off course or dropped lower, losing distance they'd labored hard to gain. The red female bellowed in fury.

The copper and song dragon fled toward the mountains to the north, zigzagging in an attempt to avoid their pursuers' conjured flares of flame and lightning, showers of acid and hailstones, and bursts of blighting darkness. Occasionally, the fugitives sent their own attack spells sizzling back to singe one of their foes, or tangle its wings in a mammoth spiderweb. For the most part, though, they wove defensive enchantments. The copper conjured several illusory images of himself to befuddle his assailants. The song drake cloaked herself in a protective aura of light.

The riders clinging precariously to the "benevolent" dragons' backs evidently lacked the magical skills to cast any powerful spells of their own. Whenever the vertiginous chase afforded them a target, however, they loosed arrows that flew straight and pierced deep.

It didn't matter, though. Nothing they could do mattered. Malazan and her subordinates were going to catch them. Indeed, she was nearly close enough to stop casting spells and use her fiery breath when a thick, pearly fog swirled into existence around her.

She could have dispelled the magical cloud, but she'd drawn so close that she chose to drive onward instead, trusting to hearing and scent to guide her to her prey. Then she plunged into the second sort of vapor concealed within the drifting coils of the first. Her belly twisted with nausea. Elsewhere in the mist, her lackeys retched.

Beating her wings, defying her dizziness and the cramping in her guts, she climbed above the fog bank, whereupon her sickness ended as abruptly as it had begun. Better still, she could see the copper and song dragon once more. They were only a little way ahead, and had finally dropped to the same altitude as their pursuers.

Malazan cried to her warriors, urging them forward but scarcely caring if they heeded or not. In her present savage humor, she was sure she could kill a copper and a song wyrm all by herself and enjoy the exercise.

She sucked in a breath, spewed forth her fire, and caught the copper square in the blaze. One of his wings burned away like paper. Wreathed in flame, the screaming dwarf fell from his back. She flew on and drove her talons into the copper's body.

At that instant, his body exploded into dozens of small, darting copper-dragon masks, which laughed derisively before bursting. The song drake, her rider, and the plummeting dwarf vanished at the same time.

Illusion. A trick to divert and delay. Malazan climbed once more, cast about, and spotted the real copper and song dragon beating their way into a pass. A moment later, another mass of fog flowed into existence to hide them from view.

They'd increased their lead significantly, but perhaps not enough. If Malazan invoked the godlike anger she could summon at will, brought the blood-sweat seeping forth to glaze her scales, it would magnify her already prodigious strength and stamina. Then she could surely overtake them, and rip them to pieces when she did.

The problem was that she didn't no how long it would take, or what might happen in her absence. Accordingly, fiercely as her instincts goaded her to pursue, she wheeled and led her subordinates back to the monastery.

A little weary from the chase, she landed on the high crag that was her customary perch. Soon, much to her displeasure, Ishenalyr came gliding to light unbidden beside her.

The ancient green with the long, high crest and rows of hornlets over the eyes was smaller than Malazan, but larger than any other wyrm participating in the siege. He stank of the poison smoke he could exhale at will, and bore arcane runes and sigils carved on his scales.

Malazan had enhanced her natural abilities by learning to use the ferocity that was a fundamental part of a dragon's nature. As she understood it, Ishenalyr had mastered certain petty tricks by walking a different path, a discipline that involved stifling one's passions as well as self-mutilation. It sounded perverse and stupid to her, and was one reason she disliked him. The main cause, though, was the way he critiqued her strategies and second-guessed her orders, his clear though not quite openly declared conviction that Sammaster should have chosen him to command the company.

The "hidecarved" green had been on the ground when the song and copper dragons made their approach, and thus hadn't participated in the chase. Accordingly, he appeared fresh where she was battered and winded, and that ratcheted her antipathy up yet another notch.

Still, he could prove a useful tool to crack the monastery open, and so she managed to hold back the fire warming her gullet.

"What?" she demanded.

"I wanted to make sure you were all right," said Ishenalyr in his prissy, superior way.

"Your 'concern' is an insult," she spat. "What could puny creatures like that do to me?"

"Apparently," said Ishenalyr, "outwit and evade you."

"I would have caught them had I cared to chase them any farther, but it was sufficient to drive them off. In case you've forgotten, the reason we're here is to destroy the monks and their archives."

"Still, it's remarkable that the dread Malazan let enemies escape. I hope frenzy isn't rotting your faculties."

"That's two insults," she said. "I beg you, puke up a third." Rather to her regret, he prudently stood mute. "Why should I absent myself from the battleground just to kill a couple of our 'kindly' kin? Such creatures are doomed one and all to permanent lunacy. Isn't that as cruel a fate as any I could give them?"

It pleased her that, for all his glibness, Ishenalyr couldn't come up with an argument for that.

The blue dragon was dead, but its conjured storm howled on. Yagoth Devil-eye had found an overhang of rock under which he could sit, hold court, and stay relatively dry. There was only enough room for one to lounge comfortably, though. Those who came to confer with him had to stand in the cold, pelting rain, and he rather liked it that way.

At the moment, the human and halfling awaited his pleasure. Bundled up in their hoods and cloaks, their layers of "civilized" clothing, they looked puny and effete as such little vermin generally did, but they'd already demonstrated during the fight with the drake that the appearance was misleading. They were two of the rare human or demihuman bugs who might prove a match for an ogre in a one-on-one fight.

The question was, what in the name of the Great Claw did they want? Their presence surely portended something important. They'd arrived at the same time as the blue wyrm, and Yagoth had never in his life seen a dragon of that color before, hadn't even known that they existed. The reptile must have been an omen, but of what, he wasn't yet sure.

When he'd observed everything about the strangers that two eyes could reveal, Yagoth closed the left to peer with the blood-red one alone. His shaman powers had awakened after a manticore ripped open his face, and occasionally the blemished eye revealed secrets imperceptible to normal sight. Often enough, its unblinking stare made folk quail, and that could be useful, too. But it failed to show him anything unusual, and the human and halfling bore its regard without flinching.

Yagoth growled, "Who are you?"

"I'm Pavel Shemov," said the human, "a servant of the Morninglord, as you already noticed. My companion is Will Turnstone."

"My people are hungry," said Yagoth. "Tell me why I shouldn't 'dump your arses in the stewpot.'"

Will grinned. "I didn't realize you heard that."

Yagoth spat. "I hear everything I need to hear."

"It would be foolish to kill us," said Pavel, "when we can help you."

"How?" the ogre asked.

"Do you know what a Rage of Dragons is?" the human asked.

"I'm not stupid, sun priest. Don't hint that I am."

"I didn't mean any insult," Pavel said. "If you know what a Rage is, you likely also know we're in the middle of one. Flights of wyrms are rampaging across all Faerûn, not just Thar. What you may not know—Will and I only recently discovered it ourselves—is that this Rage is the worst ever. In fact, it's so bad, it's never going to end of its own accord."

Yagoth snorted. "Ridiculous."

"I assure you, it's so. Perhaps you know a spell to sort truth from lies. If so, cast it. I won't resist."

The shaman frowned, pondering. Pavel really did sound sincere. Which didn't necessarily mean he knew what he was talking about, but unlike many of his kind, Yagoth was too canny to dismiss the learning of human scholars and spellcasters out of hand.

"Even if it is true," Yagoth said, "so what?"

"In ancient times," said Pavel, "the wise knew things about the Rage that we modern clerics and wizards have forgotten. Will and I belong to a band of folk trying to recover that lore so we can use it to restore the wyrms to their senses."

Puzzled, Yagoth cocked his head and asked, "You think *I* know the cure?"

"No," Pavel said. "No living person does. If the knowledge still exists, it's preserved in all-but-forgotten shrines and the like. Will and I came to Thar seeking one such site."

"Only it wasn't where my idiot partner expected it to be," said Will.

"I have a map . . ." Pavel paused as if trying to judge whether Yagoth knew what such a thing was. "But I hesitate to take it out where I'm standing. The rain will soak it."

Yagoth wasn't sure whether to laugh or take offense at the lanky man's effrontery. He shifted over a bit and said, "Squeeze in under the rock, then, if you've got the nerve."

Many humans, Yagoth knew, would have hesitated to come so close, and once they did, might well have gagged at what they claimed was the stink of an ogre's warty skin. Pavel, however, simply said, "Thank you," and entered the cramped space without any display of trepidation or distaste.

The human produced a piece of parchment from inside his mantle, unfolded it, and held it for Yagoth to see.

"This is the lake," said Pavel, pointing, "that your clan passed a few days back. I thought the site would be there, but all we found were the worn remnants of a few standing stones. Yet, unless I'm completely mistaken, the ruin must be somewhere in this region—" he drew a circle with his fingertip—"and it should be near a body of water."

Yagoth leered, comprehending at last. "You think I can point you in the right direction."

"Can you?" Pavel asked. "This is your country, and I suspect that, as a shaman, you have some interest in old places of power."

"Even if I can," Yagoth said, "why should I?"

"My guess," said Will, a drop of water escaping the top edge of his hood to drip across his face, "is that you're trying to lead your tribe to a place of safety. Caves, maybe. Unfortunately, it's pointless. Over the long run, there won't be any safe havens. The wyrms will keep roaming and killing till they've eaten us all, and I guarantee, you ogres may think of yourselves as big and strong, but you're just a mouthful of lunch to a dragon, the same as halflings and humans."

Yagoth glared at him and said, "We've killed the drakes that threatened us."

Will glanced back at the scene behind him, at the ogres bearing enormous, grisly wounds, and the females wailing for those slain outright by the blue wyrm.

"Right, on second thought, you're doing splendidly. Forget I said anything."

"The point," said Pavel, "is that your folk and mine have a common interest in ending the Rage, so why not help us do it? It won't cost you anything."

"It could cost the lives of my followers," Yagoth said.

Pavel's brown eyes narrowed. "I don't follow."

"I know where there's a second lake," Yagoth said, "with ruined temples overlooking it. I could mark the location on this badly drawn, misleading map of yours. But you still wouldn't find it hidden among the hills. You'll only reach it if we ogres turn around and take you."

Pavel and Will exchanged glances. Yagoth was sure he knew what they were thinking: Spending an hour or two among "savage," man-eating giant-kin was a daunting prospect. Lingering for days in their company might be tantamount to suicide.

Yet Pavel turned back to Yagoth and said, "If you're willing, we'd be grateful to have you as our guides. Since we're going to travel together, may I use my skills to tend your wounded? I don't mean to disparage your own abilities, but there are more injured folk than any one healer can manage alone."

Yagoth smirked and said, "I guess you don't want any sick ogres slowing down the march. Don't worry, they wouldn't. I wouldn't let them. But do what you want."

In point of fact, it was a good idea. Yagoth's patron Vaprak, a god of carnage and destruction, was niggardly when it came to granting healing magic to his shamans. A priest of soft, nurturing Lathander might do more in a day to restore the strength of the troupe than Yagoth could do in a tenday.

Though Pavel's services wouldn't lull Yagoth into dropping his guard, or make him falter when the time came to kill the human and his insolent halfling friend.

Thar had once been the site of a mighty kingdom of ogres and orcs, one so ancient that even they only vaguely remembered it. That bygone age had indeed left a scatter of ruins behind, if one knew where to look. According to legend, buried in those haunted sites were enchanted weapons and other valuable relics.

So Yagoth found it plausible that Pavel and Will truly had come seeking some sort of long-lost treasure or lore, and once they located it, he'd dispose of them and seize the booty for himself. Even if they were after exactly what they claimed, he saw no reason to permit them to carry the secret away. For in that case, the prize was essentially the power to control dragons, wasn't it, and Yagoth could rise high wielding a weapon like that. He could unite and rule the warring tribes of Thar like old King Vorbyx come again, with a blue wyrm for his emblem.

In Raryn's opinion, the trouble with magical fog was that no one could see through it from either side. As he and Chatulio flew onward, he kept peering backward. He invariably saw that nothing had poked a reptilian snout through the cloud Kara had conjured to shroud the mouth of the pass. Still, he would have felt more secure had he possessed some way of knowing what lay beyond the mist—of verifying that the chromatic dragons, that colossal red and the others, truly had abandoned the chase.

In fact, the dwarf was so busy looking over his shoulder and casting about in general—because his experience as a hunter had taught him that flying predators could appear just about anywhere—that it took a while for Chatulio's muttering to snag his attention. The gods only knew how long the copper had been ranting under his breath.

"Stupid," Chatulio snarled, "stupid, incompetent, useless. Crazy!"

He used one forefoot to rake at the other. The talons drew blood.

"Don't!" Raryn said, patting the base of the copper's neck as he might gentle a pony. The gesture felt wrong—Chatulio was a sentient being, not an animal—but he had to try to reach his companion somehow.

"Crazy!" Chatulio repeated.

He slashed himself again.

"No," Raryn insisted. Dorn and Kara were flying ahead of their comrades. Raryn considered calling out to them for help, but he had a feeling Chatulio might react badly to that. "The Rage had you for a second, but you're all right now."

"I'm supposed to be the illusionist," Chatulio said. "The trickster. The sneak. My magic should have slipped us past the chromatics, but I've lost my cunning. The frenzy has eaten it away."

"It was just bad luck," Raryn said. "When spell fights spell, the outcome is always uncertain. I'm so sorcerer, but even I know that."

"Then I was going to throw away my life, and yours, too. At that moment, I didn't even remember you were on my back. I just wanted to kill something. Kara and Dorn had to risk themselves to save us."

"Back at the village," Raryn said, "it was Kara who became confused. It's happening to all of you, and there's no point in feeling ashamed. Don't you see, exaggerated self-hatred is simply another way the Rage gnaws at you."

"You don't know," Chatulio said. "It's not happening to you, so you can't understand."

It seemed to Raryn that the dragon was waxing even more hysterical. What if, wracked with self-loathing, Chatulio decided simply to fold his wings and fall out of the sky? In all likelihood, neither of them would survive. The ranger realized he'd better involve his other comrades after all. If nothing else, maybe Kara could shackle the copper's will with another charm.

Raryn drew in a breath and placed two fingers before his mouth to whistle, but Chatulio twisted his neck and said, "What's that?"

Chatulio's enormous body and outstretched wings largely obstructed his rider's view of the landscape directly below. Raryn had to shift forward to see what the copper had noticed, but then he spotted it easily enough. A dead human lay amid a tumble of rocks on an escarpment.

"We should take a closer look," Raryn said.

The corpse had distracted Chatulio from his poisonous self-absorption. Maybe, if the diversion lasted for a while, the copper wouldn't slip back into the same mood.

Raryn whistled, and Kara's head whipped backward. Maybe she thought he'd signaled to warn that the chromatics had reappeared, and he made haste to reassure her.

"We're all right," he shouted, "but Chatulio spotted a dead man. We want to see if we can figure out who he was, and what he's doing out here in the middle of nowhere."

"All right," the song dragon said, and her lustrous lavender eyes narrowed.

Raryn had a hunch she'd just noticed the fresh blood on Chatulio's forefeet, but if so, she evidently decided not to mention it.

Still keeping an eye out for signs of pursuit, the drakes wheeled, glided, and set lightly down on the steep incline where the dead man lay. Raryn and Dorn swung themselves down from the reptiles' backs, and they all clambered toward the body. With their sharp talons and prodigious strength, the wings and tails they poised to enhance their balance, Kara and Chatulio moved almost as nimbly as they would on a horizontal surface. Raryn had learned to climb on the icy crags of the Great Glacier, and he too had little difficulty. It was Dorn who floundered, slid, and sent loose pebbles and dirt bouncing and streaming down the mountainside. In the dwarf's opinion, the big human with his iron limbs wasn't clumsy, but he thought he was, and accordingly, he acted like it. Fortunately, in combat he forgot to limp and lurch.

The corpse was burned and blistered, as if by a black or green dragon's corrosive breath. The disfigurement made it difficult to tell much about the victim, but it looked to Raryn as if he'd been relatively young, and had dressed all in gray. Judging from the bloated belly, and the leakage around the mouth and nostrils, he'd been dead for a few days, though the local animals, evidently disliking the acidic tang underlying the commonplace reek of putrefaction, had left him alone.

"Poor man," Kara sighed.

"Poor monk, maybe," said Dorn. "This Monastery of the Yellow Rose is dedicated to Ilmater, isn't it, and the servants of the Broken God wear gray."

"I think you may be right," Chatulio said.

"So," Dorn asked, "what is he doing out here instead of in the stronghold?"

"The monks travel all over Damara on various errands," Kara said. "Perhaps he was simply away from home when the chromatics arrived to lay siege to the place."

"Maybe," the half-golem said, sunlight glinting on his iron arm and half-mask. "But there's another possibility. Many castles are built with secret tunnels underneath. Maybe this lad used such a passage to come out. If so, we can go in the same way."

"If we can find it," Chatulio said.

"Raryn can backtrack him," said Dorn, "even over these rocks."

"I'll try," said the dwarf, though he recognized, as his comrades perhaps did not, that even if he found the hidden gateway to a subterranean path, there was a good chance the road would only take them to their deaths.

FOUR

26 Mirtul, the Year of Rogue Dragons

"I don't understand" Taegan said, "why this dreary subject fascinates you so."

"Just as I don't comprehend," Rilitar retorted, a crystal goblet of a passable Sembian white in his hand "why it seems to embarrass you."

"I wouldn't put it that way." Taegan paused to hack into his handkerchief. "It's just that the lives of avariels are simple. Primitive. There's little to say about them."

The wizard shook his head. "I can't believe that. I'm not one of those elves who arrogantly believes our race superior to all others. But our longevity does afford us certain advantages. It gives us perspective, perhaps even wisdom, time and continuity to develop subtle arts and rich traditions. That's why it's difficult for me to credit that the life of any elven community, no matter how small or isolated, could be as drab as you suggest."

"You say that, but we have both forsaken our kin to dwell among humans."

"I wouldn't put it that way," Rilitar said, echoing his guest's turn of phrase with a smile. "I wanted to see the world, and learn what other races had to teach, but I certainly didn't leave because I disdained my people or homeland. Cormanthor is the loveliest place in Faerûn, and one day, I'll return."

Taegan wondered if the great forest held any elven cities as magnificent as the long-vanished one he had, with Amra's guidance, visited in a dream. If so, he almost thought he'd like to see it, an impulse that caught him by surprise. He put the odd notion aside to try to turn the conversation in a more useful direction.

"How did you wind up in Thentia?" he asked. It was an innocuous question intended to pave the way for others that might, in one way or another, prove more revelatory.

"Well," Rilitar began, and above the ceiling, something crashed.

Inwardly, Taegan winced. He'd accepted Rilitar's supper invitation partly so he could surreptitiously unlock a second-story window. While he kept the mage occupied, Jivex was supposed to sneak inside and see what he could discover in Rilitar's library and conjuration chamber. It sounded as if the faerie dragon had knocked over a piece of crockery or glass.

Rilitar sprang to feet, snatched a piece of leather from one of his pockets, and chanting, twirled it through a mystic pass. For an instant, light shimmered across his body as the spell enclosed him in an aura of protection then he ran for the stairs. Hoping to look just as startled and concerned as the wizard was, Taegan grabbed his sword from the cloak rack and dashed after him. He prayed that Jivex had the sense to beat a hasty retreat back out the window, or, failing that, at least make himself invisible.

Then he smelled smoke, and felt warmth emanating from overhead. The rustle of flame mixed with a grating buzz.

Jivex hissed. Taegan realized the faerie dragon was fighting something.

Taegan and Rilitar reached the top of the stairs and dashed on. The mage threw open the door to his workrooms, releasing a swirl of acrid smoke. Beyond the threshold crouched a creature like a horsefly the size of a donkey with a sneering caricature of a human face. The apparition stood shrouded in flame, but the blaze neither consumed its flesh nor appeared to cause it any distress. Its shivering wings produced the ambient drone. It seemed to be peering at empty space, but Taegan suspected it had actually oriented on the invisible Jivex. Chanting, it thrust out one of its forelegs, which, the bladesinger observed, somewhat resembled a starving man's withered arm. Fire exploded from its fingertips, momentarily outlining the faerie dragon's form as it splashed against him.

"It's a chasme," said Rilitar. "But—"

Taegan shoved past the wizard and charged.

Still glimmering with their own pale inner light, shards of what had evidently once been a crystal ball crunched beneath the bladesinger's boots. The fierce heat inside the room made every forward stride a test of will. The chasme with its great blade of a proboscis and tufts of coarse hair sprouting from its leathery body skittered around to face him. His stomach turned over.

The creature was trying to cripple him with a charm, but he exerted his will, refusing to be sick, and the nausea disappeared. He thrust his sword at the chasme's burning head.

The point glanced off.

"It's a demon!" Rilitar shouted. "You need an enchanted weapon!"

The chasme pounced at Taegan, clawing and biting, and he retreated out of range. It scuttled forward to renew the attack, but then he heard the flutter of Jivex's wings as the little dragon streaked past him, and the demon jerked back. Taegan could imagine his small comrade, heedless of the fly-thing's halo of flame, snapping and raking at it to give him a chance to get clear. At the same time, Rilitar pelted the chasme with a barrage of conjured snowballs.

The bombardment didn't seem to injure the demon, but it spun toward the wizard anyway. Taegan hastily began a spell to imbue his blade with magic.

"I don't know how you got in here," Rilitar said, "but I'm sending you back to the Abyss."

Raising his hands high above his head, he shouted the first line of what was presumably a spell of banishment.

The demon smirked and started an incantation of its own.

Taegan's sword trembled and whined as his enchantment sank into the steel. Rilitar finished his chant with a dramatic flourish of his hands and the air of a duelist confidently driving home the killing stroke. But as far as Taegan could tell, the magic had no effect, and while Rilitar faltered in surprise, the chasme completed its spell.

A bright swarm of spiders, each apparently a creature of living flame, rippled into existence around Rilitar's feet. They scuttled over his shoes and started up his ankles.

The chasme started growling another incantation. Wishing the ceiling was high enough to allow him to use his wings, Taegan rushed the demon.

The chasme tried to back away out of range, but the cluttered workroom hampered its ability to maneuver. Taegan closed with it, feinted high, and cut low. His sword sliced the fly-thing's thorax, and it stumbled over the precise meter of its recitation, botching the spell.

The chasme shrieked and assailed him furiously, ripping with its blazing claws, biting with its fangs, and gouging with its long, pointed snout. Taegan parried, dodged, and rattled off an incantation. Power crackled and tingled over his body. As a result, the chasme should see him as a blurred, wavering figure, and have more difficulty aiming its attacks.

Warded thus, he waited for a chance to take the offensive. The demon pounced at him, raking at his head, overextending itself. He parried hard with the edge of his blade, gashing its wrist, then plunged the point into the juncture of its head and thorax.

The thrust would have killed most mundane creatures, but the fly-thing wasn't done. It thrust out its uninjured forelimb, and a beam of crimson light leaped from its fingertips. Taegan almost twisted aside, but not quite. The magic grazed him, and he felt too weak to hold his sword up.

He lost his balance and fell on his rump. The chasme lunged at him.

It would have had him, too, except that Rilitar, who'd somehow rid himself of the blazing spiders, attacked it with a burst of intense cold that made it recoil and extinguished some of the fires burning in the room. At the same instant, the still-invisible Jivex spat a plume of his sparkling breath into the demon's eyes.

At which point, it evidently decided it had had enough. It turned, hurled itself at a casement, smashed through, and flew off into the night.

"I win!" Jivex crowed.

"Quick," gasped Taegan to Rilitar, "can you break the spell the spirit cast on me?"

"I'll try," the moon elf said.

He declaimed words of power and slashed one hand through an intricate figure, leaving a flickering trace on the air. Taegan's strength flooded back, and he scrambled to his feet.

"Perhaps I can catch it," he said.

"I'll come with you," Rilitar said, then scowled.

"You're right," Taegan said. "You need to extinguish the rest of the fires."

He hurried toward the ruined window, leaped into the dark, spread his wings, and climbed. Jivex appeared beside him. The faerie dragon evidently realized his invisibility didn't work against the chasme, so it was pointless to maintain it.

"I didn't find anything," Jivex reported, "and the nether-spirit jumped at me out of nowhere."

"At which point, it bumped into the scrying orb?"

"No. I knocked that off its stand myself, on purpose. I figured you'd hear it smash, and come running."

"Next time, break something less expensive," Taegan said as he scanned the rooftops of Thentia spread out beneath him.

He'd half expected the chasme to extinguish its corona of flame, but having flown high enough, he could see it still burning like a shooting star as it fled across the city. Nothing could be easier to track.

The trick would be overtaking it. He spoke words of power and swept a bit of licorice root through a cabalistic pass. His muscles jumped as the enchantment stabbed through them. Jivex hissed.

But the discomfort was fleeting, and afterward they flew faster, gradually closing the distance to their quarry—until the chasme peered back and snarled. The space between them darkened, clotted somehow, hiding the demon from view.

An instant later, Taegan made out why the air had blackened, but his momentum was such that he couldn't veer off in time. He plunged into the mass of flying locusts. They were all over him, stinging, blinding, and suffocating him. Somehow one worked its way halfway inside his mouth, thrashing and seemingly trying to crawl down his throat.

The onslaught was unbearable, and he could think of nothing but escape. He hammered his wings and climbed above the insects. Shrilling in disgust, Jivex struggled free a moment later.

The chasme had increased its lead, but not by too much. Perhaps they could still catch it. Except that just then it vanished in front of a dark, shuttered, dilapidated house on the edge of town.

When Rilitar answered the door, Taegan noticed that the mage had strapped on the belt with the sheathed wand.

He also had charred patches on his shoes, breeches, and lounging robe, but except for a blister or two, didn't appear to be burned himself.

"May we come in?" Taegan asked.

"It's nice that you both ask for permission this time," Rilitar said, stepping aside. Jivex almost certainly understood the sour comment as a reference to his own illicit entry earlier that evening, but it failed to faze him. Silvery wings shimmering, he flitted past Rilitar and started nosing curiously about the vestibule.

"Come on," the moon elf said. He ushered his callers into the same comfortable, oak-paneled room where he'd entertained Taegan before, then poured everyone a fresh glass of wine.

The wizard took a sip of his drink and asked, "Did you kill the chasme?"

"Alas, it escaped us," Taegan said.

"It translated itself into Scattercloak's house," Jivex said, sitting on the table and craning his neck to lap at his wine with a forked tongue.

Taegan smiled wryly. "That's one interpretation of what we observed. How did you fare, Master Shadow-water? Did the fire destroy any notes or other materials required to study the Rage?"

"Nothing critical," Rilitar said. "We'll come back to Scattercloak, but first I need to understand the two of you. When we met, Maestro, I had the feeling you didn't particularly relish my company. That's why it surprised me when you accepted my dinner invitation. But now I understand the reason. You opened a window so your friend could sneak in and snoop through my possessions."

"I humbly apologize," said Taegan, "and beseech you not to take it as a personal affront. I would have done the same to any of your colleagues. And will, as opportunities present themselves."

"Why?" Rilitar demanded.

"Because I suspect one of you is secretly a member of the Cult of the Dragon. Which is to say, a traitor to his fellows, and to Kara's enterprise. If Jivex and I can find a copy of the *Tome of the Dragon* or some other incriminating item, that will establish who it is."

"Why would you believe such a thing?"

"Not long ago, one of you wizards was killed by something that both tore and burned the body. It seems likely that our friend the chasme was responsible, and came here to murder you as well. Perhaps it glimpsed movement upstairs as Jivex poked about, assumed he was you, and popped in for the kill."

Rilitar frowned and said, "That does sound reasonable."

"Yes, and it refutes the hypothesis that your associate perished at the hands of an entity she herself fished out of the netherworld. You weren't doing any conjuring when the demon appeared."

"If Lissa did summon the chasme, it could conceivably have lingered on this plane after it killed her."

"In that case, how likely is it that it would coincidentally invade this particular home? Isn't it more credible that one of you magicians is sending it against his colleagues? If you find it difficult to credit, pray, consider this: The brass wyrm seemed entirely rational, then fell into frenzy all at once. I know from personal experience that a spell exists to over-whelm a metallic dragon's mind in precisely that way, and that Sammaster has entrusted the charm to certain of his agents."

"But it we had a traitor in our midst all along, wouldn't he have tried more often to hamper us?"

"Would he? Put yourself in his place, surrounded by shrewd, magically talented folk who'd unite to destroy you in an instant if they knew your true allegiance. At first, when the investigation into the Rage began, you might simply watch and wait, hoping it would come to nothing. Even later on, when it looked as if it might actually bear fruit, you wouldn't just attack constantly, relentlessly, lest your enemies find you out. You'd only strike when you felt certain no one would discern the source of the assault."

Rilitar shook his head. "You came to this conclusion the day you arrived here. That's the reason for this alleged weakness in the lungs that doesn't seem to hinder you when you fight."

"Yes," Taegan said. "If I was going to unmask Sammaster's agent, I needed an excuse to linger in town."

"And you've told no one of your actual intent?"

"Who was I to trust, when any of you could be the cultist? True, a number of wizards fought the brass, but even the traitor could have done that, or pretended to. It would have made him appear loyal to the cause, and perhaps the wyrm might still have killed a mage or two, or destroyed some vital papers, before it succumbed to your spells."

"Well," Rilitar said, "you don't lack for confidence, I'll give you that. I don't discount your abilities, Maestro—or yours, either, Jivex—but to imagine that the two of you alone could outfox a wizard as canny and powerful as a member of our circle . . . well, let's just say it's by no means a sure thing."

Taegan grinned and said, "I'm not quite as cocky as I sometimes appear. I knew it would be difficult, but what was the alternative? Fortunately, we've had a stroke of luck tonight. The chasme's intrusion here would seem to prove that you at least are trustworthy. Ergo, I trust I can count on you to help find the traitor."

"I'll help, certainly. But if you saw the chasme disappear into Scattercloak's house, then you've identified the cultist already."

"Not necessarily," Taegan said. "It appeared to orient on Scattercloak's place, but when it disappeared, it actually could have jumped anywhere, couldn't it?"

"Well, perhaps."

"So why lead Jivex and me on a chase across town when it could have translated itself at any time? My guess is that it wanted us to assume Scattercloak is its master."

"But Scattercloak argued against continuing our inquiry."

"What's more, I gather no one likes or trusts him very much."

Rilitar snorted. "How can you trust a person when you've never seen his face, aren't even certain if he's male or female, and don't understand the reason for all the secrecy?"

"However justified your feelings, it all combines to make him the perfect scapegoat."

"I suppose, but are you sure it isn't him?"

"No," Taegan admitted. "Despite all my snooping, I'm not certain of anything. But you know your colleagues better than I. Who do you think it is?"

"I can't imagine. Phourkyn? No. I'm only guessing him because he's haughty and obnoxious. Sinylla? She's learned so much so young, one can almost imagine a legendary archwizard like Sammaster secretly tutoring her. But she's such a sweet lass, I could never believe it. Darvin?" Darvin Kordeion, Taegan had learned, was the plump mage who liked to dress in white and who, like Scattercloak, had urged discontinuing the investigation. "He strikes me as too nervous and timid."

"It's conceivable," Taegan said, "that our traitor might adopt a public persona markedly different from his true nature, if that would help divert suspicion."

"I suppose. Anyway, along with Firefingers and me, that's the roster of the most powerful mages, the ones who might have a fair chance of laying a curse on a brass dragon right under their colleagues' noses and getting away with it."

"What about Firefingers?" Taegan asked.

"He's lived in Thentia since Selûne lit the sun, and has a stainless reputation. No, it's impossible that it could be him."

"My wine glass is empty," Jivex announced.

Rilitar smiled, rose, and picked up the bottle.

Taegan was feeling increasingly discouraged, but trying not to give in to it. "Have you noticed *anything* strange?" he asked.

"Well, the chasme."

"What, specifically?"

"First off, its aura of flame. Chasmes don't usually have that. Perhaps its master enchanted it to help it destroy our notes and such. If the demon sets fires wherever it goes, then with luck, it wouldn't have to single out important papers to burn them up."

"Would the enchantment require a master of fire magic?"

"Firefingers is scarcely the only one of us to make a study of the properties of the essential elements."

Taegan sighed. "Well, it was worth inquiring. What else about the chasme was peculiar?"

"It was a wizard itself. It used magic above and beyond the innate abilities of its breed. But to my mind, the strangest thing of all was its resistance to wards and banishment. No tanar'ri should be able to enter my house unless I summon it myself. I have protections. Yet the chasme evidently experienced no difficulty, and when I tried to send it back to its own world, it laughed at me. Somehow, it knew the spell had no chance of working."

"What do you conclude from all of that?"

Rilitar shook his head. "At this point, I don't know what it means. I'm not much of a thief-taker, am I?"

"You're doing as well as I am," Taegan said.

"Look," Rilitar said, "I understand why you wanted to poke about in secret, but now that we're both certain there is a traitor, and that he intends further killing, we have to warn the other mages."

Taegan replied, "I don't like it much, but you're right."

"We can downplay the fact that you're trying to ferret out the killer."

"No. To the Abyss with it, make me a target. Perhaps, in the act of striking at me, the killer will reveal himself."

"I think you are as cocky as you seem," Rilitar said. He crossed the room, opened a handsomely carved maple cupboard, brought out a long, straight, relatively slender sword, and presented it to the avariel. "So take this. We can't have you pausing to enchant your weapon every time some malevolent spirit attacks you."

Taegan gripped the sharkskin-wrapped hilt, pulled the sword from its silver-chased green leather scabbard, came on guard, and experimentally thrust and cut. Diamond-shaped in cross-section, the gleaming blade was light and exquisitely balanced, with a needle point. He felt a shade stronger, a hair quicker, even a bit bolder, wielding it, a manifestation of the potent magic infusing the steel.

It was, in fact, the finest sword he'd ever handled, a weapon sharp and sturdy enough to cut through mail or a dragon's scales, but that responded to his manipulations as quickly and precisely as the rapiers he'd regretfully left behind in Impiltur.

"I hesitate to accept such a princely gift," he said.

"Please," Rilitar replied. "I'm no swordsman, so it's no use to me. It's an elven blade I enchanted when Firefingers first got me involved making gear for Dorn Graybrook's hunters, but for one reason or another, none of them wanted it."

"Well, I do," said Taegan, extending his hand. "May sweet Lady Firehair bless you."

"What do we do next?" Rilitar asked.

"Convene a meeting, announce that you magicians have a traitor in your midst, watch to see if the wretch somehow betrays himself—not that I believe we could possibly be so lucky—and be wary in the meantime."

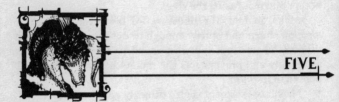

FIVE

27 Mirtul, the Year of Rogue Dragons

Dorn kept wanting to blink, as if his eyesight was cloudy. It wasn't. It was just different. Colors were muted, altered, or entirely faded to shades of gray. Yet, thanks to the enchantment Kara had cast on him, he could see clearly despite the darkness.

Employing his harpoon like a walking staff, Raryn stalked along at the head of the procession. His white goatee and long hair, like Kara's moon-blond tresses, seemed almost to blaze in the gloom.

It had taken Raryn a long, weary time to backtrack the dead monk to the hidden tunnel entrance. The poor wretch had stumbled a long way before succumbing to his burns. But after resting, and using some of their precious healing potions to ease the hurts the chromatic dragons had given them, the seekers had headed down the passage.

Which, after a final twist, opened out into a sizable cavern. Stalactites stabbed from the arched ceiling, and other spikes and lumps of limestone jutted above the uneven floor. The cool air stank of guano, evidence of a colony of bats somewhere close at hand. Indeed, Dorn thought he heard one or two of them fluttering about.

"Curse it!" Raryn snarled.

Dorn wasn't accustomed to seeing his usually placid partner betray such agitation. The half-golem had been serving as rearguard, but concerned, he sidled around Kara and Chatulio—whose long, serpentine body nearly plugged the tunnel—to draw even with the dwarf.

"What's wrong?" asked Dorn.

Raryn pointed with a stubby finger, indicating three openings in the chamber walls ahead. "That, that, and that."

"What about them?" asked Dorn.

"Which is the right way?" Raryn said. "I was hoping we wouldn't have to make such choices, though really, I knew better. We're miles from the monastery. The monks couldn't have dug a single straight tunnel all this distance. What they could do was find a way into a honeycomb of caves beneath the mountains. Unfortunately, such places are always mazes."

"Perhaps," said Chatulio, "the monks made signposts to find their way through."

"No," said Dorn, "not if they want their secret road to remain a secret. Plenty of intelligent and unfriendly creatures spend much of their lives in caves. But Raryn, I still don't see the problem. Why can't you just puzzle out which is the right way?"

"Because I'm not that kind of dwarf," Raryn said. "I'm the only example of the arctic variety any of you has ever seen, so maybe you forget, I didn't grow up underground."

"You're still the best tracker and pathfinder I've ever seen," said Dorn.

"Like any scout, I'm good in country I understand, which for me is someplace under the open sky. Below ground, I'm a tenderfoot again."

Chatulio laughed. "And here I thought I was the joker."

Kara said, "I don't believe it, either."

"Nor I," said Dorn, "and who knows you better than me? You can do this."

Half hidden by his bushy mustache, Raryn's mouth quirked upward in a somber smile. "All right. I owed you a warning, but I'll try."

∽∘∾

"Everyone's here," Rilitar said.

Taegan nodded and turned to the wizards standing or sitting about their workroom in various attitudes of curiosity and impatience. He spread his wings a bit as if stretching, then folded them with an audible snap. It was a trick he'd learned as a fencing teacher, to draw an audience's attention and make them fall quiet.

"Worthy mages . . ." he began.

"I want to say right at the outset," interrupted Phourkyn, head cocked slightly to bring the glare of his single eye directly to bear on Taegan, his slicked-back hair giving off the sweet scent of pomade, "how inappropriate it was for you, Maestro, to command any of us to attend you. You lack the authority, and so, for that matter, does your fellow elf."

Some of his colleagues growled their agreement. Perched on one of the rafters, Jivex made a spitting sound, expressing his disgust at their show of pique.

"Yet you indulged me," Taegan said. "I thank you for that, and hope to repay your kindness by saving your lives. A demon tried to kill Rilitar last night. I'm certain it was the same tanar'ri that slew Lissa Uvarrk, and am just as sure we haven't seen the last of it. It will keep on trying to destroy one or another of you, at moments when it—or the warlock controlling it—hopes to find you alone and vulnerable."

The wizards all started clamoring at once. Taegan raised his hands for silence until the babble faded, then gave the assembly an abridged account of the battle with the chasme, omitting any mention of the chase that had ended in front of Scattercloak's house.

Afterward, Firefingers, looking not merely elderly but troubled, perhaps even frail for the first time since Taegan had met him, said, "Plainly, this is cause for concern, but I'm loath to believe that any member of our fellowship could be a traitor. Surely we can find a likelier explanation."

"Such as another mage?" said Sinylla, looking fresh and pert as usual in her silvery vestments and crescent-moon pendant. "One unknown to any of us, lurking here in town."

"It's not impossible," Taegan said, "but I'm currently gazing at a chamber stuffed full of powerful wizards. It makes little sense to assume, without a wisp of evidence to support such a supposition, the covert presence of yet another unless we can establish the innocence of each of you."

"We know of the shadow Sammaster left in his writings," said Phourkyn, "to possess any who tries to read the text by magical means. Perhaps he bound a chasme in the folio to provide a second trap, and our investigations released the thing without us even realizing."

"I doubt it," Rilitar said. "Neither Lissa nor I had tried to unravel Sammaster's cipher in a good long while. We were concentrating on the lore Kara and her allies have recovered from the ancient shrines. Why, then, would a tanar'ri charged with protecting the secrets of the lich's notes attack us in preference to someone who was still working on them?"

Pink-jowled and sweaty-faced in his white and silver robes, Darvin Kordeion said, "I warned you all that no good would come of persisting in these inquiries, but nobody listens to me."

"Because you're a coward and a fool," Phourkyn said.

"For once," said Scattercloak, shrouded in his mantle, head bowed so no one could see under his cowl, "you and I agree. But in this instance, Master Kordeion was correct to worry."

"Murder is the Watchlord's business," called one of the lesser mages. "We should inform him right away."

"No," Taegan said. "For the sake of keeping the peace, he'd forbid you to continue your studies as he nearly did before. No one can tell him anything. If someone does, I'll take it as proof that the informer himself is Sammaster's agent, and deal with him accordingly."

Phourkyn sneered. "Don't flatter yourself that a mere bladesinger could 'deal' with me, Maestro, or with a number of these others. But that aside, I agree with you. What's the point of whining to Gelduth Blackturret? Does anyone believe him capable of contending with a threat powerful enough to menace us? We have to protect ourselves."

"Or abandon our inquiries," Darvin said.

"We've already discussed that," Firefingers said, "and determined it would be irresponsible."

"Worse than that," Phourkyn said, "giving up would constitute a craven surrender to our foe."

"I weary," said Scattercloak, "of the manner in which you constantly presume to pass judgment on the rest of us. It's not your place to define the course of wisdom or honor for your fellows."

"Maybe not," said the one-eyed mage. "It's certainly a waste of time trying to recommend honor or courage to you."

"Blood and dung!" Taegan exclaimed. "Dorn and his comrades warned me that you lot love to squabble, but it's accomplishing nothing. I suggest we turn our attention to safeguarding this enterprise. Rilitar and I have some ideas in that regard."

Phourkyn snorted. "I've already explained, Maestro, you're not in command here."

"I'm aware of that," Taegan said. "But Master Shadowwater and I have had a little time to ponder this matter. You haven't. For that reason if no other, it makes sense for you to listen to our recommendations."

"Yes," said Firefingers, "I concur."

Phourkyn spread his hands in a curt gesture conveying that, though it would likely prove a waste of time, he was willing to humor the senior wizard.

"Each of you" Taegan said, "needs to make himself as safe as he can. To the extent possible, keep defensive enchantments in place, and carry your arcane weapons wherever you go. Bodyguards, be they conjured spirits or hired bravos, may also prove useful."

"Surely," said Scattercloak in his emotionless, artificial-sounding voice, "this is obvious."

"What's obvious," one of the lesser mages murmured to another, "is that if you really want to be safe, you'll clear out of Thentia."

"Right," said the second warlock, "and then a dragon flight catches you on the road."

"Perhaps," said Taegan, "what I say next will seem less obvious. Most of you pursue your studies not just here, but in your own homes, your own sanctuaries—"

"Because we all have private spells and resources," Phourkyn said, "which we're reluctant to reveal. So of course we labor in secret. We're wizards! You can't expect us to do all our work together in one room, like apprentices under a master's supervision."

"I'm not suggesting that," Taegan said. "But henceforth, no pages from Sammaster's folio, or other materials relevant to your investigations, can leave this room. Moreover, we need to make an inventory of what we have, and employ a clerk to keep track of it. With luck, it will insure that the traitor doesn't steal or destroy vital information."

"I'll provide the clerk," Firefingers said.

"I also advise," Taegan continued, "that each of you submit to an interrogation conducted by one of the Moonmaiden's priestesses. I trust Sinylla Zoranyian and her sisters in the goddess's service can arrange it discretely, without the Watchlord finding out. Perhaps, employing spells to sift truth from falsehood, the Silver Lady's servants can identify the traitor."

"Not a chance," Phourkyn sneered. "Any accomplished mage can flummox such piddling enchantments."

"I think," said little Jannatha Goldenshield, a trace of anger in her voice, "that you underestimate Selûne's power." Taegan had learned that Jannatha and her sister Baerimel Dunnath, the third mage in service to the House of the Moon, were Sinylla's cousins.

"It's worth trying," Taegan said. "I know wizards are jealous of their secrets, but surely you can trust Selûne's handmaidens to restrict their questions to the matter at hand."

"Nevertheless," said Scattercloak, "I refuse to submit to such an interrogation."

"Well, you would, wouldn't you?" Phourkyn said. "It's remarkable, isn't it, how daintily we've danced around this matter, without anyone coming out and saying what's in all our minds. If someone in our circle is a scoundrel, then surely the likeliest subject is our resident ghost, the enigma whose face we've never seen. I think it's time to remedy that."

"Don't try," said Scattercloak.

"No," said Taegan, "don't. It's unnecessary, just as it's unnecessary for you, Master Scattercloak, to submit to questioning. I didn't want to reveal this, but it looks as if it may be the only way to prevent a violent altercation. I already know for a fact that, like Rilitar, Scattercloak, Baerimel Dunnath, and Esvelle Chernin are innocent."

"How do you know?" Phourkyn demanded.

"I can't explain just yet," Taegan said. "It would prevent me from using the same method to investigate the rest of you. So I ask you to trust me. I promise that if you do, I can eventually unmask the culprit."

The one-eyed enchanter shook his head. "Why should we trust you?"

"Because he kept Samdralyrion from incinerating you with his fiery breath," Rilitar said.

"I think Maestro Nightwind has given us sound advice," Firefingers said. "I'm inclined to take it."

And though many of the other mages demanded to have their grumbling, quibbling say, that seemed to be the consensus in the end.

Afterward, Taegan and Rilitar took a stroll through Thentia's teeming streets to unwind from the stresses of the conclave. The bright spring sun was warm, and though, after years spent in exquisite Lyrabar, Taegan could find nothing to admire in Thentia's bluntly utilitarian architecture, he, as always, enjoyed the bustle, chatter, and even the occasional stinks of a human city. Jivex flitted about, snapping insects from the air and eliciting cries of wonder from passersby.

Taegan was likewise an object of curiosity. He noticed a pretty lass staring at him in fascination, spread his wings to give her a better look, then offered a smile and a gallant bow. She blushed, turned away, then glanced back as he'd known she would.

Rilitar chuckled and said, "I'm amazed you have any thought to spare for flirtation."

"I don't have to think," Taegan said. "By now, it's a reflex. I trained myself to act the consummate rake to attract wealthy young men to my academy."

"Didn't the mask ever chafe?"

"No, because it wasn't a mask. I became what I wanted to be."

"If so, I'm happy for you, but still surprised it's that particular achievement that seems to give you such satisfaction. It seems a trifling accomplishment compared to mastering bladesong. If you think about it, Faerûn is full to overflowing with well-dressed louts who know how to guzzle brandy, chase whores, and shake a dice cup. People who can wield a sword with one hand while weaving spells with the other are extraordinarily rare."

Taegan realized he'd never thought about it that way, but felt disinclined to say so.

"Fencing," the avariel said, "bladesong, manners, wit, a knowledge of fashion, wine, and cuisine, are all brightly polished and equally splendid facets of the perfection that is my humble self."

"If you say so." Rilitar glanced around, checking for eavesdroppers, then continued in a more confidential tone, "The meeting seemed to go well."

"I'm glad you think so. I'm frankly bemused at the reception we encountered. Even a mage like Phourkyn, who ultimately seemed to agree with us, couldn't bring himself to admit it until he did his share of scoffing and sneering."

"For the most part, the human wizards are independent to the point of eccentricity or even perversity. They bristle when anyone tries to give them direction, no matter how benign the intent. The important thing is that they finally did fall in line with our suggestions, thanks in large part to Firefingers's support. We should give thanks to the Lifegiver that he at least is sensible."

"Did you observe anything," Taegan asked, pausing on a corner while an ox cart creaked past, "to point the finger of suspicion at anyone in particular?"

"No."

"Alas, neither did I."

They strolled onward.

"I have to say," Rilitar said, "you caught me by surprise when you announced that Scattercloak, Baerimel, and Esvelle are innocent."

Taegan smiled and said, "I surprised myself, but it seemed the right ploy."

"But how did you clear them?"

"I already explained why I think Scattercloak is in the clear. For their part, Baerimel and Esvelle are two of the less powerful mages. It seems unlikely that they can conjure demons that are somehow impervious to the wards of their more accomplished colleagues."

"That's it? You acknowledged that you could be wrong about Scattercloak, and it's also possible that Baerimel and Esvelle are more formidable than they've ever let on."

"That's true, and if I've just declared Sammaster's agent innocent, no doubt he or she is pleased. But consider the situation if, as I think likely, it's someone else. In that case, the traitor knows I was right about Scattercloak and the ladies, and accordingly, he has to wonder if I truly do possess some infallible means of unmasking him. My hope is that the threat of it will provoke him into attacking me, and thus revealing himself."

Rilitar shook his head. "You seem quite cheerful for a fellow inviting his own murder."

"Because our adversary doesn't have it all his own way anymore. He has to worry about our own feints and genuine attacks. We're fencing now, and that's a game I understand."

Raryn dropped to one knee and peered at a patch of pale fungus on the cavern floor. Something had crushed the edge of the soft, lumpy stuff. The dead monk's foot? He thought so, but the way the fungus was already growing back, blurring the shape of the track, he couldn't be sure.

He was fairly certain the path he'd chosen wasn't actually heading toward the Monastery of the Yellow Rose. It had veered too far to the east, which didn't mean it wouldn't ultimately swing back around again, but how was he to know?

He felt anxiety gnawing at him, and frowned it away. Just do your best, he told himself. That's all anyone can do, in any circumstance.

"I believe we're still on the right track," he said, straightening up.

"Let's leave another marker," Chatulio said. He murmured a rhyming cantrip, then scratched the wall with a talon—the claw cut the stone as if it were tallow—and drew an arrow.

They hiked onward, Raryn in the lead, Kara next, the copper third, and Dorn bringing up the rear.

At times, the way opened out into great vaults adorned with fantastic confections of stone, some of the stalactites and stalagmites delicate as lace or frothing sea foam, some ponderous as ancient trees. At other moments, the walls pressed in close, and hanging or rearing masses of rock choked the tunnel like rows of fangs. To negotiate one especially tight squeeze, Chatulio cast a spell that shrank him to half his former size.

Finally the explorers stepped out into another enormous, lofty-ceilinged cave. A crevasse ten paces wide split the chamber floor, but a rope bridge spanned the chasm.

Raryn sighed with relief. Surely the monks had constructed the bridge, which meant he and his friends had taken the right turns so far. Kara clasped his shoulder in congratulation.

Striding with renewed energy, the seekers hurried forward. Chatulio spread his wings to fly across the chasm. Raryn gripped one of the guide ropes, made to step onto the bridge, then hesitated.

"Hold on!" he said.

"What's wrong?" asked Dorn.

"We figured something might be lurking along the way," Raryn said, "the something that killed the monk. Well, it's here, somewhere."

He didn't know how he knew, but trusted the hunter's intuition that had saved his life on more than one occasion.

Chatulio's nostrils flared. "I do smell something," he said.

A thick gray fog clotted the air. Kara started singing a spell, and Chatulio chanted his own words of power. Certain the mist was intended to mask a foe's advance, Raryn came on guard with his harpoon and listened. From long experience, he knew Dorn must be doing the same thing, though he could barely see the half-golem, or any of his comrades, within the clammy vapor.

Raryn heard a rapid scuttling. He pivoted toward the sound, and when the creature lunged out of the fog, the dwarf drove his harpoon into its chest. The beast—some sort of enormous reptile—retaliated with a snap of its dagger-sized fangs. He jumped back out of range and snatched his ice-axe free of the straps securing it to his pack.

A second later, the fog disappeared as quickly as it had materialized. Raryn assumed Kara had wiped it from existence with a counterspell. The effect of Chatulio's magic was to sear their assailant with a burst of flame.

That creature, Raryn observed, appeared to be one of the wingless dragons called landwyrms, albeit a runtish, cave-dwelling variety he'd never encountered before. Its scales were a mottled gray that no doubt helped it hide in its environment of stone.

Dorn set himself in front of it, iron limbs forward, sword cocked back. Kara sang a crackling flare of lightning into being to stab into its neck. Taking flight with a snap of his wings, Chatulio spat acid to sizzle and smoke along its spine, eliciting a roar of pain and fury. Raryn chopped at its flank. But while evading its sudden wheeling attacks, its attempts to trample him, claw him, or bash him with its tail, the dwarf did his best to keep watch, also. Landwyrms lacked breath weapons, and likewise the magical prowess of true wizards, and that made it unlikely that this particular creature had burned the unfortunate monk.

A second reptile—a sinuous, narrow-winged drake with dark, lustrous scales—scrambled up out of the chasm. Evidently goaded by frenzy, it and the landwyrm had joined forces to slaughter whatever prey they could catch in their sunless domain.

"Watch out!" Raryn called.

A split second later, the dark dragon spat forth a plume of vapor.

Chatulio and Kara were the targets, and both tried to dodge, the copper with a beat of his wings to carry him above the breath attack, and the bard by flinging herself to the side. Still, the streaming corrosive fumes blistered them both, and Kara dropped to her knees, coughing and retching.

Raryn felt a stab of dismay. Then the landwyrm rounded on him, and he had no more time for thought.

He landed two solid chops to its mask, but couldn't quite score on an eye. He evaded several strikes and raking attacks. Then Dorn must have clawed or sliced the landwyrm badly, because it spun away from Raryn for another assault on the half-golem.

Raryn risked another glance around. Kara lay on the cavern floor. The dark dragon thrashed and snarled, a swarm of stinging, pinching scorpions encrusting its body—or the semblance of scorpions, anyway. Actually, it was one of Chatulio's illusions. The copper himself was swelling, returning to his original size, wobbling in flight as the transformation made him momentarily awkward.

Raryn hacked at the landwyrm until it whirled toward him again, then scrambled backward, not quite quickly enough. Its forefoot leaped at him, and he wrenched himself aside.

The last-second evasion turned what would otherwise have been a mortal blow into one that simply slashed his polar-bear hide armor and the skin above his ribs. Ordinarily, such a superficial wound wouldn't balk him. But it made him instantly weak and light-headed, sick, as if the landwyrm's claws were venomous.

The dragon snapped at him. He managed to jump back out of range, but in so doing, lost his balance and fell on his rump. The landwyrm reared, perhaps intending to flop down and crush him.

Then, however, it pivoted and lunged after Dorn, who must have attacked it ferociously indeed to distract it from making a kill—and who might pay for it with his life.

Accordingly, Raryn had to get back into the fight, but it took all his stamina just to clamber back to his feet, after which, dizzy and panting, he had to pause to gather the strength for further exertion. At the same time, the landwyrm slammed one clanging talon slash after another into the iron half of Dorn's body. The blows failed to penetrate the enchanted metal, but knocked the big man staggering and reeling, making it all but impossible for him to strike back.

Raryn raised his ice-axe, took a step toward the land-wyrm, and a wave of vertigo spun the cavern around him and nearly dumped him back on the floor. But if he couldn't aid Dorn, maybe Chatulio could. He cast about, seeking the copper, then cursed.

Because Chatulio couldn't help. He was still busy fighting the slim dragon with the dark, shimmering scales. It had rid itself of the phantasmal scorpions, and the two wyrms wheeled beneath the cavern ceiling like pair of colossal bats, maneuvering, using stalactites for cover, blazing away at one another with bursts of conjured frost and flame, and spurts of their corrosive breath.

It occurred to Raryn to use one of his ranger charms. He didn't know whether it would counterattack the malaise engendered by the landwyrm's touch, or even if he could articulate it properly in his dazed and feeble state, but it was worth a try.

The landwyrm knocked Dorn down onto his back, then snapped at him. Dorn whipped his iron arm across his body in time for it, and not his flesh, to catch the dragon's teeth. When the reptile's jaws clashed shut on the spiked and bladed metal and it realized what it had, it snarled, bore down hard, and lashed its head back and forth and up and down, trying either to crumple the enchanted prosthesis into uselessness or jerk it away from the meat and bone to which it was anchored.

It succeeded at neither, though the effort pounded Dorn against the floor. Finally the landwyrm hissed in frustration, then, as a notion seemingly struck it, laughed through clenched jaws. Dorn's arm still clamped between its teeth, dragging the half-golem along, it scuttled toward the chasm, and Raryn realized it had decided to dispose of its well-armored foe by flinging him into the depths. Dorn stabbed at it with his sword, but without his feet planted, couldn't exert the force to do any more than prick its rock-colored hide.

The landwyrm had nearly reached the crevasse when Kara lurched up onto her knees, singing words of power. The final, sustained note swelled louder and louder until the stone beneath the landwyrm's shattered into chips and pebbles, and it floundered in the treacherous footing. The conjuration had evidently taken all of Kara's remaining strength, for she collapsed facedown.

Still, she'd delayed the landwyrm long enough for Raryn to complete his own spell. For a moment, a fresh wind, smelling of verdure, gusted through the cave, and he felt connected, almost rooted, to the earth. Up the link surged an exhilarating wave of vitality that washed his sickness away.

He bellowed a war cry to attract the landwyrm's attention, then charged. His greatest fear was that it would go ahead and toss Dorn in the abyss before turning to face him. It was what Raryn would have done in its place. But maybe frenzy had eroded its battle sense at least a little, for, still dangling Dorn from its jaws, it pivoted.

Raryn avoided two claw strikes, meeting the second with a counterattack that drew a spurt of blood and half-severed a toe. That was good as far as it went, but he needed to get at the landwyrm's vitals, not just its extremities. He retreated, and when it started to follow, instantly sprang forward. The maneuver brought him within striking distance of its chest and he swung with all his strength, trying to shear through scale and ribs to the heart and lungs.

He drove in three blows before the reptile threw itself down, and he had to scurry to avoid being crushed beneath it. His feet slipped in the rubble shattered by Kara's spell, and he nearly didn't make it. The landwyrm tried to scramble back to its feet, but seemed to lack the strength to raise itself. The dozens of wounds it had suffered were taking their toll. It seemed surprised at its weakness, and before it could collect itself, Raryn lunged and buried his axe in the underside of its neck. The landwyrm collapsed.

Raryn immediately looked around to find out how Chatulio was faring. For a second, he only saw the remaining cave-dwelling dragon, gliding, seeking its foe. Then the copper flapped out from behind a massive stalactite several yards ahead of it. The slender subterranean drake spat a plume of its roiling corrosive breath. Caught squarely by the burst, the target exploded into a flock of giggling, flatulent pixies.

At the same moment, Raryn spotted the real Chatulio, no longer flying but walking upside down on the cavern ceiling as easily as a spider. Since the copper had distracted his adversary with a phantasm, he was able to smother the subterranean wyrm in a sheet of his own smoky breath. To Raryn's surprise, the dark reptile's scales didn't char and bubble at its touch, but when the slender wyrm wheeled to face its attacker, the ranger perceived that the assault had nonetheless had an effect. The cave-dweller's movements were slower than before.

Conceivably it could have cleansed itself of the enchantment with a counterspell, but Chatulio didn't give it the chance. He sprang from the ceiling and seized the other dragon in midair.

Grappling and thus unable to fly, they plummeted to the cavern floor with a prodigious slam that, amazingly, stunned neither. Entwined, snarling, grunting, rolling to and fro, they tore at one another with fang and claw.

His normal quickness unimpaired, Chatulio could rip more often than his adversary, and over the course of the next few heartbeats, the difference told. Finally he caught the cave-dweller's sinuous neck in his jaws, and with one convulsive effort, bit it in two. Gore fountained from the stump.

His exposed skin bruised and scraped, Dorn yanked his iron arm free of the landwyrm's fangs, breaking one in the process, then clambered to his feet.

"Are you all right?" Raryn asked.

Dorn ignored the question to rush to Kara. Raryn followed.

The half-golem rolled her over onto her back, and snarled at what he thus revealed. Kara's lavender eyes peered groggily from a field of raw, seeping burns, and Raryn reckoned it exceptional luck that the dark wyrm's breath hadn't seared them blind as well. It had spattered her scalp, though, singeing patches of her moon-blond hair away and fouling her with the stink.

Dorn extracted a healing draught from his belt pouch and held it for her to drink. But either she was too addled to understand or too feeble to swallow. She choked, and coughed the clear liquid out to run down her blistered chin.

Then something gave a rumbling growl. Dorn and Raryn lurched around. Standing over the headless corpse of his erstwhile foe, Chatulio glared at them. Raryn realized the agitation of combat had brought madness bubbling up inside the copper's mind.

"Easy," Raryn said, "easy. The fight's over now, and we're your friends. You don't want to—"

Chatulio roared and stalked forward.

Raryn took hold of the vial in Dorn's hand. "You've got to hold him back," he said, "while I help Kara. Her magic's the only thing that can calm him."

Dorn grabbed his sword, jumped up, and advanced. Chatulio pounced and slashed with his foreclaws. Dorn tried to twist aside. The talons still rang on the iron half of his body, and knocked him staggering.

Raryn couldn't watch whatever would happen next. He had to concentrate on Kara. He recited the charm that had augmented his own vigor, and as before, a forest-scented breeze gusted through the cavern. Kara shifted her limbs, and the dullness left her eyes.

Raryn offered her the healing elixir. She guzzled, only to retch it out once more.

A few yards away, Chatulio conjured a flare of yellow light that made Dorn shout in pain, then followed up with a sweep of his tail. The hunter barely managed to jump over the blow which would otherwise have shattered his leg of flesh and bone.

"Drink slowly," said Raryn to Kara. "It's the only way you'll get it down."

The bard gave a feeble nod.

Chatulio clawed. The attack clanged on iron, failing to penetrate, but hurling Dorn back against a massive lump of a stalagmite. He sprawled atop it, waving his sword, seemingly unable to rise. The impact had knocked the wind out of him at the very least.

Chatulio reared above him, throat swelling as he readied his breath weapon.

Kara finally managed to swallow some of the potion. Smooth new skin flowed across some of her blemishes, and her breathing eased a little.

"Prop me up," she whispered, "so I can sing."

Raryn heaved her up into a sitting position, but wondered if she'd be able to sing even so. She was still so weak. But her vibrant voice emerged as rich, sweet, and precisely cadenced as ever, the melody charged with a power that supplanted the fear and desperation in the ranger's mind with calmness and a profound feeling of good will toward his companions.

Until the song broke off abruptly, in the middle of the fifth line. Kara slumped in Raryn's arms, her head lolling.

Still, she'd endured long enough. Her power had quelled Chatulio's frenzy for a little longer, anyway.

"I'm sorry!" the copper cried. "I'm so sorry. Dorn, are you all right?"

The human demonstrated that he was by clambering off the stalagmite and turning to Raryn to ask, "How is she?"

"Still alive," said the dwarf, "but in need of more help than my charms and our elixirs can give. They'll have real healers. in the monastery."

"Then let's move out," said Dorn.

They trekked onward through the stony labyrinth, Chatulio bearing Kara on his back. Raryn remained uncertain of their course. True, he'd guided his comrades correctly as far as the rope bridge, and maybe that was cause for optimism, but it was no guarantee that he wouldn't stray from the right path eventually.

As he peered for a sign, or paused to ponder a choice, he could feel Dorn's urgency like heat from a fire. His friend was all but frantic to reach their destination. But the big man never demanded that he hurry. He knew a ranger needed time to exercise his craft.

At last they wove their way through a field of stalagmites, rounded a sharp turn, and beheld an incline. At the top was a ledge, and at the back of that, a large, iron-bound door set into the cavern wall.

Chatulio ran up the slope as easily as if he were loping on a flat surface. Unwilling to be left behind, Dorn scrambled up the incline as fast as he could, digging his iron claws into whatever handhold presented itself. Raryn brought up the rear.

Dorn clambered past Chatulio's dangling tail and up onto the shelf, where the copper had risen onto his hind legs to make more room for his companions.

"I knocked," Chatulio said, "and called out, but no one's answered yet."

"Don't worry about it," Dorn said as he pulled back his iron fist to punch the door.

"No," Kara groaned from her perch atop Chatulio's spine.

She sang an arpeggio that momentarily made Dorn feel a strange, poignant yearning to yield to her in some unfathomable way. The door did surrender itself, quivering and clanking as locks and latches disengaged. Spent, Kara seemed to slump back into semiconsciousness.

Dorn thrust the door open to bang against the wall. On the other side was a shadowy corridor of worked stone, lit by a few magical lights set at regular intervals. Affixed to the wall like torches in sconces, shining with their own steady golden luminescence, the enchanted lamps were roses sculpted from crystal.

"Looks like a Monastery of the Yellow Rose to me," Chatulio said.

Dorn strode down the hallway bellowing that they needed a healer. His companions scurried after, Chatulio filling the passage. The seekers passed dozens of storerooms, and chambers filled with ranks of towering bookshelves, before a gangly, shaven-headed boy on the verge of manhood stepped from a doorway. He was dressed simply, all in gray, and had a wooden amulet carved in the form of bound hands—Ilmater's emblem—dangling around his neck. He goggled at the strangers, his eyes widened in panic, and he whirled and ran.

"Wait!" Dorn shouted. "We're friendly!"

It did no good. The youth had unexpectedly come face-to-face with a dragon—and a monstrosity with iron limbs—while wyrms had the monastery under siege. Naturally he believed the worst.

Not wanting the novice to raise the entire fortress against them, Dorn gave chase, but realized almost immediately that he couldn't overtake him. The boy was a good runner, and had too much of a lead.

Then a shaft streaked past Dorn and hit the youth in the knee. It had been a tricky shot in the cramped confines of the corridor, especially with the half-golem between the bow and the target, but not impossible for an archer as adept as Raryn. The blunt fowling arrow knocked the boy down.

Dorn sprinted and threw himself on top of the novice. The boy screamed until the hunter backhanded him.

"Shut up!" Dorn snarled. "Shut up, look at us, and think, damn you! I've got you down helpless on the ground and I've got spikes and claws on my hand. If I wanted to kill you, I'd smash your skull and that would be that. The dwarf could have shot you with a sharp arrow. The drake could have sprayed you with his breath. But he's a good dragon. A copper. If you try, you can see the color of his scales even in this light."

The monk peered, squinting, and some of the fear faded from his expression, which still left him looking too weary and care-worn for one so young.

"Who . . . who are you?" he asked.

"Friends," said Dorn. "We came through the caves, but we ran into trouble. Our companion needs a healer. Right now."

"The clerics are all on the upper levels," said the boy. "Everyone is, except the youngest neophytes, the wounded, and those of us charged to mind them."

"Take us."

"You don't understand. You can't hear it this deep in the rock, but the wyrms are attacking. The priests are busy fighting them. No one can break away to—"

"Shut up!" said Dorn. "Listen. My comrades and I are good at killing dragons. We'll kill some for you now, to pay for the healing Kara needs. But somebody is going to care for her. Otherwise, we'll help the wyrms bring this pile down around your ears."

The monk swallowed and said, "Come on, then."

Limping, he led them to a broad staircase that, zigzagging back and forth, carried them higher and higher. As they scrambled upward, Dorn started to hear the cacophony of the battle raging above his head, the sounds weirdly distorted by the tons of intervening stone, but recognizable nonetheless. The roars and hisses of dragons, and the boom and sizzle of their breath. Their human prey crying out in desperation, and screaming in agony.

For a moment, much as he lived for the satisfaction of killing wyrms, he also flinched from what was to come. He was weary from clambering and trudging through the caves, and sore all over from the beating the landwyrm had given him, in no condition to plunge into a new fight. But he reckoned he had no choice.

So don't be weak, he told himself. Don't be tired. You don't have any right to be. Softness is for people, and you're not one anymore. You're a thing of metal, built for killing. Just go do it.

Finally the monk opened a triangular-arched door, admitting a gust of smoky air, the stink of burned flesh, and sunlight. After his hours underground, Dorn had to squinch his eyes to slits and wait for them to adjust to the brightness.

Once they did, he peered out into a courtyard. High walls surrounded it, and a net made of rattling chains with barbed hooks attached covered the top. Other such constructions stretched between towers like enormous spiderwebs. Together with mystical barriers—floating sheets of flame, clouds of spinning blades, planes of seething light—conjured by the monastery's spellcasters, the nets made it difficult for the wheeling, swooping dragons to fly or fight in the air immediately above the stronghold.

Yet the mesh couldn't stop the scourge of their breath, or the relentless pounding savagery of their sorcery. Sometimes it even failed to hold back the reptiles themselves, if they were eager enough to break through.

A colossal green plummeted at one of the wall-walks and the curtain of chain strung above. The drake's momentum tore the net loose from its moorings, and it slammed down atop the battlements tangled in the wreckage, with the hooks embedded in its scaly hide. That should have hampered it, but when monks came running to engage it, it struck and clawed at them with all a wyrm's horrific speed. Its strength was such that the chains simply snapped like threads to accommodate its movements. It clawed two monks to death in as many seconds, flinging their tattered bodies off the wall to thump down in the courtyard.

Dorn rounded on his guide and asked, "You'll help the lass?"

"Yes," said the youth.

Dorn ran out into the courtyard, nocked an arrow, and let it fly. It pierced the green's neck, but not deeply enough to do much damage. Raryn shot it in the chest, but that too was only a pinprick. It caught the wyrm's attention, though, and the green lifted its head in the way that meant it intended to use its breath weapon.

Dorn and Raryn waited for it to start spewing forth its billowing cloud of poison before flinging themselves to the side. Had they dodged too soon, the green would simply have adjusted its aim. Even so, Dorn's exposed skin burned, and his eyes flooded with tears. But he didn't think he'd inhaled any of the muck to rot away his lungs.

Blinking the water from his eyes, he took another shot, and as he did, noticed the arcane sigils cut into the green wyrm's scales. It was evidently one of the draconic mystics called the hidecarved, with the special abilities that implied.

Dorn cast about, spotted a stairway to the top of the wall, and ran toward it. His archery hadn't done much to the green, but maybe he'd fare better with his sword.

As he clambered upward, Chatulio pounced out into the courtyard and spat his acid upward to spatter the green's mask. At last the chromatic seemed to feel a hurt. It screamed and thrashed.

Hoping to take advantage of its momentary incapacity, the monks on the battlements attacked it with javelins, flails, and naked fists. A man in gray robes and a red skullcap dived beneath its throat, slashed with a sickle, and somersaulted clear beneath a shower of gore. The green shuddered and swayed. The defenders plunged in again, even more furiously, trying to administer the death blow.

"No!" Dorn shouted. He could tell it wasn't hurt as badly as it pretended, and if what he'd heard about the hidecarved was true, in another moment it might not be hurt at all.

Some of the monks heeded his warning and pulled back. The others were too intent on the attack.

When the green invoked the magic of the runes scarring its body, the gash in its neck closed. Knitting flesh shoved out arrows and spears as those punctures likewise healed themselves.

Full of strength, all but whole once more, the green exploded into motion, biting, raking, swatting with its wings and bashing with its tail. Taken by surprise, even monks, with all their trained nimbleness, couldn't dodge. Some perished instantly. The rest, stunned, reeling, surely would die in another instant, unless someone distracted the wyrm.

Dorn bellowed a battle cry and charged down the wall-walk. He was keenly aware that the elevated path was a wretched place to fight a dragon. He had nowhere to side-step. But it was too late to worry about that.

The green stretched out its neck to snatch the half-golem up in its jaws. Dorn stopped short, gripped the hilt of the bastard sword with both hands, and cut the creature's long, curving jaw. It hissed and lunged forward, trampling a shrieking, wounded monk in the process. Dorn scrambled back just quickly enough to avoid the same fate, came on guard with his iron hand leading, and snapped his knuckle-spikes into the green's snout.

He'd been lucky these first few moments, but knew it couldn't last. The dragon was going to kill him unless somebody came to his aid.

Fortunately, someone did. The green jerked its head around and stared at empty air. Dorn assumed it was gawking at some terrifying phantom of Chatulio's devising. He took advantage of its distraction to cut at its neck.

At the same time, Raryn chanted one of his ranger charms and shot another arrow. The shaft plunged into its flank all the way up to the fletchings.

The green roared, turned, spread its wings, and sprang into the air.

"My spell softened up its scales," Raryn called.

Dorn started to answer, but then glimpsed motion from the corner of his eye. He flung himself flat, foiling the attempt of another diving wyrm, a young red, to pluck him from the battlement.

And the fight roared on.

Such was the frantic confusion of the battle, and so crushing the exhaustion and suffering the dragons left in their wake, that Cantoule didn't hear about the newcomers until an hour after the reptiles broke off their attack. Then it required considerable self-discipline for him to keep from complaining because no one had alerted him sooner.

What he did instead was smile, thank the novice who'd brought him the tidings, and swing himself up off his cot in the infirmary. His burned leg throbbed in protest, but he ignored the pain. It meant nothing compared to the glow of hope the news had kindled in his heart. Pain, after all, had become a daily occurrence, while hope was such a rare emotion that he hadn't truly expected ever to feel it again.

He hiked across a courtyard, taking a wary, reflexive glance at the black and starry sky even though sentries kept watch along the battlements. After a battle, the dragons usually retired for at least a day or two, to heal and replenish their spells. Once in a while, though, hoping to catch the defenders napping, they launched a fresh assault in a matter of hours. Thus, the monks could never drop their guard.

Cantoule found three of the newcomers lounging outside the dining hall, at the center of a clump of curious, chattering young monks. One of the neophytes soon noticed the thin, sun-bronzed, aging Grand Master in his gray vestments, red skullcap, and yellow rose-embroidered sash. The youth announced his presence to the others, whereupon the crowd parted before him, affording him a clear look at the strangers. And a strange-looking trio they were.

The wavering light of a nearby fire glinting along the sinuous curves of his body, the copper dragon gave Cantoule a gap-toothed grin.

"I'm Chatulio," he said. "The grumpy half-iron fellow's Dorn Graybrook, and the dwarf's Raryn Snowstealer. Judging from the way these young ones made way for you, you must be somebody, too."

Cantoule bowed and gave them his name. "I'm the Grand Master of Flowers, the senior monk here, and in other circumstances, I'd welcome you with every courtesy. From what I'm told, your courage deserves no less. But I must know immediately: You came through the caves?"

"How else?" said Dorn, the half-golem, with a surliness that seemed more habitual than directed at anyone or anything in particular.

"Then are others following behind you?" Cantoule asked.

"I'm afraid not," said Raryn, the squat, broad-shouldered dwarf.

Cantoule shook his head, puzzled. "But we sent our messenger to find help. No offense, but he wouldn't have stopped with just you. He was supposed to fetch an army."

"I'm sorry to tell you this," Raryn said, "but he didn't have a chance to fetch anybody. Dragons climbed up from deep below the mountains to hunt the caves. One of them dealt him a mortal wound. He managed to keep going just long enough to make it out onto a mountainside, where we found his body. It showed us you must have a secret way in and out of the monastery, and since we needed to come here, we backtracked him through."

Cantoule felt a piercing disappointment. He took a deep, slow breath, enduring and mastering the emotion, as Ilmater taught. Refusing to let it rot into soul-killing despair.

"I'm sorry to hear that," he said. "We'll dispatch another messenger immediately."

"Don't bother," said Dorn. "No one will come."

Cantoule cocked his head. "I trust you're mistaken. The king himself is a friend to our order."

"Gareth Dragonsbane's dead," the half-golem said, and the novices babbled in shock. "The orcs of Vaasa and any number of dragon flights have overrun Damara. Your nobles and knights only care about protecting their own fiefs." He paused a beat. "I'm sorry, but it's true."

It became even harder for Cantoule to hide his dismay, but with so many of his flock gazing on, depending on him for leadership, he tried his best.

"I regret to hear it," he replied.

"The news isn't all bad," Raryn said. "We slayed the wyrms that killed your messenger. The way out is clear. Those who wish can flee the stronghold."

Dorn glared at the dwarf as if Raryn had just committed some foul betrayal. But the small, white-haired warrior bore the hostile regard without flinching.

"They have a right to know," he said.

"We have other guests," Cantoule said, "travelers trapped here when the wyrms first appeared. They may wish to leave—so may novices who have yet to swear their final vows—but we monks are pledged to defend this sanctuary, and we'll remain."

Until the end. For it seemed they had no chance after all, and would give their lives as martyrs. In the eyes of Ilmater, no service was more blessed, but even so, for Cantoule, it was a bitter thing that the stronghold, which his predecessors had defended against countless threats, would fall on his watch. Kane, he thought, should have stayed and run the place himself, or failing that, picked someone else. Someone who could defeat dragons.

"It's good you're staying," said Dorn, "because we have to hold the drakes back until our friend Kara and Chatulio here finish their studies. Let me tell you why wyrms are laying siege to the monastery."

Blunt and curt, he laid out the facts like a man chopping wood. Yet perhaps his very lack of rhetorical flourishes made his words more persuasive, for bizarre as his story was, Cantoule found that he believed it.

"By the ever-flowing tears," he murmured.

"Yes," Raryn said, "you've been fighting for more than you realized. All Faerûn is depending on you, even if nobody knows it."

"We'll die to the last man," Cantoule promised, "to give you the time to find the lore you seek."

Dorn spat.

Cantoule frowned at him and asked, "Do you doubt our resolve?"

"No," the half-golem said. "I saw how bravely you monks fought in the battle we just finished. But your job isn't to serve yourselves up for the slaughter. It's to slaughter the stinking wyrms."

"What are you getting at?"

"You have to fight better."

Cantoule had tried all his life to cultivate humility, as the creed of Ilmater recommended, yet even so he felt a twinge of outraged pride.

"The Monks of the Yellow Rose are generally considered highly proficient at the martial arts."

"You are good, considered as individuals, but that's the problem. Every monk fights like he's the only defender on the battlements."

"Our philosophy of combat teaches a fighter to take full responsibility for his own well-being, even against multiple opponents attacking from every side."

"Maybe it works against lesser foes," said Dorn, "but the only way to fight dragons is to operate as a team. I'll drill you on the tactics."

"We'll also," Raryn said, "teach you where to hit them to do the most damage, and how to tell when they're getting ready to breathe or spin around, when to get in close, and when to get away . . . tricks like that. They make a difference."

"You'll slow the dragons down," said Dorn, "and spill more of their blood than you would otherwise. That's all we can promise."

"It's enough," Cantoule said, bowing. "It's a great gift."

Dorn scowled. "Don't thank us yet. We've got more to say. Those chain nets are a clever idea. So are the floating obstacles your spellcasters conjure in the air. But they aren't enough to cancel out the advantage the wyrms' wings give them. Attacking from on high, they're killing you with their magic and breath weapons, and the javelins and sling stones you toss up in response scarcely bother them at all."

"Then what's the answer?"

"You have to give them the walls and courtyards," said Dorn, "and fight on inside your great keep and the vaults beneath."

"You can't be serious," Cantoule said. "Every inch of the monastery is sacred ground. Even the smallest shrines and chapels contain holy relics and—"

"Move your treasures deep into the mountain. Truly, that's the only way to protect them for even a little while longer."

"Dorn's right," Raryn said. "Make the dragons fight us on foot, at close range, on ground we know better than they do. Set traps and ambuscades. That way, we can hold them back for a long time. Keep fighting outdoors, and we won't last another tenday."

"But," someone said, "to let evil profane the temples and gardens? The thought is unbearable!"

"No," Cantoule said. "The Crying God teaches us that nothing is truly unendurable, except to turn one's back on righteousness and duty. Our duty now is to hold the wyrms back from the archives long enough for our new friends to discover the secret they seek. Goodmen, we'll do as you advise."

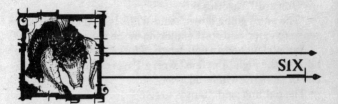

SIX

2 Kythorn, the Year of Rogue Dragons

Folk often called the sixth month the Time of Flowers, and even gray, desolate Thar had grudgingly put forth the occasional white or scarlet blossom. As far as Will was concerned, it might as well have spared itself the effort. The sprinkle of wildflowers did nothing to make the ruins rising by the dark, stagnant lake in the hollow among the hills look any more inviting, nor could it make the chilly, moaning wind sound cheerful. The halfling suspected that if he listened hard enough, he might catch the voices of ghosts inside that melancholy wail.

Many of the ogres gazed down at the vista of leaning towers and broken colonnades with the same uneasiness it inspired in him. In their eyes, the site had always been a forbidden place, and it still felt taboo to them even though their shaman had ordered them there.

Indeed, the only folk who actually looked eager to descend into the warren were Yagoth Devil-eye and Pavel. The former leered down at the ruins as if they were a foe sprawled helpless before him. Leaning forward on his roan horse, the priest of Lathander peered intently, already trying to glean secrets even from hundreds of yards away.

"Onward!" Yagoth said.

"The sun's going down," said Will. "It might make more sense to camp and start exploring in the morning."

Yagoth laughed an ugly laugh. "I forget, you little nits are blind in the night. But don't worry. Pavel can make light. Or one of us ogres will build a fire."

The halfling said, "Suit yourself."

He urged his pony down the trail, and Yagoth and Pavel followed. The giant-kin was taller shambling afoot than the lanky human was astride his steed.

Once the procession reached the broad, straight central avenue running the length of the complex, Will perceived a resemblance to places he'd visited before. To all appearances, the servants of various gods had built their temples in proximity to one another, as a lure to crowds of pilgrims who wanted to sacrifice to multiple deities, or consult more than one soothsayer.

But the shrines honored deities no halfling or human would choose to venerate. Misshapen idols crouched as if to spring, brandished severed heads, sank their fangs into hearts torn from their enemies' breasts, or committed carnal atrocities on the bound and crippled bodies of their prisoners. Hideous faces sneered from friezes, cornices, and entablatures. Will recognized some of the deities so memorialized, including one-eyed Gruumsh, chief god of the orcs, Yurtrus of the pallid hands, their ruling power of suffering and death, and Vaprak, the ogres' own ferocious patron.

All the stonework, though worn by wind and crumbling under the weight of time, was exquisite, and Will found himself more inclined to credit Yagoth's claim that Thar had once been a kingdom worthy of the name. The skill manifest in the carving, however, did nothing to render the subject matter any more palatable. Indeed, to civilized eyes, it was uniquely disturbing to see exceptional craft employed to celebrate vileness and obscenity.

"This place is big," one of the ogre females grumbled. "Where do we start?"

Pavel pointed down the avenue to the huge structure at its terminus. The building was square and black, already almost featureless in the failing light.

"In the largest and no doubt most prestigious temple of all," he said. "If you noticed when we were looking down on it, it's the focal point for the entire complex."

Yagoth said, "Good, little sun priest. Find the magic. Make me happy."

∽∾∾

Malazan watched with mounting impatience as her minions explored the monastery grounds. The dragons stalked the battlements with surefooted grace, crouched on their bellies to peer into the doorways of the outbuildings, reared on their hind legs to peek into upper-story windows, and prowled through gardens and greenhouses sniffing for the scent of their vanished prey, treading rows of blueberry bushes and beds of yellow rosebuds beneath their feet.

Soon the gigantic red wearied of their foolishness. She roared, the bellow echoing off the castle walls and the mountains beyond, and the lesser wyrms came scrambling to attend her. She jerked her head to indicate the immense white central keep, a bewildering tangle of spires and galleries that somehow resolved itself into architectural harmony.

"Are you all idiots?' she demanded. "You won't find any prey out here. The monks have shut themselves away in there."

"I agree," said Ishenalyr. "This is how human defenders fight a siege. When they can't hold their outermost defenses any longer, they fall back to the next ones in."

Malazan felt a pang of annoyance that the hidecarved had presumed to explain what she could just as easily have elucidated herself. It felt like another subtle challenge to her authority. Reminding herself once again that Ishenalyr was too useful a weapon to break prematurely, she swallowed down the fire seething in her gullet.

"It seems the monks have decided to die like rats cowering in a hole. That's fine," she said as she swung around toward the largest set of double doors opening into the keep, a portal high and wide enough to accommodate dragons. "Somebody, open that."

A fang dragon laughed, and like a bony-plated gray-brown battering ram, his forked tail flying out behind him, hurled himself at the doors. He rebounded with a crash and an look of surprise.

"They're enchanted," Ishenalyr said, "but I can wipe away the spell."

"Don't bother," Malazan said.

She hurled herself at the leaves, massive constructions of hardwood reinforced with bronze and steel just as the fang had done. But she was bigger, heavier, and immeasurably stronger, and neither the ancient timbers nor the magic buttressing them could withstand her. The doors flew inward, shattered, torn from their hinges.

On the other side was an immense temple adorned with sculpture, frescos, and stained glass windows celebrating the deeds and dominion of Ilmater. Even the high, vaulted ceiling bore paintings. All the art was masterfully rendered, and despite the adoration of the god of the weak and defeated that constituted its pathetic theme, Malazan coveted it as she coveted all treasure. After she became a dracolich, she'd carry it to her lair—or leave it where it was and lay claim to the monastery to be her new palace. The notion of a red dragon occupying Ilmater's house tickled her. That would really give the Crying God something to weep about.

But it was a pleasure for another hour. At the moment, she had monks to butcher and libraries to burn. She stalked forward down the center aisle, peering, listening, sniffing for prey, while her followers filed in behind her.

Rising from the marble floor almost to the ceiling, columns of soft white light shimmered into existence to bar the dragons' path. In a moment or two, they resolved themselves into giants aglow with their own inner radiance. Some resembled human females in every respect except their stature and the flawless perfection of their beauty. Others were male, with feathery wings sprouting from their shoulder blades. Still others walked on two legs, gripped their swords with fingers and thumbs, but sported the heads of bears or wolves. They all regarded the wyrms with a sort of calm, cold ferocity.

"Leave this place," said the winged colossus standing directly in front of Malazan, extending his blade of glittering diamond at her head. "Ilmater commands it."

Without turning her head, Malazan could sense her minions hesitating. Because to all appearances, the creatures before them were archons, celestial champions of the princes of light, and huge enough to dwarf even a dragon.

Still, Malazan herself laughed. Because she could neither smell the archons, hear hearts beating and lungs pumping in their chests, nor feel any palpable force of holiness radiating from inside them. She snarled a counterspell and smeared the illusory figures into nothingness like doodles scratched in sand.

When the glamour dissolved, it revealed the monastery's true defenders, standing in ranks at the far end of the temple. Most were monks, supported by priests and wizards who likewise served Ilmater, but the copper wyrm and the song dragon, along with the dwarf and half-golem who'd ridden them, waited there too.

Malazan still didn't understand how that peculiar foursome had slipped into the fortress, and that irked her. But once they were dead, their trickery wouldn't matter anymore.

As she chose a spell to soften the defenders up, Ishenalyr strode up beside her.

"Go easy," he said.

"Are you stupid, or a coward?" she snapped. "That's the greater part of our enemy's strength arrayed down there, and I mean to kill them fast, before any of them has a chance to flee."

The green hitched his wings in a shrug and said, "Very well. As you command."

Malazan seared the defenders with a rain of conjured acid. Her followers blasted them with shadow and ice. Humans dropped, seared, withered, or shattered. Even the song drake and the copper reeled beneath the punishment.

Her scales sweating blood, Malazan charged, and her warriors plunged after her. She spat her flame, and more humans dropped, including the hulk with the iron limbs. She raced on, seized the song dragon's neck in her jaws, and that was when she knew. . . .

The second illusion was far more convincing than the archons had been. The monks and their allies made all the noises and gave off all the odors they should, with even the mouthwatering aromas of seared flesh and spilt blood arising at precisely the right moment. Yet now Malazan recognized that they too were merely phantoms, because the song wyrm's crystal-blue neck was as light and insubstantial as cobwebs between her fangs.

"Watch out!" a red male cried.

Several of the columns supporting the transverse arches which in turn bore the weight of the ceiling turned brown, sagged, and flowed. The monastery's actual spellcasters, plainly lurking somewhere close at hand, had transformed them from marble to mud. At the same time, some other mage or cleric conjured a miniature earthquake. Waves lifted the floor as if it were the surface of the sea. A chunk of painted stone plummeted from overhead to punch a hole in Malazan's wing.

She realized the whole ceiling was going to fall. "Back!" she bellowed. "Back!"

Her followers wheeled and bolted toward the door, trampling and tearing at each other in their desperation to scramble through. She didn't see Ishenalyr. Evidently he'd hung back when the others charged, and it had enabled him to be the first to bolt to safety.

Conversely, Malazan, who'd led the advance, had the farthest to run. A prodigious quantity of sculpted rock fell on her, one chunk bashing her spine, another shattering against the top of her skull, shards stinging and blinding her eyes.

It only seemed to take an instant for her to recover from the shock of it, but when she did, she didn't see living dragons in front of her anymore, just a grinding, crashing chaos of disintegrating stonework. She drove forward, over the flattened, twisted body of a fang wyrm crushed under blocks of debris. Chunks of the ceiling hammered her over and over again.

But she was too angry for the punishment to stop her. As she neared the door, enough stone fell all at once to bury her entirely. Though the impact was excruciating, the weight enough to immobilize any lesser creature, she roared, heaved, lashed her wings, and exploded up out of the pile. A final spring carried her out into sunlight and safety.

Her followers gawked at her with manifest awe at her survival. Well, some of them. Though he didn't permit it to show in his manner, she suspected Ishenalyr was regretting her escape, and taking what solace he could in the countless wounds marring her scales.

"You," she growled to him. "You knew it was a snare, but you let me rush into it anyway."

"I simply had a feeling something was amiss," the green replied. "I didn't know what, and when I tried to suggest we proceed cautiously, you rebuffed me."

She realized it was so, but it failed to mollify her. He would have tried harder to warn her if he'd really meant to save her.

Well, it was one more offense for which he would atone in agony when the time came. At the moment, much as she loathed him, she hated the monks and their allies even more, for they were the ones who'd tricked and hurt her.

"Find another way in!" she screamed to her minions. "Fast!"

———— ✺ ————

Will held forth the "torch" Pavel had made for him by kindling a magical light at the end of the stick. The warm golden glow was steadier than the wavering sheen of fire, an advantage when a thief was looking for tiny telltale signs of hidden snares and doorways.

At the moment, the light revealed a long, broad stretch of corridor leading up to an imposing stone door framed by twin statues of Vaprak of the Claws, bestial god of the ogres, brandishing his greatclub. The black and bone-colored tiles on the floor, laid out in a subtly irregular pattern, each bore an inlaid ivory rune at the center, though it was hard to make out the symbols where white lay on white.

Will turned to Pavel and Yagoth. "Can either of you read those signs?" the halfling asked.

"I believe," Pavel said, frowning, "they represent various entities and principles of light. The idea is that we have to trample that which is good to demonstrate our fitness to enter deeper into the heart of evil."

Some of the ogres at the rear of the process growled at the scorn in the cleric's voice and Yagoth snarled, "That's a weakling's way of thinking about the gods . . . but you might be right."

"The point is," said Will, "do you read anything that suggests which symbols are safe to tread on?"

The human priest and ogre shaman pondered the question for a time.

"No," Pavel admitted at last.

Will snorted. "Why did I even bother asking? I've had to do all the work so far." As far as he was concerned, it was a fair statement, for it was he who'd discovered the hidden stairs to the crypts below the temple, and defeated the mantraps designed to kill intruders. "No point expecting either of you to prove useful at this late date."

"Maybe," said Yagoth, "we've passed the last of the traps already."

"Or maybe," said Will, "if you step in the wrong spot, something will pop or spray out of one of those concealed notches along the walls and kill you." He pointed with his torch to indicate the grooves, but suspected his companions didn't really see them even then. It needed a burglar's eye. "You can stroll on out there and put it to the test."

Yagoth scowled, his crimson eye glaring. "Maybe I'll just toss you and see what happens."

"A brilliant idea, considering you need me to find the way through."

The shaman spat, "Be quick about it, then."

Will squatted down and peered out across the tiles, looking for the signs of wear that would identify a true stepping stone, and the minute deviation in height, slant, or wider separation from its fellows that could betray a false one. Gradually, he distinguished the former from the latter through the first few rows, and that was enough to reveal the overall pattern.

"Your forefathers lacked subtlety," he told Yagoth, straightening up. "They left too many triggers embedded in the floor. A truly cunning trapper wouldn't have bothered building so many. He would have known where to lay a smaller number so they'd still catch any dunce who blundered through."

"How do we get by?" Yagoth growled.

Will used his torch to point at a white square marked with a sigil resembling a curved trident with an axe blade mounted on the butt.

"You tread on these," said the halfling, "and these alone."

"Prove it," the ogre said.

"As you wish."

Will walked out onto the tiles.

At first Yagoth was happy to let him lead, but after a few paces, tramped out ahead of him. Maybe he thought the display of boldness necessary to safeguard his position among his fellows.

Then Will saw it.

"Freeze!" he said—and felt a certain disappointment when Yagoth chose to heed him.

"What's wrong?" the ogre said.

"I didn't give your ancestors enough credit," said Will. "The other white squares with the trident mark are safe, but not the one you were about to tread on. You want the black one up cattycorner, with the sword-and-wings design."

Yagoth closed his unblemished eye and glared at Will with the scarlet one.

"You want me to step wrong," the ogre said.

"No," said Will. "The white tile is offset from where it ought to be. Look, since I can't see through walls, I can't tell you everything about this big, intricate trap we're standing in the middle of, but I have a sense of it because I understand that such contrivances require symmetry. The builders must distribute weight evenly, and support it properly, lest everything drop through the floor. Mechanisms need room to operate, and must stand in the right attitude to threaten a particular area. It's plain to me where we need to step. I'll lead again, if you want."

Yagoth sneered and set his foot on the sword-and-wings.

"You're welcome," said Will.

The builders had carved still more sigils into the towering stone door, but as far as Will could tell, they were just writing, not anything dangerous. The portal wasn't even locked in any mechanical way, but even Yagoth, shoving with all his strength, couldn't budge it.

"Allow me," Pavel said. He murmured a prayer, brandished his sun amulet, and for an instant, warm, red-gold light illuminated the hallway, as if the company stood beneath the open sky at dawn. "Try it now."

Yagoth gave the door another push, and it swung easily.

Beyond the threshold was the chamber they sought, a cavernous repository of ancient lore. A single glance sufficed to reveal that those who'd amassed the knowledge hadn't been much for paper. A few books were in evidence, standing on shelves or lying on worktables, but the greater part of the accumulated wisdom took the form of stone and clay tablets with columns of graven hen-scratchings marching down their faces. Indeed, stacks of the slabs stood everywhere, and Will winced at the thought of how long it would take Pavel to examine them all. Though maybe he wouldn't have to. Perhaps Sammaster had left the important ones grouped together.

Yagoth growled with impatience and shoved past Will into the library. The halfling and Pavel stepped in after him, and the rest of the ogres followed. The giant-kin gawked and muttered to each other.

Then Pavel shouted, "Stand ready! Something's going to manifest."

Will pivoted. Saw nothing but tablets, dust, and shadows, and asked, "You're sure?"

"Yes," Pavel said. "I feel a balance of forces shifting. Sammaster left one of his own traps here."

Well, thought Will, readying his warsling, at least that meant this was one of the truly important sites.

But when the air split not once but twice, and a pair of shapeless horrors, lumpy and half liquid like stew, came pouring, humping, and splashing out, the thought provided little consolation.

<hr>

Dorn found Kara in the quarters the monks had assigned her, a small, sparsely furnished guestroom. The soft glow of an oil lamp gleamed on her silver-blond tresses, which had taken on a patchy appearance. The healer's magic had washed away the burns on her scalp, but the hair she'd lost was just starting to grow back. He wondered if they'd both live long enough for him to see it restored to its former loveliness.

Supposedly the guestroom was a place for Kara to rest from her studies in the archives, but in point of fact, she'd brought a stack of ragged, stale-smelling volumes and scrolls back with her, and she sat at the desk bowed over one of them. Dorn raised his hand to rap on the half-open door, but before he could, she turned around in her chair.

She'd detected his presence with a dragon's razor-keen senses. His muscles clenched, but she smiled at him and the welcoming light in her lavender eyes made the surge of revulsion subside.

"I take it," she said, "you're done drilling your troops for the night."

"I wanted to go on, and the monks were game, but Raryn said all the training in the world won't help them if they're too tired to fight when the wyrms come again."

"Raryn's wise."

Dorn grunted. "Anyway, with nothing better to do, I reckoned I'd sample the blueberry wine the brothers make." He hefted the bottle, drawing attention to it. "It's supposed to be good, and I thought you might like to try it, too." He felt awkward then. "But you're working. I'll leave you to it."

"No," she said, rising, "please stay. The words are dancing in front of my eyes. I need a break, and I'd love some wine." She picked up the earthenware cups the monks had provided to go with her pitcher of water. "These will do for goblets."

He extracted the cork, then poured. His hand shook a little, and he nearly slopped wine over her fingers.

The wine was good, sweet, but not overly so. The problem was that Dorn couldn't guzzle it without pause, and between sips, the silence ached, demanding someone fill it. He was surprised Kara didn't. As a bard, she had a knack for small talk that he so sorely lacked, but she seemed to be waiting for him to take the lead.

"I think the drakes will attack tomorrow," he managed eventually.

"Can we hold them?" she asked.

"I have a surprise planned for them at the next bottleneck. But if they don't break through the first time, they will eventually. They're going to shove us down into the cellars pretty soon."

"And I've found nothing yet. Or maybe I've already read the right book, and didn't realize what I had. Arcane texts are often subtle. They speak in parable and metaphor, and I feel so stupid with frenzy nibbling at my mind."

"Your mind is fine, and you've got the other scholars in the stronghold to help you. You'll find it."

He lifted his human hand to touch her face, then hesitated.

But before he could pull back, she took his fingers in her own and said, "I appreciate your faith."

"Of course I have faith in you," he said. "In fact, for a while now . . . it's likely foolish of me to tell you. But according to Raryn, I'm a fool if I don't, and if one of us had died down in the caves, without me ever having said it . . . well, maybe that would have been bad."

"You're such a brave man. Why does it frighten you so to declare your feelings, even when you already know mine?"

"I don't know," he said.

"Well, perhaps it doesn't matter. But I have another question: It no longer bothers you that I'm a dragon?"

"No." He hoped it was true. He wanted it to be.

"Then let's not waste any more time," she said, and opened her arms to him.

Her kisses tasted of the blueberry wine, and he marveled at how they could be so urgent and tender at the same time, and at how many she gave and how she savored them. None of the whores who'd rented him their charms had prolonged the initial phase of coupling in so sweetly tantalizing a way. It made him realize that, in fact, he knew nothing of actual lovemaking. The gift Kara offered would be nothing like the brutish rutting he'd known before. It would be the ecstasy celebrated in a thousand songs, which, until that moment, he'd never understood.

"Unlace my gown," Kara whispered, her voice husky.

Fumbling, trembling, he unveiled her slim white body, and she reached to undress him. For a second, he wanted to stop her. She was as beautiful as Sune Firehair, and he, with his scars and iron parts fused to flesh, was grotesquely ugly. Yet she didn't seem to find him so.

She knelt on the oval rug in the center of the floor and tugged on his hand to guide him down beside her. Maybe she thought the weight of his half-metal body would break the cot, or perhaps she wanted more room. Either way, it was fine. Lightheaded, he simply wanted to go on touching her, and for her to continue touching him.

Apparently it still wasn't time for the final joining. She gently pushed him down on his back, kissed his lips, then started working her way down the human half of his chest. He gasped and shivered at the pleasure of it.

Until he felt her teeth.

It surprised him, because she hadn't done anything the slightest bit painful before. But some of the harlots had given him love bites, and Kara apparently relished the same practice. Unwilling to say or do anything to diminish her pleasure, he tried his best to enjoy the sensation even as she bit him harder and harder.

When she plunged her teeth deep into the flesh of his belly, the pain of it stabbed through him.

"No," he said. "You're hurting me!"

He took hold of her head and tried to lift it away from his body.

Kara snarled like an animal, and resisted. She snapped at him anew, caught more flesh between her teeth, and jerked her head back and forth as if trying to tear it free.

She was a dragon, however human she appeared, and she was trying to eat him alive. In a spasm of fury and loathing, he cocked back his iron fist for a punch that would shatter her skull.

But no. He hit her with the back of his human hand instead, and when she still wouldn't let go, slapped her harder still.

She jerked her head up. Her pupils were diamond-shaped, and her bloody teeth, long and pointed. A wave of sparkling blue washed away the rosy flush in her cheeks. She scrambled up his body, reaching for his throat with nails extending into talons.

In another moment, she'd revert entirely to drake form, then tear him apart. He slammed an uppercut into her jaw.

The punch stunned her, and she collapsed on top of him. He tumbled her onto the floor, reared above her, reached for a choke hold, then saw the fight was over. The glittering blueness had left her skin. The wide amethyst eyes had round pupils.

"I'm sorry," she whispered.

He didn't know how to respond.

"I didn't mean to do it," she said. "It was the Rage. Evidently, the . . . the excitement gave it an opening. Do you understand?"

"I should go." He picked up his breeches.

He dressed facing away from her. It was easier that way, though not much.

For one moment, he hadn't felt like a freak. He'd imagined he could partake of the same joys and comforts as ordinary folk. He supposed it had needed the boundless guile and cruelty of a dragon to rekindle hopes he'd abandoned years before, then crush them once more.

Well, he wouldn't give Kara the chance to hurt him again. He'd keep on protecting her for the mission's sake, but let the Black Hand take him if he spent any more time blathering with her, or listening to her songs.

He strode to the door, then, when he reached it, hesitated.

Anger had been his friend for most of his life. He'd come to cherish it as armor against the grief, pain, and loneliness that might otherwise have destroyed him. Yet, the emotion twisting inside him felt contemptible and self-indulgent, an excuse to concentrate on easing his own hurts while ignoring a comrade's injuries.

He turned around. Kara still sat on the floor where he'd dumped her, silently weeping. The sight of it wrung his heart, and he hated himself for nearly abandoning her to her shame.

"I'm sorry," he said, "It's not your fault. It's mine. I shouldn't have taken so long, sorting my feelings out. Why don't you get dressed, and we'll sit, talk, and drink the rest of the wine."

They did, and when the bottle and the well of conversation alike ran dry, they simply held hands. Raryn found them thus when he came to tell them Chatulio had disappeared.

Thrashing and writhing, Sammaster's guardian creatures spilled from rents in the empty air. In that first instant, with only the single enchanted torch providing light, Pavel had difficulty discerning what manner of abomination they were, but then his mind made sense of them despite the gloom and their nauseating, bewildering lack of stability and symmetry.

Each was as tall as an ogre but bulkier. They looked as if a god had shaped several chromatic dragons out of mud, then, disliking his handiwork, squashed the separate figures into one lump. Their bodies were a patchwork of black, white, azure, green, and scarlet scales, with several misshapen reptilian heads protruding from the squirming central mass. They had no limbs as such, but extending and retracting, hardening and softening, their flesh, where it made contact with the floor, heaved them across the stones.

Such horrors were called squamous spewers. Having identified them, Pavel also had a good idea of what was about to happen, but not enough time to shout a warning.

One spewer roared, a thunderous sound that shook the underground chamber and made a couple of the long-armed, short-legged ogres bolt in terror. The other guardian opened the jaws of its various heads, and an eye-stinging stink suffused the air. The creature spat jets of acid, and giant-kin screamed, their warty hides sizzling and smoking.

Chanting and brandishing his sun amulet, Pavel conjured into being a floating mace of crimson light. The weapon flew at a spewer and hammered it.

Will spun his warsling and let fly. The skiprock cracked against one malformed head, then rebounded to strike another.

Yagoth charged and drove the point of his spear deep into the same creature's rippling, amorphous form.

"Fight, curse you!" the ogre shaman bellowed.

The remaining ogres shouted their war cries, a clamor as fearsome as a spewer's roar, and surged forward. Pavel conjured a second flying mace to fight alongside the first, ripped a spewer's hide with a shrill whine of magical sound, then evoked a flash of golden light intended to sear a portion of the creature's strength away.

But whatever he and his allies attempted, the spewers didn't falter. Their snapping fangs inflicted ghastly wounds, but the real terror came when, every few seconds, one of them left off biting to spit a breath weapon from its mouths.

Pavel abruptly glimpsed brightness at the corner of his vision. He tried to fling himself aside, but the plume of flame brushed him even so. The hot pain threw him to his knees.

His body wanted to lie still, recover from the shock, but in a battle, such inertia could be fatal. He forced himself to raise his head and peer about, then gasped in dismay.

The same blast of fire that had burned him had felled several ogres. The spewer responsible crawled forward on its seething, semi-liquid base, jaws gaping to tear the life from the helpless giant-kin.

Will sprang between the creature and its intended victims. His curved hornblade slashed back and forth, splitting the creature's hide. It snapped at him, three heads striking at almost the same instant, and he dodged frantically.

"Help me, charlatan!" he cried.

Pavel scrambled forward, rattled off a prayer of healing, and his hand glowed red. He pressed it against the grimy, mole-studded, sour-smelling flesh of one of the fallen ogres, and the creature groaned and stirred.

"Get back in the fight!" Pavel told it.

He scuttled on to heal a second one, wasting precious moments before realizing the creature wasn't just incapacitated but dead. He prayed over a third, a female, and waking, she cringed and threw her forearm over her eyes, as if the spewer's fiery breath was even then leaping at her.

The ogres Pavel had healed started picking themselves up. He darted forward to stand beside Will and drove in, striking with his mace, and jerking himself out of the paths of the gnashing fangs that leaped at him from every angle. The spewer stretched one of its necks like dough, arching it up over his head, and Pavel never even realized it until its fangs pierced his back. He lunged forward, and though the abomination ripped away his manta ray cloak and part of his brigandine, perhaps it hadn't savaged his shoulder too badly.

He struck the spewer another blow, and it responded by spitting jets of pearly frost. The cold pierced him to the core, and he reeled. A dragon head reached for him, and he feared he couldn't recover his balance in time to fend it off.

Fortunately, he didn't have to. The female ogre he'd healed rushed the spewer and chopped at its extended neck with her flint axe. The blow nearly severed the head, and at last the foul thing hesitated.

"Now!" Will shouted. "Kill it now!"

He, Pavel, and the ogres lunged in, cutting, stabbing, and bashing. The spewer collapsed, seeming not to topple so much as dissolve.

Pavel pivoted toward the remaining guardian just in time to see it spit flares of crackling lightning at Yagoth and its other opponents.

"Now that one!" the human gasped. "Let's finish this!"

He and his allies swarmed on the spewer. After a moment, it opened its jaws, and the cleric poised himself to dodge another blast of its breath weapon. What gushed out, though, was blood. The spewer shuddered, then slumped down as its fellow had done.

Pavel sighed, relaxing, momentarily dull-witted with relief. When Yagoth yanked the spear from the spewer's corpse, hefted it, and cocked it back, he almost failed to register the significance.

Almost, but not quite.

"Will!" he bellowed.

The halfling had his back turned, but heeding Pavel's warning, he tried to spin away from the spot where he was standing. But the long, heavy lance was already streaking through the air, and for once, Will's agility wasn't enough to snatch him out of harm's way. The spear slammed him onto the floor.

Pavel sprang toward his friend.

Snarling, crimson eye blazing, Yagoth snatched a dead ogre's war club from the floor and swung it in a horizontal arc.

Pavel tried to duck, but was too slow. The weapon smashed into his brow, and the world went black.

———— ⌒∞⌒ ————

As the spear hurled Will off his feet, he was already angry with himself. He'd assumed the ogres meant to betray their civilized partners eventually, yet Yagoth had still caught him by surprise. He hadn't expected the attack to come before Pavel identified the tablets containing the ancient elven secrets, or a second after they'd all finished fighting a difficult battle together, for that matter.

Which meant Yagoth had chosen his moment well. As a former outlaw, to whom duplicity had been a way of life, Will felt a certain grudging admiration.

Mostly, though, he was terrified. He twisted his head to see if the spear had dealt him a mortal wound. No, probably not, unless he simply bled out by and by. The weapon's broad flint head had driven so deep into his shoulder that the tip was sticking out the other side, but it hadn't pierced his heart or lung.

It had to come out, though, and right away—before the ogres came to finish him off. He couldn't fight or maneuver with the long, heavy lance sticking out of his body, so he gripped the shaft with both hands, feeling how little strength remained in the one below his damaged shoulder, and pulled.

Until that moment, the injury hadn't really hurt, but then the pain jolted him. He gasped and let go of the weapon. When he jerked his hands away, the spear bobbed slightly, producing a second flare of agony.

Footsteps slapped against the floor. The ogres were closing in.

He made himself take hold of the lance once more. Gritting his teeth, he dragged on it as hard as he could. An ogre with a face so studded with warts as to leave hardly any clear space between leered at him and raised its club.

The bludgeon hurtled down and the spear pulled free at the same instant. To avoid the giant-kin's attack, Will had to roll onto his crippled shoulder. It hurt so badly he blacked out for a moment. Yet his body must have kept moving even while his mind was absent, for when he came to his senses, he was on his feet.

Praying that Pavel was weaving some mighty ogre-slaughtering spell, he cast about for his friend. Alas, the human sprawled motionless in the pool of blood seeping from his head.

Will was on his own. His sword arm dangled uselessly, not that he was currently in possession of his hornblade anyway. Filthy with gore, the blade lay out of reach where he'd dropped it when the spear pierced him.

He realized he had no hope of killing the surviving ogres, or of getting Pavel out of there. He'd need all his skill, and the blessing of every halfling god, just to escape by himself.

The ogres advanced, trying to encircle him. He drew his dagger with his off hand and faked a lunge to the right, then darted left instead. The trick caught the giant-kin by surprise, and he slashed a hamstring as he sprang past one of his foes. The ogre fell down howling.

Will grinned, but knew that one lucky stroke meant little. Soon, his strength would start to fail. He had to be out the door before that happened. He drew a deep, steadying breath and advanced toward the ogres barring the way.

A giant-kin aimed its spear to jab at him, and in that instant, Will sprang between its legs. That flummoxed his foes, and he was able to run another stride before two more ogres shambled into striking distance. He sidestepped so that one of his opponents was blocking the other, jumped above the low sweep of the greatclub that would otherwise have shattered his legs, and scrambled three steps nearer to the exit.

Yagoth snarled words of power, and magic filled the air with a carrion stink. Will's muscles seized up. Caught in mid-stride, he pitched off balance and cracked his head against the floor.

He knew from watching Pavel cast similar spells that the paralysis was in his head. He could break free by exerting his will. Yet his struggle to do so produced only trembling.

An ogre loomed over him.

Brandobaris, help me! Will prayed.

Perhaps the Master of Stealth was listening. In any event, Will had control of his body once again. He flung himself sideways just in time to avoid the axe stroke that would have sheared off his head. The flint blade crashed and struck sparks against the floor.

Will scrambled up and on, zigzagging unpredictably, making the ogres flounder into one another's way, using their hugeness against them. Yagoth snarled another incantation, and for an instant, Will's stomach squirmed with nausea, and dizziness tilted the floor beneath his feet. But then the curse lost its grip on him, and a second after that, he reached the door. He plunged through and ran down the corridor.

The ogres scrambled after him. What had been a kind of deadly dance became a race, and no doubt they expected to win. Their legs, though stunted in proportion to their height, were nonetheless longer than his.

But if he could stay ahead of them for long enough, he hoped to prove them mistaken. It depended on whether they, in their fury, had forgotten about the trap protecting the hallway. If so, they'd tread on the triggers, and suffer the consequences.

It seemed a good notion. Until the shadows closed in.

The only light in all the crypts shined from Pavel's enchanted torch, which Will had set down to fight Sammaster's abominations. With every stride, the glowing stick receded farther behind him. By the time he reached the trap, the corridor would be so dark that he wouldn't be able to distinguish the safe tiles from the others.

He felt a surge of despair, and strained to stifle it. He still had a chance. He'd studied the trap already. The layout was in his memory. If he was as cunning a thief as he'd always reckoned himself to be, he should be able to set his feet properly whether he could see the marks on the tiles or not.

Just enough faint illumination remained to indicate where the black-and-white pattern began. He sprinted out onto the tiles without hesitation, springing from one spot to the next.

Rapidly narrowing his lead, the ogres followed.

A thrown knife whizzed past Will's head. Then the corridor shook and groaned as counterweights dropped behind the walls, and hidden mechanisms lurched into operation. He ran on, and sensed more than saw something leaping to seal the space ahead of him. He didn't think he'd stepped on a trigger. He hadn't felt a tile hitch down beneath his weight. But one of the ogres had, and evidently, when anybody hit one, the whole enormous trap served up all the death it had to offer, all at once.

Somehow Will managed to run even faster. Metal clashed behind him. When he was certain he'd passed beyond the array of tiles, he risked a glance back.

It was so dark that it was hard to tell exactly what had happened at his back. But it seemed as if enormous blades had sprung from the hidden notches in the wall, to stab or slice through anything in their path. Ogres hung impaled, or lay maimed and dismembered beneath the sharp metal. The smell of their blood filled the air. Those who still clung to life whimpered and shrieked.

But one voice roared and cursed in rage instead of pain. Yagoth was apparently unharmed. Fortune had placed him at the rear of the pursuit, where he was able to stop short when the mantrap began the slaughter.

Will regretted the shaman's survival, but at least the blades still blocked the corridor. That would give him the chance to complete his escape.

If he could stay upright a while longer. Unfortunately, he felt as if the strength was draining out of him.

He had a vial of healing elixir. He would have drunk it before, except that the giant-kin hadn't allowed him the opportunity. He fumbled the little pewter bottle out of his belt pouch and poured the lukewarm, tasteless liquid down his throat.

It helped a little; steadied him and made him more alert. It didn't close the wound in his shoulder, though. In fact, with his mind clearer, the gaping, ragged puncture throbbed more painfully than before.

He crept onward, through absolute darkness. At least he'd deactivated all the other mantraps. He didn't have to worry about setting them off, though getting lost was a different matter. If he blundered down the wrong hall. . . .

No, he told himself firmly, he wouldn't. He was a burglar, proficient at navigating in the dark and holding the floor plan of any building he explored fixed in his memory forever after. He'd find his way.

Footsteps shuffled, and deep, harsh voices growled from ahead of him. Apparently some of the ogres Yagoth had left aboveground had heard their chieftain shouting, and were coming to investigate.

Will was adept at hiding, but he wouldn't be able to use his skill if, blind as he was, he couldn't locate any cover. As the giant-kin drew nearer, he groped along the wall, and finally found a shallow niche with some sort of many-armed statue in it.

He squeezed in beside the sculpture, and the ogres tramped by seconds later, close enough for him to smell the sour stink of them, though he still couldn't make them out in the gloom.

Not that he cared. What mattered was that they strode past without noticing him.

Will skulked on, and spotted light shortly thereafter, though, if he hadn't spent the past few minutes in utter blackness, he might not have recognized it as such. The feeble gleam spilled through a broad rectangular doorway and down the flight of stairs connecting the vaults and the temple above. A pair of ogres slouched silhouetted in the space, where Yagoth had evidently instructed them to stand watch.

Will placed one of his last remaining skiprocks in his warsling. He couldn't use the weapon as adroitly with his off hand but he was going to have to try. He spun it and let the enchanted stone fly.

The missile cracked against the head of the hulking guard on the left, and the ogre fell backward. The skiprock should also have rebounded to strike the other giant-kin, but it missed. The creature oriented on Will, hefted its axe, and charged down the stairs.

Will yelled and ran up toward his foe, stopped abruptly for just an instant, then raced on. The brief pause was supposed to throw off the ogre's aim and timing, and maybe it did, because the creature's weapon whizzed past Will's head. He threw himself against the ogre's shins.

With only a halfling's height and weight, he could never have knocked such a huge foe off balance if it weren't in motion. But the ogre was, and its own momentum enabled him to trip it. It flipped over him and tumbled to the bottom of the stairs.

Unfortunately, the impact also blasted pain through his crippled shoulder. For a moment, black spots swam through his vision, and he felt consciousness slipping away. He fought to hold on, and succeeded somehow.

Below him, the ogre bellowed. He supposed that was better than if it was climbing up after him, but if the clamor summoned other members of the troupe, it might still be enough to put an end to him. He scurried on to the top of the stairs.

The temple proper was an enormous hall filled with grotesque demonic statues and altars equipped with fetters placed to hold a human-sized sacrifice. Except for the hulk the skiprock had felled, no other ogres were in view. They were still in awe of the place, and none had entered but those Yagoth had ordered inside.

But that was sure to change in a matter of seconds. Will could still hear bellowing from the bottom of the stairs, which meant the creatures outside could, too.

The expedition had camped to the west, on the grand avenue leading up to the primary entrance. Will scurried toward a lesser doorway opening to the north.

As he rushed through, he heard ogres scrambling into the shrine. Had they spotted him in that final instant before he disappeared? Apparently not, for they didn't come chasing after him.

He climbed a hillside, trying to remember that it was still vital to stay hidden. It was hard. His mind was dim, like a candle guttering out. His limbs felt like lead. It was all he could do just to set one foot in front of the other.

Soon the moment arrived when he couldn't even do that anymore. He fell on his face, struggled, failed to rise, and finally crawled under a bush. He resolved to rest with his dagger in hand, but discovered he'd dropped it somewhere along the way. Seconds later, he passed out.

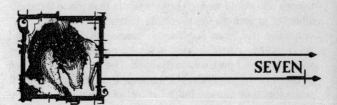

SEVEN

4 Kythorn, the Year of Rogue Dragons

"This is boring," Jivex whispered.

"Hush," Taegan replied.

"You need to think of a better plan," the faerie dragon said. "We should be doing something."

"We are," Taegan said, though he wasn't at all certain it was so.

Jivex snorted, sprang up off the stool Selûne's clerics had provided for him, and flitted about the conjuring chamber snapping moths from the air. The marble shrine was currently open to the night sky—the roof slid back in a cunning way that even the most accomplished builders in Lyrabar would have admired—and the lamps, silver crescents and circles glowing with a soft white magical light, lured a fair number of insects. Evidently annoyed by his darting to and fro, Phourkyn One-eye regarded the drake sourly. Sureene Aumratha, a tall, handsome, middle-aged woman with moon-blond hair almost the exact color of Kara's—though in the human's case, the hue came out of a bottle—smiled briefly before resuming her interrogation of the mage.

Sureene was the high priestess of the House of the Moon, and considered a formidable mistress of divine magic. In theory, she could weave enchantments that made it impossible for anyone to lie, particularly when her goddess was watching. Yet even so, Taegan suspected Phourkyn had been right to maintain that he and a number of his fellow wizards knew how to cheat the spell. The avariel had chosen to observe the interviews in the hope that he might sense it when someone dissembled, whether Selûne's power revealed it or not.

Probably it was a forlorn hope, but the truth was, he'd run out of other ideas. He and Jivex had spied and snooped to the extent they were able, and patrolled Thentia from the air, watching for the chasme with its halo of flame. Taegan had encouraged the magicians to report any suspicions they harbored of one another—and what a catalogue of petty grudges and grievances that had produced—and maintained constant vigilance while waiting for the tanar'ri to attack him. All of it had been to no avail.

Taegan tried to draw a little comfort from the reflection that the demon hadn't tried to kill anyone else, either. Rilitar had optimistically posited that Taegan had thrown a scare into the traitor, and so the dastard feared to act. But the winged elf couldn't believe it. Over the course of the past few months, he'd crossed swords with more than his fair share of Sammaster's agents, and in most cases, they'd proved to be as tenacious as they were malevolent. His current foe was either weighing his options or biding his time, like a fencer who makes a show of relaxing in the hope of prompting his opponent to drop his guard, then attacks the instant an opening appears.

"Are we done?" Phourkyn demanded.

"Yes," said Sureene.

"Am I the traitor?"

"No."

"What a relief."

Sureene's generous mouth with its coating of shiny white cosmetic tightened at the sarcasm, but she chose not to make an issue of it.

The lamplight gleaming on his pomaded raven hair, Phourkyn rose and turned to Taegan. "Unless you have further business here, Maestro, perhaps you'd care to walk out with me." His single dark eye shifted to Jivex. "And your companion, too, of course."

In fact, Taegan would seize any opportunity to try to take the measure of one of the eccentric—and in some cases, virulently antisocial—mages.

"You honor me, Master Wizard, and it's a splendid evening for a stroll. Come along, Jivex."

"I'm almost ready." The small dragon with his iridescent scales swooped, and snapped another moth from the air.

"I daresay you'll find a plenitude of bugs outside," said Taegan. "Enough to sate even your gluttony."

"You can't catch your prey," Jivex sulked, "so you don't want anybody else to catch anything, either. But all right."

They bade farewell to Sureene, Phourkyn with his customary brusqueness, Jivex cheerfully, and Taegan with all the subtly flirtatious courtliness Impiltur had taught him. Then they withdrew.

Lyrabar was a city of magnificent temples. Thentia had only the House of the Moon, but as he and his companions traversed its spacious galleries and chapels, their footsteps echoing, Taegan conceded that at least it was a worthy one. Everywhere, the glow of the enchanted lamps gleamed on silver vessels and alabaster carvings, or illuminated the paintings of the night sky adorning the high ceilings. The air smelled of frankincense, the incense competing with the pungent apple smell of the unguent in Phourkyn's hair. Yet for all its grandeur, the temple had an empty, shadowy feel to it. Taegan supposed that when Selûne walked the heavens, most of the clerics repaired to the gardens to worship her.

"So," said Phourkyn after a time, "you can't catch your prey?"

Taegan grinned and said, "Jivex and I merely like to banter. I assure you, I'm well on my way to laying hands on Sammaster's agent."

"In that case," the human said, "your behavior puzzles me."

Up ahead, Jivex landed on a statue of the Lady of Silver bearing a mace in one hand and a sextant in the other. He crawled around on her for a moment, nosing at a sculpted fold in her robe, then, butterfly wings shimmering, sprang back into the air.

"How so?" Taegan asked.

"If you have your own infallible means of identifying the cultist," Phourkyn said, "why watch while Sureene interrogates us? Indeed, why put her to the trouble at all?"

"My method of ferreting out the traitor requires time. It's possible Sureene can identify him more quickly."

"I'd like to know what your method is."

"Yet you yourself are averse to sharing your secrets, so perhaps you'll be tolerant when others display the same inclination."

"I know the limits of the magical system you claim to practice, Maestro. But if you can truly probe the minds of accomplished wizards, you're far more than a bladesinger."

"Back home in Lyrabar I'm celebrated for my modesty, and I simply can't find it in my meek and humble heart to claim to be anything grander. Though I will confess that Jivex and I slew a dracolich, so take that for whatever you feel it's worth."

Phourkyn grunted, then after a pause said, "You don't like me very much, do you, avariel?"

"I scarcely know you well enough to like or loathe you. I appreciate the fact that you recognize the need to aid Kara."

"Throughout my life," Phourkyn said, a brooding note entering his voice, "I've rarely cared what anyone thought of me. Most people are dull-witted vermin, either cowering mice or vicious rats. Certainly nothing that ought to concern an archmage as he strives to expand the limits of his Art."

"That may be a sound philosophy, but I'd be leery of propounding it to the rodent who cooks your food, unless you want her seasoning it with spittle."

Phourkyn scowled and said, "My point is this: I don't want you to misread me. While I care nothing for the average dolt I encounter in the street, I am concerned about the future of the world. I won't stand idly by while flights of wyrms in frenzy hammer Faerûn's cities into rubble, or hordes of dracoliches rise up to enslave mankind. In other words, you can depend on me."

Taegan was still trying to decide how to respond when the first cry for help shrilled from an arched doorway on their right.

～～∞〜〜

As he walked among his wicked kindred, Chatulio reflected that most spellcasters who considered themselves skilled illusionists had barely acquired the basics of the discipline. Perhaps they too could have cloaked themselves in the appearance of a black-scaled skull wyrm, right down to the flaking, decaying hide on the cheeks. They might even have managed the acidic smell. But could they have cast the far subtler enchantment that blinded the evil drakes to the fact that this particular black hadn't been a part of their host from the start? Chatulio thought not, and the fact that he'd accomplished the trick with the Rage gnawing at his faculties made the achievement even more impressive.

It was the Rage that had prompted him to flee the monastery, back through the caves. His every instinct had warned that if he didn't, he'd soon turn on the small folk. It had pained him to depart without explaining the reason to Kara, Raryn, and Dorn, but he'd suspected it might be even more painful to say good-bye.

Once he'd escaped the mouthwatering scent of human flesh, his beleaguered mind cleared a little, and it occurred to him that, chromatic dragons being the vain and quarrelsome creatures that they were, he might still be able to help the defenders of the Monastery of the Yellow Rose, even from outside the walls. It would be dangerous. The attacking wyrms were almost certain to see through his disguise eventually, and tear him apart. But that would be a good thing. He needed to die before frenzy took him and he started slaughtering the innocent, though the Rage wasn't bothering him much at the moment. It had faded to an irritating but tiny whine at the back of his mind. He supposed his current escapade was responsible. Some pranks were so funny, they could even stave off madness for a while.

Chatulio cast a charm to make his every pronouncement seem wiser and more important. He then advanced toward a trio of wyrms, a young red, a yellow-eyed fire drake glowing like iron fresh from the forge, and a magma drake with crimson optics, black claws, and hide like cooling lava. All three were creatures of fire, and crouching together, they threw off heat like a furnace, driving back the chill of a mountain night. They were eating some shaggy, curly-horned sheep they'd killed, and hissed and showed their fangs to warn Chatulio away from their repast. He shook his head to convey that he had no intention of trying to claim a portion, and they suffered him to approach. He hunkered down among them, then waited for them to finish gobbling meat, crunching bone, and slurping marrow.

When they did, a conversation started, and inevitably it turned to the siege. Baffled and enraged by how long it was taking just to root out a nest of feeble humans, the dragons could talk of little else. They had to pick at the wound to their pride.

Speaking of wounds, Chatulio noted that the fire drake still bore scabby gashes and punctures on its flank.

"I hear," the disguised copper said, "that we may attack again, as soon as the moon sinks behind the peaks."

As he'd hoped it would, the fire drake snarled, "I'm still hurt!" It rose and turned to display its injuries.

The red said, "The half-iron warrior mauled you, didn't he, with those spikes on his hand. He hurt me the same way. Before this is over, I'm going to roast him slowly."

"Some say," Chatulio said, "the healers among us have secretly pledged their loyalty to Ishenalyr. So, if you're willing to grovel to the hidecarved as well, they'll attend to you first, and if they run out of spells before they get around to the rest of us . . . well, that's just our hard luck."

"By flame and shadow," rumbled the magma drake, "that isn't fair! Those who fight the hardest should receive healing first, and that's not Ishenalyr and his ilk. They hang back. I've seen it. Why would Malazan stand for this?"

Chatulio hitched his wings in a shrug. "Maybe she's afraid of Ishenalyr."

The red sprang to his feet. His throat swelled with the promise of fire, and sulphurous smoke streamed out of his nostrils and mouth when he roared, "Malazan fears nothing!"

Chatulio was certain the red felt no affection for the ancient female, who treated all her troops with an arrogance that bordered on outright contempt. But apparently he'd rather give his loyalty to a leader of his own kind than to the rune-scarred green. Or simply to the dragon he regarded as the mightiest and most savage of them all.

Chatulio inclined his head in a gesture of submission. "As you say. Malazan fears nothing. I spoke as a fool. But alas, I'm not the only fool among us. Someone should warn her that if she wants everyone to go on respecting her, she should squash the hidecarved like the impudent bug he is."

"I'd like to see that," said the fire drake. "By all the princes of the Abyss, I would."

"Well," said Chatulio, drawing himself to his feet, "you've had your suppers. I still need to catch mine, so I'll bid you farewell."

He withdrew, but not to forage. That could wait until after his enchantment of persuasiveness wore off. Instead, he insinuated himself into another gathering of wyrms on the opposite face of the mountain, midway between the fortress and the glacier below. The ice glowed in the moonlight.

Before long, he found the chance to say: "The reds and their cronies are grumbling again."

"Grumbling?" growled an earth drake, its massive body more like a rocky outcropping than the usual sinuous dragon form, its jade eyes gleaming.

"They claim," Chatulio said, "they bear the brunt of the fighting, while certain others engage the humans timidly, and turn tail at any little hurt."

"Which 'certain others?'" demanded a fang dragon with an irritable snap of its stunted wings.

"Those who look to Ishenalyr for leadership."

"Nonsense," snarled a green, reeking of the corrosive poison that was its breath weapon. "If I take my cues from Ishenalyr, it's because he's crafty, and senses when the humans have set a snare. What's the point of blundering recklessly into trouble, as Malazan routinely does?"

"I agree," Chatulio said.

"If the fire wyrms say we don't fight as hard as they do," said the earth drake, "will they use that as an excuse to deny us our fair share of plunder at the end?"

"No one had better try to deny me anything," said the green.

"We all feel that way," Chatulio said, "but if Ishenalyr is gone by then, can the rest of us stand against Malazan and her supporters?"

"Gone?" asked the fang wyrm, crimson eyes glaring from amid the rough, bony plates on its head.

"Malazan knows Ishenalyr is more cunning than she is," Chatulio said. "She knows we know it, too. Don't you think she worries that we'll renounce her and declare the hide-carved our chief instead? Well, it's obvious enough how she can prevent it, and if she fears to face Ishenalyr in a fair fight, perhaps she can find a way to ensure he dies while attacking the monastery."

The green said, "Ishenalyr should strike first."

"Perhaps he will, if he realizes she's plotting to destroy him. I hope he knows. I hope someone has warned him."

And so it went. The frustrated, suspicious dragons danced to Chatulio's tune so readily it was all he could do to stifle his laughter.

———— ✺ ————

The rows of columns running down the sides of the corridor were just far enough apart for Taegan to spread his wings, and so he flew, with Jivex streaking along a yard or two ahead of him, and Phourkyn's running footsteps pounding at his back.

"There!" Jivex cried.

"I see her," Taegan replied.

Evidently drawn by the same cries for help that had brought him, her usually impish face grim, petite Baerimel Dunnath stood before the entrance to a room, declaiming a rhyme and sweeping her dainty hands through cabalistic passes. Though not a priestess, the mage nonetheless wore a silvery gown, no doubt to honor the goddess to whom she'd pledged her service.

Taegan landed beside her. Jivex hovered, his wings a blur.

Beyond the arch was a music room, with risers along one wall where a choir might stand, concentric half-circles of chairs to seat an orchestra, and a miscellany of instruments—lyres, dulcimers, glaurs, yartings, and a towering silver-stringed harp—waiting for someone to play them.

Perhaps Sinylla Zoranyian had entered the chamber to do precisely that, but another matter had taken precedence. Cloaked in a protective aura of light, blood staining her argent vestments, clutching at a chair to keep herself upright despite her gashed, burned legs, she conjured a barrier of floating, spinning blades into being. The chasme snarled a counterspell in its vile buzz of a voice, and Sinylla's creation vanished. The demon followed up with a flash of flame that slammed her back against the wall.

It seemed clear that, her powers notwithstanding, Sinylla was losing the fight. Baerimel plainly thought so too, and was frantic to aid her cousin. The problem was that something invisible to the eye but unyielding as granite to the touch sealed the doorway, and probably the chamber's sole window as well. Apparently Baerimel could neither dissolve the barrier nor drive a spell through it.

Taegan hoped that one of the charms he carried ready for the casting could succeed where she had failed. It was a pity he'd outdistanced Phourkyn, a more powerful magician, but he didn't have time to wait for the one-eyed human to catch up.

"Take hold of me," he said, "both of you."

Baerimel gripped his forearm, and Jivex's talons dug into his shoulder.

He rattled off the incantation, and the world jumped. Abruptly he and his allies were inside the music room. At once, the heat of the chasme's corona of flame pounded at him, and the drone of its wings was louder. The demon oriented on them, and Baerimel's knees buckled. She fell heavily, knocking over a music stand and scattering the pages. Obviously, the chasme had afflicted her somehow.

"Well," said Jivex, "she was a lot of use."

Soaring up to the ceiling, he stared at the chasme, whereupon a crust of golden dust spread across the demon's head, covering its round, bulging eyes.

"Rouse her if you can," Taegan said.

He rushed the fly-thing, intent on attacking while it was blind. The avariel thrust his sword deep into the place where the tanar'ri's head joined its torso. It was surely a grievous wound, but not enough to render the demon helpless. When he tried to pull the blade out of its body for a second attack, it gripped the sharp steel with its spindly fingers, and heedless of the cuts it thereby inflicted on itself, held the weapon in place. It snarled an incantation, and lightning flared down the sword into Taegan's arm. He convulsed, time skipped, and he found himself lying on his back.

Free of the blindfold of glittering dust, the chasme pounced at Taegan, fangs bared, hands poised to seize him. The avariel was still dazed from the hurt he'd taken, but a duelist's trained reflexes flung him out of the way. He rolled to his feet, rattled off a rhyme, and lashed his hand through the proper passes. Several exact duplicates of himself, each mirroring his every move to perfection, sprang into existence around him.

The chasme clawed at one of the images, which instantly burst into nothingness. The demon jabbed with its long, pointed snout and obliterated another. By that time, however, the real Taegan had maneuvered to within reach of the sword still jutting from the fly-creature's neck. He grabbed the hilt, yanked it free, and went on the offensive once more.

The chasme wasted another attack on one of his phantoms, and Taegan half severed one of its hind legs.

Awake again, Baerimel conjured a wave of light that seemingly failed to affect it.

Jivex breathed a plume of sparkling vapor over its blazing body. Taegan caught a stray whiff of the sweet-smelling stuff, and for an instant felt giddy, but the fly-thing merely gave a grating snarl of annoyance.

Still slumped by the wall, Sinylla started croaking an incantation. Unfortunately, no doubt due to her injuries, her voice faltered, and the cadence was ragged. It seemed unlikely that she'd succeed in creating whatever effect she intended.

Attacking the chasme with wizardry was a chancy proposition anyway. The fly-thing possessed a measure of resistance. It couldn't shrug off the bite of Taegan's sword, though, and he lunged at it once more, while simultaneously weaving another defensive spell.

He cut it twice while it raked, snapped, and gouged away the rest of his phantoms. Sinylla's incantation simply stumbled to a halt, as if she'd fainted. Baerimel hurled silvery darts of force that blinked out of existence when they touched the chasme's mantle of flame. Jivex swooped in and out of the cloud of fire to claw at the demon's veined, membranous wings.

Then Taegan plunged his sword into its chest. Its front legs crumpled, dumping its hideous, long-nosed parody of a human head on the floor. He raised his sword high for a decapitating stroke, and as soon he stood still and opened up his guard, the fly-demon sprang up at him. It had only pretended to be crippled, to lure its foe into a vulnerable stance.

Its momentum hurled Taegan to the floor, with the tanar'ri on top of him. No doubt he would have perished instantly, if not for the enchantment he'd cast to ward himself. It had created an invisible shield to hover between himself and his foe, and it was actually that barrier the chasme was crouching on. The plane of force blocked the first of the demon's ripping claw attacks, and kept Taegan from coming into full, lethal contact with its halo of fire.

But the shield could only save him for a moment or two. His only real chance was to kill the tanar'ri before it killed him. Unable to use his sword properly in such close quarters, he took hold of it partway down the blade to wield it like a poniard. He stabbed and stabbed, and the chasme caught hold of his shoulder, its fiery talons plunging through his brigandine to pierce and burn the flesh beneath. Realizing it hadn't achieved quite the hold it wanted, it released him to reach for his throat.

He realized another second would tell the tale. After that, one of them would be dead.

Then, however, Phourkyn shouted words of power, and green light pulsed through the air. The chasme jerked, screamed, and leaped off Taegan.

The avariel gripped his sword by the hilt and scrambled to his feet, but not quite quickly enough. The whine of the chasme's wings crescendoed into a deafening thunderclap that knocked Taegan, Phourkyn, and Baerimel staggering and tumbled Jivex through the air like a leaf in a gale. It bounced Sinylla where she lay inert on the floor.

The chasme scrambled through the window and took flight. Taegan inferred that Phourkyn, panting, flushed, and sweaty-faced from sprinting through the temple, had used a counterspell to wipe away the magic blocking the door, and in so doing, had unsealed the window as well.

Taegan took stock of his wounds and burns. They already smarted, and were likely to prove excruciating once the exhilaration of battle faded, but he'd functioned with worse.

He pivoted toward Phourkyn and Baerimel and asked, "Can either of you fly?"

"I don't have the spell ready," Phourkyn said.

"Nor I," said Baerimel. "Besides, my cousin—"

"Of course. Help her." Taegan looked to Jivex, whose scales were singed and seeping fluid. "Are you all right?"

"We're never going to catch the demon," Jivex said, "if you stand around asking stupid questions."

He flew out the window, and Taegan followed.

Winter having yielded its dominion to spring, the night air was pleasantly cool, not frigid. It felt good on Taegan's blistered face. As he and Jivex pursued the chasme west over the rooftops, he brandished his sliver of licorice root, recited the proper incantation, and the jolt of the magic made his muscles jump.

Jivex hissed at the momentary discomfort. "Don't you know any other spells?"

"None to make us fly faster. Do you want to catch the chasme or not?"

"Yes, if it doesn't disappear. Why do you think it hasn't?"

"Perhaps we wounded it severely enough that it lacks the strength to play that particular trick."

"Maybe," the faerie dragon said. "I did tear it up pretty badly."

The chasme swooped down toward a large, slate-roofed building with a spire at each corner and a square open space at the center. It was the home and trading emporium of a pair of Zhentish merchants, disliked and mistrusted by many folk in Thentia, but tolerated for the coin their dealings in spice and perfume brought in. Did the chasme expect to find refuge inside?

The demon dived down into the central cavity, and Taegan and Jivex plunged after him. The air around them smelled of the merchants' aromatic wares, and of the night-blooming jasmine in the garden below. The white flowers, statuary, and gravel paths gleamed in the moonlight, and an artificial brook gurgled. Taegan reflected that he'd fought a good many duels in such pleasant, seemingly peaceful environs, and hoped he was about to fight another. He needed to rid Thentia's mages of the chasme for good and all.

But the demon wheeled, laughed, and vanished a bare instant before he could close to striking distance. He cursed.

"We can break into the house," Jivex said.

"We don't know that's where the chasme actually went."

"It must have come here for some reason."

The drake was right, so what might be the explanation?

Taegan realized that he and Jivex had followed the chasme down into what amounted to a box. It was a good place to lay a snare for enemies who flew. He gazed upward. Creatures with jutting reptilian jaws and barbed, serpentine tails scrambled from their hiding places in the corner towers, unfurling their rattling leathery wings and leaping into the air. From past experience, Taegan knew they were abishais, devils with draconic traits.

"Look up," the avariel said,

Jivex hissed, "Well, at least I get to kill something."

May Lady Firehair make it so, Taegan thought. For in truth, there was a lot of abishais, and he'd already expended some of his most potent spells.

A blue abishai hurtled down at him. He couldn't see the color of its scales in the dark, but knew its scaly hide must be azure from the sparks sizzling and popping on the sting at the end of its tail. He waited until, fangs bared, talons poised to rend and tail to stab, it was nearly on top of him. Then he beat his wings and so jerked himself out of its path. As it streaked past, he cut at its head. An ordinary weapon wouldn't hurt an abishai, but the sword Rilitar had given him was far from that, and it split the devil's skull. The baatezu plummeted, slamming down in a flowerbed with a sickening thud.

Taegan cast about, seeking his next foe. Its scales dark as pitch, reeking of the acid sweating from its sting, it was just above and behind him, its clawed, misshapen hand streaking at his wing. The avariel folded his pinions, dropping lower to dodge, and thrust backward over his shoulder. It was an awkward stroke with little strength behind it, but the best he could manage when he didn't have time to spin around and face his adversary.

The abishai's talons ripped a shiny black feather or two from his wing, but failed to shred the muscle. His point drove an inch or so into its chest. It snapped its batlike wings, jerking itself up off the steel, and Jivex swooped down on its head, clawed away its eyes, and took flight once more. Shrieking, the baatezu flailed blindly about itself. Taegan left it to flounder while he sought a foe who still posed more of a danger.

Sune knew, they weren't hard to find. He killed a white abishai no taller than an avariel, though considerably thicker in the torso, then one of the gaunt, towering reds. The former had a sting covered in frost, the latter, one burning like a torch. As he fought, he doggedly labored to gain altitude, to take away the devils' advantage in height and to climb above the surrounding walls, where he'd have more room to maneuver.

Meanwhile, Jivex used his talons and fangs when he deemed it necessary, but mostly employed his magical abilities to fight at range. He repeatedly became invisible, then revealed himself once more in a new location, leading some of the abishais on a maddening chase that prevented them from swarming on Taegan. The faerie dragon also conjured a sheet of pearly fog to shroud several of the reptilian devils. After they flew out of the mist, they seemed slower, addled, more easily confused by the flashes of light and sudden blaring noises Jivex created to befuddle them. He even managed to bind the will of a green, which changed sides and defended him until other fiends ripped it apart.

Still hard-pressed, the faerie dragon then summoned two gigantic owls. Each bird shimmered out of empty air, swooped, and drove its talons into an abishai.

Taegan had learned that Jivex could only call such allies to his aid about once in every lunar cycle. Thus, it was a weapon to hold in reserve for moments of dire need. That moment surely was at hand.

The owls only survived for a few heartbeats, but acquitted themselves well before the abishais killed them, and by taking some of the pressure off Taegan, enabled him to soar above the roof of the Zhents' mansion.

He caught an updraft that carried him higher, forcing the remaining devils to follow. Then, without warning, he dived, spitted a black abishai through the chest, yanked his blade free, and veered, dodging a red's blazing stinger. He wheeled and hacked off one of the devil's wings. It plummeted.

He killed two more baatezu. Somehow Jivex sent one hurtling down as well, to impale itself on the pointed apex of one of the corner turrets, where it whimpered and writhed for a second before going limp. Taegan peered about, seeking the next foe, and realized he and the faerie dragon had accounted for them all.

Then the vitality flowed out of Taegan all at once, and his wounds ached. Exhausted, he lit on the rooftop and sat there gasping. Jivex landed beside him.

"Did you see how brilliantly I fought?" the faerie dragon asked.

Taegan grinned and replied, "Like Torm the True himself. Still, we were lucky."

Jivex sniffed. "Speak for yourself. What now?"

"Give me a moment to catch my breath, slave driver." He struggled to think despite his weariness. "I don't see how we can catch the chasme now. Rilitar may want to examine the dead devils, if the corpses don't just melt away. I want to talk to the folk who live in this mansion. But both those things will keep. Right now, let's return to the House of the Moon. We could both benefit from a priestess's healing touch." He smiled. "Especially if she's as comely as Sureene Aumratha."

Taking their time, conserving what remained of their strength, they flew back to the temple. Though the chasme had escaped him once again, Taegan tried not to feel frustrated. He'd wanted the traitor to make another move, and the whoreson had. It was possible the cultist was going to suffer for it. But even if that was so, whatever sense of satisfaction Taegan might otherwise have evoked within himself died stillborn when he heard the sounds of lamentation rising from the temple.

He peered through the window into the music room, where Baerimel sobbed. Jannatha held her in her arms and did her best to comfort her, even though, to judge from her anguished expression, the older sister was equally grief-stricken herself. Covered with an ivory-colored cloak, the cause of their pain still lay where she'd fallen. Sinylla had perished of her wounds.

EIGHT

Yagoth hesitated to hit Pavel too often. Ogres were simply too strong, and humans, too fragile. He didn't want to kill the sun priest prematurely.

What he could do was jerk Pavel up off his chair and give him a good shaking. That was enough to rattle the cleric's bones, jab pain through his battered body, and presumably, keep him from meditating. Accordingly, Yagoth performed the petty torture every couple minutes, enjoying the way his captive gasped and cried out, until another ogre appeared in the library doorway and gave him a nod, to indicate that the sun had risen completely above the hills to the east.

Every priest petitioned his god for spells at a particular hour sacred to the deity. Naturally, the Morninglord communed with his servants at dawn. Stop a sun priest from making contact with

Lathander at that time, and you denied him the chance to renew his magic.

Yagoth had likewise taken other measures to render Pavel helpless. He'd confiscated the human's armor and weapons, including the enchanted mace he carried tucked in his own kilt. He'd tethered one of Pavel's ankles to his chair. His best trick, though, had been to break the sun priest's leg, splint it crooked, then use one of the few healing spells Vaprak granted him to fuse it in place that way. Pavel couldn't possibly run with it bent and twisted as it was. He'd be lucky to hobble.

"Work," Yagoth growled. "Find something useful, and I'll give you food and water."

Pavel sighed. "I already discovered what Sammaster learned here, and shared it with you, too."

"That's useless."

"I explained from the start, the pieces of the puzzle are scattered across Faerûn. We never expected to find the entire secret here, just a portion of it. But if you let me take it back to Thentia. . . ."

"You'll profit, and I'll gain nothing."

Pavel's face tightened with pain, perhaps a sudden twinge from the scabby cut and purple bruise on his forehead. "No one will profit, or rather, the whole world will. Stopping the Rage will benefit everyone, ogres included."

Yagoth grumbled, "Even if you're telling the truth, that isn't good enough."

"Preserving all Faerûn from devastation and tyranny 'isn't good enough?' That's insane."

"Thar was a mighty kingdom once. It's my destiny to restore and rule it, as great Vorbyx did. Vaprak has given me signs. He guided me to a place of power, and gave me the tools—you and your dead halfling friend—to find and understand the lore the ancients left here. Now you're going to read every tablet, every parchment. Read until your eyes bleed. Read until you can teach me how to enslave dragons, or give me some other secret to win my throne."

"What if there's nothing here that will serve?"

"There is."

"Just suppose there isn't. At the end, if I've done my best, will you set me free, to return to Thentia and help end the Rage?"

"No. If I can't have what I want, then let the whole world go down in blood and ruin. What do I care?" Yagoth leered. "But if you help me, you can go free."

He doubted Pavel believed him, but perhaps the human wanted to. It had been Yagoth's experience that captives who were suffering and desperate would sometimes seize and cling to any hope, no matter how absurd. In any case, it did no harm to try to motivate the sun priest by whatever ploy came to mind.

"You already rule your tribe," Pavel said. "If you want to wind up with even that many subjects, release me now, before another dragon flight happens along and massacres them."

Yagoth scowled, picked up a stack of tablets, and dumped them clattering on the table in front of the human.

"Read," said the ogre. "Read or go thirsty, and starve. Look for mention of a blue dragon."

"There won't be one. I realize the blue wyrm seemed like a portent to you, but it wasn't. It was just one more drake wandering far from its normal habitat under the influence of the frenzy."

Yagoth smacked Pavel with the back of his hand. The human flew from his chair. Since Yagoth had tethered him to the seat, the length of rawhide jerked it over, too, to bang against the floor.

Alarmed, the ogre stooped to peer at his prisoner. He hadn't meant to strike Pavel. He'd simply gotten tired of listening to the human argue, until finally his patience snapped. But if he'd killed the wretch. . . .

Pavel groaned and rolled onto his side. Yagoth heaved a sigh of relief.

The carved and polished wooden amulet floated at the center of the pentacle chalked on the floor, and Rilitar prowled around it, peering, muttering under his breath, and periodically making a sinuous mystic pass. Each such gesture briefly produced a pattern of multicolored light, hanging in empty air like a chart on a wall.

Taegan watched intently, eager to hear what Rilitar would say. The avariel had worn the pendant under his clothing for some time. According to the elf wizard, the talisman was somewhat akin to a magic mirror capable of catching and holding the reflection of the first demon, devil, or elemental spirit that approached it. Except that the amulet didn't register an actual image, but rather, truths concerning the entity's essential nature. Or something like that.

His iridescent hide still singed and raw in a couple spots, Jivex crouched on a tabletop, among a mortar, pestle, alembic, and jars of powder, iron filings, mushroom caps, and dried leaves. At first, possibly enjoying the displays of colored light, he'd watched Rilitar work with considerable interest. But half an hour later, his serpentine tail switched restlessly, threatening to send a piece of glassware or crockery flying with every flick.

Finally Rilitar plucked the amulet from the air, recited a rhyme, and broke the border of the pentacle with a scuff of his toe. Taegan could tell from the magician's scowl that his report would be less than satisfactory.

"Is there nothing?" the avariel asked.

"Well," Rilitar said, "I wouldn't say 'nothing,' but we don't have what I hoped we'd get. Normally, if a wizard repeatedly used a chasme as his conjured agent, the demon would bear . . . well, call it his arcane brand. But if it was there, the charm couldn't read it."

"So what does that mean?" Jivex asked.

Rilitar shrugged and said, "I don't know. Perhaps the chasme's master erased his signature. I don't know a spell to do that, but maybe he does."

Taegan smiled wryly. "All this ambiguity makes my head ache. I much prefer thinking about fencing, where one has only so many ways to stick or cut a man, and he, only so many means of defense."

"Whereas," Rilitar said, "in wizardry, the possibilities are almost limitless. That's what makes the Art so beautiful, so magnificent, but it poses problems when you're trying to solve a magical puzzle."

"Did the amulet reveal anything else?"

"Yes, but I don't entirely know what it means."

Jivex snorted. "What else is new?"

Rilitar chuckled at the gibe. "If it's any consolation, friend dragon, much as my lack of insight vexes you, it's a greater frustration to me, because it wounds my conceit. But be that as it may, the chasme's aura differs from that of any tanar'ri I've ever encountered. That's why wards don't hold it at bay, and banishments don't drive it from our plane of existence. The spells don't recognize it for what it is."

"That raises a question," Taegan said. "If Sammaster's minion can mask a fiend's essential nature, why not use the same trick on the abishais? He could have sent all his conjured assassins romping through the House of the Moon, the clerics' protections notwithstanding."

"Well, he did use the abishais to set up an ambuscade for you and Jivex, in case you appeared to interfere in his plans."

"But that was just a secondary ploy. His primary objective was to murder Sinylla, and she was a formidable spellcaster. He would have been more assured of making the kill if he'd sent all his servants after her, and really, just as likely to eliminate the dragon and me if we turned up. The point of luring us into the merchants' garden was to limit our ability to maneuver, but being inside the temple was even more confining. No, I think he failed to disguise the abishais' natures because he couldn't. For some reason, he can only work that trick with the chasme." He hesitated, then grinned ruefully. "A discovery that ought to lead us triumphantly on to infer the traitor's identity, except that it doesn't seem to be happening."

"No," Rilitar said, "it doesn't. We have an abundance of curious facts, but no idea what they mean. Perhaps we should go question the Zhents."

When they exited the wizard's house, the morning sky was clear, and the air, warm. Crying and singing their wares, vendors pushed carts of marigolds and peonies and glistening perch, trout, and mackerel, through the streets. As Jivex flitted about, the latter kept attracting his interest, and soon he swooped and snatched a fish. Taegan had expected no less, and already carried a coin in his hand to appease the outraged seller.

Afterward, he said to Rilitar: "I feel we're close. The answer is before us. We just haven't spotted it yet. We will, though."

"But not in time to help Sinylla."

Taegan felt a pang of sadness and anger, the latter emotion directed less at the chasme or its faceless master than at his own inadequacies.

"No, not in time for that," the avariel said. "We came so close to saving her! If only a healer had reached her a little sooner, I believe she would have pulled through. But 'if only' does no good. The truth is, I failed the poor lass, after more or less guaranteeing that everyone would be all right."

"You mustn't blame yourself. Knowing the risks, she chose to fight this fight. I'll miss her, though. She was a true prodigy, at both arcane and priestly magic. I'd never seen her like before, and doubt I will again."

Which meant, Taegan reflected glumly, that of all Thentia's scholars, Sinylla might have been the one whom Kara's venture could least afford to lose.

"Yet for all her talents," Rilitar continued, "she was blithe and unassuming, full of mirth and kindness. Nearly all her fellow wizards liked her, and you've met us, Taegan. Half of us don't like anybody."

"That half including Phourkyn," the avariel said, "but he fought to save her. Perhaps he did save me. He drove the chasme back when it had me down and was reaching for my throat."

"So we can cross him off our list of suspects."

"It would appear so. He couldn't have conjured or psychically directed the chasme at the same time Sureene was interrogating him, could he? But if it isn't you, him, Firefingers, Sinylla, or Scattercloak, then who? Fat, fretful Darvin in his pretentious robes of white? A supposedly less powerful member of your circle? A stranger lurking somewhere in town? The possibilities rattle around in my skull like dice in a cup."

"I should have been there," Rilitar said, "to stand with you and help protect Sinylla."

"No," said Taegan, "that's unacceptable. If I'm not permitted to blame myself, then neither are you. You're not Helm the all-seeing, and couldn't know the traitor would strike when and where he did."

"You're right," Rilitar said. "It's just hard to see Sinylla perish so young and full of promise. Humans live such brief—"

A shadow swept over them, and folk started to clamor. Taegan looked up, just in time to glimpse enormous wings beating, a flash of bronze scales in the sun, and the human figures, tiny by comparison, clinging to the dragon's spine. Then the wyrm vanished behind a tall building.

"That's Wardancer," Rilitar said, "one of Kara's seekers. But where's she headed? Firefingers's tower is the other way."

Taegan's intuition supplied the answer: "She and her riders are headed the same place we are. Come on"

He spread his wings and leaped into the air.

Will opened his gummy eyes, surprised to find he was still alive. It was hard to be particularly happy about it. His wounded shoulder hurt too badly, especially since infection had set in, causing greenish pus to ooze from the ragged puncture and painting red streaks on his skin.

Trying to block out the throbbing pain, he warily lifted himself up from the depression in the ground and peeked through the thorn bushes. Then he sighed with relief, because the dragons were still there, crouching on the moor, shuffling about, snarling and ranting to themselves like the mad things they were. Had they wandered off while he was unconscious, it would have been just as disastrous as if they'd discovered him passed out in his hole.

The four wyrms on the heath were greens, one huge, old one and three that, though smaller, were still colossal compared to a halfling, human, or even an ogre. Maybe they'd laired in the great wood that was Cormanthor on the southern shore of the Moonsea, or in the Border Forest to the west, before frenzy launched them on their aimless journey.

Wherever they'd come from, they hadn't had an entirely easy time getting so far. Some of their prey had put up a fight, slashing and stabbing holes in their hides. Probably that was why they'd stopped to rest, though left to their own devices, they wouldn't bide for long. The Rage wouldn't let them.

If Will could only have been certain they'd go tearing off in the proper direction, it would have made his life easier. But as he had no way of knowing, he had no choice but to resume his labors.

He waited until none of the greens were looking in his direction. Then he popped up, whirled his sling, and hurled one of the mud balls he'd shaped. Blessed Mother Yondalla, but it hurt to move quickly! Biting back a gasp of pain, he dropped down once more.

The mud ball thudded in the sparse grass with a softer, more ambiguous noise that a stone would have made. The greens whirled and charged toward the noise, then, growling to one another, prowled about the vicinity from which it had issued.

That was all right with Will. He was twenty yards away.

But then the biggest wyrm decided to sweep a larger area. It stalked away from its fellows on a spiral path that would bring it within a stride or two of the depression where he lay hidden.

If he wasn't mistaken, he'd be downwind of the reptile, and he'd rubbed himself with juice crushed from the proper leaves to deaden his scent. Still, he was all but certain the green would smell his festering wound when it came close enough, glimpse him despite his screen of thorn bush, or simply hear the pounding of his heart. Yet all he could do was lie perfectly still and hope. He surely couldn't run. The wyrms would spot, pursue, and overtake him in a matter of seconds.

Nostrils flaring, forked tongue flickering, horned and crested head twisting this way and that, the green loomed above him, close enough for him to distinguish the reptile's individual scales. Gleaming despite the layer of heavy gray cloud attenuating the sunlight, they made an intricate mosaic of jade, olive, and emerald, of all the myriad hues of leaf and moss. As Will held his breath, trying not to cough or gag on the stink of the wyrm's corrosive poison, he thought that if, as seemed likely, it was his time to die, at least the last thing he'd ever see was beautiful.

The drake arched its head forward. In another instant, it would peer over the thorn bushes. Then one of the other wyrms called to it. The big green spat a little puff of vapor that rotted away the uppermost fringe of the bushes, pivoted, and strode to rejoin its comrades.

Will waited until the reptile made it all the way back. Then he crept south, found a new hiding place, and in due course threw another mud pellet, drawing the dragons after him again.

Afterward, he decided that was enough. He hoped he'd lured the dragons close enough for his purposes, and in any case, the same simple trick couldn't fool even demented wyrms for long. Keeping low, he skulked away from them, up a hill and down the other side, toward the hollow containing the black lake and the temples of the infernal powers.

The ogres were still camped in front of the grandest shrine. Will looked for his pony and Pavel's horse, but saw neither. The giant-kin had likely eaten them.

It was yet another stroke of misfortune, but there was no point fretting over it. Will sneaked on to a green, corroded bronze statue of an eyeless, four-armed demon positioned partway down the hillside. Crouching behind it, he might stay hidden for at least a few heartbeats.

He placed a stone in his warsling and let it fly, to crack against the head of the sentry lounging just a few yards away. The ogre dropped to one knee, and dazed, rubbed its bloody forehead. Will clipped the guard a second time, and it toppled forward onto its face.

Will turned is attention to the brutes in the filthy, slovenly camp below. They could eat skiprocks until the supply ran out. Despite the handicap of slinging with his off hand when he was sick with pain and fever, the missiles rebounded properly, bashing multiple targets with each throw. Will grinned.

I'll bet now you wish you'd taken the trouble to track me down, he thought, instead of just assuming I'd bleed out. Now roar and hoot, you brainless, treacherous louts.

They did bellow. The only problem was that soon, one of them pointed and shouted that there, there was the half-ling! Will glanced behind him. The crest of the hill was still empty.

How could that be? He was sure he'd drawn the dragons close enough to hear all the commotion. Unless they'd flown away as soon as he lost sight of them, and of course, that was exactly how his luck was running.

He cowered behind the statue for as long as it was practical, popping out to sling stones, ducking back to avoid the spear and rocks the ogres threw at him. When the giant-kin were a few strides away, he scrambled backward, making them chase him farther.

He knew it would only be a little farther. He couldn't stay ahead of them for long.

He jerked himself out of the path of a thrown hatchet. A pair of ogres pounded at him, spears leveled. He wished he still had his hornblade, or at least his dagger.

Then, behind him, something screeched, loud enough to shake the earth. The ogres froze, eyes wide with dread. Will didn't have to look around to know what they had seen.

━━━━━◦◦◦◦━━━━━

By the time Taegan and Jivex reached the cobbled plaza in front of the Zhents' mansion, Wardancer had deposited her riders on the ground and taken flight once more, to circle above the house. The bronze was watching to make sure nobody sneaked out the back way.

Baerimel, Jannatha, and to Taegan's surprise, Darvin Kordeion and Scattercloak stood before the front entrance, a high, black-enameled door reinforced with iron. Had they already knocked, demanding admission? If so, the Zhents had opted not to respond. Scattercloak, hooded and shrouded as ever, stood before the panel, reciting an incantation in his emotionless voice, and lashing one hand, covered almost to the fingertips by a long, flopping sleeve and gloved in gray leather beneath, through a mystic figure. The magic accumulating in the air made shadows twist and twitch where they lay on the ground.

"Stop him," Taegan said, "without hurting him."

"Right," Jivex said.

Hovering, the faerie dragon stared at Scattercloak, and a brassy note blared through the air. It was loud even where Taegan was standing, and judging from the way the wizard flinched, it had sounded right beside his ear. The shadows stopped writhing the instant he botched his spell.

He and his fellow mages rounded on Taegan and Jivex.

"What's wrong with you?" demanded Darvin, his snowy robes shining in the sunlight. "Help, or stay out of this."

Rilitar appeared in the center of the square, vanished once more, and an instant later, materialized at Taegan's side. The puff of air thus displaced rustled the avariel's feathers.

"Please, wait," the elf wizard said. "What do you intend?"

"Isn't it obvious?" Baerimel asked. Judging from the redness in her eyes and the tangles in her hair, she'd wept most of the night away. "Maestro, you said the chasme led you to this house."

"It means nothing," the bladesinger said. "The first night I encountered the chasme, Jivex and I followed it to Scattercloak's house before it winked out of sight."

That silenced them all for a moment, and during that hesitation, something blocked the sunlight streaming from on high. Taegan had to stifle the instinct to cower, even though he realized it was one of Kara's allies swooping down.

Wardancer touched down with considerable agility in what was, for her, a cramped space. The tip of one scalloped wing brushed a shower of russet paint flakes from a wall, but otherwise, she did no damage. Up close, she smelled like the sea, as bronzes often did.

"What's wrong?" the dragon asked. "Why haven't you battered down the door and hauled the Zhents out?"

"As I was just endeavoring to explain," Taegan said, "that's not a sound idea."

"According to Baerimel," Wardancer rumbled, "they drove Samdralyrion mad, resulting in his death, then murdered little Sinylla. I was fond of that child."

"We don't know that they're to blame," Rilitar said. "In fact, Maestro Nightwind and I very much doubt it."

"Because you're obsessed with the notion that a member of our own circle is responsible," Scattercloak said, "even though you have no proof. Now, it seems, you mean to point the finger of suspicion at me, even though the fencing teacher already declared me innocent."

"No," Taegan said, "I remain convinced of your innocence." He'd forfeit any influence he had over them if he admitted to being fallible or uncertain. "The point I was endeavoring to make is that our enemy consistently strives to make us suspect the wrong person."

"I've lived near and beneath the Moonsea for centuries," said Wardancer. "I know the Black Network and the evil it does. If the folk in this house are Zhents, then I can readily believe they're responsible for our woes."

"I confess," Taegan replied, "I'm a stranger to this region. But from what I've gleaned, though the lords of Zhentil Keep are tyrants, and their troops, brigands and pirates, most of their subjects are simple farmers and craftsmen, like the majority of folk in any land. It's likely the merchants who live here have no more harm in them than the average fellow born and bred in Thentia."

"Have you never heard of spies?" Darvin asked.

"I have," Taegan said, "but please, think it through. If by some chance the merchants are agents of the Black Network, then they can't serve the Cult of the Dragon also. The one conspiracy has nothing to do with the other."

"You don't know that," said the wizard in white.

"Yes," Taegan said, "I do. It's obvious to anyone who makes the effort to ponder the matter calmly. It's true that early on, the Zhentarim sought to exploit the Rage to further their own ends, but that's scarcely the same thing as wanting dracoliches to overrun the world. The Zhentish lords want to conquer it themselves."

"It comes down to this," said Scattercloak. "I intend to do everything possible to ensure my safety."

"I take it," said Rilitar, "that in your mind, 'everything possible' encompasses breaking into the merchants' home, dragging them forth, interrogating them under duress, or perhaps simply murdering them out of hand. Well, I have bad news for you. Those things aren't possible, unless you kill me first."

He placed his hand on the wand he wore sheathed on his belt.

"Trust elves," said Darvin, "and their convoluted way of thinking to make any situation worse. If your forefathers hadn't created the Rage, we wouldn't be in this mess in the first place."

"True," said Taegan. "Though all of us save Wardancer would be slaves to dragon kings, but I doubt you'd find it a pleasant existence. Those ancient mages *liberated Faerûn*. We're each and every one of us in their debt. It's scarcely their fault that, millennia later, Sammaster corrupted their work."

It seemed strange to hear himself extolling the accomplishments of elves, when he'd always considered his race to be of little account. But he was simply giving the spellcasters of eld their due.

"If you had to bear the curse of frenzy," Wardancer said, "you might well think their enchantment already partook of corruption. Still, there's justice in what you say, and I'm glad I possess no thralls. In a sense, when the ancient elves delivered the small folk out of bondage, they freed the metallic drakes as well, to find a cleaner way of living, even if the means exacted a price for our liberation."

"This is all irrelevant," said Scattercloak.

"Perhaps," Taegan said, "so let's return to the issue at hand. Which is that dragons attract attention, and accordingly, much of Thentia is watching us at this very moment, peeping from windows and around corners. What will people think if you force your way into this house and harass or slay the inhabitants?"

"The inhabitants," said Darvin, "are Zhents."

"It wouldn't matter," said Taegan, "if they were trolls. Folk would still decide that the town mages have grown cruel and arrogant. That they'll commit any crime or atrocity that strikes their fancy, without regard for the law. The burghers will likewise conclude that the dragons who keep calling at Firefingers's tower are of the same mind, and at least as dangerous."

"You know what the upshot will be," Rilitar said. "The Watchlord and the noble families will bar dragons from entering the city. They may even seek to expel us wizards.

We'll lose our homes, and more importantly, be unable to continue our studies. All Faerûn will suffer if that befalls."

"Let Master Shadow-water and I interview the spice traders." Taegan grinned. "I can virtually guarantee that they'll be happy to cooperate with us after we chivvy four hostile arcanists and an angry dragon away from their door. Perhaps we'll have Sureene use her magic to question them as well. If they have anything to say that can illuminate our present difficulties, we'll obtain the information, I promise you."

Darvin sneered. "With Sinylla lying on her bier, what are your pledges worth?"

"No one could honestly guarantee that your work would be devoid of risk," Taegan said, "and I didn't. I do promise that I'm close to identifying the traitor."

"By what method?"

"Avariel wizardry," Taegan said. "The secret magic of the sky."

If anyone else had claimed such powers for his reclusive kind, living like barbarians in the depths of the wilderness, he would have laughed. Though, it occurred to him, it was his own people who'd taught him bladesong, and it at least was far from a primitive discipline. Humans certainly had nothing comparable.

In any case, the important thing was that, with luck, Darvin and his allies wouldn't realize that his pretensions to mysterious and far-reaching occult abilities were merely a bluff.

Baerimel started silently crying, the tears sliding down her cheeks. "I just wanted to do something. I need to. Sinylla was my cousin. I was right there with her. I should have been able to save her. But . . ."

"I understand" Taegan said. "I was there, too, and we will avenge her. But not by lashing out at random. Not by bringing Kara's enterprise to ruin. That would mean our enemy had won."

Baerimel gave a jerky little nod and whispered, "I know."

"So do I," Jannatha said.

Wardancer grunted. "If Sinylla's own kin say to pull back, then I'll honor their wishes."

Taegan arched an eyebrow at Scattercloak and Darvin and asked, "What of the two of you?"

"I too relent," said Scattercloak, "for now."

"Hold on," said Darvin to his cloaked and hooded colleague, "I still think—"

Scattercloak vanished.

Darvin's pudgy face turned red at the other mage's rudeness, and presumably, the frustration of having his intentions thwarted. He turned on his heel and stalked away.

Taegan didn't relax until Baerimel, Jannatha, and Wardancer departed as well. Then he slumped with relief.

"For a while there, I thought we were all going to wind up brawling in the street."

"I could have beaten them," Jivex said.

"I admire your martial fervor," Taegan said with a smile, "but that's not the point. Win or lose, it would still have been a disaster. You'd think the others would comprehend that. Wizards are supposed to be wily."

"Exactly," said Rilitar, "too wily for anyone to fool or threaten us. Thus, when it happens, it's alarming enough to stifle our reason and panic us. We have to unmask Sammaster's agent soon, my friends. Otherwise, one way or another, our enquiry is doomed."

"I know." Taegan said

"Shall we go ahead and knock on the merchants' door?" the magician asked.

Taegan shrugged and said, "I'm reasonably certain it's pointless. Unless my instincts are in error, the abishais simply commandeered the Zhents' towers and garden without their knowledge. But I suppose we'd better go through the motions."

Will was closer to the onrushing greens than any of the ogres. If the wyrms didn't gobble him up first, it would be because he was so much smaller. He threw himself to the ground to make himself less conspicuous still.

The giant-kin, conversely, shouted and screamed. A few bolted. Others hurled spears and stones, or scrambled forward brandishing flint-headed axes and clubs.

As a result, the greens ignored Will to rip into the ogres. Even so, he was in danger. An enormous scaly foot plunged down and jolted the ground less than a yard from the spot where he lay curled in a ball. Had it stepped on him, it would have squashed him to jelly.

Kara, the halfling thought, I deserve a bonus for this. If we ever see each other again, dig deep into that purse of gems you carry.

As soon as the wyrms raced by, he jumped up and ran, trying to swing around the reptiles. It wasn't entirely possible. The dragons kept whirling and lunging unpredictably to attack ogres that were seemingly out of reach. Closing the distance in an instant, the greens snatched up the giant-kin, bit them into pieces, or clawed them to tatters of bloody flesh and shards of shattered bone.

A wyrm spun around and glared directly at Will. Well, he thought, I still think this was a good idea, even if it isn't working out. Hating the spastic clumsiness of his crippled arm, he fumbled a stone into his warsling for one final and surely futile cast.

But before he could let the missile fly, an ogre hurled an axe that stuck in the dragon's mask just below its eye. The green snarled and pivoted to pounce at its attacker. Will scurried on toward the largest temple.

Not all the ogres had forsaken their camp in front of the structure to chase Will up the hillside. Of those who'd remained, some were dashing to join the fight. Others had begun to retreat toward the shelter of the huge stone pile.

Most of them never even made it to the broad flight of stairs leading up to the primary entrance. A winged shadow swept across the ground, a plume of acidic vapor washed over them from on high, and they reeled and fell, their warty hides charred and blistered. In the mad confusion of the slaughter on the hillside, Will hadn't even realized that one of the greens had taken to the air. But it had, and employed its breath weapon to deadly effect. It plunged to earth to crush more victims beneath its hugeness, then struck and ripped at any prey that yet survived.

Will sprinted around to the south side of the temple and through one of the secondary entrances. The urge to keep moving, to get below ground where the dragons couldn't follow, was like a goad jabbing at him. Still, he forced himself to hide behind a pillar and wait until the path was clear.

After a minute, Yagoth and three of his warriors pounded up from the vaults. Will had assumed some guard would run to inform the shaman and any of his followers who happened to be attending him of the battle outside, and plainly, that was what had happened.

Now go out, fight, and die, the halfling thought. And sure enough, Yagoth bellowed "Vaprak!" and led his minions charging out the door.

Will descended into the tunnels and groped his way through the dark until faintness and vertigo overwhelmed him. He struggled to cling to his senses, but passed out anyway.

When he woke, it took him several seconds to recall where he was, and why. Even afterward, he still felt so weak and sick that he feared it was addling him, that he no longer accurately recalled the layout of the crypts.

Though it went against all the instincts he'd acquired as a thief, he decided to call out. Why not? If any ogres remained underground, he was likely dead in any case.

"Pavel!" he cried. "Pavel!"

His voice emerged as a feeble croak, and it seemed clear that nobody, whether human or ogre, was likely to hear it.

But after a moment, an answer echoed out of the blackness: "Will!"

The halfling heaved a sigh of relief. He'd assumed Yagoth had kept Pavel alive, but that wasn't the same thing as knowing, and until that moment, he hadn't.

"Keep talking, charlatan," Will replied. "It will help me find your worthless arse."

"All right," Pavel said. "Yagoth assured me you were dead, but I didn't believe it. I knew I'm not that lucky."

Will staggered toward the sound until light blossomed in the gloom, glinting on the contours of the twin idols flanking the entrance to the secret library. The halfling quickened his pace, tripping over the ogre corpses that still littered the floor. The enormous blades that had killed them clanked beneath his boots. The surviving giant-kin had torn them from their mountings.

The source of the light turned out to be a torch in a sconce, enchanted to burn forever with a cool greenish flame. When it illuminated Pavel, Will winced. Seated on a chair beside a table heaped with stone tablets, the priest looked exhausted and half-starved. The gash and livid bruise on his brow were surely painful. But it was even more disturbing to observe his crooked leg. The filthy ogres had crippled him.

"You look like something somebody dumped out of a chamberpot," said Will. "I mean, even more than usual."

"I can honestly say the same of you. What kept you?"

"I couldn't get past all the ogres until I worked out how to create a little distraction. Let me untie that tether, since you're plainly too stupid to figure out the knot."

"All right, and while you do that—"

Out in the corridor, the broken blades rattled. One of the ogres was coming, and had likely heard Will and Pavel's voices.

Will scurried to the rear of the chamber and hid in the shadows beneath a table. He placed a stone in his warsling.

Red eye glaring, the normal one squinched shut, Yagoth shambled through the doorway. Dragon breath had scalded his warty, branded hide, but the injury didn't appear to be slowing him down any. He held his spear leveled in his hands, and had Pavel's mace tucked in his kilt.

"Show yourself, little rat!" he bellowed. "I know you're in here!"

"No one's here but us," Pavel said. "Are you hearing voices? I keep telling you, you're insane."

Yagoth ignored the taunt and started prowling around the room. "I understand the trick you played, halfling. My people are dead because of you. But I'll still achieve my destiny. After I kill you, and the sun priest finds me the weapon I need, I'll make myself chief of another tribe, and build my kingdom from there. The banner of the blue dragon—"

Will lunged out into the open and hurled the rock.

It was supposed to put Yagoth's scarlet eye out. Instead, it glanced off the ogre's low, blemished forehead, leaving a bloody graze, but no more. Yagoth roared and charged.

In better times, Will could have slung another stone before his foe took two strides, or dodged and tumbled with such agility that Yagoth would have found it difficult to score a hit on him. But in his current state of decrepitude, he could manage neither. He scrambled back beneath the cover afforded by the table.

Which vanished instantly, when Yagoth grabbed hold of the furniture and tossed it aside. Tablets crashed down everywhere, some shattering against the floor.

Snarling, Yagoth stabbed repeatedly with his spear, and Will gave ground. The halfling realized his opponent was pushing him into a corner, but lacked the speed to maneuver out of the box. In another moment, he'd have his back to the wall, and most likely, the lance in his vitals an instant after that.

"Flee!" shouted Pavel.

Brilliant idea, thought Will. I would, if I had anyplace to flee to.

But bellowing in anger and surprise at his own behavior, it was Yagoth who shambled backward. Will belatedly realized that Pavel had afflicted the ogre with a magical compulsion.

Most likely, it would only last a moment, but maybe that was time enough for another cast. Will dropped a stone into the sling and let it fly.

The missile hit the mark. Yagoth screamed and clutched at his ruined eye. As he reeled, his foot landed on a fallen tablet. He slipped and fell.

Will rushed him, and thumb-gouged Yagoth's good eye. The ogre howled and flailed blindly. Will ducked, seized a tablet in a two-handed grip, and pounded Yagoth over the head with it. After two blows, the shaman slumped down motionless, but Will kept on hitting him until he hammered his skull out of shape.

Then he turned to Pavel and wheezed, "What was the point in waiting so long to cast a spell?"

"I had to decide who I disliked more, you or Yagoth. Well, actually, I only had one chance. Once the ogre realized I could work magic, he'd knock me out immediately if he could. Thus I needed to choose my moment carefully."

"I take it," said Will, "that he imagined you didn't have any spells prepared."

"He abused me every morning at dawn, to keep me from praying, but he underestimated my ability to concentrate, and the strength of my bond with Lathander. I managed to acquire a few spells despite the harassment."

"So why didn't you use them to escape? Too lazy, or too gutless?"

"Too lamed. I couldn't fix the injury by myself. For that, I'll need your help. Once I'm untied, and I've mended your shoulder, I'll lie down on the floor, and you'll re-break my leg with my mace. Pulverize the bones if that's what it takes, just as long as you can straighten the limb when you're done. Then I'll heal myself. Can you do it?"

Will supposed he had no choice, though the thought of inflicting such agony on his friend made him feel queasy.

He forced a grin and asked, "Are you serious? It's exactly the kind of thing I've always wanted to do."

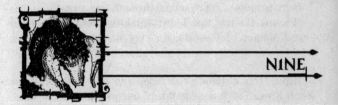

9 & 10 Kythorn, the Year of Rogue Dragons

The crashing echoed along the tunnels, down the stairwells, through the archives, storerooms, and tombs. Dorn knew what the disturbance was, because Raryn had skulked up to the surface to scout it out. In undisputed possession of the mountaintop, the dragons were employing their strength, breath weapons, and wizardry to demolish portions of the stronghold.

Like Dorn, Cantoule was standing watch behind the makeshift ramparts where they planned to oppose the wyrms the next time the reptiles attacked. Looking as dirty and exhausted as everyone else, the skinny, sun-bronzed Grand Master of Flowers flinched at a particularly loud bang that might have been a whole tower collapsing.

"Why?" Cantoule asked. "Why are the dragons doing this?"

"Maybe," said Dorn, "they're just venting their anger that it's taking so long to kill us. Or, they mean the noise to keep us from sleeping. Or, they hope the destruction of the castle will demoralize us."

"It's demoralizing me," Cantoule said. "They're defiling sacred ground I swore to protect."

Dorn grunted. "We've talked through this already."

"I know. It's just that I keep thinking that if Kane were Grand Master of Flowers, it never would have come to this."

"Kane?"

"King Dragonsbane's comrade, who helped destroy the Witch-King. The wisest monk of our order, and the most accomplished fighter. By rights, he should have presided here. But he loved wandering too much to stay in one place, and so chose me for the position. Now evil is destroying everything he gave into my keeping."

"That's self-pity talking," said Dorn, "and it isn't helping you or anybody else."

Cantoule blinked as if the half-golem had slapped him, then smiled wryly and said, "Perhaps you're right. Ilmater teaches that virtue lies in fidelity, not in success. Still—"

Something roared. It was more or less what Dorn had been waiting for, but as he started to string his longbow, he realized with a stab of dread that the noise had reverberated from behind him.

"Come on!" he shouted to the monks manning the barricade. "All of you! No, wait." He pointed. "You four stay here, just in case. But the rest of you, run!"

He wheeled and plunged through the arched doorway behind the fortification and down a length of hallway. His companions sprinted after him.

As Dorn ran, his iron foot clashing against the polished stone floor, he despised himself for the idiot he was. In retrospect, it was obvious why some of the dragons had spent the last couple days knocking down sections of the citadel overhead: to disguise the noise and vibration of their comrades digging into the mountain, thus bypassing whatever fortifications, traps, and guards waited to hinder them. Dorn had observed burrowing dragons among the attacking force, yet still hadn't anticipated thats particular tactic.

As he and his companions dashed down a staircase, a fierce yet lovely battle anthem, a defiant answer to the invading dragons' bellowing, rose to meet them. Kara had evidently reached the site of the breach. Dorn was glad someone so formidable had showed up to oppose the malevolent wyrms before they pushed any farther into the vaults, but was likewise fearful that the intruders would overwhelm her.

While he and his fellow sentries raced through the cellars, other folk came running from their new, improvised barracks, kitchen, mess hall, and chapel to join them. The cacophony of combat led them all to an ossuary, a series of chambers where the polished bones of previous generations of monks, assembled into intricate designs, adorned the walls and ceilings of a skull room, a vertebra room, a pelvis room, and so forth.

The crypts were too cramped for archery. Dorn set down his bow and quiver so they wouldn't get in his way, drew his hand-and-a-half sword, and advanced into the first vault, a repository of foot bones arranged into gleaming white roses. His comrades surged after him.

Inside the ossuary, the mingled crashing, roaring, and the soaring strains of Kara's song were deafening. The rooms shook. Jarred loose from their fastenings, bones rained down to batter Dorn's head and shoulders. Dust filled the air, to choke him and sting his eyes.

It was disorienting, and for a moment, he had the crazy feeling that somehow, he'd blundered right past the combat without noticing. Then he spotted it an instant later.

Digging with no way of knowing precisely where it would end up, a huge earth drake with a thick, lumpish body, craggy gray-brown hide, and shining green eyes had found its way into an area too small to contain it. It had needed to knock and scrape away sections of ceiling, and the dividing walls between chambers, just to squirm partway into the ossuary. The space was really too confining for Kara as well, but slender and nimble, she was better able to maneuver than her massive foe. It had black burns all over its mask and chest where she'd seared it with the lightning in her breath, while she only had a single set of bloody claw gashes on her shoulder.

Which meant that so far, the situation wasn't as disastrous as it might have been. But peering under the earth drake's belly, past its stamping legs and lashing tail, Dorn glimpsed other dragons, waiting to pour into the cellars as soon as their comrade cleared the end of the burrow. Meanwhile, several yards away, a scaly, obsidian-clawed forefoot, mottled black and red and throwing off heat like a blazing hearth, smashed through a section of wall. A magma drake was on the verge of breaking in as well.

Striving to make himself heard above the noise, Dorn bellowed, "Form into squads! Those with spears and polearms, attack the fiery one!"

Anyone who tried to battle the magma drake with a shorter weapon would come away with burns.

Anyone but Dorn.

His iron half would shield his vulnerable flesh from the worst of the heat, as long as he kept the artificial side forward, and so he advanced on the magma wyrm.

With a grinding roar, the wall crumbled into rubble, loose bones, and grit. Red eyes blazing, the drake thrust its wedge-shaped head and long neck into the breach, then set about the task of squirming its dark wings and shoulders through. Impatient for the burrowing dragon to clear the way, other wyrms snarled and hissed behind it.

Dorn dashed forward to stop its progress. The heat pounded at him. Grateful that, unlike a red, the creature couldn't breathe flame, he rammed his knuckle-spikes into its snout. It jerked its head back, exposing the underside of its neck, and he clawed away a handful of flesh.

It snarled and bit at him, and he sidestepped. The drake snatched at him with its forefoot, and again he tried to dodge. That kept the black talons from stabbing into his torso, but the reptile still bumped him and knocked him staggering. It instantly grabbed for him once more, and its digits closed around him.

He caught his balance and heaved with all his strength. Even so, he might well have failed to break the reptile's grip, except that the effort drove the spikes and blades of his iron hand into its flesh. It screeched and snatched its foot back, and in that instant, before it could return to a fighting stance, he took the hilt of his sword in both hands and cut at its throat. The blade bit deep, blood gushed to sizzle and steam on the floor, but he knew he still hadn't inflicted a mortal wound.

Streaming white hair and polar-bear hide armor shining in the gloom, Raryn rushed up beside him to thrust with his harpoon. Monks assailed the magma drake's flanks. Dorn wished he knew what was happening in the other half of the battle, but didn't dare turn away from his adversary to look. At least Kara was still singing, thus, obviously, still alive.

The magma drake lurched forward, looked backward, and snarled. Dorn realized that the wyrm behind it had tried to shove it out of the way. He and Raryn immediately sprang forward to attack while it was distracted. Both scored solid hits, but the dragon still wouldn't die.

Raryn scuttled underneath the drake and plunged the harpoon into its belly. The wyrm slammed itself against the floor, willing to risk driving the lance in deeper to crush its attacker. Raryn dived free, but lost the harpoon in the process. He yanked his bone-handled ice-axe from the straps securing it to his back.

The weapon's haft was too short. "Go fight the other dragon!" Dorn called.

Raryn ignored him. He lifted the axe and rushed the magma drake, too full of battle-fury to care if the heat of it burned him.

They fought on. For an instant, Dorn thought the magma drake was finally faltering, then perceived that it was gathering itself for a supreme effort. It surged forward, and at last its charcoal-colored wings pulled free. With a thunderous crack, it lashed them up and down at the enemies on its flanks, catching the monks by surprise. A couple still managed to spring out of the way, but the rest dropped beneath the battering pinions. Raryn and Dorn rushed the drake, and for once not trying to strike with its fangs, it heaved the head at the end of its long neck in a horizontal arc, just as a warrior might swing a flail. The attack caught both the half-golem and the arctic dwarf by surprise, and bashed them tumbling across the floor.

Dorn rolled into a broken section of wall. He hit hard, but the flare of pain meant nothing compared to his horrified awareness of what was about to happen. In another second, the magma drake would force itself all the way into the chamber, all the wyrms at its back would come pouring in after it, and nobody was in position to stop it.

Then he saw that one man was.

Hands empty and open, Cantoule stepped into the dragon's path. The thin, aging Grand Master of Flowers looked as small as a child's toy in front of the immense creature, and as incapable of doing it any harm. Knees bent, feet at right angles, he swirled his arms through some sort of focusing, preparatory movement.

The dragon struck at him, head hurtling down from above, jaws gaping to bite him to shreds.

Cantoule shifted just far enough to the side to avoid the attack. Then, before the magma drake could lift its head again, he drove the heel of his palm into the side of its red-hot mask.

Dorn was certain the blow had done no damage through the dragon's scaly armor. Why in the name of his martyred god had Cantoule discarded his weapon?

But the magma drake shuddered, then groaned. Its legs buckled, and its head and wings flopped to the floor. It looked dead, impossible as that seemed.

That was good as far as it went, but the defenders were still in trouble. Left to their own devices, the dragons trapped behind the carcass would shove it aside. Indeed, the body was already hitching forward.

Kara sprang in front of it, reared, and braced her forefeet against it. Presumably she'd already finished dealing with the earth drake. Or else she believed the magma wyrm's burrow presented the greater threat.

Whatever she thought, her strength and weight, prodigious as they were, couldn't long hold back the might and mass of all the wyrms pushing from the other side, but luckily, she intended more than that. She opened her jaws and spewed a bright, crackling flare of her breath into the magma drake's corpse, which jumped as if the blast had jolted it back to life.

Behind the barrier of lifeless flesh and bone, other drakes screeched in pain. The magma wyrm's body would have blocked most breath weapons, as it largely stopped the yellow flame the next reptile in line within the burrow spat back at Kara. But the essence of lightning infusing a song dragon's exhalation could evidently penetrate obstacles to burn targets hidden behind them.

Kara couldn't use her breath continuously. It needed time to renew itself. But she was also adept with spells for conjuring thunderbolts. Singing, she evoked several in a row, to blaze through the magma drake's corpse and down the tunnel. Her mostly unseen targets bellowed in agony and rage. A smell of roasting meat rose from the dead reptile's charring body.

Then everything started shaking again, even harder than before.

Dorn cast about to find out why. As he pivoted, he finally got another look at the earth drake. Still half in and half out of its burrow, the head partly severed, it was dead, and sealed in a mass of ice as well. Kara must have conjured the latter to plug the tunnel more effectively, and apparently it had worked. No other wyrms had driven through.

At the rear of the ossuary stood half a dozen of the monastery's resident priests and visiting wizards, chanting in concert. Though it had taken them some time to reach the battlefield, their intent was obvious. They meant to spark another earthquake to collapse the invading dragons' burrows.

Dorn thought it a good strategy, but it had one drawback. Even the most adroit spellcaster couldn't target such an effect with the same precision that an able swordsman could aim a thrust or cut. Which meant his allies might well collapse the ossuary, too.

"Pick up the wounded," Dorn shouted, "and clear out!"

He snatched up a dazed, bloodied, blistered monk, threw him over his shoulder, and hauled him toward the exit. His considerable strength notwithstanding, Raryn's short arms and legs made it awkward to carry anything as big as a human being, but he too managed to drag an injured man along. Kara shrank back into human form, perhaps to make it easier to flee through the cramped rooms, perhaps so the immensity of her dragon guise wouldn't block her comrades as they endeavored to retreat. Blood from her shoulder wounds began to soak her dress.

They and their comrades ran, while the floor rose in waves, threatening to trip them. As he scrambled into view of the doorway leading out of the ossuary, Dorn half-expected to see it jammed with terrified, madly struggling men. But the monks were too brave and disciplined for that, and just in case they weren't, Cantoule, the arm he'd used to strike the magma drake singed and blistered from fingertips to elbow, lingered there to make sure folk passed through one at a time, in good order.

Once they made it out of the ossuary and withdrew a few yards down the corridor, the tremors felt less violent. Dorn inspected the walls and ceiling, then looked down at Raryn.

"Have we fallen back far enough?" the half-golem asked. "Will this section of the tunnel hold?"

Raryn, who bore genuine blisters on the brick-red cheeks and forehead that always looked painfully sunburned, smiled a crooked smile and replied, "I told you, partner, I'm not that kind of dwarf. Someone else will have to judge how sturdy the stonework is."

With a deafening rumbling and crashing, the ossuary collapsed. Dust burst from the entrance like another blast of dragon breath, followed instantly by a surge of rubble. But the corridor didn't cave in, and after another moment, the tremors stopped.

One of the younger monks gave a cheer. Dorn kept staring at the spill of broken brick and bone, and the sections of wall around it. He maintained his watch for another minute before concluding that, in fact, no dragons were going to come exploding out of the ruined ossuary. Probably, when the earthquake started, they'd fled back down their burrows to safety.

He turned to Kara, to gauge how serious her cuts were, and to see if, in the aftermath of the violence, frenzy was gnawing at her reason. Sensing his concern, she gave him a reassuring smile.

"I'm fine," she said. "I just need healing."

She started to turn away, toward the priests who'd already started ministering to the wounded.

"I'll come with you," said Dorn.

"No! I mean, you don't need to."

From that, he knew the combat had stirred the monstrous urges and appetites of the Rage, and she didn't want him to glimpse the shameful madness seething inside her. But it appeared she had it under control, so he reluctantly allowed her to hurry away by herself.

Cantoule murmured a prayer or mantra, and the burns on his arm began to fade, leaving patches of smooth skin paler than his dark tan.

"That was close," he said.

"I should have guessed the wyrms would try tunneling," Dorn said.

" 'That's self-pity talking, and it isn't helping you or anyone else.' "

Dorn surprised himself by smiling. It made the human side of his face hurt, and he realized that he, too, was burned to some degree.

"I mean it," Cantoule said. "Nobody's infallible. The dragons would have slaughtered us all tendays ago if it weren't for you and Raryn."

"They would have butchered us today if you hadn't killed the magma drake. With your empty hand no less. I can't believe this Kane you so admire could have done any better."

"Ilmater lent me his strength. To him belongs the glory." Then Cantoule grinned a grin that, just for a moment, made him look as boyish as the youngest of the novices in his charge. "It was a nice technique, though, wasn't it?"

The Monastery of the Yellow Rose was so huge that, even after the dragons had spent two days demolishing portions of it, plenty of spacious halls, chapels, and galleries remained. The majority of the wyrms, many of whom customarily laired in caves and ruins, had accordingly chosen to quarter themselves indoors, and Chatulio was glad. When everyone had camped on the mountain, out in the open air, he'd worried that someone would grow curious about the black who kept drifting from one clique of dragons to the next. With walls obscuring his movements, spreading suspicion and rancor was somewhat less dangerous, though he would have persisted no matter how great the risk.

The Rage was sinking its talons into him once again, alternately manifesting itself as an urge to attack Sammaster's minions and as an almost uncontrollable need to laugh when a gullible chromatic swallowed one of his lies. He wanted to see his labors bear fruit before his reason crumbled.

So he whispered, insinuated, and aspersed through the night. Following the failure of the day's assault, the wyrms were in a vile humor and eager to believe any calmuny. The only drakes he stayed clear of were Malazan and Ishenalyr. He feared that they, the most powerful, would see through his illusory disguise, or failing that, recognize his true intentions. But with luck, other dragons would repeat his lies to both the red and the hidecarved green.

Just after dawn, Malazan roared, summoning everyone forth from his repose. Her call led her underlings to a garden, still bright and fragrant with gold, crimson, and purple flowers despite all the trampling it had endured. It was one of the few places in the stronghold spacious enough to hold the entire horde comfortably.

Malazan perched on the roof of a shrine with a marble statue of Ilmater, complete with scars and twisted limbs, inside. The structure was only barely large enough to support her. Those wyrms who obeyed her not merely out of fear but because they trusted her leadership congregated around her. Many were reds and fire drakes.

Ishenalyr took up a position at the opposite end of the garden, and those who wished he were commander assembled around him. Most were other greens and the like, wyrms whose essential natures partook of earth and stone instead of flame.

A third group of dragons stood apart from the other two. These were drakes who hadn't chosen a side, and as Chatulio hurried to join them, he was pleased to see they numbered only a few.

"It is time to speak," said Malazan without preamble, "of stupidity, cowardice, and disloyalty."

Ishenalyr snorted, masking the scent of the flowers with the sharp smell of his acidic breath.

"By all means," said the green, "let's speak of stupidity. Of war captains devoid of cunning."

Malazan's throat swelled with the threat of fire and she said, "It was your witless suggestion to tunnel into the mountain."

"It nearly worked. It did work as well as the series of frontal assaults you ordered, exactly where the humans expected us to come . . . where they built their ramparts and laid their snares."

"My way enables us to bring more of our strength to bear at once. It's pushing the monks deeper and deeper into the vaults. Soon they'll have nowhere left to retreat. Soon we'll reach the books Sammaster wants destroyed, and we will have won."

"How many of us will die in the meantime?"

"Three of us perished today, attempting your scheme, and I notice that one was the magma drake, and the other, a red."

"What are you implying?"

"That as usual, you and your kind hold back, and leave the dragons of flame to bear the brunt of the fighting."

"Nonsense," Ishenalyr said. "It was just bad luck the red didn't make it out of the tunnel before it collapsed. Either that, or he was a weakling."

The dragons massed around Malazan bristled.

Looking at all those glaring eyes and bared fangs, Ishenalyr belatedly recalled the prudence for which he was known.

"Great lady," he said, "this squabbling accomplishes nothing. You're the leader. I've never disputed that. I simply sought to aid our campaign by devising a new tactic. If our best diggers had survived, I might suggest we try it again, but as it stands, the point is moot. Instead of casting recriminations, why don't we consider our next move?"

"You'd like that, wouldn't you?" Malazan replied. "To grovel to my face, only to resume conspiring against me as soon as my back is turned."

The green rolled his eyes. "What do you require of me, then? How can I convince you your apprehensions are groundless?"

Malazan sneered. "If you mean what you say, give me your submission. Open your mind and spirit to me, and let me bind them with enchantment."

It was the turn of Ishenalyr and his faction to glower, hiss, and dig their talons restlessly in the turf.

"You can't be serious," the hidecarved said. "No wyrm would permit another to so enslave him."

"You will," said Malazan, "or you'll leave this place. But if you forsake our endeavor, you'll forfeit your hopes of becoming a dracolich. Sammaster's lackeys will never transform a deserter."

"I think," said the green, "that I'll have to avail myself of another option: to slay you. Sammaster won't care who leads our force to victory. He'll reward me as readily as you."

Malazan laughed, and a glaze of blood seeped across her deep red scales.

"So be it, then," said the great red dragon. "I'd hoped to put off killing you for a while longer. I thought you could be useful in your way. But oh, how I've yearned for the moment when I could finally burn away your insolence."

With a crack, she unfurled her gigantic wings, casting much of the garden into shadow, and leaped into the air. Ishenalyr took flight a split second later.

Chatulio studied the wyrms who'd given their allegiance to either the colossal red or her rune-scarred rival. If only they'd follow their chieftains' lead and fight each other, it might mean the salvation of the monastery.

For a moment, as they crouched, showed their fangs, spread their wings, it looked as if it was going to happen. Then one of the uncommitted wyrms, a spurred and fork-tailed fang dragon, flapped its stubby wings and leaped between the two factions.

"No!" it snarled. "There's no need for all of us to battle. Malazan and Ishenalyr will settle the issue, one way or the other."

The other reptiles hesitated, then, warily, a bit at a time, abandoned their aggressive postures.

Chatulio felt a bitter disappointment, which threatened to warp into fury, into an overwhelming need to assault the fang wyrm. Shivering, struggling to quell the anger, he gazed upward at the aerial duel.

Malazan and Ishenalyr climbed, wheeled, and snarled incantations. Magic droned through the air, and a web of glowing red strands shimmered into existence around the hidecarved's body, tangling and constricting his wings. He plummeted.

But not far. He abandoned the half-completed spell he'd been reciting to rattle off a different word of power, whereupon his fall slowed to a gentle drift downward, as if he were no heavier than dandelion fluff. He thrashed, squirmed, and wriggled his head and neck free of the luminous scarlet strands.

Malazan roared, swooped over him, and spewed her flaming breath as she streaked past. Chatulio could feel the heat of the flare even from the ground, and winced in involuntary sympathy. It seemed impossible that Ishenalyr or any other creature could survive such a devastating attack.

But the green did endure, and twisting his neck, responded with a blast of his own toxic, corrosive breath weapon. The plume of vapor washed over the underside of Malazan's body, and after she passed, Chatulio saw that Ishenalyr was unscathed. Some enchantment, or power granted him by his hidecarved mysteries, evidently rendered him impervious to his enemy's fire. Malazan, conversely, bore burns on her belly, legs, wings, and tail. The shock of having been wounded made her momentarily clumsy as she wheeled and climbed.

Ishenalyr heaved himself clear of the net of light, beat his wings, and rattled off another incantation. Rain hammered down from the empty air above Malazan, and she roared at the searing acidic barrage before swooping clear.

She hurtled at Ishenalyr, plainly trying to close with him and bring her fangs and talons to bear. The green fled before her, leading her out over the shining whiteness of the glacier.

His voice faint with distance, Ishenalyr snarled a rhyming spell with which Chatulio was unfamiliar. It made something happen—the copper felt magic prickle over his scales—but he couldn't tell what.

Meanwhile, Malazan declaimed her own incantation. The wispy cirrus clouds streaking the sky grumbled and flickered in sympathy with the spell, just as if they were thunderheads. Plainly, if the red couldn't burn her foe with fire, she meant to do it with lightning.

But when the dazzling, twisting bolt leaped into being, it didn't blast across the intervening distance to strike Ishenalyr. Originating a yard or two in front of Malazan's jaws, it stabbed backward to blaze though her head and down the length of her body, illuminating her from inside like a paper lantern, casting the shadows of her bones. As she convulsed, Chatulio surmised that Ishenalyr's most recent charm had been magic devised to turn an attack spell back on its caster.

For a moment or two, Malazan's wings beat spastically, out of time with one another, and she lost altitude before she managed to level off. Ishenalyr wheeled, flew over her, and spat his smoky breath weapon.

The fumes washed over her mask, charring her crimson scales, and she screeched in pain. But then she gave chase, and when Ishenalyr veered, she compensated. Evidently she'd squinched her featureless, radiant yellow eyes shut in time to save her sight.

But, Chatulio wondered, did it matter? Malazan had sustained ghastly injuries, and had yet to score on her opponent.

Above the monastery, Ishenalyr wheeled back around toward his pursuer. He'd decided it was time for another attack. Malazan's throat swelled. She cocked her head in the manner of a drake intending to use a breath weapon.

Chatulio wondered if injury and rage had so addled her she no longer recalled that her flame was useless against the hidecarved. Then, a trickster himself, he sensed that she was trying to outfox her adversary.

Shrewd and wary as he was, Ishenalyr should have sensed it as well. But red dragons had the power to tamper with an enemy's mind, and perhaps she employed that ability as, leathery, purple-edged wings pounding, she hurtled closer. Or maybe, after hurting Malazan so badly while coming off entirely unscathed himself, the hidecarved felt too utterly in control to imagine she might still pose a threat. In any case, it was obvious from the way he slowed, simply floating on the wind, that he was inviting her assault. He wanted to draw her close so he could land a particularly devastating riposte.

Malazan spat her flame. It crackled over Ishenalyr's serpentine body, and he howled in shock. At some point, the red had surreptitiously cast a spell to invest her breath with some crippling power in addition to its heat.

Ishenalyr still didn't look hurt, though, merely stunned and shaken. He raised one wing high and tipped the other low, veering off, trying to distance himself from Malazan until he could recover his composure.

With a sudden burst of speed, the like of which she hadn't exhibited hitherto—had she also cast a charm to make herself fly faster?—the gigantic red streaked after her foe and plunged her talons into his body. Clinging to him, she seized the root of one emerald wing in her jaws, bit down, and sheared the limb away from the hidecarved's shoulder.

Tangled together, ripping at one another, they dropped. Malazan beat her wings in an effort to slow their descent. They slammed down on the apex of a peaked roof with a prodigious crash, tumbled down the side, and fell on to the ground.

The duelists sprang to their feet and assailed one another with tooth and claw. As they struck and scrabbled, Ishenalyr's wounds began to heal, new scaly jade hide sealing over the gashes and stanching the flow of blood.

Chatulio thought that, Malazan's superior strength and size notwithstanding, the hidecarved, with his regenerative capabilities, still possessed the advantage. Eventually he was going to wear the red down, especially since she was still suspceptible to his occasional blast of searing, poisonous breath.

But no matter how he tore and burned her, Malazan wouldn't fall, wouldn't stop lunging at him. She shredded his mask and neck, he healed them, and she did it again. The cuts began to close once more.

Malazan lunged. Chatulio realized the red had discerned that her foe had to concentrate briefly to mend his hurts, and during that instant, he was slower. Vulnerable. Catching the base of his neck in her jaws, she heaved him onto his back, sprang onto his chest, held him pinned with her forefeet, and clawed with the back ones, flinging chunks of bloody flesh and lengths of broken rib.

She plunged her head into the enormous wound she'd created. When she lifted it, she clasped Ishenalyr's heart in her fangs. She turned, displaying it to all the assembled dragons, then chewed it to rags and swallowed it down.

"I lead here!" she bellowed. "I, Malazan! Who disputes me?"

The other wyrms lowered their heads in submission. All of them but Chatulio.

He knew he ought to do the same. But really, Malazan just looked too ridiculous, striking imperious poses while burned to a crisp and sliced to ribbons. Snickering welled up in his throat. He tried to hold it in, but to no avail. In another moment, he was shrieking with laughter.

Other dragons stared at him in amazement. Abandoning Ishenalyr's corpse, Malazan glided forward. Was anger still making her sweat gore? Her wounds were bleeding so profusely, it was impossible to tell. For some reason, that seemed funny, too, and Chatulio guffawed, not trying to hold the mirth in anymore. It was too late anyway.

"Reveal yourself," Malazan hissed, and the words wormed their way into his mind.

For a moment, it seemed natural to do as she asked, and he dissolved his skull wyrm disguise.

"A copper!" someone snarled.

"Not just any copper," Chatulio replied. "The copper who manufactured the feud that divided your force. I was hoping all you idiot newts would slaughter each other, but I'll settle for what I got."

He whirled, spitting his breath on the nearest wyrms to make them sluggish, spread his wings, and sprang into the air. He knew he couldn't escape, but that was no reason not to make them work for the kill.

Malazan snarled words of power. Another glowing net sprang into existence around Chatulio, binding his wings. He fell back to earth, and the chromatics stalked toward him.

Perhaps he could have managed one one more blast of his breath, or a swipe of his talons, before the end, but he realized he could put the time to better use. He rattled off a spell, and the entire mountaintop rang with peals of disembodied laughter, to mock his enemies as they ripped him apart.

When Kara heard the disembodied laughter, she quickly surmised it had something to do with the vanished Chatulio. The bright gods knew, he was the one person of her acquaintance who could see something comical in every situation, even a nightmare like the siege.

The echoing sound led her upward through the cellars before it faded to silence. Since she didn't encounter the copper along the way, nor anyone who had, she wondered if the laughter had actually originated out under the open sky.

It was difficult to see how, though. The attacking wyrms were in possession of the mountaintop. Chatulio would have had better sense than to fly into the midst of them, wouldn't he?

Perhaps not, if frenzy had consumed his mind, and she suspected that fear of such a calamity was what had prompted him to run away, so he wouldn't harm his friends. She hurried to the narrow spiral staircase Raryn used to sneak up and scout the surface. The shaft was too cramped for any of the evil dragons to negotiate, and so far as the defenders could tell, their foes hadn't even noticed the steps where they rose to their summit in one of the monastery's outbuildings.

She found Dorn and Raryn at the lower terminus of the stairs. Grimy, bruised, and haggard, the half-golem was fully armed. Apparently he'd been standing watch. Raryn had his ice-axe, but not his bow, white fur-covered armor, or the rest of his gear. He'd probably been off duty, and come running without taking the time to equip himself in full.

Dorn frowned when he saw Kara.

"You're not coming," he said.

"I am," she replied.

"If you get yourself killed up top, who'll pull the old elves' secrets out of the archives?"

"I fight the chromatics when they make an assault."

"That's necessary. This isn't."

"It is for me. Chatulio is my friend."

Raryn looked up at Dorn. "You aren't going to change her mind," said the burly dwarf.

Dorn grunted. "Then let's get this done."

As they climbed the stairs, Raryn leading, Dorn following, and Kara bringing up the rear, she strained her senses for any warning sign that they were headed into a trap. She didn't detect any, but she did hear snarling, and smell the tang of blood. Because of the Rage, the odor made her head swim, her mouth water, and her guts twist with self-loathing.

Nothing lay in wait for them in the outbuilding. Like the rest of the structures comprising the monastery, it was a fine example of the stonemason's craft, pleasingly shaped of creamy stone and adorned with intricate round stained glass windows, even though it was, in its essence, simply a gardener's shed, with hoes and pruning shears hanging on pegs, flowerpots stacked in the corner, and sacks of fertilizer tingeing the air with a dungy scent. Still struggling against frenzy, Kara wished the stink was potent enough to mask the unsettling, arousing aroma of gore.

She and her companions crept to the doorway and peeked out. She caught her breath. The growling came from several dragons devouring the body of another. So eager were the wyrms to rip their meal apart and gobble down the shreds that much of it was already unrecognizable. But Kara could still make out some coppery scales glinting in the sunlight.

Fury swelled inside her. She hated the chromatics for desecrating the body of her friend, almost as much as she despised herself for craving a portion of the feast. She had to make Sammaster's minions pay for the atrocity. She focused her mind to trigger the shift from human to draconic form.

Somehow—perhaps he noticed a change in her posture—Dorn sensed her intent, took her by the forearm, and turned her around to look her in the eyes.

"No," he whispered.

For an instant, she fully intended to strike him down for interfering with him, but then resentment gave way to shame.

"I'm sorry," she said.

"It's all right," Dorn replied, gruff and awkward as always when trying to give comfort or reassurance.

"The madness is so close to the surface now," she said, "all the time."

"You'll beat it," he said.

"Look beyond Chatulio," Raryn murmured.

She tried. The knot of squirming, lunging dragons in the foreground largely blocked her view, but by craning and ducking, she caught a glimpse of the portion of the garden on the far side of them.

Torn by fang and claw, the immense hidecarved green lay dead on the ground. Nobody was eating him yet, perhaps because his slayer had reserved the body for herself. Said killer was surely the ancient red—Kara had heard her underlings call her Malazan—commanding the attacking force. Burned and blistered, nearly as mangled and bloody as her vanquished foe, she lay in a bed of purple blossoms. Two smaller dragons, who evidently possessed priestly powers, crawled around her, hissing charms to close her wounds and renew her strength.

"Now," said Raryn, "back down the stairs. We've lingered long enough."

When they reached the vaults, Kara said, "Somehow, Chatulio tricked Malazan and the green into dueling. I'm sure of it."

The dwarf nodded. "I think so, too, which means he won a victory before the enemy laid him low."

"He eliminated one of their two most powerful fighters," said Dorn, "and sorely hurt the other. Even with healers tending her, she won't be fit to lead another attack for a while. The copper bought us some extra time."

I'll make the time count, Kara thought. I promise you, Chatulio.

As if to mock her pledge, a picture of all the tomes and loose parchments she had still to examine—shelf upon shelf, rack upon rack, chamber after chamber—rose up unbidden in her mind.

TEN

15 Kythorn, the Year of Rogue Dragons

In Thar, the infrequent trees were runt-ish growths twisted and gnarled by the wind. Still, the specimen on the benighted hilltop was substantial enough to support the naked corpse of an orc. Dangling from rawhide lashings, its eye sockets emptied by some hungry bird, reeking like the carrion it was, the goblin kin with its piggish face bore multiple cuts on its chest and belly. No doubt one of them had been the death of it. Above the marks of combat, someone had carved a crude representation of a horned, leering face with crossed scimitars beneath. Pavel reckoned it was the emblem of a rival orc tribe, who'd likely killed the creature for entering their territory, then hung it there as a warning to other would-be trespassers.

"Well," said Will, "are we ready for this?"

He stood with his hand on the pommel of his horn-blade. They'd found the curved, enchanted hunting sword in the grip of a dead ogre, and Pavel's sun amulet among Yagoth's possessions, after the flight of greens moved on. In the priest's opinion, that was about the last piece of good fortune that had come their way.

In the time since the extermination of the ogre troupe, the two searchers had tried to make their way back toward Thentia, but without horses, progress was slow. Time and again, they had to deviate from their course to avoid marauding dragons, or encounters with orcs and giant-kin.

He wished he and Will had traveled in the company of one of Kara's rogues. How glorious it would be to soar straight out of that wasteland on the wings of a dragon. But the Great Gray Land was just to the north of Thentia. He'd never imagined it would be so difficult to journey from one to the other, and thus it had made sense to employ all their flying allies to explore more distant sites.

Finally, desperate to make some headway, he and the halfling had resolved to sneak across orc territory under cover of night. The problem, of course, was that goblin kin could see in the dark. But not as far as a man could see in the daylight, so it was possible the hunters' woodcraft would see them through.

"I'm ready," Pavel said.

"Want to cast a spell of silence?" asked Will.

Pavel shook his head. "If something's sneaking up on me, I want a chance of hearing it. I can creep quietly without enchantment helping me."

Will snorted. "You 'creep' like a three-legged ox, but have it your way. I'll lead. You keep ten paces behind me, unless I wave for you to close it up."

They skulked forward, keeping to high ground but not the crests of the low hills. They didn't want to silhouette themselves against the sky.

In that sky, Selûne and the stars floated unseen above a layer of cloud, though a bit of their light suffused through to keep the night from being entirely black. The wind whistled, colder than by day. It made Pavel's leg ache. Though Will had done a good job of straightening the limb, the priest walked with a slight hitch, and suspected he always would. Well, perhaps the ladies would think it heroic and therefore alluring.

He and Will skulked along for perhaps an hour. Then the one-time thief raised his hand signaling a halt, and scurried back to join his human comrade.

"What?" Pavel whispered.

"Orcs, I think. A hunting party, maybe. I can't see them yet, just hear them. They're over there—" he pointed—"and headed in this direction."

Pavel listened intently, and heard nothing but the moaning of the breeze. Still, he was sure Will was correct. The halfling's ears were keener than his.

"So we hide and wait for them to pass by?" Pavel asked.

"Yes." Will pulled the warsling from his belt. "And fight if they spot us. Come on."

They crouched behind a clump of brush. Heart beating faster, reviewing the spells he carried ready for the casting, Pavel kept trying to detect some sign of the approaching orcs. It came abruptly: a fierce baying, followed immediately by a clamor of brutish voices.

"You didn't tell me they had dogs," Pavel said.

"I didn't know," Will said. "Until the beasts picked up our scent, they didn't make any noise. We're in for it, pretty boy. Try not to wet yourself."

He placed a stone in the pocket of his sling.

"Let me enchant that, you larcenous flea," said the cleric.

Pavel murmured a prayer, flourished his pendant, and touched it to the rock, which then glowed with a red-gold light. The halfling rose and let the stone fly.

When the glow illuminated the oncoming orcs and the several huge dogs bounding ahead of them, Pavel winced. Maybe, as Will had assumed, they'd set forth as a hunting party, but if so, it was a large and well-armed one. Pavel thought it more likely they were raiders who embarked at first to attack a neighboring clan, but then grew more intent on prey discovered closer to home.

Will slung a stone, and one of the hounds fell, its momentum tumbling it head over heels. Rattling off an incantation, Pavel thrust out his arm. A ray of light leaped from his hand to burn another dog to ash.

Javelins flew out of the dark. One of them missed Pavel by inches and made him yearn for his enchanted brigandine, damaged by the squamous spewers, then destroyed utterly when Yagoth tore away what remained.

He could conjure a form of magical armor for both Will and himself, but decided that before he attempted the spell, they needed to finish neutralizing the dogs. Big, shaggy brutes, the four who survived had nearly closed the distance separating them from their prey.

Will hurled stones and dropped two more. Pavel conjured tingling, crackling power into his hand. A rod of congealed crimson phosphorescence shimmered into being in his grasp. When a hound lunged into range, he snapped his arm as if he held the butt of a whip, and a lash of red lightning blazed into being to strike the canine. The dog convulsed and collapsed, stinking of burned meat.

The remaining beast sprang in, and Pavel had to leap aside to avoid its slavering jaws. He lashed it with the sizzling whip, and it too went down.

The orcs charged.

Will hurled more stones. Pavel chanted, brandishing his amulet. When it glowed red-gold, he touched it to the halfling's shoulder. The light leaped to Will's body to surround him with a shimmering aura that would help deflect a blade. Pavel just had time to repeat the operation and provide himself with the same protection before the first orcs scrambled into striking distance.

Pavel and Will fought back to back, so no foe could attack either from behind. The lightning whip would last a few more heartbeats before the spell ran out of power, so for the time being, the priest struck with that, using the mace in his off hand as a shield to bat away thrusting spear points and slashing scimitars.

He killed one foe, then another. He assumed Will was faring at least as well. But more orcs kept coming, swarming around them, and he wondered if he and the halfling would be overwhelmed. What a bitter joke it would be if they, who'd survived encounters with scores of creatures commonly accounted more dangerous, fell to goblin kin.

As he battled on, he silently prayed to Lathander for succor. Until something swept over the combatants on the ground, momentarily blocking the moonlight that leaked through the clouds and plunging them all into deeper gloom.

A huge, dark, and bat-winged reptilian form slammed to earth, the impact jolting the hillside. Scarlet eyes shining like hot coals, it snatched up an orc in its jaws, the two elongated upper fangs toward the front of its maw piercing the goblin kin through. The wrongness, the unnatural corruption Pavel felt seething inside the dragon, made his guts clench.

"It's Brimstone!" Will exclaimed.

Since he wasn't a priest, he lacked Pavel's sensitivity to the undead, but he too had recognized the vampiric smoke drake—perhaps by the wyrm's stink of sulfur and ash.

Brimstone laid about himself, rending orcs with his talons and smashing them with his tail. For the time being, though, his jaws were occupied. He kept his first victim impaled on his longest fangs, and a nauseating sucking and slurping sounded from his mouth as he drained the goblin kin's blood.

The orcs screamed and fled, scattering in all directions. Plainly, they were no longer a threat, but Brimstone kept attacking them anyway, pouncing from one to the next like a dog in a ratting pit. After a time he spat out the bloodless corpse in his jaws, and apparently still thirsty, snatched up another swine-faced warrior in leather and mail.

By the time he drank the life from that one, all the orcs were either dead or had run far away. Brimstone pivoted, and the fiery light in his eyes dimming a little since the slaughter was through, gave Pavel and Will a sneer.

"Behold, priest," he said. "You pray to your god for deliverance, and I appear. Aren't you going to thank me?"

Taegan floated on the wind, above the lights of Thentia, and when the air currents carried him south of the town, the black expanse of the Moonsea. From time to time, luminous, translucent phantasms wavered into view around him, then faded out again. For the most part, they were representations of the local wizards, their images in full or just their faces painted large. The show was supposed to make him look like a seer using "avariel wizardry, the secret magic of the sky" to search for the identity of the traitor.

The truth, of course, was otherwise. Hovering near him, shrouded in invisibility, Jivex cast illusions to create the spectacle. With luck, Sammaster's agent saw the lights flickering in the night sky, and they'd provoke him into making an attack.

That was assuming Taegan hadn't already demonstrated the hollowness of his threat to unmask the wretch by erroneously proclaiming his innocence. Two days ago, to keep the pressure on, the bladesinger had announced the names of four more magicians whose loyalty he'd supposedly established beyond question. According to Rilitar, the folk in question were spellcasters of comparatively modest abilities, lacking the arcane might to operate as Sammaster's agent did, but it was impossible to be sure. After all his prying and pondering, Taegan still wasn't certain of anything.

Hence the need to draw the enemy out, dangerous though the tactic was. Rilitar had wanted to stand guard over Taegan as he attempted it, but the bladesinger had deemed it a bad idea. Invisible or not, the more folk who lurked in his vicinity, the more likely it was that the traitor or his minions would somehow detect their presence. Accordingly, when

Phourkyn had asked the elf wizard to meet with him to discuss some esoterica one of Kara's rogues had discovered etched on a ceremonial anvil in a long-deserted dwarven stronghold, Taegan had insisted that he go.

The avariel was carrying a pair of charms that Rilitar had prepared for him, however. One was a silver ring imbued with magic that gave the wearer the ability to see the invisible. Thus, he perceived Jivex as clearly as ever, and as the faerie dragon cast the glowing semblance of Firefingers's grandfatherly countenance against the dark, he abruptly glimpsed the chasme as well.

The fly-thing surged into view progressively from proboscis to rump as its body penetrated the effective area of the enchantment. It was diving from on high, out of the glittering haze of Selûne's Tears, and had quenched its halo of flame. Perhaps it didn't know how to make the blaze invisible.

Since Taegan had spotted the danger, the other charm Rilitar had given him, a golden brooch cast in the form of an eye, had presumably detected it, too, and was sending a psychic signal to its maker. The elf would rush to the scene of the confrontation as soon as his magic could carry him there. Meanwhile, Taegan simply went on hovering as if nothing was wrong, luring the chasme into striking range.

It snarled, leveled off out of its dive, and wheeled, putting distance between itself and its foe. Its shroud of flame erupted around it, drawing a hiss from Jivex, who hadn't been aware of its presence until that instant. Somehow the demon realized Taegan had spotted it.

The bladesinger gave chase, and so did Jivex. Taegan rattled off the spell to augment their speed. As the magic jolted through his muscles, he wondered what was keeping Rilitar, who represented the best hope of defeating the tanar'ri's power of instantaneous travel.

The chasme swooped low, over the spires and peaked roofs of the town. Just as it began a tight turn, Jivex stared at it intently, and slipped a bit of his natural magic past the tanar'ri's natural resistances. A layer of powder spread across the chasme's long-nosed caricature of a human face, sealing its eyes. Startled and blind, it swung too wide and smashed into a conical spire, then dropped to the rooftop below, where it lay unmoving.

Taegan and Jivex raced on to the rooftop, where the bladesinger landed. Any swordsman, even an avariel, struck hardest with his feet planed. Pinions spread for balance on the treacherous incline, he advanced on his motionless foe. Butterfly wings a glimmering blur, Jivex streaked along beside him.

The chasme vanished. Taegan cursed. He assumed the demon had recovered its wits and translated itself to a different location, but Jivex thought otherwise.

"It was an illusion!" the dragon snarled. Perhaps, as a being adept at creating such mirages himself, he'd belatedly recognized a phantom for what it was.

In any case, the purpose of the glamour could only have been to lead him and Taegan where the chasme wanted them to go. The bladesinger poised his wings to propel him back into the air.

The rooftop split open beneath him, and his feet plunged through. The shingle-covered planks snapped shut, stabbing jagged wood into his ankles, holding him fast like fanged jaws. He cried out at the shock.

Wings buzzing, the chasme—the real one, presumably—clambered over the apex of the pitched roof of a neighboring house. Jivex oriented on the tanar'ri, but hesitated for an instant as if uncertain whether to engage the demon or help Taegan free himself. It gave the chasme time to target the faerie dragon with a spell.

Jivex's flickering wings—and the rest of his body—abruptly stopped moving. He dropped from the air and rolled down the roof, nearly dropping off the edge before he came to rest. He trembled as he struggled vainly to overcome the magically induced paralysis.

Heedless of the pain it caused him, Taegan strained to drag his feet from the crack. When that didn't work, he started quickly reciting his spell of translocation.

The air around him darkened. Locusts swarmed all over him, crawling inside his clothing, biting him, cutting off his air. Startled, repulsed, he stumbled over the cadence of his incantation, and the magic failed.

Unable to see what he was doing, he hacked at the trap of wood securing his feet, but failed to free himself. With his off hand he flailed at the locusts, but that too accomplished nothing.

He wished again that Rilitar would come, but realized the wizard never would. Somehow the chasme had detected and neutralized the talisman that was supposed to summon him.

The locusts bit again and again. Each attack was little more than a pin prick, but in the aggregate, the effect was crippling. As consciousness began to slip away, Taegan felt a bitter anger, directed primarily at himself, that he'd been so thoroughly outwitted and outplayed.

Pavel wondered how Brimstone could tell that he'd prayed to the Morninglord for succor, but he was reluctant to ask, or to give the vampiric drake the satisfaction of responding to his taunt in any other way.

Instead, he said, "What do you want?"

Brimstone snorted, thickening the smell of smoke that surrounded him, and answered, "What I've always wanted: to defeat Sammaster. I told you I'd emerge from seclusion when I deemed it necessary."

So he had. But the priest had doubted the promise, and not just because, of all of Kara's allies, Brimstone was the strangest and by far the most sinister. Bound to the purifying sun, every cleric of Lathander despised the undead, and in the normal run of things, did his utmost to destroy them whenever they crossed his path.

"Something's different," murmured Will. "Make another light."

The glowing stone Pavel had enchanted previously lay somewhere behind the drake, which made it difficult to see him as anything more than a silhouette.

Pavel hesitated for a beat, then decided that, though they were still technically in hostile territory, the chances of any more orcs attacking while Brimstone was on the scene were minute. He recited the prayer, and ruddy light shined from the head of his mace.

The illumination revealed all the details Pavel recalled with such loathing, the serpentine form, charcoal-colored scales with their maroon highlights, and jet-black dorsal ridge. But it showed something new as well. A huge and seemingly flawless ruby gleamed at the center of a diamond-studded platinum collar encircling Brimstone's neck.

Will let out a whistle. "Nice," he said. "If you could see your way clear to part with that bauble, I wouldn't ask for any other payment."

It was a suggestion that glossed over the fact that Kara, not the vampire, was, in theory, the hunters' employer, though they'd long since passed the point where coin was their principal reason for helping her.

Brimstone showed his fangs, and his eyes burned brighter.

"I suggest you spare me your impudence, halfling, considering that I have no need of you. It's the sun priest I require."

Pavel frowned and asked, "Require for what?"

"To accompany me into Damara."

"That's out of the question. Our errand was a success. We've learned something important, and we have to get back to Thentia to tell Firefingers and the other mages."

"You'll report your discovery in due course. First, you must assist me. Otherwise, our cause will fail."

"I guess you'd better tell us about it," said Will. He pulled up a handful of coarse grass and used it to wipe orc blood from his hornblade.

"As you'll recall," said Brimstone, "I'm a scrier, and of late, I've used the ability to keep track of events throughout the North. Thus, I know that disaster has overtaken Damara."

Pavel felt a pang of dismay. "What's wrong? Have dragon flights ravaged the realm?"

"No. Or rather, Damara has suffered such assaults, but that's not the greatest danger threatening it. The giants and goblin kin of Vaasa have once again overrun your homeland."

"Impossible. The Gates hold them back, and if they somehow circumvented them, Dragonsbane and his army would crush them."

"The Gates and the king alike have fallen to treachery. Most people believe Gareth Dragonsbane is dead, and nobody else can persuade the barons to fight as one. Every petty lord seeks to protect his own holdings. But they can't survive that way. The Vaasans are sweeping all before them."

Will eyed the smoke drake and said, "It almost sounds like you care, but I can't figure out why."

Brimstone sneered. "I shed no tears for slaughtered shepherds or farmwives raped to death. But Karasendrieth and her agents have many sites to explore in Damara. If the country is crawling with giants and goblins, it will be impossible."

Pavel shook his head, trying to assimilate what Brimstone had told him. Like most Damarans, he'd grown up thinking of Dragonsbane as an invincible hero, almost a demigod. It was nearly impossible to believe that anyone or anything could vanquish the paladin monarch, or destroy Damara's hard-won freedom, peace, and prosperity in a matter of tendays. Yet, profoundly as Pavel mistrusted the vampire, it was difficult to see why Brimstone would lie about such matters. What would he have to gain?

"You said," observed the priest, "that the majority of folk believe the king is dead. Does that mean he isn't?"

"Yes," said Brimstone. "I hope you have wit enough to

realize it isn't a coincidence that the creatures of Vaasa invaded at this time. Sammaster stirred them up to cover his tracks, and agents of the Cult of the Dragon, positioned close to the king, struck Dragonsbane down with a spell that sundered his soul from his body. Fortunately, I learned the same enchantment during the time I made common cause with the lich."

"So I'm guessing you know how to lift the curse," said Will. "Good. But how does the charlatan here come into it?"

"I think I know," said Pavel, "assuming he's telling the truth. Brimstone needs to get close to the king to cast the counterspell. But Dragonsbane is a champion of the bright powers, and his officers are as devout as he. They'd never permit an undead to approach their master in the hour of his infirmity. Except that the wyrm believes that if I, a Damaran born and a servant of Lathander, vouch for him, they may allow it after all."

"Yes," said Brimstone. "This is why I scried for you and sought you out. If you're willing to help, climb onto my back and let's be gone while we still have some hours of darkness left. My wings will carry us swiftly, but I can't fly by day."

"I need a moment," Pavel growled.

He turned and stalked a few paces down the hillside, and Will trotted after him.

"Is there a problem?" the halfling whispered. "Don't you believe him?"

Pavel sighed. "That's the problem. I think I do. Which means spending days in his company . . . touching his undead flesh as he bears us northward. It will grind at me."

"We got used to traveling with ogres, and their personal habits were pretty disgusting."

"For a priest of the Morninglord, this will be infinitely worse."

"Don't give yourself airs. It's not like you're much of a priest."

Pavel chuckled. "Well, perhaps it won't be so unbearable at that. After all, I tolerate your hideous face, boundless stupidity, and myriad other deficiencies. If I can do that, I should be able to endure anything."

"Then shall we go and mount our trusty steed?"

"Not quite yet. I want to tell you something first, about Brimstone's collar."

"Now you have my full attention."

"When we first met him, I speculated that he could never stray far from his hoard, that he was bound to it as a common vampire's tied to its grave or coffin. I still believe that's true."

"Then how did he fly all the way from Impiltur to Thar?"

"I think he can travel because the choker's a talisman linking him to his treasure trove. On a mystical level, it is the entire hoard."

"So it sounds like I'm not going to be able to talk him into presenting it to me for services rendered."

"The point is that, this far from his cave, it's vital to his existence. If he ever turns on us, remember that."

❦

Taegan woke from a nightmare of locusts to a reality equally frightening and considerably more painful. He lay fettered spread-eagled atop a torturer's table in what appeared to be a shadowy cellar lit by a couple of smoky, guttering tallow candles. He hurt all over from the insect bites, but that stinging was nothing compared to the throbbing agony in his ankles where the spikes of wood had pierced him, ripping flesh and splintering bone.

He cast about for Jivex, and flinched when he saw him. Their captor apparently hadn't possessed any shackles sized to hold a faerie dragon, and had therefore restrained the reptile by stretching out his wings and nailing them to the wall. Jivex had countless bloody locust bites spotting his iridescent hide. His head dangled at the end of his long, flexible neck. He was unconscious, and perhaps that was a mercy.

Taegan heaved at the chains securing his wrists. The only effect was to drag his lacerated ankles against the metal cuffs encircling them. Despite himself, he gasped at the jolt of agony produced by the pressure.

Afterward, as he lay panting, footsteps clopped above his head. Perhaps he'd made sufficient noise to alert his captor to the fact that he'd awakened. He drew a deep breath, composing himself. A rake of Lyrabar was always dauntless and suave, even when caught at a disadvantage.

A pale figure descended the wooden stairs at the far end of the cellar. It shined as pale as a ghost in the gloom, though the steps groaned beneath its weight. Then Taegan blinked the tears of pain from his eyes and recognized that all the whiteness was simply the snowy, silver-trimmed attire clothing Darvin Kordeion's pudgy form.

"Bravo, Master Kordeion," the bladesinger said. "Could I rise, I would bow. Could I bring my palms together, I'd applaud."

Darvin scowled and cocked his head. "You're in no position to mock me."

"I assure you, derision is the farthest thing from my mind. It was cunning of you to draw Jivex and me into another snare, and more artful still to mute the call that would have summoned Master Shadow-water to our aid. But when you intuited that Jivex was once again trying to blind the chasme with his golden dust, incorporated the effect into your illusion, and used it to maneuver us to precisely where you wanted us, that was a little stroke of genius." Taegan smiled. "Or am I congratulating the wrong party? For it was the chasme the dragon and I were actually fighting. Does the demon make its own decisions in combat, or follow instructions given in advance? Or perhaps you control its actions from moment to moment, as if it were a rapier in your hand."

Darvin snorted. "Still trying to find out all about me?"

"I like to satisfy my curiosity whenever possible. Particularly when it could be the last morsel of pleasure ever to come my way."

"That's unfortunate, because I'm the one who's going to ask the questions."

The wizard advanced to the table. Up close, he smelled of some sweetish soap, perfume, or unguent. He lifted his hands. On the middle finger of each was a steel ring with a little barbed point on the inside. When he clasped Taegan's head between his palms, the blades pierced his temples.

It was only a little sting, but Taegan could somehow sense the magic burning inside the steel. He was certain the rings had the power to do something to him. Probably something hideous.

"Now," said Darvin, "tell me about this avariel divination you claim to practice. Was it truly yielding information that eventually would have identified me as Sammaster's ally?"

Taegan intended to say that yes, given a little more time, his mysterious powers would indeed have unmasked Darvin. At that point, he didn't know what good the lie would do, but one deceived an adversary whenever possible. Then, however, the magic in the rings pulsed, creating a startling sensation of warmth inside his head.

"No," he said. "I'm no seer. It was merely a pretense, to draw you—or at least the chasme—out of hiding. Master Shadow-water hoped that if I killed the fly, something of its essence would cling to my sword, and that in turn could be used to discover your identity. If not, we still would have deprived you of your weapon of choice."

Taegan understood: The rings compelled him to tell the truth. He supposed it could have been worse—he'd assumed they were instruments of torture—but he dreaded the coercion nonetheless, dreaded where it might lead. Though that probably didn't matter either.

Darvin scowled in manifest disgust at having been taken in.

"Please," Taegan said, his voice honeyed with false sympathy, "don't feel badly. You out-tricked me in the end."

"Yes," said the human with his round, pink face, "I did, and whether you practice divination or not, it's worth the effort to be rid of you. Firefingers and the other fools didn't even realize they had a traitor among them until you showed up to warn them."

"Before you do something irreversible to me, may I point out that I possess a fortune in jewels. It's yours if you spare me, and should suffice to buy you any life you care to lead. I daresay it'll be superior to the existence Sammaster promises, lording it over your fellow men but groveling before dracoliches."

Darvin sneered. "You understand nothing. Nothing at all."

Well, Taegan thought, that isn't quite true.

"But you needn't worry," the magician continued. "You won't die tonight. I'm going to feed you and the drake restorative elixirs to heal your hurts, give you a pair of boots to replace the ones I ruined, and teach you a new spell before I release you."

Taegan grinned. "How chivalrous. I sensed that underneath it all, you possess a gallant heart."

Darvin shook his head. "As I said, Maestro, you truly comprehend nothing. You and your comrade will leave here as my slaves, your wills shackled, though you'll have no memory of encountering the chasme, or me, tonight. You'll go about your business as before. But the next time Karasendrieth or one of the other rogues pays a visit, and we wizards assemble to hear what the dragon has discovered, you'll recite the incantation I'm going to teach you."

Taegan felt a chill. He did his best to keep dismay out of his voice when he said, "The words of power that thrust a wyrm into full-blown frenzy."

"Exactly. When the Rage erupts in his mind, your Jivex may run amok as well, slipping from my control. But you won't, and you'll have more work to do. As the drakes attack, in the confusion, you'll murder Firefingers, then Rilitar, then Scattercloak, then any other magician you can reach. Except me, of course. You'll keep on killing until someone slays you in your turn. Having witnessed your prowess in battle, I think you may commit considerable mayhem before you expire."

Taegan inclined his head. "You flatter me."

Darvin glared as if irked by the bladesinger's refusal to evince any distress at the ghastly picture he was painting.

"You understand what it will mean. More mages butchered. Another deranged dragon slaughtering humans in the heart of Thentia. The meddler who promised to keep everyone safe revealed as an enemy himself."

"Alas, no," Taegan said. "Someone will realize I was acting under magical duress. How could I be the Cult of the Dragon's agent? I wasn't even in Thentia when the first murder occurred."

"Who's to say when you actually sneaked into town? In retrospect, it will seem telling that you were in the workroom when Samdralyrion went mad."

"If you'll recall, I fought the brass, as I fought to save Rilitar and Sinylla."

"You failed to protect the latter. Maybe you were merely putting on a show." Darvin smiled unpleasantly. "It comes down to this: The wizards will see you turn on them. Afterward, assuming any survive, they'll be too full of horror and grief to think any deeper than that.

"In any case," the man in white continued, "convincing everyone you were Sammaster's ally all along, convenient as it will be for me, is merely a side benefit. The true objective is to eliminate the most learned wizards, demoralize any who remain, and motivate the Watchlord to command us to suspend our investigations. After that, it won't matter what lore Karasendrieth and her friends unearth in ancient crypts. They won't have anybody to interpret the information."

"It's an interesting strategy," said Taegan, then he bucked, tearing the barbed points out of his skin, throwing his weight against his fetters, hoping the chains would at last break away from the wood.

But they didn't, and Darvin simply caught hold of his head once more, jabbing the steel points back into his brow. Heat flowered inside Taegan's skull, and he went limp.

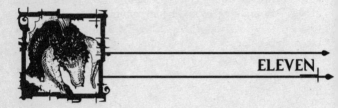

ELEVEN

25-26 Kythorn, the Year of Rogue Dragons

Kovor Gemetsk straightened Pavel's red and yellow vestments, then stepped back to inspect the result. Will hooted.

"It'll take more than that to make him respectable," the halfling said. "You'll have to do something about the slack-jawed look of imbecility."

The stooped old priest with his bald, spotted pate, Pavel's mentor from the beginning of his novitiate until the day he departed his temple forever—or so he'd imagined—made a sour face at the gibe. "The truth is, the robes aren't draping properly."

"I'm not used to such clothing anymore,' Pavel replied. "But glories of the sunrise, does it matter how I look? I've come bringing help in a time of crisis."

"It always matters what kind of impression a person creates at Court," said Kovor, "at least if he wants anyone to pay attention to him. Particularly 'in a time of crisis.' "

Pavel felt his nervous irritability twist into a twinge of shame. He owed his former master far too much to grouse at him.

Kovor's most recent kindness had been to arrange an audience with the queen for his long-lost protégé, and flying across Damara, even by night, had convinced Pavel just how urgently he needed to speak with her. Fires dotted the ground below as the Vaasan horde plundered, and burned whatever they didn't covet or couldn't stuff into their sacks. Cries rose up to grieve him, brutish voices howling with glee and human ones wailing in anguish. It seemed that only Heliogabalus, the royal city itself, remained unscarred by marauders. Maybe that was because a goodly number of troops still garrisoned the capital. Or perhaps the goblins hoped the absent "Zhengyi" would reemerge from the shadows to lead the assault.

The doors leading to the throne room, tall panels of polished green, red-speckled bloodstone that were plainly the product of enchantment, swung open, jarring Pavel from his broodings. A herald thumped the butt of a staff on the floor and announced, "Kovor Gemetsk, Patriarch of the Temple of the Dawn, Pavel Shemov, priest of the Morninglord, and Wilimac Turnstone, hunter."

The three advanced into a hall spacious enough to hold scores of petitioners. Paladins of the Order of the Golden Cup, armed with halberds and swords, stood guard along the walls. Gonfalons agleam with gems hung from the rafters, but by far the most impressive jewels were the two high-backed thrones, also sculpted from chalcedony, on the dais at the far end of the chamber. The larger of them—the king's—was vacant. Christine Dragonsbane, his queen, sat in the other. Half a dozen dignitaries clustered around the pedestal to attend her. With one exception, those gentlemen wore trappings indicating that they too were either paladins or clerics sworn to the service of the Crying God, and that was as Pavel expected it to be. Ilmater was Damara's principal deity.

Lathander too received a measure of the people's devotion, but not nearly as much.

The newcomers bowed, and held that posture until Christine bade them rise.

"Welcome," said the queen, a comely woman in her middle years with clear blue eyes and plaited auburn hair. With its upturned nose and dusting of freckles, her heart-shaped face seemed made for joy and laughter, but held only care and sorrow. She wore a brooch shaped like an oak leaf that, to Pavel's knowledgeable eye, revealed her to be an initiate in the druidic mysteries rather than a worshiper of Ilmater. "Master Shemov, Goodman Turnstone, you're both strangers to this hall. But Kovor vouches for you, and says you have important information to report. If so, then tell me, please."

"Yes, Your Majesty," Pavel said, "and I pray you'll bear with me if my account seems strange, digressive, or even wholly irrelevant at times. The threat facing Damara is a more complicated matter than you may suppose, and I seek to explain it in such a way as to make it comprehensible."

Christine sighed. "Time presses, Master Shemov. A hundred matters demand my attention. But give us your tale."

Employing all his rhetorical skill, Pavel proceeded to offer an abbreviated version of it. He avoided all mention of Brimstone, though. He'd have to speak of the undead dragon soon enough, but he wanted to enlighten his audience as to the basics of what had befallen Damara—and all of Faerûn—first. When he finished, the queen, her officers, and even Kovor, who hadn't known what his student meant to say, regarded him with manifest astonishment. And skepticism.

"So you claim," said a white-haired but robust-looking knight, "that it isn't Zhengyi who led the goblins against us, but another lich impersonating him?"

The speaker bore the emblem of the Golden Cup on his surcoat, and Pavel, who'd been told whom he might expect to find advising the queen, inferred that he was Brellan Starav, commander of the order of holy warriors.

"Yes, Milord," Pavel said.

"That's preposterous. Every foe we've captured vows that the Witch-King himself oversaw the taking of the Gates."

"That's why they call it 'impersonating,'" said Will. When Brellan shot him a glare, the halfling blandly added, "Milord."

"It would explain why Zhengyi vanished afterward," said the one officer not wearing religious regalia, a handsome, foxy-faced man, of mixed human and elf blood by the look of him, with a belt of pouches encircling his narrow waist. It was the sort of garment favored by wizards to hold spell components, or by expert housebreakers like Will to hold the tools of their trade. If the tales were true, that fellow, Celedon Kierney, Damara's spymaster, was both. "What could the genuine Witch-King possibly have to do more important than completing the reconquest of Damara? But if he isn't really Zhengyi and his true concerns lie elsewhere . . . it makes sense."

"So all the slaughter and destruction across our realm were just a ploy, a single gambit in a greater game a madman is playing with all the dragons in the world?" Brellan shook his head. "That's . . . unimaginable."

"It certainly tweaks our Damaran pride," Celedon said. "But consider something else. Sergor Marsk and his fellow traitors attained positions close to the king because I put them there, an error for which I will never forgive myself. I had my reasons, though. The dastards enjoyed remarkable success gathering intelligence and conducting strikes against the bandit army. Perhaps they managed that because someone was feeding them information about the brigands. It's questionable that the real Zhengyi would have so betrayed his allies. But an impostor, who cared nothing about preserving Vaasa's strength over the long haul, might well have done it."

"For the moment," said Drigor Bersk, "let's imagine this tale is true." Huge and scar-faced, plainly a warrior by nature if not vocation, the high-ranking cleric gave the lie to the popular notion that all priests of Ilmater were skinny from fasting and mild as milk in their demeanor. "Does it change anything?"

"Believe me, Milord," Pavel said, "it's of the utmost practical importance. Thus far, I've been vague as to how I know Sammaster usurped the mantle of the Witch-King."

Celedon smiled and said, "Yes, you have. I intended to get into that."

Pavel took a deep breath then said, "We—Karasendrieth, her circle, and the folk who've pledged to aid them—have an ally I haven't mentioned yet. Long ago, he was one of Sammaster's associates, and understands the lich's mind. He's a master scrier, and spied on developments in Damara and Vaasa. He is, in fact, a smoke drake and a vampire, who calls himself Brimstone."

Christine, her officers, and Kovor all gawked at Pavel. Then several of them started to speak at once, but Will raised his voice to cut through the babble.

"Brandobaris's knife, idiot, you left out the important part! Brimstone may be a vicious, bloodsucking wyrm, but he can wake Dragonsbane!"

"Is this true?" asked the queen.

"He says so, Your Majesty," Pavel replied, "if certain requirements are met. For starters, it will be necessary to allow him into the presence of the king."

Brellan peered intently at Pavel, and the hunter realized he was using his paladin powers of discernment.

"You have a taint on you," said the knight. "I'm surprised that I didn't smell it before. The question is, does it simply come from consorting with the undead, or does the rot run deeper? Are you merely a dupe, or have you deliberately set your feet on the path of evil?"

"I'm a Damaran," Pavel said, "who's willing to get his hands dirty to help his liege lord and preserve his native land from devastation. I'd hoped all of you would feel the same."

"I might," said Christine, "if I were certain of this undead wyrm's intentions. But Gareth slew dragons, and was a tireless destroyer of vampires and their ilk. How can I assume this Brimstone truly means him well?"

"Your Majesty," Pavel said, "I beg you to believe that I am by no means naturally inclined to credit whatever Brimstone tells me. But it's plain that for the moment, his intentions are benign."

"So you say," Brellan said, "but who are you? A stranger, who forsook his temple and homeland so long ago that only Kovor remembers you. How can we trust you? Besides, if he could give us his counsel, the king would never consent to our trafficking with an undead wyrm, whatever the vampire's intentions. No paladin of Ilmater would ever make common cause with a creature as foul as any demon, or use unclean means to achieve even the noblest end."

Celedon frowned. "I'm not quite so certain of that. With respect, Milord, you weren't with His Majesty in the old days, when we fought to drive out Zhengyi. I was. I recall him turning a blind eye to one or two instances of petty wickedness when it was necessary to strike a blow against the greatest evil we knew."

"But is it necessary?" asked Drigor. "His Majesty has Master Kulenov and some of the ablest healers in Damara working to lift the curse afflicting him."

"How's that going?" asked Will.

Drigor glared at the halfling. "The point," said the scar-faced man, "is that I see no reason to abandon hope in people we trust and take a chance on an abomination simply because a pair of vagabonds recommends it. Who agrees with me?"

With the exception of Celedon, all his fellow officers clamored in support of their fellow servant of Ilmater.

Christine regarded the folk arrayed before her with troubled eyes. "I mean no disparagement to anyone here when I say I wish Dugald, Kane, and all Gareth's comrades from the early years were here to advise us. But we've had no word of them since the Vaasans swept into the realm, and wishing doesn't make it otherwise." She sighed. "Of course, even if they were here, it would still be my decision, wouldn't it?"

She turned her gaze directly on Pavel and said, "Master Shemov, I can't look at a person's spirit as paladins can. My gifts are of another sort. But I take you for a good man and a shrewd one, and it's certainly true that nothing the mages and physicians have attempted so far has produced the slightest change in my husband's condition. Accordingly, my counselors and I will meet this Brimstone, and if he passes muster, he may attempt his cure."

Pavel bowed and said, "Thank you, Your Majesty."

"As the queen commands," said Drigor, "so be it. But Master Shemov, Goodman Turnstone, be advised that if your undead drake attempts any treachery, you too will answer for it. In full measure."

———— ❧ ————

Kara's song echoed through the vaults and cellars. As Dorn would have expected, it was beautiful. He doubted the bard could sing a false note if she tried. But it was also chilling, a wild, mad wail of rage and anguish.

Several hours earlier, Sammaster's dragons had attacked, and pushed the defenders of the monastery deeper into the tunnels. But that wasn't the worst of it. Despite all the precautions Dorn had taken to keep his spellcasting allies out of harm's way, Malazan had managed to shred two able priests with her talons and incinerate one of the most powerful magicians with her fiery breath before the monks finally turned their assailants back.

It was a catastrophic loss, and though Dorn knew it had only been a matter of time before the foe achieved such a success, he still couldn't help feeling that if he weren't a worthless fool of a freak, he would have found a way to prevent it.

Accordingly, hoping her company would ease his self-reproach, he'd decided to seek out Kara. By so choosing, he'd surprised himself. He'd never been one to reach out to others for solace. He'd always thought it better to hide his hurts behind a scowl, perhaps so other people wouldn't exploit the vulnerability, or think him any more contemptible than they did already. But today he'd craved whatever comfort the song dragon had to give.

But it sounded as if she needed consolation more urgently than he did. His iron foot clanking on the floor, he raced through the archives until her lament led him into her presence.

Kara had scored her cheeks with her nails, and the tears from her amethyst eyes streamed across the raw red striae. She stood behind a long table covered with musty-smelling books and curling brown sheets of parchment. Motes of dust floated in the air above them.

"What's wrong?" said Dorn.

Kara ceased her singing to draw a ragged breath. "Why, nothing," she said in a bright, brittle voice. "I've found the lore Sammaster harvested from these libraries."

Dorn tried to understand. "Then . . . that's good, isn't it?"

"You'd think so, wouldn't you, considering how many brave monks died to win me the time to do my studying."

The hunter felt a surge of impatience. "Just tell me the problem straight out. Can't you read the cursed things? Is it another cipher?"

"It might as well be," she said. "The texts constitute a grimoire of sorts, but not in a straightforward sort of way. The authors recorded the spells, rituals, and explication of the underlying thaumaturgical principles in a series of obscure symbolic allegories. It would take months to derive the actual incantations.

"Which, obviously, means the material is worthless," she continued. "Because we don't have months. We'll be lucky to hold out another tenday."

"Then we need to carry the books out of here," said Dorn, "and back to Thentia. That's feasible. The caves are clear."

She laughed. "Oh, but that's the heart of the joke." She pointed to one of the books. "Turn back the cover."

He hesitated. He wasn't used to handling books, and they were plainly old and fragile. He took hold of the sheet of flaking leather with the fingers of his human hand and lifted it with care.

But not enough care. The cover crumbled.

"They're all in the same exquisitely delicate condition," said Kara. She picked up a parchment and gave it a slight shake. It vanished in a puff of dust. "You would have laughed to see how slowly and cautiously I moved, just to shift them from their shelves to this table. They'd never survive any sort of journey across country, and thus, they're useless."

She cocked back her arm to lash the books and papers with the back of her hand.

Dorn lunged, caught her wrist in his iron fist, and wrenched her away from the table.

"Are you mad?" he said.

She laughed. "Of course I am. Frenzy's eating my mind. If it weren't, perhaps I would have found the lore sooner, or maybe I could interpret it quicker. But as it stands, Chatulio and all those valiant men have died for nothing, because what's left of me isn't clever enough to complete her task. I've failed you, my people, the whole world."

"Enough!" Dorn shouted. "You haven't failed yet, and you won't. Just stop the self-pity, buckle down, and solve the puzzle."

"It's impossible."

"I don't care. Do it. Raryn, the monks, and I will buy you all the time we can. We'll die to the last man if that's what it takes. You just hold up your end of the bargain." He tried to soften his tone. "I know you can. You can do anything you set your mind to. You're the wisest, cleverest person I've ever met. Every day, I marvel at the things you know and understand."

She sighed and said, "All right, my love. I'll try."

<hr />

It had proved more expedient to carry Dragonsbane out into the benighted, torchlit courtyard than to accommodate a creature as huge as Brimstone inside the castle. Looking as if he were merely sleeping, the king lay bundled up in blankets on a couch with a goodly number of his retainers clustered protectively around him. All who were knights or men-at-arms stood fully equipped for battle. Pavel, who himself wore a new brigandine and carried a new buckler courtesy of the royal armory, had explained that some of his companions would require their weapons, but knew they would have brought them in any case, for fear of the vampiric dragon.

Seated on a sort of portable outdoor throne, Christine nodded to one of the paladins, who, his face a rigid mask of barely contained loathing, presented a rag doll for Brimstone's inspection. Standing between the smoke drake and Will, Pavel saw from the puppet's crown and beard that it was meant to represent the king.

"Yes," said Brimstone in his sibilant whisper of a voice, "I was correct." He loomed over the rest of the company like a child among his toys. "Sammaster and his lieutenants use fetishes like these to sunder a victim's body and soul and imprison the latter on the Plane of Shadow."

Pudgy Mor Kulenov regarded the dragon with skeptical eyes. "That seems an excessively elaborate way of eliminating an enemy," the wizard said. "Why not just kill him?"

"Some men, indeed, most paladins, are resistant to death magic," Brimstone said. His crimson eyes glowed a little brighter, and his breath stank more strongly of burning, at the wizard's expression of mistrust. "But few folk can withstand this curse."

"Besides," said Celedon Kierney, who wore a short sword and light leather armor in addition to his belt of pouches, "if the Cult of the Dragon had murdered the king, we could have crowned someone else, who might just conceivably have rallied the barons to his banner. By simply crippling His Majesty, the traitors made certain the realm would remain in disarray."

"At this point," said the queen, "it doesn't matter why our enemy chose this particular weapon. What's important is whether we can heal the wound it inflicted."

"I believe so," Brimstone said. "Now that you've admitted me to your husband's presence, I can use that proximity, along with the doll, to transport several companions and myself into the dark world. We should arrive close to the place where his spirit is imprisoned. But it won't be easy to liberate him. We'll have to contend with the guards."

"What sort of guards?" asked Drigor Bersk. The brawny, scar-faced priest wore a full suit of plate and carried a long-handled warhammer in his fist.

"Dragons indigenous to Shadow," Brimstone said. "Sammaster has a pact with them."

"So," said Brellan Starav, also wearing plate and bearing a tall rectangular shield emblazoned with the sign of the golden cup, "you want to lead a company of the most able captains Damara has left into the netherworld, there to risk their lives fighting wyrms. Vampire, if this is a trick. . . ."

"I know," Brimstone snapped, his red eyes flaring, "I'll regret it. How much time do you posturing fools intend to waste, delivering the same threat over and over?"

"Brandobaris knows," drawled Will, "it's starting to bore me too."

Will had likewise reequipped himself. The armorer had even found him a fresh supply of skiprocks.

"We're going to do as Brimstone recommends," said Christine, "for I believe his plan represents our only real hope. Sir Dragon, how many comrades can accompany you on the journey?"

"A dozen," Brimstone said, "two of whom will be Master Shemov and Goodman Turnstone."

Celedon frowned. "You have the flower of Damaran chivalry arrayed before you."

"I have two experienced dragon killers standing beside me," Brimstone retorted. "They're going. It only remains to choose the rest."

"I'll send no man unless he's truly willing," said Christine, "not on a venture as perilous as this." She surveyed the assembly. "Who—"

As one, the king's men stepped forward, bring a momentary smile to the queen's pretty but careworn face.

"Thank you, gentlemen" she said. "Now I must select."

"Your Majesty," said Celedon, "I insist on going. First, because I'm one of Gareth's oldest comrades. Second, because it's my fault the dragon cultists got close enough to the king to harm him."

"I'm to blame as well," said Mor Kulenov. "The traitors were magicians under my command. I should have realized what they were doing. I too plead for the opportunity to atone."

"I don't have the same reason to offer," said Drigor, "but send me, also, Your Majesty. You know I'll pull my weight."

"Yes," said the queen. "I choose the three of you."

"And me, surely," Brellan said.

"No, Milord," Christine said, "I'm sorry." He stared at her in amazement bordering on outrage. "But you said it yourself. We gamble the lives of Damara's best. I'm not prepared to risk all of you. Someone must remain to advise me and command our army if the worst befalls."

Brellan bowed stiffly. "As Your Majesty commands."

Christine selected six more champions, paladins mostly. Then a lanky youth with a pox-scarred face, perhaps the least impressive-looking of all the men-at-arms gathered there under Selûne's silvery gaze, could contain himself no longer.

"Please, Your Majesty," he cried. "I beg you, give me the last place."

Celedon regarded the young man with a sympathetic expression, then said, "Your eagerness does you credit, Sir Igan. But you only won your spurs a few tendays back. Every other warrior here has more experience than you."

"Pardon my frankness, Milord," Igan snapped, "but if you and Master Kulenov are going because you failed the king, then surely I can request the same privilege based on the fact that I saved him."

Celedon looked momentarily taken aback, then smiled at the young knight's show of spirit.

"You did save him," said Christine, "and perhaps you'll be lucky for him a second time." She turned to Brimstone. "You have your dozen."

"Good," said the dragon. "All of you, stand in front of me." The twelve obeyed. "First, I'm going to cast an enchantment that will enable you to see in the absence of light. It's dark in Shadow, and if you carry torches or lanterns, Sammaster's allies will notice, as will every other predatory creature for miles in every direction."

He rattled off an incantation in the Draconic tongue.

Magic crackled through the air, and for an instant, Pavel's eyes stung. But when he blinked his tears away, he could see across the courtyard almost as clearly as if it were day, though the night still dulled most colors to gray.

"Now," said Brimstone, "we're ready to depart."

The second whispered incantation took considerably longer, and the words of power made Pavel's skin crawl, even though, for the most part, he couldn't understand them. Gradually, the shadows within the high walls deepened. Then they lengthened and shifted from side to side. On the final phrase, they reared up from the ground and raced toward the would-be rescuers like gigantic waves converging on a ship at sea from every direction at once.

Pavel stiffened, his body anticipating the shock of impact, but he felt nothing at all when the blackness swept over him. When the shadows collided, they instantly disappeared, and he could see that the courtyard and castle were gone as well.

He and his companions stood beneath a black sky devoid of stars or moon. A seemingly lifeless wasteland, the arid ground all sand and gravel, lay around them. Towering masses of rock jutted from the earth, making it impossible to see very far in any direction, and transforming the desert into a maze. The air was chilly. All colors withered to blacks and grays, and in many instances, what had appeared light in the mortal world had gone dark, and vice versa. Will's face was sooty, while his lovelocks were the color of bone.

"I can't see as well as I could before," the halfling said.

"Because, it isn't just dark, simpleton," Pavel said. "We're immersed in the essence of darkness, the very *idea* of it. Brimstone's enchantment can't wholly compensate for that."

Will snorted. "I should have known it would take more than a trip to another world to stop a charlatan spouting gibberish."

Celedon looked up at Brimstone, whose charcoal-colored scales looked bleached and leprous in that strange place.

"What now?" the spymaster asked.

Brimstone still had the rag doll. The talisman looked tiny in his claws. He stared intently at it for a few heartbeats, then said, "Your king is this way." He indicated the proper direction with a thrust of his wedge-shaped head.

"If you were to fly above these pillars of stone," Celedon said, "you might see exactly where he is."

"I might also attract attention," Brimstone said, "even cloaked in the subtlest obscurement any of us can cast. I prefer to stay on the ground for now."

"If we're going to march," said Will, "I'll scout ahead."

"I'm a fair hand at sneaking about," Celedon said.

"But as Brimstone said, I stalk dragons for my living while you're the king's officer, too important to do the most dangerous job when someone else can manage."

"He's right," Drigor said.

Celedon pulled a wry face. "Nobody ever lets me have any fun anymore. But very well. Thank you, Goodman Turnstone."

Will grinned and said, "When we get back, thank me with a wagonload of those bloodstones you folk are so fond of. For now, just give me a couple minutes' head start."

He skulked away, his boots silent on the sand and pebbles, and melted into the gloom.

While the rest of them waited, Drigor cast a blessing on the company that washed the anxiety from Pavel's mind and left a cool, confident alertness in its place, even as it sent a surge of vitality tingling through his muscles. Some of the paladins prayed, enhancing their own personal capabilities, and Mor Kulenov presumably did the same with a spell that made his robes and staff shimmer. For some reason, the glow lingered for an extra moment in his tuft of beard. Brimstone bared his fangs at the display of light.

Then they set forth after Will. Except for the noises they couldn't help making themselves—the clink of plate and mail, the creak of leather, whispered consultations—the dark world was silent. Sometimes Pavel thought he glimpsed something stirring from the corner of his eye, but when he turned and peered directly at it, the flicker of motion disappeared.

Then, abruptly, the instincts he'd developed during his years as a hunter whispered that something was wrong. And when Will came scurrying back a moment later, he was certain he was correct.

"What is it?" Brimstone whispered.

"Dragons," said Will. "Two of them, moving in on you. They didn't see me, though, so they won't realize we're expecting them."

"At least one will try to attack from above," Brimstone said. "Perhaps I can intercept him, and take him by surprise." He rattled off a spell and faded from view. An instant later, the snap of his wings and the gust of air they displaced revealed that he'd taken flight.

Pavel turned to the king's men. "Don't bunch up," he told them. "Strike at a drake when it's turned away from you, and get away when it pivots in your direction. Remember, though, that no matter where you're standing, the creature's dangerous. It can shatter your bones with a flick of its tail or a beat of its wing. It can blast you with its breath or a spell from yards away."

"Good advice," said Drigor. "Now, stand in a circle. We want to make sure the creatures can't creep up on us."

Pavel peered into the darkness, searching, until a hiss from overhead distracted him. He looked up, at a triangle of dragon breath livid against the featureless black sky. At the wide end, a vague bat-winged shape screeched and floundered in flight as the plume of hot smoke and embers washed over it. At the narrow point of origin, a second such form, rather more distinct, burst into view. The act of attacking had breached Brimstone's cloak of invisibility.

The vampire started snarling an incantation. His opponent beat its wings, hurtled at Brimstone, but missed, as if the smoke drake's breath had blinded it.

Pavel realized that if one shadow dragon had been on the verge of attacking, the other probably was, too, for surely they intended to make a coordinated assault. He hastily returned his attention to the ground.

Even so, he almost missed seeing the wyrm, its head raised and its throat swelling to discharge its breath weapon. Though huge, the shadow dragon had a mistiness to it, almost a translucency, that rendered it virtually invisible in the gloom.

"It's there!" Pavel shouted, pointing with his mace. "Look out!"

He and his comrades flung themselves to the sides. Still, when the wyrm spewed its horrifying breath, the expanding, billowing streak of shadow caught Mor Kulenov and five knights inside it. The magician screamed and fell to the ground. The warriors staggered.

With appalling speed, the dragon charged the men it had afflicted. It plainly intended to slaughter any survivors before they could shake off the effect of its breath, and no one was in position to block its path.

But Will whirled his sling, and despite his target's ghostly indistinctness, the skiprock evidently hit a sensitive spot, because the shadow dragon balked. That gave Pavel time to conjure a flying luminous mace into existence to pound at the reptile's head. Lashing his hands through the proper figure, Celedon engulfed the creature in an explosion of fire.

Afterward, Pavel couldn't tell how badly they'd hurt it. Its murky vagueness made that as difficult as aiming an attack at it. But it must not have liked the punishment, for instead of rushing on forward and so inviting more harassment, it stood still.

Pavel realized it was casting a spell, or invoking some innate power. He prayed that a blow from his conjured mace would break its concentration, but on its next swing, the floating weapon missed the reptile in its mantle of gloom. Will fared better. Pavel heard the skiprock whack against the dragon's hide. But by itself, the impact likely wouldn't suffice to stop the wyrm from doing as it intended.

The ambient darkness both deepened and seemed to fray into tatters, which spun around the battlefield as if caught up in a whirlwind. It had been difficult enough to see before. But Pavel, all but blind, felt a queasy upswelling of vertigo as well.

As he tried to deny the dizziness, the shadow drake hissed an incantation. Cramps jabbed through his muscles and guts and made him stagger. He silently called to Lathander, and the sickness passed, but then he felt blood on his face. The magic had done more than make him momentarily ill. It had clawed at him as well.

Elsewhere in the whirling, leaping darkness, barely visible, men kneeled or lay retching on the ground. They had yet to shake off the sensation of sickness, and thus, for the moment, they were helpless.

The shadow dragon charged.

Celedon met it with a crackling flare of lightning. Brandishing his warhammer, Drigor called to the Crying God and produced a barrier composed of floating, spinning blades. The wyrm plunged right through it. As before, the chaotic darkness and the reptile's blurred, inconstant form kept Pavel from discerning whether the magic was truly doing it any harm. At any rate, the spells didn't stop it, and an instant later, it sprang close enough to strike with fang and claw.

Pavel swung his mace at its ribs. He was certain he'd score on it, but the gloom deceived him, and he was actually out of range. The dragon turned, and he jumped backward, barely evading a rake of its talons.

He kept retreating and circling, avoiding the head and forefeet, until the wyrm pivoted to attack another foe. Then he charged, struck, hit—and the dragon vanished. He realized he'd attacked an illusion. The reptile had conjured phantasmal images of itself, creating another layer of defense to bewilder its foes.

An instant later, its dark breath washed over him, and the strength drained out of his limbs. His legs buckled, dumping him on the ground. He wasn't in pain, precisely, but felt a sickening sense of violation, as if a portion of his very life had been ripped away.

The shadow dragon raced at him and all the other foes it had just afflicted. Its phantom duplicates lunged along beside it. Pavel tried to scramble back onto his feet, but saw that he wouldn't make it in time.

Drigor and Igan rushed in on the wyrm's flank. The priest's hammer stroke simply eradicated another image, but the young knight's sword appeared to cut deep into the true drake's scaly hide. Will tumbled underneath the wyrm's belly and drove the hornblade in. The wraithlike reptile struck, clawed, and stamped at its assailants.

Shaken though he was, Pavel had to aid his comrades. He heaved himself to his feet, gripped his sun amulet to commence an attack spell, then realized the invocation wasn't in his memory anymore. In addition to whatever other harm it had done, the wyrm's breath had burned away a portion of his mystical abilities.

Silently praying to the Morninglord, he charged. Swung his mace, and missed. Somewhere in the wheeling, fragmented darkness, Celedon shouted a rhyme. Darts of light streaked through the gloom, diverging in flight to strike every possible target. All the dragon's false images burst at once.

Heartened, Pavel struck and missed again. The shadow wyrm whirled, and he flung himself flat to keep its tail from pulping his skull, then instantly had to roll to keep it from trampling him. Its stamping feet jolted the earth.

Had the creature slowed down at all? It didn't appear so, and Pavel struggled to quell a surge of fear. He lurched to his feet and attempted another prayer.

Thanks be to Lathander, the incantation was still in his head. Warmth glowed through him, calming his mind and cleansing pain and fatigue from his body. He saw the spectral dragon more clearly. Its form didn't shift and waver as much as before.

He rushed it, struck, and connected, the mace crunching into its scales. Igan sliced its neck, and blood jetted. Underneath the drake, Will cut another gash. The reptile lurched down to crush him, but he rolled clear before its ventral surface slammed against the ground.

The dragon tried to rise again, but floundered. Igan hacked into its neck. It screamed and convulsed, nearly rolling on top of Pavel before he leaped backward, then it lay still.

Pavel had the same reaction he often felt at such a moment, a numbed inability to believe the seemingly unstoppable creature had finally succumbed to its wounds. He was still trying to credit it when someone bellowed a warning.

The other half of the battle still raged high in the air. He looked up to see a serpentine shape with a tattered, crippled wing plummeting straight at him and Will. It looked solid, not shadowy, which meant it was Brimstone, not his foe.

Will dived. With his extraordinary agility, perhaps he'd make it out from under. Pavel recognized he had no chance of doing the same.

The falling Brimstone eclipsed the dead black sky. Then, just before he hit the ground, his body dissolved into smoke, a sulfurous mist suffused with stinging embers that shrouded the man he would otherwise have crushed.

Brimstone's transformation revealed the other shadow dragon, swooping after him like a falcon attacking a pigeon. When the vampire turned to vapor, his assailant immediately turned its attention to the folk on the ground. Its throat swelled as it prepared to spit a spray of poisonous, devastating shadow.

A prone man heaved himself to his knees. Without bothering to rise any farther, plump Master Kulenov, evidently at least partially recovered from his immersion in dragon breath, jabbered an incantation. On the final word, he whipped a quirt, evidently one of the spell foci he carried concealed in his voluminous robes, through the air.

The shadow wyrm screeched, and its wings flailed out of time with one another. Flying clumsily, it leveled out of its dive, wheeled, and veered off. To Pavel's eyes, it seemed dazed, but only for a moment. Then it oriented on Kulenov, and hurtled at the wizard. Kulenov's nerve broke. He wailed and turned to run.

At the same instant, the cloud that was Brimstone drew in on itself and coalesced into solidity. The smoke drake's wing was still torn, but not as badly as before. He flexed his legs, then beat his pinions as he sprang into the air.

The shadow wyrm was swooping low, and all its attention was on Kulenov. Otherwise, Brimstone, with his mangled wing, probably couldn't have intercepted it. But he did, and plunged his fangs and talons into his adversary's body.

Tangled together, unable to fly, they crashed to earth and rolled over and over. Until Brimstone caught the shadow dragon's throat in his jaws.

The shadow wyrm thrashed madly for a few seconds, nearly shaking the vampire loose, but then its struggles subsided. Even after it stopped moving, Brimstone clung to it, slurping and guzzling its blood. The stolen vitality knit together the lacerations in his wing and closed his other wounds.

Relieved and repulsed in equal measure, Pavel turned his attention to the rest of the company, and winced at what he found. Five of his comrades were manifestly dead, and four more, wounded. Intent on aiding one of the injured, he took a step forward, but weakness abruptly overwhelmed him. He swayed and would have fallen if Drigor hadn't caught hold of his arm.

"You took a full dose of shadow dragon breath, didn't you?" said the burly priest of Ilmater.

"Yes," Pavel gasped.

"Once we get back to the palace," Drigor said, "I can restore you. Just hang on till then." He turned to his other surviving comrades. "Whatever cures or other magic you want to cast, do it fast. We need to get out of here."

Eyes gleaming, Brimstone lifted his gory mask away from his prey and rumbled, "You're right. The battle raised too much commotion. Other shadow wyrms are surely coming."

In another minute, they were on the march, scurrying through the columns of stone. For Pavel, the frantic scramble was a brutal test of endurance. He panted, his head swam, and the eternal night of the Shadow Deep seemed even darker than before.

At the head of the column, Celedon said, "Can't we go any faster?"

"No," Brimstone growled. "It takes me time to choose the correct path." They rounded another outcropping. "But behold!"

Squinting, Pavel could just make out a relatively low hump of rock with a ring of standing stones at the top. At the center of the circle was the rarest of all phenomena in that universe of gloom, a point of pale phosphorescence.

"This is the place," said Brimstone. "Come on."

Pavel felt as if it required the very last of his stamina to clamber up the rise. Climbing beside him, Will eyed him with concern.

"Are you going to make it?" the halfling asked.

Pavel nodded. He supposed that to truly reassure Will, he should have responded with an insult, but he couldn't spare the breath.

The light they'd spotted from below floated at the center of the ring of menhirs. It was Dragonsbane's spirit, gleaming, semitransparent, and motionless, seemingly in a deep slumber like his physical body back in the mortal realm.

Pavel knew that by rights, the soul of a great paladin ought to shine more brightly. But an egg-shaped weave of crisscrossed shadows surrounded the king's essence, trapping and dimming the radiance.

Igan scowled and reached for the black web as if he thought to break it apart by strength alone.

"Don't touch that," Brimstone snapped, "unless you want to rot your arm off. I'll open it."

The dragon hissed words of power. Magic whined through the air, and made fresh blood trickle from the nicks on Pavel's face. The dark prison faded for a moment, then clotted back to its former condition.

"I thought you knew how to do this," said Will.

"I do," Brimstone snarled.

He recited the incantation a second time, but achieved no more than before.

"I can break it," said Mor Kulenov.

Staff held high, he declaimed a counterspell. A screech of wind lashed everyone's clothes. The mound shuddered and groaned. Yet the black mesh held.

Will studied the sky.

"More dragons," he said, "coming fast."

He extracted a skiprock from his belt pouch. Celedon rounded on Brimstone.

"It's now or never," the spymaster said.

"My spell should work," the vampire said. "But if Sammaster himself enchanted the fetish . . ."

"Light," Pavel croaked. "Light drives out dark. Somebody conjure a flash at the same time Brimstone works his spell."

"I'll try it," Drigor said, and produced a flare so bright it made Pavel squinch his eyes shut. Still, the shadow prison remained.

"The wyrms are just about close enough to start throwing their own charms," Will reported. "I'll wager those will work."

"We'll attempt it again," said Pavel, raising his sun symbol, "only this time, I'll summon the light."

Drigor shook his head. "My friend, you're sorely wounded, and I've advanced farther in the mysteries than you. If it didn't work when I—"

"Your light," Pavel snapped, "isn't Lathander's light." He glared at Brimstone. "Your incantation is longer than mine. You begin."

The dragon snarled words of power. Pavel tried to judge when to chime in with the opening of his prayer. It was more difficult than it should have been. He felt so weak and muddled.

Yet he and Brimstone finished at precisely the same instant, and a ray of red-gold light blazed from his amulet to strike the web of shadows. Striking in concert with the force of the vampire's spell, it seared away the strands of darkness. The radiance of Dragonsbane's spirit shined forth in all its glory, and the translucent figure vanished.

"Can we go home, too?" called Will. "Preferably soon?"

Brimstone began a new spell. Half a dozen dragons dived and spewed shadow from their gaping jaws.

But it never reached their targets. The dark world spun, dropped away, and Pavel and his companions stood in the torchlit courtyard once more. Christine and her retainers exclaimed at their sudden reappearance.

Pavel turned toward the couch and its occupant. Whereupon anguish and frustration stabbed him to the heart, for the king looked exactly the same as before.

But then Dragonsbane's eyes flew open, and he bolted upright.

"Lances—!" he rasped, then peered about in confusion.

Celedon murmured an incantation and flicked one hand through a cabalistic pass. A large, luminous, three-dimensional map of Damara and the surrounding territories shimmered into existence to float three feet above the ground. Small, stationary images of goblins, giants, mounted knights, spearmen, and archers stood about the landscape like tokens on a game board.

"Our intelligence concerning the enemy's whereabouts is incomplete," the thin, sly-faced spymaster said. "But as you can see, the scouts report that the Vaasan horde has dispersed to plunder. Still, the majority remain in the duchies of Brandiar and Carmathan, all within a few days' march of one another. They'd have little difficulty recombining into a single force, and I believe they'll soon do precisely that, to assault Heliogabalus."

Still slightly ill from his exposure to dragon breath, but vastly improved thanks to Drigor's ministrations, Pavel shuffled and craned with the foremost captains and royal officers in Damara for a clearer look at the map. It had surprised him when he, Will, and Brimstone received a summons to the council of war, especially since the vampiric drake's participation required another open-air palaver in the benighted courtyard. But evidently the king felt they'd played such a significant role in his rescue that it was their due.

Like Pavel, Dragonsbane was still trying to shake off the lingering effects of an ordeal. The magic of the priests of Ilmater had kept the monarch's body alive in his soul's absence, but couldn't entirely compensate for the lack of water, food, and exercise. As a result, Dragonsbane stood leaning on a gold-headed cane. Pavel prayed that the king's strength would return quickly. The gods knew, the man was going to need it.

As he studied the map, Dragonsbane's face was tight and grim.

"So much devastation," he said, "and the representation doesn't even show the damage to the fields and crops."

"I've conferred with the elder druids," said Queen Christine. "They say it's not to late to insure a reasonable harvest, one large enough to stave off famine in the months ahead. They'll petition the earth and weather to yield all the bounty they can. But the farmers must return to their labors soon."

"Which requires chasing the goblins out of the barley," said Will, standing on tiptoe to see over the top of the map.

Dragonsbane smiled for just an instant. "That it does, Goodman Turnstone, that it does."

"It's obvious we have no choice but to fight," said Brellan Starav. "But we need to lay our plans in the knowledge that the Vaasans have us greatly outnumbered."

"We'll send forth riders tonight," said Dragonsbane, "to every noble hiding on his estate with a company of guards. With luck, some of them will reach the royal army in time to make themselves useful."

"With respect, Your Majesty," Drigor said, "we told people right along that you weren't dead. Nobody believed our reassurances."

"Because folk assumed that if I truly was alive, I'd get up off my arse and drive out the invaders," the blond-bearded monarch said. "Now, the heralds can proclaim that the king is riding to war. Maybe that will make a difference."

"You realize," Celedon said, "the goblins and giants will learn of it as well."

"Good. We don't have time to defeat a hundred raiding parties one by one. We need our foes to merge into a single army, which we can then smash at one go. Demoralized, any survivors will run back to Vaasa, or at least the protection of the Gates."

Drigor grinned a grin that made his harsh, scarred features even more forbidding. "A nice trick if we can manage it."

"Trickery," said Dragonsbane, "is what I have in mind. Even a proper army will often disintegrate in fear and confusion if attacked unexpectedly on the flank, or better still, the rear, and goblins, though fierce under the right circumstances, aren't disciplined troops. So here's what I propose. We'll split our force in two. One half, with me at its head, will proceed across country with no attempt at stealth. With some maneuvering, it can probably arrange to engage the enemy around here—" he pointed with the ferule of his cane—"to the west of these hills."

Brellan, nodding, said, "I understand. The second half of the army sneaks north and hides behind the rise. Once the battle begins, and Your Majesty's command fixes the Vaasans in place, the rest of Damara's protectors take the creatures from behind. We crush them with a convergent attack."

"Maybe," said Will.

The commander of the Paladins of the Golden Cup scowled down at the halfling. "Do you see a problem with His Majesty's strategy?"

Will shrugged. "I'm no knight, just a hunter, but I've had a few brushes with goblin kin out in the wild. They may not be 'disciplined troops,' but they're not idiots, either. They know how to look after themselves in hostile country. They're liable to send scouts into those hills, spot the second force, and spoil your big surprise."

Brellan stood silent for a moment, pondering, then said, "Curse it, you're right."

"Then how about this?" said Dragonsbane. "My company will engage the enemy farther north, then flee the field with the Vaasans in hot pursuit until we reach the final battleground. That will deny them the opportunity to investigate what waits behind the hills. Does that meet with your approval, Goodman Turnstone?"

"I'm not sure it meets with mine," Celedon said. "You've more than once observed that retreating in good order while under attack is one of the most difficult tasks any force can undertake. If the goblins' harassment renders you incapable of standing and fighting a second time when you reach the right patch of ground, your strategy fails."

"It's a chancy plan in a number of ways," Dragonsbane admitted, "but also the best I can devise. If anyone has a better one, by all means, let's hear it."

The company stood silent for a moment.

Celedon grinned and said, "I guess that's it, then. We'll just have to hope for the favor of Lady Luck."

Brimstone arched his serpentine neck, bending his crimson-eyed mask closer to the king.

"I can't improve on your scheme," the smoke drake whispered, "but I can suggest an embellishment."

Dragonsbane surely loathed vampires as profoundly as the other paladins and priests in the assembly, but unlike them, he didn't allow even a hint of that revulsion to show in his expression.

"Please," he said, "tell us."

———— ∞ ————

Weary as she was, Kara no longer trusted herself to handle the ancient documents with the delicacy required. Fortunately, the mindless, shapeless, invisible helper she'd conjured was immune to fatigue. She willed it to turn the page, and the brown, brittle leaf slowly shifted without crumbling.

Eyes aching, squinting at the crabbed, faded characters that kept trying to blur, she read to the end of a nonsensical tale in stumbling iambic heptameter. At the conclusion, the butterfly knight flew into a misty field of marigolds and emerged transformed into a kestrel.

By all the notes ever sung, what was it supposed to signify? Had the knight, by changing from insect to bird, become a higher form of life? Or, by becoming a predator, had he lost his innocence? And in any case, what agency produced the metamorphosis?

It was hopeless. Kara didn't understand and she never would. She felt another urge to smash the mocking, worthless books to dust, and this time, Dorn wasn't there to stop her.

But the thought of him was.

He believed she could solve the puzzle, and even with the Rage gnawing at her mind, she couldn't betray his faith in her. She drew a ragged breath, calming herself, and returned to her labors.

Hours passed, somehow seeming both to drag on interminably and to hurtle by. Her phantom servant ceased to be, and she invoked another. A neophyte brought her a tray of bread and beans. She tried to eat, but a single taste made her stomach churn, and she set the rest out of the way on the floor.

And through it all, she accomplished nothing, until at last, she pushed back from the table and closed her eyes. She needed a different approach, but what could that possibly be? Reading was reading, wasn't it?

Well, perhaps not. She was studying the allegories as a human scholar might, pondering every image, symbol, and apparently meaningless incident as she read. But she wasn't a human scholar. She was a song dragon, and both story and magic were a part of her very essence, forces she supposedly comprehended instinctively.

She resolved to try experiencing the ancient writings as she'd experience any poem or tale. She'd stop agonizing over every nuance and see how the material made her *feel*.

Much of it didn't make her feel anything. The stories were simply too disjointed and obscure. But as she once again worked her way through the feckless wanderings of the butterfly knight, something occurred to her.

The marigolds represented fire. Their yellow was the brightness of flame, and the fog swirling around them was actually smoke.

Fire could purify. By turning an aimlessly flitting butterfly into a sharp-eyed hawk, flying purposively forth in search of prey, had it cured the character of folly? Perhaps even of madness? Was that what the poet was implying?

If he was, then other elements of the tale, and even the surrounding material, must relate to the idea of fire, physical or metaphysical, actual or notional, in a way that made sense according to the principles of magic. She read on, and though much of the texts remained entirely cryptic, nonetheless, fragmentary patterns began to emerge. Until, her heart pounding with excitement, she started to see how one might construct a spell. She dipped a quill in the inkwell and scribbled furiously on the fresh parchments the monks had provided for her use.

At last she completed a deceptively brief and simple-looking incantation. She regarded the lines with a fierce satisfaction that immediately withered into doubt.

Because she didn't actually know that she'd truly fathomed any part of the arcane writings. Perhaps her interpretation was completely false, the product of frenzy, exhaustion, and wishful thinking. Even if she had gotten part or all of it right, the majority of the information in the grimoires, all the fine and subtle points, remained impenetrable. How, then, could she possibly imagine that she'd successfully moved from a set of half-comprehended mystical relationships to the exquisitely balanced and nuanced artifact that was a functional spell?

She scowled at her misgivings. The magic would work because it had to. Because she had no time to study and tinker endlessly to refine it.

In any case, she didn't need to sit and wonder if she'd succeeded. It was an easy thing to test.

She rose and sang the words she'd written. As she reached the final notes, she couldn't help but tense. The spell was meant to draw a sort of cauterizing blaze into her mind, no less dangerous for being psychic and spiritual instead of corporeal. If she'd botched her work, the flame might sear what remained of her sanity and even her very soul away. Even if she'd gotten it right, she feared the magic's touch would be excruciating.

It wasn't, though. All she felt was a fleeting lightness, as if the spell had lifted a weight from her being.

Will and Pavel rounded a corner, and the priest stared in surprise at the old clapboard building across the street. He'd expected to find it ablaze with light and raucous with music and laughter. But except for the gleam of a candle behind a window or two, it was dark, and entirely quiet. The painted sign above the door was gone, and by the looks of it, someone had remodeled the stable to serve some other function.

"Oh, slop and dung," said Will. "I know you're hopeless in the wild, but I didn't think even you could get lost in the same town where you grew up."

"This was it," Pavel insisted, and he was sure of it. In days gone by, the building had been the Boot and Whistle, the tavern where he'd learned to drink, play cards, and chase women, as much a part of his youth as the cloisters and archives of the Temple of the Dawn. But it appeared someone had turned the place into a cheap boarding house. Pavel had scarcely thought of the establishment during the years he'd been away, but nonetheless felt a pang of sadness to find it gone.

"Oh, well," said Will, "it's a pleasant enough night, and it shouldn't be that difficult to find a mug of beer. Let's walk on."

The council of war had dragged on for some time after everyone ran out of worthwhile things to say. At the end of it all, Will and Pavel had discovered a common urge to escape the company of lords and royalty for a little while. Accordingly, they'd slipped away from Dragonsbane's citadel to visit the commoner precincts of Heliogabalus.

Pavel found he quite enjoyed the stroll. He liked hearing the accents and idioms of Damaran speech, observing the intricately carved gingerbread under the eaves of the Damaran houses, and catching the hearty aromas of Damaran cooking. They didn't make him regret the wanderer's life he'd chosen. That fed a part of his soul he could nourish in no other way. But even so, he realized a part of him had missed them.

"We helped Brimstone rescue the king," he said after a while. "We could head back to Thentia now, and perhaps we should."

"But you don't want to," said Will.

"No. Damara's my homeland and the outcome here is still in doubt. You could say it's up to Dragonsbane and his knights now, we have little more to contribute. . . ."

"Speak for yourself," said Will. "The king's going to need scouts and skirmishers, folk with our—say rather, *my*—talents to make his plan work."

"So you don't mind lingering?"

"Not if they'll pay me what I'm worth."

"That could be a problem," Pavel said with a smile. "I don't think Damara mints coins in such small denominations."

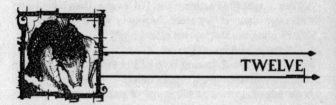

TWELVE

5-8 Flamerule, the Year of Rogue Dragons

Slathered in blood, dripping it on the stone floor, Malazan lunged at Dorn. He sidestepped, cut at the dragon's mask, and his hand-and-half sword glanced off her scales. The gigantic red lashed her head to the side to catch him in her fangs, and he leaped backward. His foot landed and skidded in wet gore, throwing him off balance. The wyrm snatched for him with her talons—

And he woke flailing. Kara was leaning over his cot, touching his shoulder gently, and had to jerk away to dodge a sweep of his iron hand.

"Easy!" she said, her moon-blond hair shining in the gloom.

"I'm all right now," he said, though that wasn't entirely true.

Awake, he suffered the smoldering sting of his burns and blisters, wounds sustained when he didn't quite manage to dodge a flare of Malazan's fiery breath. The monastery had exhausted its supply of medicinal elixirs, and even with so many of its defenders slain, didn't have enough priests to restore all those who remained to full health. Some men simply had to endure their wounds.

"I take it you were having a nightmare," Kara said.

"Yes. I fight the battles when I'm awake, then have to do it all over again in my sleep." Anxiety jolted him. "Battle. Malar's claw, are the wyrms attacking?"

He scrambled up off the cot.

"No," Kara said, taking hold of his forearm, restraining him. "Do you hear, everything's quiet?"

He felt chagrined at his surge of panic. "Right. Sorry. I guess I'm too tired to think straight."

"Everyone is," she said, smiling. "But I've discovered something nonetheless. Do you sense anything different about me?"

He studied her. Something had changed, though he couldn't quite tell what. The closest he could come was: "You seem . . . more like you were when I first knew you, in Ylraphon, and sailing down the Dragon Reach."

"I am," she said, "because I've virtually quelled the frenzy inside me. I recovered the enchantment Sammaster must use to keep the chromatics sane enough to serve his purposes. I tried it on myself, and it worked. Thanks be to Mystra that you held me to my task."

"Then . . . this is it? We win?"

Some of the elation went out of her expression and she said, "Well, no. Remember, the Rage is waxing steadily stronger. In time, the defense will fail."

"Still," he said, feeling guilty to have dimmed her moment of triumph, "it buys us more time to solve the greater puzzle. Now we need to clear out of here, and give a dose of the remedy to your fellow rogues." He sighed. "It will be hard to walk away from our comrades, but Cantoule swears the monks won't abandon the monastery, no matter what."

"We can't, either. What I've gleaned thus far is only a fraction of the secrets concealed in the ancient books. We were right that we absolutely must save them, and the only way to do that is to break the siege."

Dorn scowled, pondering the problem.

"That will take reinforcements powerful enough to make a difference against a horde of dragons," he said, "and mobile enough to get here in time. With the rogues scattered across the North, that leaves the wizards in Thentia, though I hate the thought of it. They can't unravel the answers we need if they're fighting battles, certainly not if they die in them, and they might. They're powerful, but for the most part, not veteran war mages. I don't know how many of them could handle themselves in a conflict such as this."

"I agree," Kara said. "But we have an alternative. Lareth and other dragons who accept his authority are hiding somewhere in the Galenas, hoping their magical slumber will save them from the Rage. We thought of approaching him after our expedition into Northkeep, but decided we still hadn't learned enough to persuade him that our scheme was superior to his."

"But a charm to tame frenzy, even if only temporarily, ought to convince him, and he and the other metal drakes can fly south to save the monastery." Dorn frowned and added, "That's assuming we can find the refuge."

"I hope we can. It's probably not far from the bowl where Lareth convened his parliament of dragons."

"Then that's our plan. We'll tell Cantoule, then you, Raryn, and I will leave through the caverns at once."

"I understand that our task could scarcely be more urgent. Still, now that I've cleansed myself of the Rage, do you think we could steal just a few minutes for ourselves?" She lowered her eyes. "It wouldn't be the long, sweet night I hoped for, but perhaps we'll find some joy in it even so."

Dorn felt a giddy surge of excitement. "I'm sure we will."

Dorn and Kara found Raryn standing guard behind a breastwork constructed of broken stone. The burly dwarf took one look at them, and grinned.

"It's about time," he said.

Dorn felt his face grow hot, and dealt with the embarrassment by pressing on with the business at hand.

"The three of us are leaving," he snapped.

"Why?" Raryn asked. Speaking in tandem, Dorn and Kara explained. But when they finished, the scout said, "That's good news. But I think I'll bide here for the time being. Chatulio blazed the trail through the caves, so you don't need me to find the way out again, nor to talk to this King of Justice, either, I expect. But these lads"—he waved a broad, stubby-fingered hand at the haggard, dirty-faced monks standing guard alongside him—"might still need a dragon hunter to advise them. They've learned a lot, but maybe not all our tricks."

"You realize," said Dorn, "the monks can't hold out much longer. Kara and I may not make it back in time. Or at all."

Raryn shrugged. "Folk can only do their best, and let luck decide the rest. So the brothers and I will make our stand here, you'll watch Kara's back on her journey, and we'll meet again when we can, in this life or the next."

He held out his hand and Dorn clasped it.

------ ∞∞ ------

Wineskin in hand Taegan sauntered through the tailor shop, inspecting the bales of cloth on their wooden spindles, passing judgment on each in turn.

"Hideous," he declared. "Boring. Repulsive. Though admittedly, if I wanted garments the exact color of phlegm, it would do admirably. Garish enough to burn out a mole's eyes. But wait!" He fingered the edge of an azure taffeta. "Is this from Sembia?"

"Yes, Maestro," the tailor said. A tall, thin woman with long brown hair, she appeared more amused than vexed by

Taegan's disparagement of her stock. "You won't find finer silk anywhere along the Moonsea."

"I suspect that, unfortunately, you're right," Taegan said. "Do you think you could cut and stitch it into a proper doublet for me, as opposed to one of those shapeless tunics that, for some inexplicable reason, people seem to favor hereabouts?"

"I expect I could manage."

"Then show me what you propose to line it with, and what you have in the way of fasteners."

The tailor bustled away to fetch the desired items, leaving Taegan with Jivex and Rilitar. Neither was particularly appealing company at the moment. The normally garrulous faerie dragon had grown quiet, almost sullen, of late, perhaps from the strain of resisting frenzy. The elf wizard wore a frown.

"Your expression," Taegan told him, "bespeaks a lamentable sobriety. Happily, the cure is at hand."

He proffered the wineskin.

"No, thank you," Rilitar said. "My friend, your . . . frivolity troubles me."

Taegan hitched his shoulders and wings in a shrug. "I realize my concerns may seem eccentric here on the fringe of civilization. But I'm a gentleman of Lyrabar, and in that queen of cities, we prize stylish clothes, exquisite wines, and the pleasures of the table."

"You didn't seem to care about them so much when you first arrived."

For a second, a vague anxiety stirred in Taegan's mind, for it seemed to him that Rilitar's statement was correct. Then he recognized it for the nonsense it truly was.

"I've always relished the finer things. If I didn't seem to, it must have been because I fell into slovenly habits while traveling, cruelly separated from the amenities of urban life."

"But should you let such trivialities preoccupy you when we have vital work in hand?"

"Do Jivex and I still patrol the town, seeking some sign of the chasme or its master?"

"Yes," the elf said grudgingly.

"Are we doing all else that can be done?"

"I suppose."

"Then please, permit me my petty amusements."

"If I must." Rilitar glanced down at Taegan's feet. "I suppose a visit to the boot maker is next on the agenda."

Once again, the avariel felt uneasy. "In fact, no. I like this pair."

Was that actually the case, though? The boots were cracked, scuffed, a bit too loose, and a drab shade of brown, altogether wretched accessories to any rake's ensemble.

Still, he thought, I have to keep them, precisely because they aren't right. Because they aren't even really mine. Then he realized that notion was another absurdity, and thrust it out of his mind.

Kara soared high above the bleak, snow-capped Galena Mountains. Seated astride her back, Dorn was cold despite the bright summer sun that made her blue scales sparkle like diamonds. He ignored the chill as best he could while scrutinizing the peaks below, even though it was unlikely that his merely human eyes would spot anything that her draconic sight, sharpened still further by enchantment, overlooked.

"Anything?" he called. He couldn't quite break the habit of raising his voice when riding on her shoulders, with her head extended yards ahead of him, even though he'd learned her ears were keen enough to catch it even if he whispered.

"No," Kara said, twisting her neck to glance back at him. "Perhaps I should have expected as much. Nexus is the greatest wizard among the golds. If he cast the spell to hide the sanctuary, it makes sense that we can't find it. But I'd hoped he'd erect his barriers in such a way that dragons of goodly nature would have little trouble finding their way through. Alas, that doesn't seem to be the case."

"Because of Lareth's spite, I imagine. You and the other rogues wouldn't grovel to him, so he made sure you couldn't change your minds and shelter in the refuge later on."

"I pray that isn't so. I'd rather believe Nexus had to cast the spells the way he did for some other reason."

"Either way, what do we do now?"

"Keep searching. I don't know what else we can do."

So they glided back and forth, through the morning and into the afternoon, with the same lack of success, while frustration gnawed at Dorn and did its best to make him frantic.

Though not given to introspection, he recognized that he'd changed. Freak though he was, a woman had given him her love, and while the fact that she was also a dragon was a profound irony, in the end, it didn't matter. Kara had made him happier than he'd believed possible, and in so doing, had taught him what it truly meant to be afraid.

For he dreaded losing her to the Rage as he'd never feared anything since the hour the red wyrm slaughtered his parents. The only hope of preventing it lay in finding Lareth's refuge. It was too late to turn around and fly to Thentia. Raryn and the monks would never hold out that long.

So think! he told himself. There must be a way of find the sanctuary. If Pavel were here, he could puzzle it out. Try to use logic the way he would.

Start by admitting the haven was imperceptible to human eyes, and Kara's senses, too. They hadn't spotted it by direct observation, and weren't going to.

But when they flew near it, what did they see instead? The semblance of an empty piece of ground, probably, but could the phantasm be perfect in every detail? Perhaps in the manner of a masterful painting or sculpture, but unlike a work of art, a part of Nature, even the most desolate, was never static. It was infinitely complex and constantly changing.

"Fly lower," Dorn said.

"That will slow our search," Kara replied. "We won't be able to see as far."

"It's necessary. We need to look more closely at the ground."

"If you think it will help. . . ."

She furled her crystal-blue wings and swooped. The breeze fluttered his cloak and sleeves and ruffled his hair.

"I hope it will," he said. "We're not going to bother to spy for dragons or their tracks anymore, or the glow of enchantment."

He imagined it to be a glow, anyway. He had no way of knowing what she actually saw when she perceived the presence of magic.

"Then what will we look for?" she asked.

"Pine needles that don't smell right. A rill that sounds funny as it splashes over rocks. Brush that takes a second too long to rustle when a breeze kicks up, or shadows that don't line up correctly with the sun. Anything wrong."

"Tiny anomalies in the illusory landscape. It's a good thought, and we'll try it."

And they attempted it for hours, while the sun sank in the west. Dorn began to despise himself for a fool, capable of conceiving only foolish, useless notions.

But then Kara said, "Look! Ahead and to the right . . ."

He leaned forward to obtain a clearer view past her shoulder, then said, "I don't see anything."

"Those crags yonder come together in a most peculiar fashion, too crowded and jumbled, the angles too acute. Look around, and you won't see anything comparable among the neighboring peaks. I understand now. Nexus's magic didn't cover over the refuge with an illusion, not precisely. Instead, it blinds us to the sanctuary, and so we won't wonder at the gap in our vision, tricks our minds into pulling the edges of the hole together."

Dorn very much wanted to believe her, but feared she was making too much of a mass of rock. He'd seen stone shaped into many odd formations in the course of his wanderings.

He asked, "Are you sure?"

"I hope we both will be in a second. Now that I know where to target my own magic, perhaps I can strip away our blinders."

She sang words of power, and the incantation echoed from the mountainsides. Loose stones clattered down the escarpments, and the vista before them seemed to split apart, making room for a new stretch of earth to ripple into existence. It was almost as if the mountains were giving birth. To a valley nestled between steep, rocky slopes, where dozens of metallic wyrms, their scales reflecting the sunlight like mirrors, lay motionless.

"You did it!" said Dorn.

"I accomplished the first part of it. Nexus has a second ward in place to defend the haven, though I can't determine exactly what it does."

"Can you dissolve it?"

She sang another spell, then said, "No. Not until it manifests, anyway."

"Then how do we proceed?"

"We trigger it, and cope with the result. Hang on tight."

Wheeling, she descended toward the depression among the peaks. Mouth dry, heart pounding, Dorn waited for something to strike at them. After a moment, he spotted what appeared to be an old man with a bald pate and a white beard standing on the high ground at the eastern edge of the refuge. Probably it was a dragon sentry who'd altered his form, the better to stave off frenzy. Whatever he truly was, he was waving his arms over his head, warning the newcomers away. He seemed to be shouting, too, but distance and the snapping of Kara's wings covered up the sound.

The wind shrieked, and smashed into the flyers like a battering ram. It whirled Kara end over end, and tried to rip Dorn from her back. He caught hold of the dragon's hide with his iron hand, plunging the talons into her scales. Even in that moment of terror, he hated the necessity, but had no choice except to cut her. Only the strength of his artificial arm could anchor him.

Even if she'd noticed the pain, Kara had more urgent matters to concern her. The gigantic whirlwind constantly threatened to smash her into the side of the mountain.

Her wings hammered. She had no hope of escaping the vortex, but by exerting herself to the utmost, managed to maneuver to a limited extent within it. For the first few seconds, it kept her from crashing against a cliff. She started singing a spell.

Lashed this way and that on her back, pressing himself against her body to deny the wind a purchase on him, nearly torn from his perch even so, Dorn occasionally caught a glimpse of the sentinel. The old man stood without difficulty on the rim of the valley. His robe wasn't even flapping. Evidently the gale wasn't blowing there, a circumstance that made Dorn hate him.

Kara finished her musical incantation. The vortex howled on, unaffected. She resumed her singing. Dorn's heart sank, for though he couldn't understand the lyrics, he recognized them as the same words, the same spell, as before. If it hadn't worked the first time, it seemed unlikely to prevail ever, but evidently it was the only card she had to play.

For a second, Dorn saw the guard swelling into a winged and glittering shape, with a gold's characteristic tendril "whiskers," and a proud crest running almost the entire length of its body.

As Kara reached the end of her spell, thunder boomed, and the lightning that was a part of her nature blazed from the clear blue sky. But after the climactic note, the wind shrieked on, strong as before, and hurled her on through the air.

She began the counterspell once more. Lighting flashed and thunder roared in time with the melody. Dorn felt power accumulating around her, stinging his skin. Sparks danced and popped on his iron parts.

It's going to work this time, he thought.

Then the great muscles heaved beneath her hide as she wrenched herself around in the air. A split second later, her ventral side smashed into a cliff face. As stones showered down and battered them both, Dorn understood that she'd twisted as she had to spare him the impact.

He couldn't believe it mattered. Surely the collision had stunned or crippled her, and they'd roll down the mountainside together, the long tumble bashing and grinding their lives away. But she pushed off from the escarpment, pounded her pinions, and took flight again. Even more miraculously, neither the impact nor the pain of her foreleg breaking and a shaft of splintered bone stabbing through her hide had disrupted the precise enunciation of her song.

During the final phrase, the lighting burned so bright that Dorn had to hold his eyes shut, and the thunder boomed so loud it spiked pain through his ears. But then the whirlwind died all at once, as if it had never been.

Dorn slipped his bloody claws from Kara's hide, then, as best he was able, gave her huge reptilian body a quick and clumsy embrace.

"This Nexus is no better a warlock than you," he gasped.

"I love you for saying that," Kara answered, "but we were very, very lucky."

Below them, the gigantic gold spread its wings and leaped into the air.

"I guess now we need a little more luck," said Dorn, readying his longbow. "At least I can help with this part."

"Don't shoot!" Kara said. "Not unless you're sure he means us harm. That's Tamarand, first among Lareth's lieutenants. He doesn't like needless killing."

"Unless the Rage has taken hold of him."

"He tried to wave us off," she said, "so the whirlwind wouldn't seize us. He wouldn't have, if he were eager to see us dead."

"Maybe not."

Still, Dorn put an arrow on the string. He'd spent his life hating dragons, and even though he'd come to care for one in particular, that didn't incline him to abandon his mistrust of the species as a whole.

Kara and Tamarand circled one another.

"Go away," said the gold. "After much meditation, His Resplendence decreed that you and your fellow rebels are forbidden to avail yourselves of the sanctuaries. I'm not sure of his reasoning, but it doesn't matter. You must depart, and weather the Rage elsewhere as best you can."

"I must speak with Lareth," Kara said. "Afterward, if it's his will, I'll go and never return."

"You don't understand. It will mean your death, and your companion's too. I'm already derelict in my duty for not attacking you as soon as you quelled the wind storm."

"I must speak with Lareth," Kara repeated. "If I pay for the privilege with my life, so be it. I was right, Lord Tamarand. The Rage has a cause, and a cure as well. My friends and I have discovered part of the remedy, and know how to obtain the rest. But I need the help of the dragons hibernating here."

The gold stared at her, then asked, "Can this be true?"

"Yes," said Dorn, "luckily for the rest of you. Because her discoveries are the only hope for you strutting, preening golds and silvers."

"Land," said Tamarand, "and I'll wake His Resplendence. I urge you to treat him with all the deference that is his due."

The two dragons spiraled down and lit among the rows of their slumbering fellows. Once Dorn swung himself down from Kara's back and stepped away from her, he saw that the punctures his claws had made and the broken foreleg she cradled against her breast were scarcely her only injuries. The collision with the mountainside had scraped and bloodied the entire underside of her body. In contrast, the golden scales of the larger wyrm gleamed without a single blemish, a fact that made the hunter's jaw clench in another spasm of dislike.

"I regret," Tamarand said, "that I'm no healer."

"We can attend to my hurts later," Kara said.

"I pray that's so. I'll take you to His Resplendence."

Kara and Dorn followed where he led, the crystal-blue dragon bard hobbling on three legs, the half-golem trotting to keep up with his companions' longer strides, past one immense, coiled, motionless wyrm after another. They meandered to avoid clambering over the sleepers, but Dorn soon made out where they were headed. At the northern end of the depression, somewhat separate from the other reptiles, lay a gold even huger than Tamarand—perhaps even more colossal than Malazan.

"It will only take a few moments to wake him," Tamarand said.

The words of power hissed and rumbled from his throat. For a moment, the air took on a greenish tinge, and Dorn's ears ached as if he was deep underwater.

Lareth groaned, the sound a bone-shaking rumble, and his yellow eyes fluttered open. He clambered to his feet and swung his head from side to side, peering about. He seemed confused, and Dorn felt a pang of foreboding.

Then the gold's gaze locked on Kara. His eyes burned brighter, the glow perceptible even in sunlight. He lifted his head and his throat swelled, kindling its fire.

"No, Your Resplendence," Tamarand cried, "please! I gave Karasendrieth permission to enter the refuge."

For a second, it looked to Dorn as if Lareth was going to attack anyway, but then the King of Justice turned his glare on his deputy.

"I ordered you to kill anyone who overcame Nexus's wards. Including the traitors. *Especially* them."

"With respect, Your Resplendence," Kara said, "I disagree with your plan for surviving the Rage, but that doesn't make me a traitor to my people."

"You're a traitor twice over," Lareth said. "Once for defying the decision of our conclave, and again for bringing a human here." He sneered. "If, indeed, this gruesome mix of iron and flesh is human. Whatever he is, no outsider can know the location of the refuge. That's the only way to keep it safe. Therefore, both you and he must die."

"I'm prepared to," she replied. "But first I have a tale to tell."

"I won't listen," said the ancient gold. "I've wasted enough time attending to your folly."

"Please," Tamarand said, "hear her out. She says she's found a cure for the Rage, or at least is on the verge."

Lareth snorted. "No one can cure the Rage, because it isn't a sickness. It's simply an aspect of our nature. Your judgment is failing you, my brother, and in consequence, you've nearly failed our people and me. But you can redeem yourself. Help me kill the intruders as you ought to have done in the first place."

Dorn yanked his sword from its scabbard and came on guard.

"Try it, then," he spat. "Over the past few months, I've run up a nice tally of slaughtered wyrms. Blacks and greens. Ooze and magma drakes. It might be fun, adding a couple golds to the score."

"Don't confuse us with dragons bound to darkness," Lareth said. "We're a different order of being."

"Well," said Dorn, "that's the question, isn't it? Are you really any different from the reds and their kind, or do you just pretend to be? I used to believe all dragons were cruel and selfish. I had reason. Then I met Kara, learned how gentle and kind she is, and started to change my mind. But maybe I shouldn't have. Maybe she's as much a freak among her race as I am among mine."

"Please, Your Resplendence," Tamarand said, "I can't help but think it would indeed be harsh to slay these folk without even listening to their petition. Whatever her past transgressions, Karasendrieth came here in peace."

"Very well, Tamarand," Lareth growled, "only for the sake of our friendship." He glowered at Kara. "Speak your piece, singer, and I suggest you make it convincing."

"Thank you, Your Resplendence," Kara said.

For the next hour, she recounted the story of the rogues, their allies, and their investigations, and did indeed employ all her bardic eloquence to make the complex narrative as clear and compelling as possible. Tamarand's eyes grew wide with wonder and dawning hope.

But Lareth's hostile, contemptuous glare never wavered, and at the end of it all, he simply snapped, "Now you stand thrice condemned. The third time for consorting with a vampire drake, as foul an abomination as ever stalked the world."

"What of the rest of my tale?" Kara asked, her musical voice as calm and steady as before.

"Lies," Lareth said, "or madness. It doesn't matter which."

"Can we be certain of that," asked Tamarand "without a test? Karasendrieth claims she has a charm to quell the Rage. Very well. Let her cast it on me."

"I won't have her laying a curse on you."

"I'm willing to risk—"

"No!" Lareth roared. The bellow echoed off the mountainsides, and flame crackled from his maw. "The snake wants to cast me down, and destroy our entire race! She's already subverting your loyalty. I can see it! But she won't succeed in her designs. I rule here! I, Lareth, King of Justice, and now I'll mete out justice to her and her creature!"

He spread his wings.

Dorn felt sick with dread. Lareth was mad. They couldn't reason with him, and with Kara injured, her magic already depleted by the struggle to still the whirlwind, the hunter was grimly certain they couldn't defeat the gold, either. But it seemed they had no choice but to try. Since Lareth was about to take flight, the hunter thrust his sword point-first into the ground and snatched for an arrow.

Then Tamarand cried, "Abdicate!"

Startled, astonished, Lareth rounded on him. "What did you say?"

"Abdicate," the smaller gold repeated. "You see insanity everywhere but festering inside yourself. But as your deputy, your comrade, and your friend, I must alert you, frenzy has you in its grip. I couldn't bear to believe it, but it's so. You must step down—for everyone's sake, including your own."

"Thus making you King of Justice," Lareth sneered.

"I don't aspire to your rank," Tamarand said. "That has nothing to do with it."

"You lie," Lareth said. "But I forgive you. I understand you're not yourself. But speak no more of this."

"I must. If you won't abdicate, then I challenge you for your position."

Lareth bared his huge ivory fangs. "No gold has ever perpetrated such an insolence."

"Yet the law permits it. As the keeper of our traditions, you should know it better than anyone."

"Fine, then!" Lareth screamed, spewing fire. "Have it so! I renounce you and I will kill you!"

"We'll see," Tamarand said. "Let's wake Nexus and Havarlan. The protocols require witnesses."

Nexus proved to be another huge gold, whose narrow eyes and an unusually full "beard" of fleshy tendrils gave him a look of sagacity. Havarlan, Barb—or captain—of the martial fellowship of silvers called the Talons of Justice, was a lithe drake with a number of vivid scars crisscrossing her argent hide.

When apprised of what had transpired, both dragons were appalled.

"Your Resplendence," said Nexus, "Lord Tamarand, I beg you to reconsider. Surely we can find a better way to resolve this disagreement."

"It's too late for that," Lareth said.

"My friends . . ." Havarlan began.

"Too late!" the King of Justice snarled.

Dorn edged up beside Kara. "*Is* it too late?" he whispered. "Now that Lareth's distracted, can you dose him with the cure whether he likes it or not?"

"No," she said. "Perhaps Sammaster could, but my comprehension of the spell, my mastery of it, is incomplete. For me to cast it successfully, the recipient must consent."

"Then we've got to help Tamarand. He's outmatched."

"We can't do that, either. No matter how stealthy we tried to be, Nexus would likely detect it, and this is supposed to be single combat. If we meddled to influence the outcome, all these others would turn on us immediately. Probably even Tamarand would strive to strike us down."

Dorn felt angry and sick with helplessness. "So all we can do is watch, even though our lives hang in the balance?"

"I'm afraid so."

Lareth and Tamarand stalked to the opposite ends of the cut then, with beats of their gleaming golden pinions, sprang up onto the rim. Nexus hesitated as if giving them one final opportunity to relent, then spat a flare of blue and yellow fire straight up into air. The duelists took flight.

Each dragon climbed rapidly, striving to rise above the other, and quickly recited words of power. Lareth finished his incantation first. An oval of roiling reddish-purple light, or perhaps some otherworldly flame, expanded around Tamarand, engulfing him. It looked like a gigantic, demonic mouth opening in empty air.

The younger gold screeched in pain, spoiling his invocation. He furled his wings and dived, evidently to escape the hovering magical field as quickly as possible.

The result was that Lareth achieved the advantage in altitude. He climbed even higher and declaimed a second spell. Tamarand convulsed, floundering in flight. Watching from far below, Dorn couldn't tell exactly how the magic had hurt the smaller gold, but it plainly had.

Still, Tamarand shook off the pain and struck back with a conjuration or innate power of his own. A dazzling light exploded into being in front of Lareth's mask, so painfully bright that, from Dorn's vantage point, it was as if the sun had instantaneously shifted across the sky. He squinched his eyes shut and twisted his face away.

When he looked again, through floating blobs of afterimage, Lareth was twisting his neck back and forth, casting about. Had the burst of glare blinded him? Not entirely, Dorn suspected, but Tamarand had also maneuvered to put the floating purple-red haze between them. The seething cloud wasn't opaque, but to some degree, it veiled what lay behind it, and that, combined with the insult to Lareth's eyes, seemed to have confused the elder gold as to the precise location of his foe.

Hit him now, Dorn silently urged Tamarand. Maybe he won't see it coming.

But Tamarand didn't attack. Instead, he cast what was evidently a defensive enchantment. His gleaming, serpentine body started flickering, present one instant, absent the next.

Meanwhile, Lareth succeeded in orienting on his foe, then snarled an incantation that, for an instant, made the air above him curdle and twist into leering spectral faces. He brandished his forefoot, and a jagged bolt of blackness sprang forth and hurtled unimpeded through the smoldering cloud, down at Tamarand.

Tamarand tried to dodge, raising one wing and dipping the other, but was too slow. Luckily, though, he disappeared just as the lance of shadow was about to stab him, then popped back into view a split second after it streaked by. Lareth roared in fury.

The two dragons began to conjure once more, even as they continued to maneuver. Lareth plainly wanted to close with Tamarand so he could bring his greater size and physical strength to bear. But evidently he couldn't safely enter the seething oval cloud, even though he himself had created it. Accordingly, the younger gold was doing his best to keep the magical obstacle between them.

Tamarand completed an incantation. Lareth's shadow surged up from the rocky, uneven ground below, swelled large enough to dwarf the immense creature who'd cast it, and stretching fantastically, reached for him with its claws.

To Dorn, the effect was terrifying, but Lareth seemed to pay it no mind, defying it, opposing its power with force of will, perhaps, and to good effect. The titanic phantom frayed into nothingness a moment before it would otherwise have seized him, and he had a normal shadow once more, flowing and wheeling across the mountainsides.

Lareth snarled the final phrase of a spell, vanished, and instantly reappeared on the other side of the wound in the air, directly above his foe. Wings furled, talons poised, he plummeted—straight through the space his target had just vacated.

The flickering had protected Tamarand again. But in Dorn's estimation, it was an imperfect defense. Eventually, it would fail to snatch the smaller gold away at exactly the right moment, and an attack would strike him.

Yet for the time being, it had given him the advantage in height. Popping in and out of view, leathery wings pounding and flashing in the sunlight, he climbed, widening the vertical distance separating him from his adversary. Lareth leveled off, wheeled, and gave chase.

Tamarand angled his head down toward his foe and hissed. The sibilant sound was another sort of spell. Even though Dorn wasn't the target, the magic made him feel groggy, sway, and stumble a step. Perhaps it was supposed to make Lareth fall asleep, but it had no effect on him.

"No," Kara groaned. "No, no, no."

"What is it?" asked Dorn.

"The shadow spell simply induces fear," said the bard, "and the hissing deadens the mind. Tamarand's trying to win without actually harming Lareth."

"Is he insane, too? The king's stronger. Tamarand can't afford to go easy on him."

"I know."

Lareth spewed a plume of fire upward. Tamarand veered. The flame caught him visible and vulnerable, but only the periphery of the flare brushed him, blistering and blackening the end of one outstretched wing. Unfortunately, though, the evasive maneuver cost him a precious moment of furious climbing. His foe, a more powerful flyer, was rapidly beating his way up to the same altitude.

Each gold commenced another conjuration. The magical force gathering in the air around them sent rings of distortion expanding outward across the sky, like ripples in a pool where someone tossed a stone. A shrill whine set Dorn's teeth on edge.

Tamarand reached the end of his recitation first. Lareth made a retching sound and fell silent.

"By all the songs ever sung!" Kara exclaimed.

"What?" asked Dorn.

"Tamarand's stolen Lareth's voice, and thus, his ability to declaim spells. Perhaps we were too pessimistic. Maybe if Tamarand can keep away from the king, maybe he can win after all."

Enraged, Lareth managed to lash his wings up and down even faster and draw even closer to his foe. He spat a blast of flame that would have squarely engulfed Tamarand except that the younger wyrm flickered out of harm's way.

Tamarand dived, giving up altitude for the added speed gravity provided, at the same time starting an incantation. Compensating, Lareth swooped after him.

The mad gold nearly closed with his lieutenant, and Tamarand enunciated the final word of power. He tilted his wings, and easily, or so it appeared to Dorn, dodged the claws of his hurtling foe. In the moments that followed, he widened the distance separating him from Lareth. It seemed plain that enchantment had made him faster and more nimble in the air.

Thereafter, he dueled Lareth at long range. The elder gold spewed flare after flare of fire, but each fell short. Meanwhile Tamarand assailed his opponent with a succession of spells, shafts of multicolored light and streaks of gray shadow that carved no visible wounds but made Lareth flinch and flail.

"Surrender!" Tamarand bellowed. "I don't want to hurt you, but you must see I have you at my mercy."

Lareth simply flew at him yet again. Tamarand resumed his conjuring.

The magenta cleft in the sky folded in on itself and vanished, and a moment later, Tamarand stopped flickering, as the spells that had created the effects reached the ends of their existences. Lareth vanished and instantly reappeared just above and behind his deputy.

Horrified, Dorn realized what had happened. Back at the beginning of the duel, Lareth had invested himself with the power to translate himself through space not just once, but multiple times. Obviously the spell had a longer duration than the flickering. After using it once, Lareth, frustrated by his lieutenant's ability to avoid attacks, had decided to forgo another such leap until the protective enchantment ran its course. That way, maybe he'd catch Tamarand by surprise.

As he did. His booming blaze of fiery breath seared the younger gold from head to tail. The edges of Tamarand's wings burned and flaked away like dry leaves.

Lareth plunged down and forward. Tamarand flung himself to the side. The larger wyrm's claws tore furrows in his seared, cracked hide.

Tamarand tried to evade his adversary, but their enchantment notwithstanding, his seared wings were slower than before. With his ability to shift instantly from one spot to another, Lareth had no trouble keeping up with the smaller drake. He slashed long gashes in Tamarand's flanks, bit a chunk of flesh from his shoulder, and spat fire directly into his mask.

At last Tamarand struck back in the same brutal fashion. If he hoped to survive, he had no choice. His talons ripped at Lareth. At the same time, he snarled an incantation, somehow forcing the words out in a steady rhythm despite the recurring shocks as his sovereign scored on him again and again.

Lareth evidently recognized the spell, and perhaps feared it, for he attacked even more savagely, his fangs tearing such a gaping wound in Tamarand's neck that Dorn winced, certain the hurt was lethal. But the younger gold kept chanting.

On the final word, power screamed across the mountains, and the whole world seemed to tilt. Dorn's muscles cramped, and his belly churned with nausea.

Lareth's body changed. For a second, the hunter couldn't make out how, then realized the dragon had gone utterly limp, while his flopping, sagging shape had lost definition. It was as if the bones had melted away inside him.

Such an amorphous lump of flesh couldn't extend its wings and fly. Lareth plummeted, and Dorn peered eagerly to watch the dragon king splash to pieces on the ground. But Tamarand dived and caught the other reptile. Lareth's weight was too great for the smaller wyrm to support easily, but still he managed a relatively gentle descent, his burned and tattered pinions hammering.

"Yield!" Tamarand pleaded.

In answer, Lareth's body jerked in his grasp, the limbs straightening and stiffening. Dorn belatedly recalled that for a gold dragon, or any other shapechanger, a transformation like the one the demented wyrm had endured was merely a momentary inconvenience.

Nearly restored, Lareth's claws fumbled at Tamarand. In another heartbeat or so, they'd be firm and strong enough to shred him, just as his squirming jaws would strike and spew their fire. Except that Tamarand denied them the chance. Exploiting his master's final moment of helplessness, the younger gold tore at him with fang and talon, then cast him down.

Dorn waited for Lareth to spread his wings and arrest his fall. He never did. He dropped like a stone, and disappeared into the cleft between two mountains. A moment later, a loud, flat thump reverberated.

Tamarand spiraled down after his foe and disappeared into the gulf. Nexus and Havarlan spread their wings, sprang into the air, and followed. Awkwardly, because of her broken leg, Kara lowered herself to help Dorn haul himself onto her back. Then they too flew to see what had happened.

They all found Tamarand standing before Lareth's shattered corpse at the shadowy bottom of the gorge, near a gurgling brook with mossy banks. Earlier, Dorn had resented Tamarand for being whole while Kara was injured. He had no cause for such rancor anymore. The dragon lord was even more grievously wounded than the hunter had anticipated, his hide such a blackened patchwork of gory cuts and seeping wounds that scarcely a glimmer of gold remained. The reek of blood and charred flesh utterly overpowered the odor of saffron that was his species's usual scent.

His pain was surely excruciating, yet Dorn could tell that the dragon king's most profound agony was of the spirit. As Kara touched down beside Havarlan, Tamarand raised his head and howled a long, wordless cry of lamentation. The wail echoed from the walls of the ravine.

Nexus inclined his head. "Your Resplendence," he said.

Eyes blazing, Tamarand rounded on his fellow gold. "Don't call me that! The King of Justice lies dead before you, foully murdered by a treacherous retainer!"

"The *former* King of Justice lies before us," Havarlan said, "fairly overthrown in a lawful challenge."

"I didn't want to kill him," Tamarand said. "I had no right."

"You had every right," the silver said. "What you lacked was a choice. By the end, we all recognized the necessity."

"He was the wisest and noblest of us all. He was my liege lord and my friend," said Tamarand. He turned to glare at Kara and Dorn. "May the gods curse you for coming here this day."

"Perhaps they will, Your Resplendence," the song dragon said. "Meanwhile, we have a more general blight to concern us."

"I told you not to call me that! I won't be King of Justice. I won't clamber over my brother's corpse to usurp his rank."

"If you won't claim Lareth's crown," Nexus said, "who will?"

"I don't care!" Tamarand snarled. "No one, perhaps. The silvers have no sovereign. Perhaps we golds would be better off if we didn't, either."

"I don't care a thimble of piss what you call yourself," Dorn said. "But until we end the Rage, you've got to lead. Why else did you fight?"

"He's right," Kara said. "We must save our own race, and the small folk as well. All across Faerûn, flights of our evil kindred lay waste to the land, slaughtering multitudes, destroying towns and villages, and leaving desolation, starvation, and pestilence in their wake. In their despair and desperation, the survivors wage war on one another for whatever food, shelter, and treasure remains. Meanwhile, ensconced in their secret strongholds, Sammaster and his cultists spawn dracoliches in sufficient numbers to conquer the world.

"Armored against the Rage," the dragon bard continued, "you metallic drakes can leave your havens and make your benevolent presence felt in the land once more. With your might, you can avert the calamities that threaten to drown the world in blood and darkness. That is, Milord, if you will have it so."

Tamarand stared at her for what seemed a long while. At last he said, "How quickly can you mute the frenzy in all the dragons gathered in this sanctuary?"

"I can only cast the spell a couple times each day," she said. "To do so expends a portion of my power, just like any other magic. But if I teach the charm to the three of you, and you in turn share it with others, we can help all the sleepers fairly quickly."

Tamarand turned to Nexus. "Can your sorcery translate our forces instantly to the Monastery of the Yellow Rose?"

"Not in the way you're hoping," Nexus replied, "not all at once. I can only shift myself and one other dragon at a time. Our people are simply too big and heavy for me to carry any more, and even I can only work that particular magic a few times in the course of any given day."

"I think," Havarlan said, "that if we go to fight a horde of reds and their ilk, we must arrive in strength. The chromatics will have little trouble overwhelming us if we appear a couple at a time."

"Then we'll apply Karasendrieth's remedy to the fastest flyers first," Tamarand said. "When we judge we have a sufficient number, we'll wing our way south, and pray we reach our goal in time. Let's get started."

Nexus, Havarlan, and Kara unfurled their wings. Tamarand however, made no move to do the same.

"Are you coming?" Nexus asked. "I mean to wake Marigold immediately, to tend your wounds and the bard's."

"I'll be there," Tamarand said. "I just need a moment to say farewell, and beg forgiveness."

He turned away, back toward the fallen Lareth, his grief and guilt so palpable that Dorn, who'd never in his life expected to truly regret the suffering of any dragon except Kara and Chatulio, felt a pang of sympathy nonetheless.

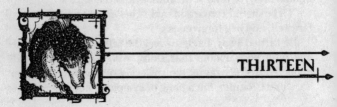

THIRTEEN

11 Flamerule, the Year of Rogue Dragons

Scimitar in hand clad in enchanted armor carved from sacred oak, Christine Dragonsbane turned her war-horse, casting about to see where she was needed next. Then her mount's head vanished, and blood gushed from the stump. The shock, the seeming impossibility of it, paralyzed her for an instant as the animal started to topple.

Recovering, she jerked her feet out of the stirrups and jumped clear. She landed hard, but without injury. As she scrambled to her feet, she realized some spell or huge, hurtling missile must have decapitated her steed.

She turned, seeking the source of the attack, then gasped. Its skin white as milk, a mane of coarse silvery hair tumbling over its massive shoulders, a creature as tall as five men tramped toward her. Even amid the shrieking chaos of the battle, it seemed unfair that anything so huge could draw so near without her spotting it until then.

The giant cocked its hand back. Christine flung herself to the ground, and when her foe threw the boulder, it flew over her head. The behemoth sneered, readied its meticulously shaped and polished club, and advanced.

Gareth hadn't wanted Christine to ride to war, but couldn't rebut her argument that if his strategy failed, she, like all of Damara's people, was likely doomed no matter what. Such being the case, the only sensible course of action was for her to lend her druidic powers to the struggle.

When her husband realized he couldn't change her mind, he'd ordered several knights to hover close to her and protect her, and they'd tried their best. But with the retreat begun, every rider had too much other work to do, for only horsemen could maneuver quickly enough to shield the spearmen and archers on foot from the goblins racing in pursuit.

A pair of Christine's scattered bodyguards galloped back fast enough to interpose themselves between her and the giant. The one to her left was a Paladin of the Golden Cup brandishing a battle-axe. To her right rode a knight armed with a long, straight thrusting sword. He had spatters of blood staining his yellow surcoat and chose to fight with his visor open, so he could see better.

The sight of those protectors endangering themselves on her behalf steadied Christine. She had to help them. She drew a breath and began a prayer to the Oak Father, lord of the forests and all wild places, and her patron deity.

The paladin charged the giant and swung his axe. The weapon chopped a gash in the creature's calf, the red crease vivid in its dead white skin. Ilmater's champion galloped on, and Christine thought he was going to get clear. But the giant pivoted with appalling speed for a brute so huge and whirled its club low like a child swiping at a dandelion with a stick. The crashing impact of the prodigious weapon flung both rider and destrier up into the air. They smashed down a dozen yards away.

The knight in the bloodstained trappings rode round and round the colossal leg his comrade had injured. He stabbed repeatedly, trying to finish the task of crippling the extremity. The giant bellowed and poised its club for another stroke, but the cavalier saw the threat and danced his horse to the side. The bludgeon whizzed harmlessly by.

Christine completed her spell. Lightning blazed down from the clear blue summer sky to blast the giant. The enormous creature jerked and flailed. But it didn't fall down, and after it regained control of its twitching limbs, it lifted its club to strike at the knight again.

Or so it seemed. But while the horseman watched the bludgeon, preparing to guide his destrier out of its way, the giant heaved its foot high and stamped down hard enough to shake the ground, crushing warrior and mount both beneath the sole of its hide boot. The knight died instantly, without making a sound. The middle of its body squashed nearly flat, its legs splayed out, but somehow still clinging to life, the war-horse screamed. The giant laughed, the noise like stones grinding together, and spun back toward Christine.

She could feel that the lightning had gathered itself again and awaited her summons. She willed it to strike, and as before, the giant jerked like a marionette at the end of a bright and jagged string. But also as before, when the paralyzing power released it from its grip, the pasty, colossal thing lumbered on toward her.

The giant flicked the club at her. She started to dodge, then discerned too late that the comparatively dainty motion had been a feint. The bludgeon snapped back the other way and bashed her off her feet.

As she sprawled stunned, breathless, hurting from head to toe, she realized that, enchanted armor or no, if the giant had hit her with its full strength, it likely would have killed her. When it bent down and reached for her, she surmised why it had chosen to delay her destruction. At some point, an idea had crept into its skull.

The giant meant to lift her high above the battlefield so everyone could see, then make a spectacle of her annihilation. It hoped the slaughter of Dragonsbane's queen would inspire the Vaasan horde, and strike terror into the Damaran men-at-arms.

As it might. The common soldiers had rejoiced when their heroic king returned to lead them. Every company had one or more of the Crying God's paladins among it to help keep it steady. But most of the men-at-arms had no idea Gareth was trying to draw the Vaasans into a trap. Had their monarch entrusted them all with the secret, the cult's spies would have learned it in short order. Thus, most of the warriors believed the army was simply running from a battle it couldn't win, and in such circumstances, it might only take butchering the queen to turn a disciplined fighting withdrawal into panicked rout.

Christine scrambled backward, but couldn't retreat fast enough to escape the giant with its long reach and stride. When its hand came near enough, she struck with her scimitar. The curved sword sliced deep into its fingers, but the injury failed to balk it. It grabbed her and jerked her off the ground. The pressure of its grip made her wooden armor creak, crack, and splinter, and crushed the breath from her lungs.

She couldn't use the scimitar to do any more damage to the fingers imprisoning her. The angle was wrong. She perceived that once again, a thunderbolt awaited her command and she called it sizzling down.

The giant stumbled and shuddered, and she too convulsed. She'd understood that, with the creature clutching her, the magic would of necessity hurt her, too, but had been willing to risk it to kill her enemy.

That still didn't happen, though. The giant set its club on the ground and started to lift her high.

Then the colossus lurched forward. The precipitous, unexpected motion confused Christine's senses for a moment, but afterward, she saw that her captor had fallen to one knee.

Igan had attacked its already wounded leg from behind.

The gangly young warrior wasn't one of the bodyguards Gareth had assigned to guard his queen, but evidently he'd noticed her peril, ridden to her aid, and struck a telling blow.

The giant wrenched itself around and swiped with the back of its free hand. Armor clanged as the blow swept Igan from his saddle and dashed him to the ground. He tried to rise, but apparently stunned, was moving too slowly. The giant made a fist and raised it high.

Christine called the lightning. The pain was excruciating, even worse than before, and she nearly blacked out. But the magic slowed the giant long enough for Igan to clamber to his feet and ready his sword anew.

The giant snarled and reached for Christine with its empty hand. She realized with a surge of terror that, enraged by the ongoing punishment from on high, it had abandoned the idea of making a show of her death. It meant to kill her without further delay, squeezing and crushing her head or wringing her body like a wet rag.

Igan, however, rushed in and slashed it across the belly, recapturing its attention. It roared and hammered its fist down at him, but he jumped back and avoided the blow. Meanwhile, Christine attempted more magic.

She feared to bring down any more lightning. She had the feeling that she herself couldn't withstand another bolt. Fortunately, she had other spells prepared. Trying to focus past the pain still burning in her tortured flesh, she recited the prayer, and power whispered around her like leaves rustling in the wind. A cloud of white steam billowed into existence, surrounding the giant's wrist like a bracelet, scalding the brute's corpse-white skin.

Startled, it jerked its arm out of the blistering vapor. At that instant, Igan leaped in and cut it again. A great gush of arterial blood spurted from the wound.

The giant doubled over, clutched at the gash with its free hand and slowly flopped over onto its side. It trembled, grasped Christine even more tightly than before, then stopped moving.

Igan helped her squirm from her attacker's death grip, hauled her to her feet, and held her up when her legs buckled beneath her. He turned and whistled, whereupon his warhorse trotted up to them.

"Until I can find Your Majesty another mount," he said, "we'll have to ride double."

He helped her up into the saddle, started to swing himself up behind her, then slipped back and fell on the ground. For a moment, she didn't understand. Then she saw the stubby goblin arrow with the black fletchings. The shaft had found the tiny gap between Igan's breastplate and gorget.

Attuned like any druid to the ebb and flow of life, she sensed that Igan was dead, but it seemed unbelievable. He was still a youth, yet already a knight, a hero, savior of the king and queen alike, dragon- and giant-slayer. How could such a life end so abruptly? With so little fuss? It was quite possible the goblin archer hadn't even aimed the shaft specifically at him.

She scowled away her consternation. Thousands of Igans would die that day and in the tendays to come, if she and her comrades didn't make Gareth's plan work. She used what remained of her lightning magic to harry the onrushing Vaasans, a sea of stunted goblins, their flat, ugly faces russet or jaundice-yellow, with giants rising from their midst like mountainous islands. When her spell ran out of power, she wheeled her mount and rode toward the center of the beleaguered Damaran army, where she could concentrate on healing herself with some degree of safety, and steel herself to plunge back into the fray.

Pondering, Malazan prowled through the garden, among yellow roses and Ishenalyr and the copper's scattered bones. The monastery's cellars weren't spacious enough for all the dragons to attack their foes at the same time. That was why the humans had retreated there, to make it impossible for the wyrms to bring the totality of their strength to bear. Which drakes, then, should accompany their leader in the forefront of the final assault?

Her instincts assured her that the attack would indeed be their last. She and her minions had already slaughtered scores of monks, and the wretched crypts and tunnels couldn't go on forever, could they?

Though, confident as she was, it was mildly troubling that no one had seen the song dragon or the warrior with the iron limbs for the past few days. Maybe someone had struck each of them a mortal blow to which they'd subsequently succumbed, deep inside the mountain where the attackers couldn't witness their deaths, but Malazan had no way of knowing that for certain.

The gigantic red spat her trepidation away, charring a patch of grass in the process. For inferior creatures, the song drake and her companion had proved themselves worthy adversaries, but whatever had become of them, they couldn't forestall the destruction of the monks and the archives any longer. Nothing in all Faerûn could do that.

A vermilion, amber-eyed fire drake swooped over the garden, disturbing Malazan's meditations. She'd given him leave to go hunting through the mountains and over the gleaming whiteness of the glacier, but he'd returned almost immediately.

"Milady!" he cried. "A company of metallic dragons . . . flying down from the north."

"Nonsense," she said. "The metals have all gone into seclusion to wait out the Rage. It's what they always do." A thought struck her. "Unless these are wyrms who failed to do so in time. In which case, they've lost their minds, and have united to go on the rampage."

It amused her to think of her squeamish kindred slaughtering humans, elves, and their ilk with all the ferocious glee of any chromatic. Perhaps it was just as well for them that the frenzy would never release them, for how they'd writhe in anguished guilt if it did!

"I doubt they'll come anywhere near here," she said.

"With all respect, Milady," said the fire drake, "it looks as if they're headed straight for the stronghold, and if I'm not mistaken, one of them is a song dragon."

"That can't be. Show me."

She spread her wings and leaped into the air. The other reptile led her north, over the river valley and toward the southernmost peak of the Galenas. Soon she saw points of light glittering above the mountains. Most were gold or silver, though not all. One was bronze, one brass, and another blue, at a distance only barely discernible against the clear cerulean sky.

"I don't understand," said the fire drake, "how this can be. Did Sammaster warn you the metals might come?"

The witless question triggered a flare of rage, and she nearly succumbed to the urge to smite him with a spell. Instead, controlling herself, she merely snarled, "Silence, imbecile! I have to think!"

However the song dragon had slipped out of the monastery and assembled her new force, she hadn't mustered as many wyrms as Malazan had followers. Despite the formidable abilities of silvers and particularly golds—might that even a red had cause to respect—the chromatics could win the coming battle. The question was, where to fight it?

Beneath the monastery? No. It would be more difficult to exploit her numerical advantage there. She and her warriors would meet the metals in the sky. She wheeled and hurtled back toward the fortress as fast as her pounding wings could carry her.

———— ❧ ————

Crouched behind a heap of broken stone, Raryn watched the fang dragon ten yards away. The mottled, gray-brown creature with its bony spurs and forked tail was one of several wyrms stationed throughout the cellars to keep the monks from reclaiming any of the ground they'd lost. For his part, the dwarf was scouting the perimeter of the territory the humans still held in order to determine when the wyrms would launch their next attack.

A long, ululating howl echoed through the vaults. The fang dragon raised its head to listen. Raryn couldn't speak the Draconic tongue, but assumed he was hearing the command to prepare for another assault. The last one, he suspected. After tendays of dogged resistance, the defense had little left to give.

He told himself he and his comrades had done their best, and that was all the gods required of anyone. It was a belief that had sustained him through every other danger and uncertainty in his life, but he found little comfort in it just then. It was a bitter thing to strive so hard only to lose at the end, thus failing his friends and all the world.

He prepared to slip away from the fang dragon and rejoin the monks. He expected the enormous reptile to remain where it was while it waited for its fellows to descend into the crypts. But instead the wyrm wheeled, the long blades at the end of its tail clattering through rubble, and headed toward the surface.

Raryn realized its departure could only mean one thing: Dorn and Kara had returned with the help they'd gone to find. Malazan had called her followers forth to meet the new threat.

Grinning, no longer feeling the weight of his fatigue or the sting of his scrapes and bruises, Raryn ran to find Cantoule. The defenders might possess only a shadow of their former strength, but whatever remained, they'd commit to the final struggle. The chromatics would find themselves assailed on every side, from the front and rear, and above and below.

Pavel and Will peered over the crest of the hill at the two armies, the littler one retreating, the bigger pursuing, darkening the plain below like enormous swarms of ants.

"That's a lot of goblins," the halfling said.

Pavel snorted. "As usual, I find myself in awe of your profound insight into the obvious. Are you wishing we'd gone back to Thentia when we had the chance?"

Actually, Will did. He didn't fear even the most vicious alley brawl or a hunt for even the fiercest creature. But he'd never marched to war before, and the prospect of hurling himself into the vast and murderous confusion churning and yammering below gave him a pang of unease. But he would have sooner have dipped his nose in tallow and lit it on fire than admit such a thing to Pavel.

"I do wish I'd left," he said, "but only to escape the fetid stink of your breath. I wonder, though, will Dragonsbane's company turn and fight when they're supposed to? Look how hard the Vaasans are pushing them. If they won't stand, the Vaasans are going to massacre us all."

"Says the master of military strategy. We're about to find out if our side can still put up a fight. The goblins have advanced to the proper position."

A moment later, Celedon whistled, recalling the pickets he'd positioned along the top of the rise, to keep watch and kill any goblin kin or giant who wandered up the hill, before the creature could discover the army hiding on the other side and alert its fellows. Will, Pavel, and the other sentries scurried to rejoin the band of skirmishers to which they'd been assigned. It took the squad a couple minutes to form up, and Drigor didn't wait on them. Other cohorts stood ready, and the hulking, scar-faced priest ordered them forward. Thus, Will had the leisure to observe the first moments of the new phase of the battle.

Drigor's command advanced to the top of the rise. With a prodigious thrumming and whistling, archers shot arrows arching across the sky. Wizards hurled blasts of flame, crackling, dazzling thunderbolts, and pale plumes of frost down the slope. Knights couched their lances and cantered toward the foe, and spearmen and swordsmen on foot trotted along behind them. Their faces red, their cheeks puffed out, trumpeters blew their horns.

Down on the plain, other bugles answered. More rapidly than Will would have imagined possible, the ragged, harried mass of Dragonsbane's company stopped fleeing and regrouped into something even a lad who'd never before been to war could recognize as an army arrayed in formation and ready to fight.

The king himself had been in the rearguard, and thus, since the company had reversed it facing, rode his white destrier in the vanguard. He brandished his sword, and a halo of light, somehow visible even in the bright sunshine, flowered around him. Will inferred that he'd used his paladin abilities to cast some useful enchantment. Damara's champion then charged his foes, and his knights surged after him.

Will sighed. The Damarans actually had a chance.

The halfling sensed a presence on his left. As he pivoted, the grizzled sergeant bent over him, the better to shout into his face.

"Are you deaf?" the Damaran roared, spraying him with droplets of spit. "I said, move out!"

He strode away as soon as Will showed signs of obeying.

"I helped fetch your king's soul out of Shadow," Will said to the warrior's broad, mail-clad back, meanwhile extracting a skiprock from his belt pouch. "You really ought to treat me with more respect."

Vingdavalac was a bronze dragon, though in the pale, steady light of Firefingers's magical lamps, his scales looked more yellow than metal-brown. According to Rilitar, that was a sign of the dragon's relative youth, and certainly, he was smaller than any of the warriors of the Queen's Bronzes Taegan had known in Impiltur, compact enough to fit inside the magicians' workroom without utterly dominating the space.

Taegan realized his mind was wandering and he made an effort to focus on the report Thentia's magicians had assembled to hear. It was difficult. Vingdavalac had a rambling, pedantic, tedious way of speaking, the room was warm and stuffy, and Taegan's head buzzed as if he had a bee trapped in his skull. He wondered if he was getting sick.

Then the droning resolved itself into words of command forgotten until that moment. He felt a stab of horror, which hardened into determination. At last he recalled how Sammaster's agent had violated him, and if he was aware, then surely he could resist.

He opened his mouth to warn the wizards and plead for their help, but couldn't force the words out. He sought to flail his arms and capture their attention, only to discover he couldn't manage that, either. He struggled to flee the tower. His legs refused to walk, or his wings, to spread.

He felt defiance fading. He strained to hold onto it, but it dwindled anyway, until nothing remained and he no longer even understood why he'd made the effort. He had a task to perform, and perform it he would. Why wouldn't he?

He murmured the opening phrases of the incantation under his breath. If no one heard, no one would try to stop him.

Or so he imagined. But then something, a duelist's instinct for danger, perhaps, warned him of trouble on his left. Trying to make the motion appear casual, he looked around. Rilitar had been standing at his side, but at some point in the past few moments, had slipped away, placing some distance between them. The elf was whispering too, his lips moving rapidly, rushing to complete his spell first.

Sammaster's ally had compelled both Taegan and Jivex into his service. Accordingly, the bladesinger pointed urgently at Rilitar. Jivex, who'd been flitting restlessly about the ceiling, dived at the elf, throat swelling with its disorienting euphoric vapor, talons poised. Taegan whipped out the magnificent sword the wizard had given him and rushed to aid the drake in his benefactor's destruction. At the same time, he continued with his spell.

Jivex spat out a plume of his sparkling breath. Rilitar jumped away and covered his mouth and nose with the collar of his tunic. It evidently protected him, for he kept on chanting, declaiming the intricate rhymes at the top of his voice. No doubt he hoped it would alert his colleagues that something was amiss, and probably it did. But surprise froze them in place and rendered them useless.

Jivex clawed for Rilitar's eyes. The magician wrenched himself to the side, and the reptile merely tore gashes in his cheek as he hurtled past. By then, however, Taegan was nearly in sword range. He sprang forward, beating his wings to lengthen the leap, and lunged.

Rilitar floundered backward, twisted, and the thrust plunged into his biceps instead of his torso. Taegan yanked the sword back and prepared to redouble. Both combatants were still reciting their spells. Magic whined in the air around them.

Taegan's point plunged at Rilitar's breast. The elf was off balance. He couldn't dodge again.

But gloved hands seized hold of Taegan's forearm and held his weapon back. The grip sent a magical jolt of pain juddering through his body, but couldn't make him stumble over his words of power. He turned his head. It was Scattercloak who'd grabbed him. Even with their bodies scant inches apart, Taegan still couldn't see even a hint of the features hidden inside the magician's shadowy cowl.

He jerked his arm free of Scattercloak's hold, then bashed the warlock in the jaw—presumably—with the pommel of his sword. Bone cracked. Scattercloak reeled backward and fell on his rump.

Taegan whirled back toward Rilitar. His instincts told him the elf presented the greater threat to the completion of his task, and therefore, he meant to finish him first. Wheeling, claws outstretched, Jivex began a second pass.

But before either attacker could strike, Rilitar shouted the final syllable of his spell. He lashed his hands apart, and power streamed from him in an invisible but palpable wave. Taegan staggered. Jivex floundered in flight.

That, however, was merely an incidental effect of the spell. The true purpose was evidently to cleanse the mind of possession, and that it accomplished. Taegan was himself again, full of gratitude for his liberation and a profound desire to exact retribution on the dastard who'd enslaved him.

When his psychic shackles broke, a portion of his memories withered, for that was the way of his adversary. The wretch sought to plan for every contingency. To layer one safeguard on another. But he hadn't done enough tampering. Taegan still knew where to aim his sword.

He pivoted, seeking his foe, then realized to his dismay that though Rilitar's counterspell had freed Jivex as well, the faerie dragon hadn't figured out what he had. As a result, the reptile was streaking across the chamber at pudgy, white-robed Darvin Kordeion.

"No!" Taegan cried. He spread his pinions, leaped into the air, and flew toward his comrade. "Darvin's not the traitor. You're attacking the wrong man!"

For a moment, it looked as if Jivex was too enraged to hear. Then, however, the drake veered off, an instant before he would otherwise have ripped the mage with his talons. Darvin stumbled backward, his eyes wide with shock.

Taegan wrenched himself around to find the real foe, then saw with a twinge of dread that the need to save Darvin had delayed him too long. It had given Phourkyn One-eye time to cast a spell.

The square-built mage with his eye patch and shiny, slicked-back hair thrust out his hand. A spark leaped from his fingers and shot across the workroom, to strike in the center of the majority of the assembled wizards, Vingdavalac, and a goodly assortment of their notes, books, and documents.

With a deafening *boom*, the point of light exploded into a spherical blast of fire. The flame didn't blaze out far enough to engulf Taegan, but the concussion tumbled him through the air and slammed him into a wall. He dropped to the floor.

Refusing to let the shock of the impact paralyze him, he struggled to his feet. On the far side of the room, some of the wizards and even Vingdavalac sprawled motionless. Taegan prayed they were simply stunned, not dead. Other mages threw themselves to the floor and rolled to extinguish their burning robes. Hissing tongues of flame danced on books and papers. Perhaps immune to the searing heat that made the bladesinger flinch from yards away, old Firefingers stood conjuring and seemingly unharmed in the midst of the conflagration.

His platinum wings a blur, Jivex swooped down to hover in front of Taegan's face.

"They just can't keep this place from catching on fire," the reptile said.

"But maybe Firefingers can extinguish the blaze as he did before," Taegan said, "if we stop Phourkyn from making any more mischief."

He cast about, spotted the treacherous mage, and flew at him. In so doing, he met the gaze of Phourkyn's single eye.

Bitter sorrow welled up inside Taegan, drowning his anger and determination, making him falter short of his objective. For a moment, the emotion, though intense, was formless, unconnected to rational thought or memory. Then he recalled his mother, father, and the other kindred and friends he'd left behind in the Earthwood. He hadn't even bade them farewell before forsaking the clan. He'd feared it would be too painful, feared they might even talk him out of his resolve, but how the callous abandonment must have hurt them!

These feelings aren't real, he insisted to himself. Phourkyn's playing with my mind. He struggled against the grief and regret, denying them, and after a second, pushed them back. They still oppressed his spirit like a heavy chain, but at least they weren't paralyzing him anymore.

He oriented on Phourkyn once again, just in time to see one of the long worktables squirm like an animal working the stiffness out of its muscles. Flexible as a serpent, spilling the tomes and sheets of parchment heaped on top of it, the table reared up on two legs with the obvious intention of smashing down on the mage. Evidently Jivex had animated it with his supernatural abilities, for he hovered, staring at it, apparently guiding it by sheer force of will.

Unfortunately, Phourkyn invoked magic of his own, and vanished. The living table crashed down on an empty patch of floor. Jivex hissed in frustration.

It was conceivable that Phourkyn's wizardry had carried him a thousand miles away. But Taegan didn't think so. Now that he'd unmasked Sammaster's minion, the time for stealthy murder and patient manipulation was over. If Phourkyn wanted to be sure of putting an end to the wizards' investigations, he had to finish the job. Such being the case, he was probably lurking right outside the tower, conceivably poised to strike at whoever exited through the door.

Fresh sadness welled up inside Taegan, stinging his eyes with tears, swelling a lump in his throat.

He snarled to quell the magically induced emotion, then called, "Come here!"

While Jivex flew to him, he murmured words of power and brandished his scrap of licorice root. His muscles jumped, and the dragon snarled, as the magic seethed through them, quickening their reactions.

"Take hold of me," Taegan continued.

He stretched out his arm, and Jivex gripped it with his foreclaws. Straining a little to support the reptile's weight, the bladesinger rattled off a second spell.

The world seemed to wink like an eye—and they were high above Firefingers's red-and-yellow tower. The open air felt cool and clean after the heat and smoke inside. Taegan beat his wings and studied the streets and rooftops below. Jivex released his arm and flitted back and forth, peering downward also.

"There!" cried the faerie dragon, his hide rippling with rainbows in the sunlight. "I see him!" He pointed by jabbing his snout in the proper direction.

"Right," said Taegan grimly.

Sword extended before him, conjuring a defensive charm, he dived. Jivex streaked after him. Below them, just outside the gateway to the spire's courtyard, stood Phourkyn. The traitorous mage began to change, to grow into something colossal. Yellow scales sprouted over his body, his ears lengthened, and his face stretched into fanged jaws. A golden eye burned on each side of his reptilian mask.

Phourkyn dropped to all fours, then each of his legs divided into two. Batlike wings erupted from his shoulders, and a serpentine tail writhed forth from the base of his spine. At the tip of the appendage throbbed a point of light.

As the magician swelled and altered, his form grew brighter and brighter, until Taegan had to squint to look at him. The air wavered around him, twisted by the creature's burgeoning internal heat.

People screamed and fled. Taegan started to veer off. He'd read of dragons like that in a book from Rilitar's library. The creature was called a sunwyrm, was hideously powerful, and it probably didn't matter a mouse's whisker whether Phourkyn was truly a drake who'd spent years disguised as a human or was a human cloaking himself in the form of a drake. As powerful was his wizardry was, he was almost certainly capable of using all of a sunwyrm's devastating capabilities either way.

Taegan could never defeat such a terrible foe. It was hopeless . . .

No, curse it, it wasn't! It was only Phourkyn's spell making him feel that it was. He and Jivex had killed a dracolich, and they could slay a sunwyrm as well.

Particularly if they struck before the dastard's transformation was complete. Until then, he might be vulnerable. Accordingly, intent on thrusting his sword deep into Phourkyn's heart, Taegan drove at his enemy with every iota of speed he could muster.

He'd almost reached the target when, wings buzzing, halo of flame crackling, the chasme sprang from Phourkyn's chest as easily as an earthly creature could pounce from a patch of fog. The fly-thing's claws were poised to rend, its long, pointed chitinous snout, to stab, and Taegan's own momentum hurled him onward into the attacks.

❦

To Dorn, in his impatience, it felt rather like a maddeningly slow and stately dance.

Soaring above the mountains, valleys, and glacier, the metals and chromatics had maneuvered and countermaneuvered for an hour, each host seeking to attain the high air, to put the chilly wind at its back, or to outflank its foe. Occasionally one dragon or another conjured a bank of fog, a floating mass of darkness, or a veil of invisibility to disguise its movements, and sometimes a spellcaster on the other side exerted himself to wipe such obscurements away. So far, though, no one had thrown a genuine attack spell.

Nor had Kara commenced one of her ringing battle anthems. Instead, she crooned a gentle ballad. He supposed it kept her relaxed, or helped her think.

For his part, he found himself incapable of relaxation, and at the moment had nothing useful to think about. He just wished the cursed wyrms would get on with it.

Then Tamarand roared, hammered his golden wings, and streaked forward. His warriors raced after him. Sammaster's minions rushed to meet them. Dorn had no idea why it was finally happening. As far as he could tell, none of the maneuvering on either side had accomplished much of anything. But he was grateful the wait was over, and thankful, too, to have plenty of arrows. He and his companions had stopped at a mountain lord's stronghold just long enough for him to demand a fresh supply from the frightened, astonished inhabitants, along with stout rope to lash the quivers, and Dorn himself, to Kara's back.

As he nocked a shaft, Kara switched to a new song, the melody bright and sharp, with a pounding beat. Though

Dorn couldn't understand the words, he sensed the magic in them, felt the enchantments bound in his iron limbs shiver in response. Sparks jumped and sizzled on his artificial hand.

Across the sky, other dragons conjured defensive wards. A single onrushing green split into five dragons as it created illusory images of itself. Havarlan's lithe, scarred argent form smudged into a blur. Arranged in a spiral, several points of white glow materialized around Malazan.

Nexus appeared behind and slightly above the chromatics. The gold's magic had translated him instantly across the intervening space. He spat a plume of fire, and a black screeched and burned in the blast. But other chromatics swiftly wheeled and spewed their own breath weapons.

Kara tilted her wings, veered, and swooped downward, sacrificing altitude to distance herself from the red and fang dragons on her flank. It seemed to Dorn as if the reptiles had sprung out of nowhere, as if they'd appeared by magic, and of course it was entirely possible they had.

Scowling away his surprise, he drew his bowstring to his ear. It was awkward shooting upward, but at least he'd positioned himself in such a way that he didn't have to worry about hitting Kara's sweeping, crystal-blue pinion. He loosed the shaft, and it plunged into the underside of the red's neck.

The scarlet reptile jerked its head back at the stab of pain. Dorn had delayed it casting an attack spell or spitting flame for at least another moment. Unfortunately, he'd had no way of balking the fang wyrm at the same time. Darts of green light flew from its outstretched claws at Kara's torso.

But they blinked out of existence just before they could touch her scales. Dorn realized she must earlier have cast an enchantment that shielded her against that particular attack.

Recovered from the arrow's sting, the red furled its wings, dived, spread its jaws wide, and spewed flame. Kara spun away from the stream of fire, turning completely upside down in the process. Dorn felt a jolt of unreasoning fear, instinct's frantic insistence that, rope or no, he was about to plunge to the earth far below. Then the sky was above him and the ground where it belonged once more, and he saw that Kara had successfully evaded the blast of flame.

Somehow she'd even looped above the diving red. Dorn tried to drive an arrow into the creature's spine, but the red wheeled in a way he hadn't anticipated, and he only succeeded in piercing its wing. Kara was more successful. Without missing a beat in her throbbing, ferocious melody, she discharged a flare of bright, lightning-charged breath to sear the chromatic's neck and shoulders. The red screeched and floundered in the air.

Wings pounding, Kara took advantage of the red's distress to climb higher above her foes. Unharmed as yet, the spurred, gray-brown fang wyrm labored after her. But like most members of its species, it was a clumsy flyer, and failed to narrow the distance.

Still, magic could leap across the gap. The fang dragon snarled an incantation, and a wave of distortion shot from its foreclaws. It slammed into Kara's ventral side like a battering ram, bashing her several yards through the air, and making Dorn fumble his grip on his bowstring before he finished drawing it back. The arrow jumped feebly, uselessly away.

Dorn was sure the impact had hurt Kara, but the pain didn't mar the perfection of her song as it birthed more of her own magic. Plummeting from empty air, huge hailstones hammered down on the red. The barrage jabbed more holes in its wings, and Dorn drove an arrow into its spine.

The crimson dragon roared words of power, and a point of light flew at Kara. She tilted her wings, veering, nearly inverting herself and Dorn once more, and when the spark exploded into a blast of fire, they only caught the edge of it.

Kara completed another spell, and a cloud of foul-looking greenish vapor boiled into existence around the red. It swooped out of the mist and kept on hurtling down and away, gliding above the glacier, its shadow gray on the gleaming ice.

Dorn peered after it, trying to determine if it was truly running away, then glimpsed motion from the corner of his eye. He jerked around. A green was hurtling toward them.

"On our right!" he cried.

Kara dodged left. Glare flashed into being. For Dorn, it was like looking into the sun, except that it was impossible to turn away. The charm the green had cast made the light flare on every side. The only defense was to squinch his eyes shut, and he didn't manage that quickly enough. When he opened them again, he saw only haze and floating blobs.

Kara's body tilted beneath him, snapping him to the side. He surmised she was trying to dodge an attack, and could only pray she'd shifted in the right direction. That she could still see, or, failing that, her other inhumanly keen senses compensated.

Something seared his skin. Reckoning it to be the green's breath weapon, he tried not to inhale, but sucked in a bit of the corrosive vapor anyway. It burned his nose, throat, and lungs, and he coughed and retched.

But the stuff didn't melt the human half of his face away, or rot his chest from the inside. Kara must indeed have dodged the worst of it.

He blinked away tears and found that his sight had more or less returned. Kara and her new adversary were circling one another. Left some distance behind, the fang dragon struggled after them until a silver-scaled shield wyrm distracted it by blasting it with a thunderbolt spell.

Dorn shot an arrow into the green's shoulder, and it replied by raking at Kara with jagged lengths of conjured darkness. Then darts of azure force pierced the chromatic's underside. It roared and veered off. Kara wheeled to pursue, spotted the fire drake winging its way at her, and turned to meet that threat instead.

As Dorn reached for an arrow, he glanced down to determine where the glowing blue missiles had come from. All the way up from the monastery grounds, it appeared. Tiny with distance, folk were scurrying around down there, loosing arrows, crossbow bolts, or spells at any chromatic who ventured into range.

For a moment, Dorn slumped with relief at knowing for certain that the monks still defended the archives—and that, quite possibly, Raryn still lived. Then he spat the soft feeling away and laid another arrow on his bow.

He and Kara traded attacks with the fire drake for a few seconds, until the chaos of the aerial battle wrenched the two wyrms apart to seek new opponents. In general, that seemed to be the way it was going to work. With dozens of dragons wheeling in three dimensions, occasionally using magic to pop from one spot to another, the action was too frenzied and confusing simply to pick a single adversary and fight it to the finish. Which made it that much harder to judge which side was winning, though already a copper lay motionless inside the monastery walls, the shattered body of a young red, its tail and one wing dangling over the edge, overfilled a ledge below the stronghold, and a black sprawled in a pool of its own blood on the glacier.

Malazan roared. Over the course of the next half minute, all three of the fang dragons broke away from the conflict in the air to spiral down toward the monastery. Evidently their commander had decided they'd be more use on the ground, putting an end to the harassment stabbing up from below.

Raryn had expected that some of Sammaster's wyrms would fly down and attack their earthbound foes. That didn't make it any less alarming to watch them coming, plunging out of a sky so streaked and scarred with flares of magic and dragon breath that it scarcely seemed accurate to call it blue anymore. It was more like a jester's patchwork rainbow of a cloak.

"Form up your squads!" the dwarf shouted. "Spellcasters, take cover inside the buildings!"

The monks and their associates scrambled to obey. After tendays of diligent training and hard fighting, they knew what they were doing. Raryn just hoped that would be enough to tilt the balance.

He scrambled behind a marble fountain, the lip grooved where one of the chromatics had used it to hone its talons. He was in position to fight in concert with the rest of his own squad, though it might not look that way to a casual observer. The group was spread out to make it difficult for a dragon to target more than one of them at a time.

Raryn murmured a ranger charm and loosed an arrow. The magic enhanced both the accuracy and the velocity of the shot, and the shaft drove so deep into an onrushing fang wyrm's mottled breast that it disappeared entirely. Quarrels and javelins flew at the creature as well. A wizard jumped up behind a window just long enough to hurl a pearly burst of frost at it, then crouched back down.

None of the attacks made the gray-brown dragon falter or veer off. It furled its wings and hurtled downward, claws poised to impale the youthful monk underneath it. The boy flung himself out of the way, and for an instant, it looked as if he'd scramble clear. But as soon as the wyrm slammed to earth, it whipped its forked tail in a horizontal arc. With a dull thunk, the long, bony blades at the end of the appendage chopped the youth's body into several pieces.

Raryn dropped his bow and grabbed his new harpoon. It wasn't as fine a weapon as the one he'd lost in the ossuary, but it would do. He cast it at the dragon's flank, the line he'd tied to the heavy fountain streaming out behind it.

He grinned for an instant when the barbed lance drove deep between the reptile's ribs. He grabbed his bone-handled ice-axe and charged.

The rest of his team rushed in, also, to assault the dragon from all sides. Each warrior attacked when the creature oriented on someone else—or at least appeared to, for the creature had a nasty habit of feinting at one foe, then pivoting to strike at another—and retreated when it focused on him.

To Raryn's mind, it was scant comfort that, so far anyway, for these first few seconds, the melee was a purely physical confrontation. Fang wyrms had no breath weapon, and if it still had any spells left, it was apparently saving them to use against the metallic drakes. But why shouldn't it? Who could fault it for believing it had no need of magic to annihilate the scurrying mites assailing it? Quick as a viper for all its hugeness, it lashed out furiously with fangs, claws, wings, and tail, the slightest brush of its razor-edged scales sufficient to flay a man or dwarf's flesh to the bone.

Raryn hacked at its side, scrambled underneath it, drove his axe into its belly, and sprang clear just before it flung itself down to crush him. A monk drove a pair of long daggers into the base of its neck. Another of Cantoule's gray-clad followers gave a fierce, resounding shout and thrust a spear straight up into the wyrm's lower jaw. The bloody head of the lance crunched through multiple layers of hide, muscle, and bone to pop out the top side, in front of the fang dragon's glaring orange eyes.

Raryn thought he and his comrades had hurt the reptile badly, but it didn't slow down. It worked its lower jaw from side to side, and the spear pinning its mouth shut snapped to pieces. It dipped its wedge-shaped head with its thorn-like encrustation of small horns and snatched up the monk who'd pierced its jaws. The spearman screamed, his flailing limbs already withering and blackening as the reptile's bite poisoned him. Forgetting Dorn and Raryn's training, another monk charged straight at the dragon's mask, perhaps in hopes of extricating his fellow from the huge, gnashing teeth. The wyrm ripped most of the organs from the would-be rescuer's chest with a single flick of its claws.

Raryn ducked a sweep of the tail-blades and chopped at the dragon's flank. The axe bit deep. The reptile jerked in pain, began to whirl toward its attacker, and tangled a leg in the rope securing it to the fountain. It howled in frustration and lunged, throwing all its strength against the line.

The harpoon tore from its flesh, and blood spurted after it. It was possible that, in yanking out the barb, the fang dragon had given itself the worst wound it had yet sustained. Still, it was free, and its restored mobility caught its foes by surprise. It pounced between two monks, shredding one with its fangs and cleaving the other with its tail blades, and whirled to find another target. Confused, suddenly terrified for all their courage and discipline, the remaining servants of Ilmater floundered backward. If they broke, the dragon would slaughter them all in a matter of seconds.

Raryn frantically rattled off another ranger charm. The grass in the dragon's immediate vicinity grew tall and wrapped around its feet and the end of its tail, binding them to the ground.

The enchantment would only immobilize the wyrm for a heartbeat or so at best. The dragon was simply too strong, and it was probably surprise as much as the grip of the restraints that made it falter. Still, Raryn had held it up for a moment, and the monks could see that he'd hindered it. Maybe that would hearten them.

"Kill it!" the hunter bellowed.

He rushed in swinging his axe, and the humans followed his lead.

The fang wyrm struck and caught another monk in its fangs. It heaved, and its tail and right forefoot tore free of the binding grass. Then it shuddered, gave a breathless little cry, flopped over on its side, and thrashed. Raryn and the monks scurried backward to avoid being crushed in its death throes.

Panting, his heart pounding, Raryn felt an upswelling of relief that the creature could no longer hurt him or anyone else. But he refused to let the emotion make him slow and stupid. The battle wasn't over, just one little part of it. He cast about to see how the rest of it was going, then cursed in dismay.

A second team of monks, led by Cantoule, had likewise killed its fang dragon. But the third such wyrm had slain many of its opponents and scattered the rest. It bounded unopposed toward a chapel with the martyrdom of the Crying God depicted in bas-relief on the facade. The spellcasters sheltering inside hurled darts of crimson light at the reptile, and conjured a wall of rippling distortion to block its path. But the missiles didn't seem to harm it, and it simply leaped through the barrier without even slowing down, as if the magical construct was no more solid than air.

If the dragon reached the wizards, it would have little trouble killing them. Raryn sprinted to intercept the wyrm. So did some of the monks. The dwarf saw that they were all too far away.

But a column of white vapor streaked down from the sky to wash over the fang dragon. Its body stiffened, locking into immobility, and off balance, it toppled onto its side. It shuddered, plainly trying to break free of the paralysis, and a shield dragon plummeted down on it like an avalanche of silver. The metallic drake ripped and tore the gray-brown reptile apart, seemingly oblivious to the cuts it suffered from the fang wyrm's abrasive hide in the process.

Its jaws smeared with crimson, the silver lifted its head. Something about the set of its eyes and the pair of long, smooth horns sweeping backward from its skull was familiar.

"Azhaq!" Raryn cried.

Azhaq turned and regarded him without any noticeable warmth. Still, he did condescend to answer, "Raryn Snow-stealer."

"How's the fight going, do you think?" Raryn asked. "Is there anything else the folk on the ground can do to help you in the air?"

"Let's see. . . ."

Azhaq raised his head to peer up at the sky, and Raryn did the same. A few moments of observation sufficed to reveal that the character of the battle raging overhead was changing.

At first, attacking primarily with spells, the dragons had fought widely dispersed, wheeling about the mountaintop, casting at whatever target presented itself from one moment to the next. But all but the eldest were running low on magic. They had to strike with their breath, or even fang and claw, and thus needed to maneuver closer to their foes. Due to that requirement, and because both sides had suffered attrition, it had become possible for a wyrm to trade attacks with a particular adversary until one of them overwhelmed the other.

Malazan with her coating of wet blood was just concluding one such duel. She spat flame, and a silver dropped, its wings burning, ruined, unable to hold it in the air anymore. The shield dragon invoked one of its innate abilities, and its fall slowed to a gentle drift downward. But that meant it could no longer maneuver, and Raryn assumed the gigantic red would have little difficulty finishing it off.

Malazan let it go, though, in favor of other targets. Purple-edged wings hammering, she climbed and turned toward Kara and Dorn.

Raryn was grimly certain his friends were no match for the red. Not by themselves. He cast about, hoping to see one of the golds or silvers rushing to their aid, but the metals were all busy with opponents of their own.

Azhaq spread his gleaming wings and said, "I'll help them."

"I'm coming with you," Raryn said.

"I have no harness to secure a rider on my—"

"I'm coming with you. I just need my bow."

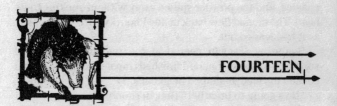

FOURTEEN

11 Flamerule, the Year of Rogue Dragons

The chasme's talons whizzed past Taegan's head. Its proboscis stabbed at his throat, and likewise missed by a matter of inches. The charm of displacement the bladesinger had invoked during his dive had thrown off the demon's aim.

But Taegan's sword missed the tanar'ri too, for he'd been prepared to strike Phourkyn, not the apparition that had leaped unexpectedly from within the traitor's swelling, altering body. Worse, his momentum slammed him into the spirit, and they fell to the ground together.

It snatched for him, to rip him with its claws and hold him while its aura of flame roasted him, and Taegan tried to scramble clear. It didn't look as if he was going to make it. But Jivex streaked at the chasme and heedless of the fire, raked at one of its round, bulging eyes.

The demon snarled and flinched back. Taegan sprang to his feet and thrust at it.

The elven sword plunged deep into the fly-thing's body. It screamed, and wings droning, leaped away.

Taegan lunged, trying to hit it again, but the attack fell short by an inch. Jivex conjured golden dust to blind the chasme, and the powder spilled away without sticking to its head. The demon flew back inside Phourkyn's torso as easily as it had leaped out.

Squinting, Taegan peered at the radiant, eight-legged sunwyrm and saw that he'd finished transforming. Phourkyn cocked his wedge-shaped head back.

"He's going to breathe!" Taegan shouted.

Wings hammering, he and Jivex hurled themselves through the air.

A split second later, something—dazzling yellow light or fire—streaked from the sunwyrm's maw. Narrowly missing both Taegan and the faerie dragon, the stuff hit the rutted mud of the street without disturbing it or even splashing. But the avariel knew it would have consumed his flesh if it had swept over him.

He simultaneously rattled off another defensive enchantment and flew with all his magically augmented speed, trying to maneuver away from the sunwyrm's jaws and foreclaws and into position to strike at the creature's flank. He poised his sword for a thrust, then, despite the glare that was half blinding him, discerned a subtle change in Phourkyn's enormous form. The mountain of golden scale and muscle blurred ever so slightly.

From reading Rilitar's book, Taegan understood what it meant. Phourkyn had just become as insubstantial as a ghost. Most attacks couldn't touch a sunwyrm in that form, but the creature could still employ its breath weapon, and it seemed likely that particular specimen would be able to use at least some of his spells as well.

Taegan had no idea how he and Jivex were supposed to cope with such an adversary. His uncertainty gave his magically created despair another opening, another chance to overwhelm him, and he felt a desperate urge to flee. But he resisted, shouted a war cry, and thrust his sword at the hollow between two of Phourkyn's ribs.

To his surprise, he felt resistance as the weapon plunged in deep, and Phourkyn roared in shock. Apparently, thanks to the enchantments bound in the steel, the elven blade could cut the sunwyrm even in phantom form.

Taegan flew on down the length of the dragon's body, stabbing repeatedly. The sunwyrm whirled, his horned head whipping around at the end of his serpentine neck, and spewed another blast of brilliant light. Taegan tried to dodge, but the stream of radiance still grazed the edge of his wing.

He cried out, and spastic with the searing pain, floundered in the air. By the time he regained control of his muscles, Phourkyn had swung into position to strike at him with all a sunwyrm's best weapons. Solid once more, the traitor reared on his four back legs and poised the four front ones to snatch and tear. Burning with the same lethal power that infused his breath weapon, the talons glowed even brighter than the rest of him.

Taegan could only dodge and wait for a chance to fly clear. One set of huge, shining claws rebounded from the invisible floating shield he'd conjured moments before. He wrenched himself out of the way of a second blow, and with a beat of his wings, jerked himself above a third one, even managing to hack off one of Phourkyn's toes before the traitor snatched his leg back.

The wound seemed to make the sunwyrm hesitate, and Taegan thought he saw his opportunity. He kept on climbing, then discerned too late that it was what Phourkyn wanted him to do. The bladesinger had been so busy avoiding the dragon's blazing talons that he'd momentarily lost track of the creature's jaws, and Phourkyn struck at him like a viper, fanged jaws gaping.

Taegan perceived with a surge of dread that he couldn't fling himself out of the way in time. Jivex, however, hurtled past him and straight into the sunwyrm's maw, past the rows of huge, pointed teeth and deeper in. No doubt startled, Phourkyn faltered, and his attack fell short. But the larger wyrm snapped his jaws shut, sealing the faerie dragon inside.

Taegan felt a senseless desire to cry out and warn Jivex not to do the gallant thing he'd just done. He was certain his friend was doomed. All Phourkyn had to do to destroy the small creature trapped in his mouth was spit his breath weapon. Unable to dodge, Jivex would dissolve in the blast.

Grimly sure he couldn't inflict enough damage in time for it to do any good, Taegan slashed at Phourkyn's neck. Then the sunwyrm's jaws flew open, and silvery wings a blur, Jivex streaked out into the open air amid a haze of blood. Evidently the larger wyrm's breath weapon hadn't yet renewed itself, and Jivex had used the delay to good effect, tearing at the soft insides of Phourkyn's mouth with fang and claw, inflicting so much pain that the traitor couldn't bear to hold him there any longer.

Taegan slashed another gash in Phourkyn's neck, and turned to fly down his adversary's flank. But with a sudden beat of his wings, the traitor sprang away from his opponents to land ten yards down the street. Phourkyn's blazing eyes stared intently, and the air around Taegan and Jivex darkened and droned as a cloud of locusts seethed into existence.

The manifestation infuriated Taegan. It seemed monstrously unfair that the chasme could still use that filthy power even when hiding inside its master's body. The bladesinger pounded his wings up and down and threw himself forward in a desperate attempt to reach Phourkyn before the insects fully materialized.

A locust bumped against his forehead. Another landed on his wrist and crawled up his arm. Then, however, Rilitar's voice declaimed words of power, and all the insects vanished. Taegan glanced around and saw the elf wizard standing in the street. Rilitar's garments were singed, and his face, raw and blistered from close contact with the flames inside

Firefingers's tower, but the topaz-tipped wand was steady in his outstretched hand.

Taegan drove onward at Phourkyn. Hurtling beside him, Jivex filled the surrounding air with the illusory images of dozens of winged, brightly clad pixies, each brandishing a miniature spear.

As fast as they were flying, Rilitar's wizardry was faster. Five spheres of light, each a different color, flashed past his allies to explode on impact with Phourkyn's body. The red orb burst into flame, another, the yellow one, into crackling tendrils of lightning, and the green, into a sizzling splash of acid. The blue sphere encrusted a patch of the sunwyrm's scales in ice, and the silver one birthed a deafening howl that split his hide like an axe.

Taegan and Jivex streaked by Phourkyn's head and along his spine. The bladesinger stabbed and cut. Jivex conjured more golden dust, which dropped away without adhering to the sunwyrm's head. The illusory pixies swarmed around his mask, however, jabbing with their spears, perhaps obstructing his sight almost as effectively as the powder would have. As Phourkyn spun sideways in a futile attempt to swing his head clear of the phantasms, the faerie dragon created a shrill whine that set Taegan's teeth on edge. The winged elf assumed Jivex had placed the source of the magical shriek right inside Phourkyn's ear, where it would prove excruciating, deafening, and inescapable.

More radiant spheres exploded against Phourkyn's breast. Taegan drove his sword into the sunwyrm's back. The huge, glowing reptile spun, attempting to swat him with a wing, but he beat his own pinions, looped out of the way, and stabbed the traitor once more.

Phourkyn jerked in pain, and Taegan wondered if the creature might actually be close to defeat. But then the sunwyrm bellowed a single word of power.

In response, the whole world seem to ring, as if Taegan was a sparrow caught inside an enormous tolling temple bell. The sensation wasn't painful, precisely, but vibrated his strength and will away, and made consciousness itself gutter like the flame of a candle in the last moments before it melted utterly. No longer able to use his wings, the avariel fell from the air, hit the sunwyrm's flank, and rolled down its contours to land heavily on the ground. Jivex thudded down somewhere nearby.

Nearly trampling Taegan in the process, Phourkyn wheeled to face his fallen foes. The bladesinger felt a dull, murky sort of fear, knew he ought to rise and fight, but was unable to translate the thought into action.

Phourkyn snarled an incantation. The swarm of pixies vanished, and the howl cut off abruptly. The sunwyrm cocked back his head to spew his breath weapon. Taegan struggled to scramble to his feet, but only managed to lift himself to his knees.

Shifted through space by his magic, Rilitar appeared between Taegan and Jivex. He stooped and stretched out his arms to touch them both, but found they were too far apart. The wizard grabbed Taegan's forearm, heaved him closer to the faerie dragon, then managed to reach the tip of Jivex's platinum wing. At the same instant, Phourkyn spat a stream of dazzling light.

Taegan flinched, but nothing hurt him. He saw that he was lying in a narrow alley, with the surrounding houses pressing in close on either side. Rilitar had translated him and Jivex away just in time. His strength rapidly returning, the avariel lifted his head to thank the mage, then gasped in dismay.

Because, while Phourkyn's breath hadn't quite reached him or Jivex, it had washed over the rescuer crouching above them. As a result, Rilitar didn't look burned so much as vivisected, as if a master torturer had flayed and whittled sections of skin and flesh away to make an intricate design. Some of the wounds appeared superficial, but others ran deep.

The wizard collapsed on his belly.

"Rilitar!" Taegan cried.

"Don't fret . . . about me," Rilitar gritted. "Kill Phourkyn."

Taegan realized the elf was right. Somebody had to deal with the traitor, or he might yet bring Kara's enterprise to ruin.

He turned to Jivex and asked, "Can you still fight?"

"Watch me," the faerie dragon said.

He sprang off the ground, and wings beating, wheeled toward the mouth of the alley.

"Wait," Taegan said. "Phourkyn doesn't know where we disappeared to. It's possible he doesn't know he hurt Rilitar, either. We'll use that against him." He looked at the surrounding rooftops, then pointed. "I'm going to circle that way. Give me a little time, then conjure an illusion of the three of us charging from the alley into the street. With luck, it'll distract Phourkyn, and I'll take the whoreson from behind."

"Get going," Jivex said.

His injured pinion throbbing, Taegan took to the air and maneuvered in an arc, striving to keep himself hidden behind shops and houses, and when he had to cross the gaps separating them, spying for glimpses of the sunwyrm. At first Phourkyn seemed to be catching his breath, and casting about for his vanished foes. Soon enough, though, he stalked toward Firefingers's tower, probably intending to hurl an attack spell or a blast of his breath through the entrance.

Before he could reach it, though, semblances of Rilitar, Jivex, and Taegan lunged into the street to confront him. The elf pointed his wand. The bladesinger and faerie dragon streaked through the air toward their foe. Phourkyn hesitated, peered at the deception, then snorted with contempt at a trick that, he thought, had failed to take him in.

By then, the real Taegan had flown up behind him. The avariel drove his sword into the center of Phourkyn's back.

Phourkyn screamed. His serpentine tail with the point of brilliant glow at the end flopped limply to the ground. His four rear legs buckled. Using the four in front, he struggled to keep from falling down, and as he swayed and stumbled, Taegan went on thrusting.

The sunwyrm whipped his head around, and Taegan dodged the strike. It was easier when he didn't have to worry about claw attacks. Phourkyn needed his remaining legs to hold his crippled body up.

Or perhaps not, for the sunwyrm spread his leathery wings and flexed the four functional legs to spring upward. Before he could, though, the earth beneath his feet rippled, turned a lighter shade of brown, and by the looks of it, changed in consistency as well, to an ooze more treacherous than quicksand. Phourkyn's feet could find no purchase in the muck, and it sucked them down at once.

At the same time, strands of jagged darkness writhed about the sunwyrm's wings, the shadow dimming their radiance. The limbs withered at its touch.

Taegan risked a glance around to find out which of the other wizards had emerged from the tower to join the battle. As it turned out, three of them had: Scattercloak, Jannatha Goldenshield, and Baerimel Dunnath. The petite, impishly pretty sisters looked ferocious. Avid to avenge their murdered cousin.

Phourkyn snapped his head around in their direction and snarled words of power. Trying to disrupt the conjuration, Taegan drove his sword into the sunwyrm's neck. Jivex streaked through the air and ripped at the larger reptile's eye. Phourkyn stumbled over his recitation. Taegan thrust home, pulled back his sword, and arterial blood spurted from the puncture.

Phourkyn vanished. Taegan swung his blade again anyway, just in case the traitor had simply become invisible, but the weapon touched nothing. The avariel cried out in fury that, at the end, his foe had eluded him.

But then Scattercloak said, "No. I forbid it."

Whereupon Phourkyn reappeared beneath Taegan as abruptly as he'd blinked away.

It was startling, but Taegan had the reflexes of a master fencer even when his wits were addled. He attacked, slicing open a prodigious gash.

Phourkyn's head splashed down into the quicksand. Half expecting the sunwyrm to rear back up, Taegan hovered warily above him. But all the traitor did was sink deeper into the muck. The yellow glare of his scaly hide dimmed.

"I don't much like it," said Scattercloak in his emotionless tenor voice, "when people commit unsavory acts and try to shift the blame onto me."

Wings pounding, Taegan rushed back toward the alley and Rilitar. Jivex hurtled in his wake.

Dorn loosed arrow after arrow. Singing her defiance, Kara wheeled toward Malazan.

It seemed suicidal. The ancient red was twice Kara's size. But in Dorn's judgment, the bard was making the right move. Over the past months, he'd learned her limits well enough to know she was nearly out of magic. Malazan almost certainly wasn't. Therefore, if Kara tried to keep away from her adversary, the chromatic would simply smite her with spell after spell, while she had no way of striking back. Whereas, if she closed the distance, it was possible she could employ her breath weapon to good effect.

The drawback to the strategy, though, was that Kara would be in range of Malazan's fiery breath as well. It was even possible that the red with her sheen of wet blood would catch the song dragon in her talons and bring her superior physical strength to bear. Dorn could only hope that Kara, being the smaller, would prove more agile in flight, or that his own presence would somehow give Kara a decisive advantage, unlikely as that seemed. He sent another shaft streaking across the sky. It flew to the target but glanced off Malazan's scales.

The red roared an incantation. The words of power made Dorn's stomach churn. For a second, the cold mountain wind blew hot.

Kara screamed and pulled her wings into her body, as if they were clenching in an uncontrollable spasm. She and Dorn plummeted. Malazan hurtled forward and down, swooping to intercept them in mid-descent, claws poised to seize and rend.

"Fight it!" Dorn shouted, simultaneously loosing another arrow.

The shaft lodged in Malazan's chest, but intent on making her kill, she didn't even seem to notice.

Painted in gore, the red's outstretched wings seemed to cover the entire sky. Dorn sunk an arrow into her flesh and snatched for another, even though the onrushing dragon was so close that he doubted he'd have time for a final shot.

Then, at the last possible instant, Kara resumed her song and unfurled and beat her wings. The action jerked her to the side, and Malazan plummeted past her. Kara blasted the red with a sparkling jet of her breath. Malazan jerked and screeched at the crackling touch of the lightning suffusing the vapor.

Panting, his heart pounding, Dorn realized Kara had tricked her foe. Recognizing the spell Malazan had cast to cripple her wings, she'd pretended the power had overwhelmed her, to lure the red into opening herself up to an attack.

A successful ploy, but scarcely a decisive one. Malazan swept her wings up and down, climbed after them, and spewed fire.

Kara tilted her pinions and spun herself out of the path of the plume of flame. Woven into the savage melody of her song, another spell from her dwindling store shrouded Malazan in a cloud of nasty-looking olive vapor, but to no apparent effect.

Kara and Malazan wheeled and swooped about the sky, and though intent on the red, Dorn nonetheless caught glimpses of the aerial battle as a whole. After repeated uses, the dragons' breath weapons took more time to renew themselves. For that reason, or because it seemed a relatively safe tactic to use against a wounded, weary, or smaller foe, a good many wyrms were finally assailing their enemies with fang and claw. A red swooped over a gold, raking gouges in the metal's scales as it hurtled past. A brass attempted a similar maneuver against a skull wyrm, but the black seized its attacker's hind leg in its teeth and yanked it close. Ripping and biting at one another, unable to fly while twined together, the dragons plummeted halfway down the sky before breaking their grapple, springing apart, and spreading their wings once more.

Dorn still couldn't tell which side was winning.

He drove an arrow into Malazan's mask, just missing the gigantic reptile's blank yellow eye. The red snarled words of power, and the longbow jerked from his grip, as if invisible hands had seized it. The ploy caught him by surprise, and though he snatched for the weapon, he failed to catch it. It tumbled end over end toward the mountains below.

Without it, he was useless, nothing but hindering weight on Kara's back.

He recognized the final spells Kara cast, one after the other. The first should have stolen Malazan's voice, but didn't take. The other made her breath blaze so brightly that it might have blinded the red, except that the chromatic dodged the blast. After that, though the bard kept chanting her song of righteous wrath, there were no more incantations threaded through the lyrics.

She veered, climbed, and swooped, accelerated and decelerated, with uncanny foresight and agility, evading the flares of flame and sorcery that Malazan hurled in her direction. Until the red howled words that jabbed pain into Dorn's ears and made them bleed. Malazan then spewed more fire, not bothering to aim it at Kara but simply blasting it into the air.

The mass of flame lingered, floating, and writhed into the shape of a dragon nearly as huge as Malazan herself. It lashed its burning pinions and streaked toward Kara.

With a pang of fear, Dorn grasped the point of the tactic. The song dragon had enjoyed some success evading one foe, but two could maneuver to trap her between them.

Malazan and her creation winged their way toward Kara, converging on her from two directions. The crystal-blue dragon faked a turn, then spun back around, swooped lower, and caught an updraft to fling her high once more.

It didn't matter. She succeeded in distancing herself from the creature of living fire, but Malazan matched her move for move. Indeed, the red anticipated her, attained a slight advantage in altitude, and close enough once more, spat flame.

Kara tried to swoop under the attack, but the flare still seared the ends of her upraised wings. The shock silenced her song and made her flounder in the air, whereupon Malazan dived at her. Dorn bellowed a warning that, he already knew, Kara was for the moment incapable of heeding.

But some invisible agency intercepted Malazan short of her target and bounced her higher into the air. The fringe of the same force caught Kara and spun her like a wheel until she managed to right herself.

Meanwhile, Dorn recognized the surge of vertigo that resulted when up and down reversed themselves, for Azhaq had once used the same power against him. He looked down and saw the silver climbing toward Malazan with Raryn astride his back. The dwarf shot an arrow into the red's belly.

Wings pounding, Malazan wheeled to escape the enchantment Azhaq had created, the treacherous, disorienting zone where things fell upward. She screeched, and her fiery conjured creature hurtled at the silver.

Azhaq didn't try to evade the apparition. He simply rattled off an incantation, and the bright mass of living flame vanished as if it had never been. Raryn loosed more arrows, driving them into the red's neck, breast, and guts.

Azhaq was an old wyrm, unscathed, with a highly competent archer mounted on his back. Kara was relatively young, wounded, and bore a rider who had no way of attacking at range. Understandably, Malazan oriented on the Talon of Justice and the tracker, and that, Dorn realized, afforded him an opportunity.

"Climb!" he said to Kara. "Swing behind and above Malazan, and get close."

"I don't need to be too close to use my breath."

"Do it!"

"I'll try," she promised, and beat her charred and blistered
wings.

Azhaq roared an incantation, and a blaze of frost streaked
up from his outstretched talons, only to melt away just before
it reached Malazan. The red laughed and growled her own
cabalistic rhyme. Gashes split Azhaq's argent hide, as if invisible blades were hacking him. As he reeled in the air, wracked
by the ongoing punishment, Malazan rattled off a second
spell. A creature that seemed part man and part gray-feath-
ered vulture materialized midway between its summoner and
the shield dragon. It gave an ear-splitting screech and dived
at Azhaq and Raryn. The dwarf drove an arrow all the way
through its spindly, crooked neck, but it didn't falter.

That was all Dorn had time to see before Malazan
reclaimed his full attention. The red plainly hadn't forgotten
her other foes, for her head twisted, seeking them. Her eyes
blazed when she saw how close they'd sneaked.

But Dorn saw with a sick, helpless feeling, that it wasn't
close enough.

He expected Kara to veer off. Malazan having spotted her,
it was the only sane thing to do. But still striving to do as
Dorn had bade her, resuming her battle anthem, she swooped
nearer.

Malazan met her with a burst of fiery breath. The song
dragon's body shielded Dorn from the worst of it, but even
so, the brush of the flame was excruciating. Quite possibly,
it had burned Kara's life away.

But he couldn't think about that. He had to act. He jerked
loose the knot securing him to Kara's back, scrambled to his
feet on her scorched, blistered body, and leaped.

He was no acrobat like Will, and when Malazan spotted
him and started to spin away, he was sure he was going to
miss, to fall and smash himself to pulp on the ground far

below. But he banged down on the red's back instead.

Malazan's scales were slick with their coating of blood, and he started to slide away into space. He snagged his iron claws in her hide and drew his bastard sword.

Malazan spat fire at him. He hunkered down, shielding his human parts behind the metal ones, and though he gasped in agony, when the jet of flame guttered out, he was still alive. He plunged his sword into the red's flesh.

The blade bit deep, but not deep enough. Malazan poised her head to strike at him. It was an awkward angle for her, straight back along her own spine, but neither could he do much in the way of dodging when he had to cling to her like a tick to keep her slippery, heaving mass from flinging him off. All he had was the forlorn hope that she'd hurt her fangs on his iron half, and flinch back.

Or so he thought, until Kara hurtled onto Malazan's neck. Though her blue hide was horribly blackened and burned from head to tail, she clawed and bit at the red with a ferocity no doubt born of desperation, and Malazan struck back at her. Locked together, the dragons fell.

Dorn kept thrusting and cutting, and ducked a random sweep of Kara's tail that would otherwise have snapped his neck.

Malazan left off biting long enough to roar three grating syllables, and afterward, any blood her attackers spilled burst into flame on contact with the air, searing them.

Dorn refused to let the pain balk him. He attacked until one particularly deep wound made Malazan convulse. The sudden jerk broke the hunter's grip on the hilt of his sword, tore his talons from Malazan's hide, and hurled him into empty air.

Here is death, then, he thought. Naturally, it had arrived only when he'd decided he actually wanted to live.

To his surprise, however, he slowed to a stop, then rose toward the blue dome of the sky. Below him, Azhaq, still on the wing despite the ghastly wounds he bore, his vulture-demon assailant evidently slain, grunted in satisfaction at making the catch. Raryn nodded at Dorn, laid another arrow on his bow, and cast about for a target. Weak and clumsy with pain but still alive, Kara laboriously climbed toward her erstwhile rider, to collect him before the magic holding him aloft ran out of strength.

But nobody moved to assist Malazan. Either dead or crippled, in any case incapable of flight, the colossal red fell like a shooting star, shrouded in the flames of her burning blood and leaving a trail of smoke in her wake. She smashed down on a mountainside. The impact flattened and deformed her body and stabbed lengths of broken bone through her hide.

Faced with the likes of Tamarand, Nexus, and Havarlan, perhaps the chromatics had been losing the battle even before their commander perished, but even if not, her destruction panicked them. Crying to one another, most sought to break away and scatter in all directions.

Dorn wondered how many would get away. None, he hoped. Let the wrathful metallics slaughter them all. Then a wave of faintness picked him up and carried him into darkness.

Shrouded in invisibility, Brimstone circled over the benighted battlefield, taking stock of the situation. It looked as if Dragonsbane's strategy had worked about as well as the king had had any right to expect. His troops had inflicted grievous casualties on the Vaasan horde.

But the majority of the goblins and giants had stood their ground and likewise butchered many a Damaran warrior through the hours of daylight, and since darkness had fallen, it was possible the balance was tilting in their favor. They could see well at night, and humans couldn't. Dragonsbane's wizards conjured fields of pearly glow to compensate, but often enough, a spellcaster on the other side extinguished them, and in any case, they couldn't light up the whole landscape.

As he listened to the clash of metal on metal and the anguished cries of the wounded and dying, rather savoring them, Brimstone mused on just how easy it would be to betray his allies and hand the victory to Vaasa. Easy and natural, for though the goblin kin and their ilk were base, dull vermin compared to him, they were nonetheless born of the same darkness. Why not aid them, then, to slaughter the miserable paladins and priests of light, and rule as their monarch thereafter?

Only because such a betrayal would do nothing to further his vengeance against Sammaster. Someday, perhaps, he would claim a throne, command legions, and make his name a byword for terror across Faerûn, but for the moment, he craved retribution more than glory.

Brimstone flew to a place where the two armies ground together and soon spotted Dragonsbane at the forefront of the Damaran host. The paladin king was surely exhausted, but no one could have told it from the vigor with which he swung his broadsword and exhorted the warriors around him to fight on.

That was good. The little drama Brimstone had devised wouldn't seem very convincing if Dragonsbane looked half dead in the saddle.

The vampire whispered words of power, shedding his mantle of invisibility and replacing it with a corona of harsh white light. The glare illuminated the puppet astride his back as well. It was simply an animated skeleton, a mindless tool, but crowned with gold and jewels and robed in ermine and purple, it looked the part of Zhengyi the Witch-King, and with Brimstone's will prompting it, would behave appropriately as well.

Brimstone swooped down over the battlefield, roaring to attract the combatants' notice. The puppet brandished its staff, and the goblins clamored to see their master finally appear. Then a dozen of them scrambled for their lives when they perceived that Brimstone intended to land on the patch of bloody, trampled earth they occupied.

His impressive advent made both sides pause in their struggles to gawk at him, and that was how he wanted it. As soon as he touched down opposite Dragonsbane, he bellowed maledictions and a challenge to single combat in a magically augmented voice that every member of the Vaasan host could hear and understand. The words, of course, seemed to rave from the skeletal figure perched on his back.

It might have been nice if the king had replied with a speech of his own, but he simply slashed his sword through the air to indicate he accepted the challenge. Conceivably his idiotic paladin code forbade him to say anything that amounted to a lie, but he was willing to act his part in a misleading pantomime and let the Vaasans draw their own erroneous conclusions.

Dragonsbane extended his blade in front of him and charged. Brimstone cast the first of the spells with which his puppet was supposedly attacking the king, invocations that filled the air with dazzling flashes, seething mists, and thunderous bangs and roars, magic that even shook the ground, but could do no actual harm to anyone.

The king cut at Brimstone. He was a talented enough swordsman to make it look convincing even though the strokes were too soft to penetrate a smoke drake's scales. Brimstone bit and clawed at the human and his horse, warning what the next attack would be with slight shifts of his head and legs. He and Dragonsbane had rehearsed their dance, but he wasn't willing to risk the human making a mistake. His fangs and talons were simply too deadly.

The hardest part was resisting the impulse to strike out in earnest, for he could feel the virtue, the sacred power, burning inside the paladin, and it filled him with loathing. He wondered if Dragonsbane was struggling against an equivalent urge.

As the drama progressed, Dragonsbane appeared to try repeatedly to strike at the figure on Brimstone's back, and the vampire always moved to shield it, or lift it out of harm's way. Until finally it was time to conjure the semblance of a burst of fire, an illusion so convincing that those nearby would even feel a flare of heat, though it wouldn't burn the man and destrier caught in the center of the blast.

Dragonsbane wheeled his horse and ran. Brimstone gave chase. The Vaasans howled to see their nemesis fleeing for his life.

Actually, though, Dragonsbane was simply achieving the distance required to use a weapon other than his sword. He turned his mount again, pulled a luminous javelin from its sheath on the charger's saddle, and hurled it.

The spear pierced the puppet through the torso, whereupon the skeleton instantly caught fire, flailed, shrieked, and toppled from Brimstone's back. To all appearances, Dragonsbane had slain the Witch-King with a holy relic, or a weapon charged with his own god-granted magic.

The Vaasan cheering died, and a moment later, a Damaran shout of triumph filled the air. Dragonsbane charged Brimstone, and his warriors surged at the goblin kin and giants.

The king beat at Brimstone with his sword. Brimstone cringed away, spread his wings, and leaped into the air. Once he climbed high enough that no one was paying any attention to him anymore, he circled above the field to witness the result of his deception.

When he'd bolted, the Vaasans around him had too, and as they blundered backward, jamming into the ranks of the creatures behind them, sometimes lashing out with scimitars and spears to force their way through, they communicated their panic to even those goblins who hadn't enjoyed a clear view of the mock duel. In a matter of minutes, the entire host was routing, and for the Damarans who rode in pursuit, killing them was as easy as slaughtering sheep.

Brimstone reckoned Dragonsbane's men still had months of campaigning ahead before they fully purged their realm of invaders, retook the Gates, and sealed Bloodstone Pass. Still, in truth, they'd already won back Damara, or rather, a vampire drake had done it for them. He grinned at the irony.

The sickroom smelled of medicines and myrrh. The silvery glow of the magical crescent-shaped lamp was too dim to sweep the shadows from the corners. Perhaps the gloom was supposed to help Rilitar rest.

Sureene had wrapped the wizard in bandages, and surely used all the healing magic at her disposal to help stanch the flow of blood from his wounds. Still, red spots stained the white gauze, the bed linen, and the mound of pillows propping him up.

Inwardly, Taegan winced to see it, but resolved to keep his distress from showing. He was certain Rilitar didn't want a display of pity.

"Hello," he said.

"We came as soon as the stupid priestesses would let us in," Jivex said.

Rilitar laboriously turned his head toward his visitors. "Our enterprise . . . ?" he wheezed.

Taegan realized what he meant. "None of your fellow mages died, and Firefingers saved most of the books and papers."

Rilitar smiled feebly, the quirking of his ashen lips just visible between two strips of bandage. "That old man knows how to talk to flame."

"Naturally, the Watchlord—speaking for the old families, I assume—wasn't happy about us fighting a sunwyrm in the street. But I pointed out that we did kill it before it harmed any of the citizenry, and that with our traitor unmasked and eliminated, we could absolutely guarantee there would be no more such incidents. Firefingers reminded him just how vital you wizards are to the security of Thentia, and the upshot of it all was that he grudgingly agreed to let you continue your investigations."

"Then we truly did defeat Phourkyn."

"You deserve the credit. Thanks be to Lady Luck that you noticed me reciting the charm of frenzy, and realized what it meant."

"Luck had little to do with it. I'd been watching you closely for a while, because you were acting strangely, going to absurd lengths to play the frivolous rake, insisting on fancy new clothes but clinging to those worn, drab, ill-fitting boots. At first, I couldn't determine what it meant. Phourkyn's enchantments were so subtle my magic couldn't detect them. But I was sure it indicated something."

"I'm fortunate his curse made me peculiar."

"I suspect it was your own mind, your own will, resisting him and signaling for help, even though you weren't conscious of it. It isn't easy to enslave an elf."

"Or a master-of-arms, perhaps."

Rilitar drew a ragged breath. "Sureene did everything she could to mend me, but says that even so, I'm unlikely to see the sunrise. Will you keep me company until the end?"

"Of course," Taegan said.

He pulled a chair away from the wall. Jivex furled his wings and lit on the corner of the bed.

"Thank you," the wizard said. "Perhaps you know a prayer or hymn, for when the moment comes."

The avariel hesitated then said, "I remember a chant from my days with my tribe. But I imagine it's a plain, crude thing compared to what true elves use in Cormanthor."

"That's fine. It will speed my spirit on its way better than any human words."

———◦༄◦———

Like all the others, the final battle left countless tasks and duties in its wake. It was late before Cantoule could slip off by himself to collect his thoughts.

As he walked the monastery grounds, the pale statues and shrines gleaming in Selûne's light, it grieved him to behold all the destruction. Yet the stronghold was enormous, and more of it remained intact than otherwise. The rest could be rebuilt.

He realized it was the same with the inhabitants. Many had died defending their holy sanctuary and the precious archives, so many that he could hardly bear the sorrow of it, yet not all. The Order of the Yellow Rose survived, and in time, other men would hear Ilmater's call and come to swell its ranks.

Meanwhile, because the brothers had endured the worst the besieging dragons could do, it was even possible that Kara and her comrades would avert a doom threatening all Faerûn.

But that was a matter too vast and mysterious for a tired man to contemplate for long. Soon enough, his thoughts returned to smaller matters. Indeed, to a petty one.

He knew that in the aftermath of the agonies the monastery had weathered, in the midst of the myriad needs that still remained, it was unworthy of him to think of himself at all. Yet he believed the Crying God would forgive him for taking a moment to recognize the truth that, in the darkest of times, his stewardship had proved sufficient. Perhaps he hadn't led his followers as ably as Kane would have, but his best had been good enough. He found a vacant chapel and kneeled before the altar to whisper a prayer of thanks.

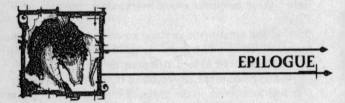

EPILOGUE

Midsummer-20 Eleasis, the Year of Rogue Dragons

Despite the dread that had engulfed the world, the burghers of Thentia celebrated Midsummer with gusto. Or perhaps, Taegan reflected, it was precisely the knowledge that a flight of rampaging dragons might descend on their town at any moment that made them embrace the pleasures of the festival with such enthusiasm.

The warm night rang with raucous music. The taverns were full to overflowing, and in every square and plaza, people danced fast, whirling, stomping dances, or watched them while ladling beer and wine from open barrels. Lads and lasses eyed one another, teased, flirted, and whispered, until eventually the couples stole away from the rest of their companions to find some privacy. Some of them didn't require a lot of it. A shadowy doorway sufficed.

To Taegan's sophisticated eye, Thentia's revels

had a crude, bucolic quality compared to the lavish, elegant Midsummer entertainments he'd enjoyed in Lyrabar. But he didn't miss the latter as much as he might have expected. It was pleasant to stroll the boisterous streets with Jivex, Dorn, Raryn, and Will, observing the flushed, bright-eyed girls in their paint and finery, and regaling the hunters with the tale of his recent adventures. Even if the telling recalled the sorrow of Rilitar's death, and he realized, required a certain amount of explaining at the end.

"Firefingers believes," the bladesinger said, "that at the start, there was a real Phourkyn One-eye. But Sammaster arranged his murder and replaced him with an impersonator. At that point, he couldn't know for a fact that the mages of Thentia would become involved in an effort to quell the Rage. You fellows hadn't yet ventured into Northkeep, then traveled here to ask for their help. But he was aware of their reputation for learning, and deemed it prudent to have a powerful, resourceful agent in place to ruin any such endeavor if, in fact, they undertook it."

Will nodded and said, "The Cult of the Dragon has spies and assassins lurking in all sorts of places. We knew that already. But let's hope they don't have many as dangerous as this. A wyrm and a mighty spellcaster . . . with a demon living inside him?"

"According to Jannatha Goldenshield," Taegan said, "certain drakes augment their strength by fusing tanar'ri with their own hearts. Generally, the spirit just stays inside them afterward, quiescent, but Phourkyn—I suppose we might as well keep calling the sunwyrm that, for want of his true name—discovered new ways of using the magic. He could separate from the chasme for brief periods of time, and send it forth to kill."

"And a fine weapon it was," Raryn said, sidestepping to avoid a running, happily squealing girl and the grinning youth pursuing her.

"Indeed," Taegan said. "The chasme and Phourkyn had become two aspects of a single being. By merging with its master, the demon acquired the halo of flame that echoed the pure destructive force a sunwyrm can channel through its breath and talons, as well as the ability to cast Phourkyn's spells. What's more, because it wasn't purely a spirit anymore, but rather a hybrid entity, wards devised to hinder demons couldn't hold it back, and since it spent nearly all its time hidden inside Phourkyn's body, Jivex, Rilitar, and I couldn't find it when we tried to track it down."

"Also," said Will, "while the chasme was killing people, Phourkyn could let himself be seen elsewhere, doing something innocuous. That alone wouldn't prove he wasn't the traitor, but it would tend to make people think he probably wasn't."

"But the drawback," said Raryn, "was that, since Phourkyn and the chasme were one, if it died, so would he. I notice that after you, Maestro, proved you could hurt it—"

"After *we* proved we could hurt it!" Jivex cried, wheeling overhead in search of mosquitoes and moths.

The dwarf inclined his head. "Your pardon, my friend. After the two of you proved you could hurt it badly, it generally kept its distance, attacking you with spells, locusts, abishais, and the like, instead of its claws and spear of a nose. But here's one of the things I still don't understand. Didn't you, Maestro, say Phourkyn drove it back when it was close to killing you?"

"That was how it seemed," Taegan replied, "but I was close to killing the demon, too. The encounter could have gone either way. The chasme broke away of its own accord, and Phourkyn seized the opportunity to make it look as if he was responsible by conjuring an impressive but harmless flash. It was one more way to create the impression that whoever the traitor might be, it certainly wasn't he. He had a cool, quick, cunning mind, I'll give him that. No wonder it took so long to discover his identity."

"How did you?" asked Will. "You said that when he held you prisoner, he appeared to you in the guise of Darvin Kordeion."

Taegan smiled. He'd hoped to save that bit of explaining for last, and conclude with something that made him look clever.

"Yes," said the avariel. "Once again, it shows how wily he truly was, how he sought to plan for every possibility. When I acted as his helpless thrall, I understood I was forbidden to hurt my master, Phourkyn One-eye. But if anyone broke my psychic bonds, as Rilitar ultimately did, I wouldn't recall that anymore. Instead, I'd remember Darvin questioning me and laying his enchantment on me, and strike down an innocent man.

"But here's where Phourkyn erred," the bladesinger continued. "He'd mastered the knack of shapeshifting into an exact duplicate of the man he'd replaced. As he spent his days in the company of shrewd and powerful wizards, no other disguise would serve for any length of time. But I gather such magic is difficult and demanding, and when he spoke with me in the cellar, he didn't think he needed to bother with it. Accordingly, he simply masked his true appearance with a lesser spell, conjuring the mere illusion of Darvin's face and form.

"Happily, he still reeked of that fragrant pomade he used to slick his hair back. Firefingers thinks he may have used it to cover his true scent. A sunwyrm in human form with a demon bound to its heart may smell a little off. Be that as it may, he also still cocked his head sideways to peer straight at me with his single eye. I retained those details when Rilitar restored me to my right mind."

"There's one thing I don't see," Dorn grumbled.

"What might that be?" Taegan asked.

"Biding here, Phourkyn was privy to all the information we brought to the wizards. That means he knew Sammaster himself brought on the frenzy that threatens all dragons, sunwyrms included. Why would he continue to help the lich after that?"

"Conceivably," Taegan said, "he'd long ago set his heart on reigning as a dracolich in the world Sammaster envisions, and decided he didn't care what means the madman used to bring it about. Or perhaps he feared Sammaster too much to cross him, no matter what."

"Considering," said Will, "how strong Phourkyn himself was, that last is not a happy thought. Here's hoping we can wreck Sammaster's plans without having to square off against the old bag of bones himself."

Taegan saw they'd nearly reached the edge of town, and in consequence, the last of the open-air parties. Zigzagging in flight to the beat of the bouncy melody arising somewhere nearby, Jivex flitted away, lit on the edge of a tun of wine, lapped at the contents with his long tongue, then wheeled to rejoin the group.

The benighted countryside seemed particularly quiet after the noisy festivities in the city. In another minute, the five companions passed a guard, one of the Watchlord's Warders, stationed on the road to keep dragon cultists, or the merely curious, from spying on the meeting Thentia's spellcasters were convening.

The wizards had little choice but to hold it in an open field, or somewhere outdoors, anyway. Too many of the dragons in attendance either lacked the knack of shapechanging or simply preferred to remain in their natural forms for them all to fit in even Firefingers's spacious workroom. Peering about, aided by the silvery, sourceless illumination someone had evoked, Taegan spotted Nexus, who'd supposedly worked wonders interpreting the vital documents discovered in the Monastery of the Yellow Rose, Vingdavalac, none the worse for the burns he'd sustained, and dark, ember-eyed Brimstone in his ruby collar. Most of the company were keeping their distance from the vampire, but Scattercloak apparently had no such qualms. He and the smoke drake murmured to one another.

As was generally her preference, Kara wore her human guise. Dorn smiled at the sight of her, though the unaccustomed expression looked as if it might pain his sullen, divided face.

Pavel stood at the bard's side, handsome as ever but looking a shade older and graver than when Taegan had met him in Impiltur. Around them were Firefingers, Darvin, Baerimel, Jannatha, and the rest of Thentia's arcanists.

Kara returned Dorn's awkward smile with a radiant one of her own, then raised her hand for silence. Taegan inferred that he and his companions were the last to arrive, so the discussion could begin.

When the drone of conversation faded, Kara said, "We've made considerable progress."

"Oh, bugger!" Will whispered. "After all our chasing about, the idiots still don't have the answer."

He probably hadn't meant for the assemblage as a whole to overhear, but perhaps he'd forgotten how keen a dragon's hearing was. A dozen towering, wedge-shaped heads swiveled to glower at the interruption.

Kara smiled wearily at her friend's impertinence and said, "I think you judge us a trifle harshly, Will. You're right, we don't have the whole solution. But we believe we have half of it."

"We think we've reconstructed the rite the ancient wizards used to curse dragonkind," Pavel said. "We don't understand everything about it, including how it was possible for an undead human like Sammaster to alter elven high magic and make it serve his will. We believe we've gleaned enough, however, to devise a counterspell that will wipe the enchantment away. Obliterating such a thing entirely is easier than tinkering with it."

"That sounds splendid," Taegan said. "What, then, do we still require?"

"Thanks to Master Shemov's discoveries in Thar," said Firefingers, "we now know that somewhere—in the far north, probably—in territory so forbidding and remote that the primordial dragon kings had no interest in it, their enemies raised a citadel where they could pursue their plans undetected. There, they cursed the wyrms, there, the magic lives on today, and only there can the spell be lifted."

Will sighed and said, "Right, and even after poring over all the information we seekers hauled out of Thar, Damara, and the rest of Faerûn, you sages still haven't figured out where the stronghold is, have you?"

"No," Kara said. "The elf mages almost certainly warded it against scrying, divination, and the like, to keep it hidden from their foes. Like the mythal they guard, those defenses probably still function today. Still, we must locate the fortress, and have little time to do it. Nexus believes that by the turning of the year, perhaps even sooner, the Rage will grow so virulent that the antidote we found in the monastery won't protect us anymore."

Taegan tried to feel resolute, as opposed to apprehensive, disappointed, and despondent. At that moment, he didn't find it easy, and judging from the glum silence that enfolded the gathering, many of the others felt the same.

Jivex, however, made a scornful spitting sound. "Are you all stupid?" the faerie dragon demanded. "Castles are big. How hard can finding one be?"

❦

On the Great Glacier, summer seemed no more than a lunatic's fancy. The howling wind could freeze an unprotected man to death in a matter of minutes, and the sunlight glaring from the ice could blind him just as quickly. Tramping along, staff in hand, robe and mantle flapping around him, Sammaster had reason to be grateful that his withered flesh and desiccated eyes were immune to such afflictions.

His musings, however, were distressing enough to compensate for the absence of physical discomfort. Somehow, over the course of the past few months, his grand strategy had begun to unravel. First, emissaries from Impiltur had gone forth across Faerûn, carrying tidings of the secret strongholds he'd established to spawn dracoliches, urging that the havens be found and destroyed, and a host of meddlers had answered the call. Next, the metallic wyrms had emerged from seclusion to aid the paladins, champions, and whomever in their struggle. The drakes were likewise striving to quell the chaos the Rage had spread across the continent, unrest the Cult of the Dragon depended upon to divert attention from its endeavors, and to weaken the kingdoms of men for the coming conquest.

The golds and silvers wouldn't have dared venture among humans unless they had protection against frenzy. Their return could only mean that, against all probability, Malazan and her underlings had failed to take the Monastery of the Yellow Rose, allowing some genius of a scholar to discover the secrets buried in the archives.

Sammaster might have been inclined to blame such setbacks on the Harpers, the Chosen, or Mystra herself, formidable enemies all who'd thwarted him before. But his instincts told him that final responsibility for his troubles lay elsewhere, with the unknown foes who'd stolen his notes in Lyrabar.

In retrospect, it was obvious he should have exerted himself to identify and destroy the wretches as soon as he discovered the theft. The realization made him grind his rotting teeth in a spasm of self-loathing, the emotion that always overwhelmed him when he made a costly mistake.

Straining to compose himself, he insisted it wouldn't matter in the long run. Knights and wizards might destroy some of the cult's secret enclaves, but they wouldn't get them all. The metallics could only slow the growth of the cancer that was frenzy, not excise it. Nobody else would ever find the heart of the Rage in time to spoil his plans, and even if someone could, Sammaster had an answer in place for that contingency as well. It was inevitable that at last, he'd win victory, vindication, and his heart's desire. At last, the glorious future Maglas had prophesied would come to pass.

But still, even if his faceless foes were, at worst, a temporary inconvenience, it was past time to find and crush them. For all his power, though, it would be difficult to undertake the chore unaided. He had too many other crucial tasks to perform, calming frenzied wyrms across the length and breadth of Faerûn, convincing them to accept the transformation into dracoliches, and shepherding them to the appropriate locations.

Fortunately, he didn't think he'd have to labor all alone, or even rely solely on his cultists. As he'd proved in Vaasa, a clever fellow could usually find someone to cozen into furthering his schemes.

He clambered to the crest of a rise and beheld his destination below him, a fortress molded of gleaming ice. With a twitch of his staff, he splashed a dragon-shaped shadow across the sky to announce his coming.

Go Behind enemy lines with Drizzt Do'Urden in this all new trilogy from best-selling Author R.A. Salvatore.

THE HUNTER'S BLADES TRILOGY

The New York Times *best-seller now in paperback!*

THE LONE DROW
Book II

Alone and tired, cold and hungry, Drizzt Do'Urden has never been more dangerous. But neither have the rampaging orcs that have finally done the impossible—what for the dwarves of the North is the most horrifying nightmare ever—they've banded together.

New in hardcover!

THE TWO SWORDS
Book III

Drizzt has become the Hunter, but King Obould won't let himself become the Hunted and that means one of them will have to die. The Hunter's Blades trilogy draws to an explosive conclusion.

THE THOUSAND ORCS
Book I
Available Now!

FROM *NEW YORK TIMES*

BEST-SELLING AUTHOR

R.A. SALVATORE

In taverns, around campfires, and in the loftiest council chambers of Faerûn, people whisper the tales of a lone dark elf who stumbled out of the merciless Underdark to the no less unforgiving wilderness of the World Above and carved a life for himself, then lived a legend...

THE LEGEND OF DRIZZT

For the first time in deluxe hardcover editions, all three volumes of the Dark Elf Trilogy take their rightful place at the beginning of one of the greatest fantasy epics of all time. Each title contains striking new cover art and portions of an all-new author interview, with the questions posed by none other than the readers themselves.

HOMELAND

Being born in Menzoberranzan means a hard life surrounded by evil.

EXILE

But the only thing worse is being driven from the city with hunters on your trail.

SOJOURN

Unless you can find your way out, never to return.

Two new ways to own the Paths of Darkness by *New York Times* best-selling author

R.A. Salvatore

New in hardcover!

PATHS OF DARKNESS
COLLECTORS EDITION
A *Forgotten Realms*® Omnibus

•

PATHS OF DARKNESS
GIFT SET
A new boxed set of all four titles in paperback
Contains: *The Silent Blade, The Spine of the World,*
Servant of the Shard, Sea of Swords

Wulfgar the barbarian has returned from death to his companions:
Drizzt, Catti-brie, Regis, and Bruenor. Yet the road to freedom will
be long for him, and his path will lead through darkness before he
emerges into the light. And along the way he will find old enemies,
new allies, and someone to love.

THERE ARE A HUNDRED GODS LOOKING OVER FAERÛN, EACH WITH A THOUSAND SERVANTS OR MORE. SERVANTS WE CALL... THE PRIESTS

LADY OF POISON
Bruce R. Cordell

Evil has the Great Dale in its venomous grip. Monsters crawl from the shadows, disease and poison ravage the townsfolk, and dark cults gather in the night. Not all religions, after all, work for good.

MISTRESS OF NIGHT
Dave Gross

Fighting a goddess of secrets can be a dangerous game. Werewolves stalk the moonlit night, goddesses clash in the heavens, and a lone priestess will sacrifice everything to stop them.

QUEEN OF THE DEPTHS
Voronica Whitney-Robinson

Far below the waves, evil swims. The ocean goddess is a fickle mistress who toys with man and ship alike. How can she be trusted when the seas run red with blood?

May 2005

MAIDEN OF PAIN
Kameron M. Franklin

The book that **Forgotten Realms®** novel fans have been waiting for—the result of an exhaustive international talent search. The newest star in the skies of Faerûn tells a story of torture, sacrifice, and betrayal.

July 2005

ADVENTURES IN THE REALMS!

THE YELLOW SILK
The Rogues
Don Bassingthwaite

More than just the weather is cold and bitter in the wind-swept realm of Altumbel. When a stranger travels from the distant east to reclaim his family's greatest treasure, he finds just how cold and bitter a people can be.

DAWN OF NIGHT
The Erevis Cale Trilogy, Book II
Paul S. Kemp

He's left Sembia far behind. He's made new friends. He's made new enemies. And now Erevis Cale himself is changing into something, and he's not sure exactly what it is.

REALMS OF DRAGONS
The Year of Rogue Dragons
Edited by Philip Athans

All new stories by R.A. Salvatore, Richard Lee Byers, Ed Greenwood, Elaine Cunningham, and a host of **Forgotten Realms®** stars breathe new life into the great wyrms of Faerûn.

FORGOTTEN REALMS®

FATHER AND DAUGHTER COME FACE-TO-FACE IN THE STREETS OF WATERDEEP.

ELMINSTER'S DAUGHTER
The Elminster Series

Ed Greenwood

Like a silken shadow, the thief Narnra Shalace flits through the dank streets and dark corners of Waterdeep. Little does she know that she's about to come face-to-face with the most dangerous man in all Faerûn: her father. And amidst a vast conspiracy to overthrow all order in the Realms, she'll have to learn to trust again—and to love.

ELIMINSTER: THE MAKING OF A MAGE

ELMINSTER IN MYTH DRANNOR

THE TEMPTATION OF ELMINSTER

ELMINSTER IN HELL

Available Now!

CHECK OUT THESE NEW TITLES FROM THE AUTHORS OF R.A. SALVATORE'S WAR OF THE SPIDER QUEEN SERIES!

VENOM'S TASTE
House of Serpents, Book I
Lisa Smedman

The New York Times Best-selling author of *Extinction*.
Serpents. Poison. Psionics. And the occasional evil death cult. Business as usual in the Vilhon Reach. Lisa Smedman breathes life into the treacherous yuan-ti race.

THE RAGE
The Year of Rogue Dragons, Book I
Richard Lee Byers

Every once in a while the dragons go mad. Without warning they darken the skies of Faerûn and kill and kill and kill. Richard Lee Byers, the new master of dragons, takes wing.

FORSAKEN HOUSE
The Last Mythal, Book I
Richard Baker

The New York Times Best-selling author of *Condemnation*.
The Retreat is at an end, and the elves of Faerûn find themselves at a turning point. In one direction lies peace and stagnation, in the other: war and destiny. *New York Times* best-selling author Richard Baker shows the elves their future.

THE RUBY GUARDIAN
Scions of Arrabar, Book II
Thomas M. Reid

Life and death both come at a price in the mercenary city-states of the Vilhon Reach. Vambran thought he knew the cost of both, but he still has a lot to learn. Thomas M. Reid makes humans the most dangerous monsters in Faerûn.

THE SAPPHIRE CRESCENT
Scions of Arrabar, Book I
Available Now

R.A. Salvatore's
War of the Spider Queen

THE EPIC SAGA OF THE DARK ELVES CONTINUES.

EXTINCTION
Book IV
Lisa Smedman

For even a small group of drow, trust is the rarest commodity of all. When the expedition prepares
for a return to the Abyss, what little trust there is crumbles under a rival goddess's hand.

ANNIHILATION
Book V
Philip Athans

Old alliances have been broken, and new bonds have been formed. While some finally embark for
the Abyss itself, others stay behind to serve a new mistress—a goddess with plans of her own.

RESURRECTION
Book VI

The Spider Queen has been asleep for a long time, leaving the Underdark to suffer war and ruin.
But if she finally returns, will things get better... or worse?

April 2005

The New York Times *best-seller now in paperback!*

CONDEMNATION
Book III
Richard Baker

The search for answers to Lolth's silence uncovers only more complex questions, allowing doubt
and frustration to test the boundaries of already tenuous relationships. Sensing the holes in the
armor of Menzoberranzan, a new, dangerous threat steps in to test the resolve of the
Jewel of the Underdark, and finds it lacking.

Now in paperback!
DISSOLUTION, BOOK I
INSURRECTION, BOOK II

Legends Trilogy

Margaret Weis & Tracy Hickman

Each volume available for the first time ever in hardcover!

TIME OF THE TWINS
Volume I

Caramon Majere vows to protect Crysania, a
devout cleric, in her quest to save Raistlin from
himself. But both are soon caught in the dark
mage's deadly designs, and their one hope is a
frivolous kender.

WAR OF THE TWINS
Volume II

Catapulted through time by Raistlin's dark
magics, Caramon and Crysania are forced to aid
the mage in his quest to defeat the
Queen of Darkness.

TEST OF THE TWINS
Volume III

As Raistlin's plans come to fruition, Caramon
comes face to face with his destiny. Old friends
and strange allies come to aid him, but Caramon
must take the final step alone.

The Elven Nations Trilogy is back in print in all-new editions!

FIRSTBORN
Volume One

Paul B. Thompson & Tonya C. Cook

In moments, the fate of two leaders is decided. Sithas, firstborn son of the elf monarch Sithel, is destined to inherit the crown and kingdom from his father. His twin brother Kith-Kanan, born just a few heartbeats later, must make his own destiny. Together—and apart—the princes will see their world torn asunder for the sake of power, freedom, and love.

New edition in October 2004

THE KINSLAYER WAR
Volume Two

Douglas Niles

Timeless and elegant, the elven realm seems unchanging. But when the dynamic human nation of Ergoth presses on the frontiers of the Silvanesti realm, the elves must awaken—and unite—to turn back the tide of human conquest. Prince Kith-Kanan, returned from exile, holds the key to victory.

New edition in November 2004

THE QUALINESTI
Volume Three

Paul B. Thompson & Tonya C. Cook

Wars done, the weary nations of Krynn turn to rebuilding their exhausted lands. In the mountains, a city devoted to peace, Pax Tharkas, is carved from living stone by elf and dwarf hands. In the new nation of Qualinesti, corruption seeks to undermine this new beginning. A new generation of elves and humans must band together if the noble experiment of Kith-Kanan is to be preserved.

New edition in December 2004